Empire of Temptation

A Small Town Mafia Romance

New York State of Mafia
Book 1

Mila Finelli

EMPIRE OF TEMPTATION
Copyright © 2025 by Mila Finelli

Cover: Letitia Hasser, RBA Designs

Editing: Jennifer Prokop

Contents

"I'd rather regret the things I've done than regret the things I haven't done."

    — Lucille Ball

Chapter One

Luca

Sant' Onofrio
Provincia di Vibo Valentia, Calabria

The car door opened and a man slid into the back seat beside me. "We have a serious problem, Don Benetti," Don Rossi said, slamming the door. "The GDF is planning to arrest you."

Rossi was the current head of the 'Ndrangheta in our region, but he was fond of hyperbole. No chance was I about to be arrested.

The Guardia di Finanza oversaw financial crimes in Italy. They were regular pains in our asses, but most of us found ways to keep them at bay. Only stupid and lazy bosses went to prison—and I was neither.

"*Cazzata*," I said calmly. "I pay them to make sure they don't."

"That was before you fucked Colonnello Palmieri's wife."

Palmieri? Why was this coming up now? I slept with Signora Palmieri a year ago when she approached me at a restaurant. I didn't

1

usually fuck strange, albeit beautiful women, but she'd pressed hard. The encounter had been fun, though not very memorable. "I didn't know who she was at the time. I had no idea she was married."

"It doesn't matter. She knows who you are and has rubbed the encounter in Palmieri's face. To get even, he's been targeting you, quietly putting a case together."

"This is the first I'm hearing of it. He can't have anything substantial."

"But he will. Your cousin Niccolò was arrested in Lucerne on a delivery run. He's being brought back to Roma and Palmieri plans to use it to his advantage. They want him to turn on you."

Merda! I was going to murder my GDF contact for not warning me of all this—right after I murdered my cousin. "I'll handle it."

"Yes, you will. But it may not be necessary. Palmieri is throwing you a lifeline."

I stared through the window, thinking. Palmieri may have amassed information on me, but I knew about him, too. I researched all of my enemies. After I learned it was Palmieri's wife who got me into bed I tried to figure out why. I still didn't know but I'd familiarized myself with every other aspect of the colonel's life. There were two things he didn't bend on: his hatred of the Italian mafia and his unwillingness to accept a bribe.

So I didn't understand this offer to help me. "Why?"

Don Rossi frowned fiercely, the lines around his mouth deepening. "Does it fucking matter? It could keep all of us out of trouble."

"It matters to me. I don't trust him. What does he want me to do?"

"He wants you to find Flavio Segreto and bring him to Roma."

This was even more confusing. A legend in Southern Italy, Flavio Segreto had been a ruthless underboss at one time, but he disappeared ten years ago after stealing money from several of the *'ndrine.* We've been looking for him ever since. "Why Segreto?"

"Remember when Palmieri's daughter was murdered two years ago?"

"Of course." The seven-year-old girl had been blown up in a car bomb on her way to school. It was big news at the time. Palmieri was obsessed with the case, using every spare moment to investigate, and all signs indicated that he blamed it on the mafia. "And?"

"Segreto carried out the hit."

"*Che cazzo?* This can't be possible. Why would Segreto come out of hiding to kill Palmieri's daughter?"

"I couldn't say, but Palmieri says he has proof it was Segreto," Rossi said.

"Impossible. I would know if Segreto had resurfaced."

"Yes, your informants are legendary. But we are not in a position to argue with the GDF. Let's give him Segreto in exchange for Niccolò, then wash our hands of it. Because if Niccolò talks, you go to prison and we are all at risk. This is bad for business."

My brain turned all this over, looking at the options from all sides. I was not a man who acted rashly. I planned and plotted and used logic. This was one of the things that made me successful as the head of a powerful criminal family. Emotions were dangerous, and I'd been raised to have none.

In the silence, Rossi asked, "Do you know where Segreto is?"

"Not exactly."

"Meaning?"

"I heard he has a daughter living in New York."

Rossi slapped the car door with his palm. "*Porca puttana!* This whole time you knew where to find his daughter? Why haven't we used her to find him?"

"Because the two are not close. There have been no reports of contact between them since I learned of her three years ago."

"So bringing her to the GDF is a waste of time."

"Not necessarily," I said. "If we bring her to Palmieri, Segreto will learn of it and do anything to get her back." As a father, I knew this to be true. I had two sons and I would go to hell and back for either of them.

"I like this." Rossi straightened his cuffs and grabbed the door handle. "See that it's done."

"I will. I'll send a man to New York to find her—"

"No! You handle this personally. There is no room for error."

I adjusted my watch and struggled for calm. "It's both foolish and dangerous for me to perform this errand. I will turn over her location once I have it and one of Palmieri's men can bring her to Roma."

"No. He doesn't want the GDF to know. This is personal, not official. We have to keep it quiet or the deal for your cousin is off."

I sighed heavily. Unhappily.

Rossi pressed. "Do you want to risk it, with Niccolò behind bars? Be smart, Luca. Take as many men as you need to stay safe and go to New York, then get this girl on a plane as quickly as possible."

Fuck me. It seemed I was flying to America tonight.

Chapter Two

Valentina

Paesano, New York
Trattoria Rustico

Business was slow.

But then business was always slow on Tuesday nights. It would pick up on Thursday and through the weekend—at least I hoped so.

Trattoria Rustico was my family's fifty-year-old restaurant, and it was up to me to ensure its survival. As manager and owner, I filled in where necessary, and these days that meant being in the kitchen.

It was impossible to keep kitchen staff for longer than a month. I suspected my head chef, Tony, was to blame, but that was a problem for another day. Tonight we had to get through dinner service.

Anne Marie, my best server, walked in, a concerned frown on her face. "Tony, I gotta have that chicken parm. What the fuck is going on back there?"

"Keep your fuckin' shirt on," Tony called from behind me. "It's coming."

I checked the time on the ticket. "They've been waiting almost forty minutes. Why is it taking so long?"

"I had to get a chicken breast from the freezer, Val. There weren't any prepared."

The fuck? How could we not have any chicken breasts ready for dinner service?

Now was not the time to get into it, though.

"Douchebag," Anne Marie muttered under her breath and went back into the dining room.

Tony placed two plates onto the pass with a snap. "Order up! Spaghetti and meatballs and penne alla vodka."

I wiped the edges of the plates and placed a sprig of parsley on each. Then I found the ticket on the line. Table four. Just as I was about to take the food to the table myself, Christina came into the kitchen. She was younger than me and a terrible employee. But her father was the mayor, and no one said no to the mayor.

She grabbed the plates of pasta from my hands. I could see something was wrong by the look on her face. "What is it?"

"The guy at table seven is, like, a serious asshole."

Great. A problematic customer was all I needed. "Is he drunk?" We occasionally got one of those if we didn't carefully track how much alcohol they were served.

"No, he's foreign. I think Spanish, maybe. He keeps asking questions about the menu and telling me how wrong everything is. Literally like I care."

"Why is he giving you a hard time?"

"Because he's a dick?" She took the plates and walked out of the kitchen.

I didn't like customers mistreating my employees. It was hard enough to find people willing to work here. I looked across the line at Tony. "You okay for a few minutes? I want to see what's going on."

"Yeah," he waved his hand at me. "I got it handled in here."

I wasn't sure about that, but I had bigger problems. My heels clicked on the floor as I pushed my way into the dining room. Seven tables were occupied, even though it was peak dinner hour. Shit. Not great.

Ignoring that for the moment, I glanced over at table seven—and nearly tripped.

Oh, wow. *Hello, sir.*

A very handsome older man sat in the back of the round booth alone, one arm stretched out along the top of the leather back. He wore an expensive-looking gray suit, and the huge silver watch on his wrist gleamed in the soft overhead lighting. Why were big watches like that so sexy on men?

A weird flutter went through my chest as I took in the dark wavy hair, the strong features, the high cheekbones. He was clean-shaven, so there was no missing the full lips or the small cleft in his chin. His jaw was a work of art. Some men were just born to stop traffic, sculpted by divinity to drive women wild, no matter his age.

Well, one of those was now sitting in my restaurant.

Fine. Okay. I could handle him. Hot or not, he didn't have the right to be a dick. Not in my restaurant.

Table Seven lifted the full glass of red wine on the table and brought it to his face. I expected him to drink, but he smelled the contents instead. Then his top lip curled and he set the glass back on the white tablecloth, untested.

The nape of my neck tightened and my skin grew hot. Was he implying my wine was bad?

Remain calm. Stay in control. I could do this. This was my domain.

I walked over to his table. "Good evening, sir. Is there a problem with your wine?"

Deep brown eyes met mine. The color of strong coffee, they were filled with intelligence and confidence. And plenty of disdain. "The *problem* is this wine is an insult to the people of Toscana."

Italian. I would know those long vowels and rolling r's anywhere.

It reminded me of my father, and a wave of irrational anger rolled through me. I swallowed it down, as I always did when thoughts of my father threatened to ruin my day. "I would be happy to get you a fresh glass. Or a different wine, if you prefer."

"I was told this is the best wine you offer."

"Maybe you would prefer a beer, then. Or a glass of whiskey."

"What I want, *signorina*, is a decent glass of wine."

Yeah, this guy was a total dick. Customer or not, I didn't need this grief in my life. "Well, there are a lot of other restaurants in Paesano. Maybe one of them has a wine that will meet your standards."

He barely blinked, his stare so intense that I felt it in the toes of my high-heeled shoes. "You are supposed to please the customer, no? Not kick them out. Perhaps I should speak to the owner."

"You are speaking to the owner."

His lips twitched, as if this information pleased him. Which made no sense. "I see. So you are the one who pretends to know my language."

I folded my arms over my chest. "What are you talking about?"

"The name of your restaurant is incorrect."

"Look—" Out of the corner of my eye, I saw the table waiting on their chicken parm standing up to leave, their expressions both angry and annoyed. Shitballs.

I hurried over to see if I couldn't get them to stay. "Mrs. Taylor, Mr. Taylor. Please, don't go. Let me go see what's holding up your food."

"Oh, Val." Mrs. Taylor grimaced and exchanged a look with her husband. "Sweetie, we really can't wait any longer. Mr. Taylor has low blood sugar and if he doesn't eat . . ."

I held up my hands, pleading with them. "I know you've been waiting on your food for a long time. I'm so sorry. What if I bring you something to tide you over?"

"We have to go," Mr. Taylor said. "There's a game on tonight."

"Well, let me send you home with some food. Salad or a dessert, maybe."

The older couple started edging away from me, heading toward the door. "That's alright, honey," Mrs. Taylor said. "We've got some leftover chicken tetrazzini in the fridge."

Damn it, this was a disaster. I followed them. "Fair enough. But the next time you visit, your dinner's on me."

"Sure, Val," Mrs. Taylor said, but it didn't sound genuine. Were they placating me to get out of here?

I waved good-bye and let them go, my shoulders slumping in defeat. Forgetting about Table Seven for the moment, I marched toward the kitchen, angry beyond words.

This is your responsibility. You're in charge. And you're failing. Get it together, Val.

Chaos met me when I pushed inside. Anne Marie and Tony were screaming at each other. Bits of the conversation started to take shape in my brain.

"—make the food as the tickets come in, bitch," Tony snapped. "I'm not playing favorites."

"Bullshit," Anne Marie yelled. "You're putting her tickets first because you're fucking her—even when it costs me customers."

Wait, were they talking about Tony and Christina? And they were . . . ? Oh god, the mayor was going to kill me.

"You're fuckin' crazy," Tony said. "No wonder your husband left you."

I legit gasped as Anne Marie snarled, "What the fuck did you just say to me?"

Tony didn't back down in the least. "You heard me."

Anne Marie grabbed a plate and hurled it at Tony's head. "You asshole!" Tony ducked and the plate hit the back wall, shattering.

I shouted, "Wait a minute! Both of you!"

"See?" Tony gestured to the broken plate. "Fucking crazy!"

Anne Marie went for another plate—but a pair of suit-clad arms suddenly wrapped around her, holding her still.

My heart dropped. It was Table Seven. And he looked pissed, his dark eyebrows pulled low, his jaw taut as he kept hold of Anne Marie.

"Let me go!" She twisted, trying to break free.

"*Basta, signora,*" he said in a commanding tone that no one—man, woman or child—would argue with.

Silence descended.

I didn't know what to say. Horror and embarrassment had taken hold of my tongue. One of my customers had broken up a fight in my kitchen. Could things get any worse?

"I am going to release you," Table Seven said to Anne Marie. "No more throwing of plates, *per favore.*"

She nodded and Table Seven let her go. Then Anne Marie held up her hands. "You know what? Fuck this. I'm done." It took only a second for her to throw her keycard on the counter. "Good luck with this asshole, Val. He's the reason no one wants to work here. He's verbally abusive and completely incompetent."

I tried to stop her, calling, "Wait, Anne Marie. Don't go."

But she was already gone, the kitchen door flapping behind her. I rounded on Tony. "Are you kidding me right now?"

He shrugged. "Eh, she's a bitch. Whaddya gonna do about it? Besides, you're better off."

That was the second time he'd called Anne Marie a bitch, and I hadn't liked it either time. And I one-hundred percent believed Anne Marie's assessment of him. Now everything made sense. "You're fired."

His jaw dropped open. "You're firing *me*? I'm the only thing holding this place together. Without me, you're fucked, Val."

"I don't care. I'm tired of the late tickets, the sloppy plates, not following directions. You are costing me both customers and good staff."

His expression twisted with fury as he slapped the metal counter with his palm. "Fire me? Fuck off! I'm the only person willing to work here. You'll never find another chef."

"You fired Tony?" The kitchen door swung closed behind

Christina as her eyes darted between Tony and me. "You can't fire him, Val."

"Why? Because you're sleeping together and you know your father won't approve, so this is the only way you can sneak around to do it?"

I heard Table Seven mutter, "*Madre di dio*," but I kept my gaze on Christina. She lifted her chin like the belligerent teenager she was. "Don't be such a bitch. He's the only reason I stayed. The tips are literal shit."

"If you don't want to work here without him, then go. Both of you, just fucking go."

Tony whipped off his apron and threw it on the floor. "You're gonna regret this, Val. Come on, baby."

My last remaining waitress threw her order pad and keycard next to Anne Marie's on the pass. "Yeah, you're fucked, Val."

The two of them marched out the back door, letting it slam shut behind them. Mike, one of the two line cooks, walked over and turned off the burners on the gas stove. "What should we do, Val?"

"Can you or Pete take over tonight?" Maybe I could wait tables. God knew I'd filled in many shifts before. Then the evening wouldn't be a total loss.

Mike and Pete exchanged a look. Neither looked particularly enthusiastic about taking over. I suppose I couldn't blame them, considering they hadn't been working here long.

Mike scratched the side of his neck. "I don't know. Tony was still teaching us."

I nodded, even though I wanted to scream about the unfairness of all this. But it wasn't Mike and Pete's fault that they weren't ready. It was like this place was cursed.

Do something. This is your responsibility.

I took a deep breath and let it out slowly. I needed to close tonight. Maybe for the entire week, until I hired another chef and more servers. "Why don't you two take off? I'll send the customers home and we'll figure all of this out tomorrow."

Ignoring Table Seven, who for some reason was still standing in the kitchen, I went to the back. John, my dishwasher, was busy loading dirty plates into the rack, his head bopping to the music blaring from his ear buds. I flicked the lights to get his attention without scaring him half to death.

He took out his ear buds and grinned over his shoulder. "Hey, Val. Everything okay?"

John was in his late twenties. I knew he'd been in jail a few years ago for stealing a car, but I didn't judge him. None of us had it perfect in this life. He was an excellent employee, and I'd pushed him for months to go out onto the floor as a server. He claimed he liked washing dishes best because no one hassled him back here.

"We're closing early tonight. And we'll probably be closed for a few days." I swept my arm in the direction of the kitchen. "Almost everyone just quit."

"Oh, shit. What did I miss?"

"It's not worth explaining. Bottom line, I should've fired Tony a long time ago."

"Yeah," John agreed, wiping his hands on a towel. "Him fucking Christina wasn't ever going to end well."

Did everyone but me know? "Why didn't you tell me?"

"I thought everyone knew."

"I'll see that you're paid until I find a new chef."

"Thanks, Val. I appreciate that." He gestured toward the stack of dishes. "I'll finish up for the night. Just bring back anything that needs washing."

"I will, and thank you."

I hurried to lock the back door, just in case any recently fired employee tried to return. Then I went to my office to turn off both the online ordering system and the phone. No sense in taking orders we couldn't fill.

When I returned to the kitchen, I found Table Seven opening a fresh bottle of wine. I nearly tripped. Like, what the hell? Yes, he looked like a contestant on a reality show called Italy's Hottest Business Daddy. But I didn't need him to witness any more of my humiliation. "What are you still doing here?"

The man rolled his hand as if the answer were obvious. "I'm pouring you a drink."

"I don't have time for that. I have to go deal with the customers."

He filled a glass halfway with red wine. "I have done that already. Have a drink, signorina."

He had? I peered through the tiny window in the kitchen door into the dining room. Sure enough, empty. "What happened? How did you clear everyone out so quickly?"

"I gave each table one hundred dollars and told them to get the fuck out. Along with your boy, the one that cleans the dirty tables."

There had been six tables other than his out there. And he sent my bus boy home, too? Who carried seven hundred dollars in cash on them?

I'd think about that later. He was standing beside me now, his expensive cologne filling my head. Why did he smell so good? A glass of wine appeared in front of my face. "Drink."

"I really shouldn't. I have a thousand things to do tonight."

"No, you don't. Take a breath and have a drink. Your problems will keep."

He made it sound so easy. But there hadn't been time in my life to take a breath, not since before my mother got sick. Who was this stranger to order me around?

Except that glass of wine looked amazingly good.

I stared at it, feeling myself weaken. I did need to relax. Wasn't that what my friend Maggie always said? And this had been a really, really shitty night.

Still, I didn't trust men bearing gifts.

I peered up at him. "Is this because you feel sorry for me?"

"No, this is because I have been in this country for two days and am still searching for a decent glass of wine. Maybe this will be the one."

Despite all my woes, my lips twitched in amusement. "Are you a wine snob?"

"I am from Italia," he said with an elegant lift of his shoulders. "Take the glass, signorina. You deserve it."

I did deserve it. Fuck it.

Our fingers brushed as I accepted the wine and I ignored the little thrill that rocketed through me. "I'll pay you back," I murmured before taking a long sip. The wine was rich and flavorful, a delicious explosion of bold fruit on my tongue. "Wow, this is good. Which one is it? The pinot noir?"

"No. I bought a decent bottle from the place next door." He went to the counter and poured his own glass. He held it up to his nose and smelled, his eyes closing in concentration. "*Bellissimo.*"

A wave of heat went through me at the Italian word in his low, pleased tone. My cheeks grew hot, so I hid my face with another drink of wine. I watched him do the same, the thick cords of his throat working as he swallowed. Why was this attractive man here?

"*Allora*, this is proper wine," he declared.

"Why are you here?" I blurted. "In my kitchen, I mean."

His dark brown gaze slid over my face, but I couldn't tell what he was thinking. There was something dangerous and enigmatic about him. "Because I feel sorry for you," he replied, confirming my earlier suspicion.

Oh, god. That was depressing.

I tapped a finger against my glass. "When I came to your table, you said the name of the restaurant was wrong. What did you mean?"

He set his wine glass carefully on the counter. "Trattoria Rustica. Not *rustico*. Trattoria is feminine."

Whatever way you spelled it, the name sounded incredibly sexy rolling off his tongue. Sexy or not, though, this was insulting. My voice turned frosty. "My family has owned this restaurant for over fifty years. No one has ever pointed out that the name is wrong."

"*Ma dai*," he muttered and dragged a hand down his face. "You know nothing of your heritage."

"Yeah, well. We live here, not there." And some of us hadn't ever visited Italy, either. I wanted nothing to do with my father or his homeland.

"That is no excuse."

I downed the rest of my wine. "Thanks for this. But if you don't mind, now I have to clean up so that I can go home and take the world's longest shower before dropping into bed and catching three hours' worth of sleep before coming back here in the morning."

He heaved a sigh at my rambling and shook his head. Like I was a ridiculous child. "You are better off. These people, they were terrible."

"True, but no one's knocking down my door to work here."

He reached for the bottle of wine and refilled my glass. "Have another drink and tell me why."

I probably shouldn't, but what the hell?

Lifting the glass, I took a deep swallow. My shoulders eased slightly and I leaned against the counter. "Because I suck at this job, apparently."

Oh, shit. I covered my mouth with my hand. Had I really said that? Normally, I had to be super drunk to start letting my insecurities show.

Maybe I should slow down with the wine.

"From what I could tell, the food and service were awful. But these things are not entirely your fault."

My lips parted as I stared at him for a long beat. "Wow. You just say whatever you want, don't you?"

The edge of his mouth kicked up, making him appear a hundred times hotter. Why did I find this man so attractive? Did I have daddy issues?

Of course I have daddy issues. I barely know my father. And I'm still grieving for my mother. I have everything issues.

Table Seven waved his elegant hand. "A habit from a young age, I'm afraid. Tell me, why are you in charge here? You are obviously young. Why are you not attending university, partying with friends?"

Did I honestly want to get into my life history with a perfect stranger?

Granted, a stranger who smelled like heaven and looked like an Italian movie star. And what was I rushing home for? An empty house, a reality show, and a carton of ice cream? Besides, John was still washing dishes in the back, so it wasn't like Table Seven and I were alone.

Another glass of wine wouldn't hurt.

Chapter Three

Valentina

"Okay, I'll have another drink," I announced. "But you have to tell me your name first. I can't keep thinking of you as Table Seven."

He stuck out his hand. "Luca DiMarco."

"Val Montella."

I put my hand in his and large fingers engulfed mine. Warm, rough skin wrapped around me. He had a strong grip—a *man's* grip. Heat rolled through me and settled between my legs.

"Val?" he asked.

"Short for Valentina."

"Ah. That is a beautiful name."

"I've always hated it. Sounds too much like 'valentine.'"

His eyebrows pulled low, like he was confused. "It is from the Roman name Valentinus, which derives from the Latin word *valens*. It means 'healthy' or 'strong.' This is an honorable name in Italia."

Oh, boy. Sexy *and* smart? My body was about to go up in flames so I forced myself to let go of his hand. Still, his touch lingered on my skin.

I shoved aside the unwelcome attraction and accepted another full glass of wine from him. I made sure not to let our fingers touch this time. "So, what do you want to know?"

"Why are you here instead of attending school?"

Leaning against the stainless steel counter, I cradled my glass in my hand. "My mother ran this place after my grandfather died. But when she died three years ago, I took over."

"I am sorry to hear this. But is there no one else? A cousin or an uncle?"

I narrowed my eyes on him. "A man, you mean?"

"An adult, I mean."

"I am an adult."

He sipped his wine and stared at me over the rim. "Barely. Regardless, you need a firmer hand with your staff. You let them speak to you as if you're a friend, not the boss."

"Maybe. But it's been hard to keep people around. I can't afford to—" I bit my lip, stemming my thoughts. "I was going to say I can't afford to lose anyone else. But in one night I've lost almost everyone."

"This can be good, no? A fresh start."

A bitter, loud laugh escaped my mouth. "Sure. Because it's so easy to hire people here." And I was running out of money. The restaurant had been operating in the red for the last eight months, using up the remainder of my mother's life insurance payout. I didn't know how much longer I could stay afloat.

"If the food and wages are good, people will come."

He was talking in circles and I really wasn't in the mood for—

My stomach chose that precise moment to make a hideously loud noise. Mortified, I froze and prayed the floor would swallow me whole. Then I put my hand on my belly, like I could stem whatever was happening in there. "Sorry. Ignore that."

He paused, glass halfway to his mouth. Then he frowned. "When was the last time you ate?"

I thought back over the day. I'd skipped the employee meal to deal with a particularly nasty vegetable supplier. Did I eat a power bar from my desk? No, it was breakfast. A bagel, I was pretty sure.

Luca sighed heavily, sounding aggrieved, and put down his glass. He took off his suit coat, then folded and placed it on the counter. Suddenly, I was distracted by wide shoulders encased in a crisp white shirt. No tie, so I could see a bit of his chest and the hair dusting his skin. Everything about him was so manly, completely different from any guy my age.

He walked around me, behind the pass, toward the gas stove. On the way he began rolling up his shirt sleeves, revealing strong forearms and tanned olive skin. I must've had more wine than I thought, because I itched to run my fingers over those forearms, trace the veins and tendons there.

He peeked into the pans left on the stove and pushed them out of the way, then searched through the utensils and cookware. He produced a clean sauté pan and set it on a burner.

"What are you doing?" I asked.

A clean apron appeared in his hands, which he wrapped around his waist. "Making you dinner."

Dinner?

No way was he cooking me food. I must've misheard him. "I'm sorry, what?"

Instead of repeating himself, he peeked into a pot of water leftover from earlier. Luca poked at the limp noodles and shook his head. "*Mamma mia,*" I heard him mutter before he carried the pot to the trash and upended it, sending the pasta and water into the garbage.

Taking a fresh stockpot to the sink, he filled it with water and set it on a burner, which he lit with a flick of his wrist. He moved briskly, efficiently, like someone comfortable in the kitchen. I almost couldn't believe my eyes.

A hot Italian man who looked like this *and* cooked? It wasn't fair. I'd practically grown up in this restaurant and I was hopeless with preparing food.

"Where is your garlic?" he asked, rummaging through the spices.

"It's there." I walked around the counter and found the container of garlic powder. "Here."

He looked at the container in my hand and his upper lip curled into a sneer. "I meant *fresh* garlic." He selected the salt and poured some into the pot on the stove.

"Fresh garlic should be in the cooler."

"Bring me a head."

Not "will you," or "can you." Just a clear order to fetch the ingredients for him. Didn't stop me from walking to the cooler, though.

"Anything else?" I asked over my shoulder with a heavy dose of sarcasm.

"Three chili peppers. And some parsley."

The inside of the cooler was a mess. Vegetables were placed with no rhyme or reason, and today's delivery hadn't even been put away yet. I sighed. Another project for tomorrow.

I searched the shelves for Luca's requests. Unfortunately, I couldn't find any chili peppers, only green bell, so I grabbed three along with fresh parsley.

He glared at the items in my hands. "Those are not chili peppers."

"I couldn't find any, so I took these. Won't they work?"

He muttered in Italian and took the parsley. "Put those peppers back."

I did as ordered. When I returned, he was expertly chopping parsley on a wooden cutting board. He handled the knife like a professional chef, but I was mesmerized by the muscles in his forearms as he worked. He looked strong. And competent.

Stop. He's too old for me. And I'm not interested.

Okay, maybe I was a tiny bit interested in those forearms.

Bending, he searched below. He dangled the giant container of olive oil in his two fingers like he was holding a dead rat. "This was made in *Texas*."

I crossed my arms over my chest, feeling defensive. "That is good olive oil."

He uncapped the container and sniffed inside. "It's shit."

"Well, that's all we have."

"This is your problem," he said, drizzling some of the oil into a sauté pan. "You don't know real food. Tell me, what is your favorite dish?"

That was easy. "Chicken Parm."

He snorted. "Not from Italia. Next?"

It wasn't? "Spaghetti and meatballs."

"Again, not a dish from Italia."

Now I was getting annoyed. "Then why are those dishes on every Italian menu in the world?"

He added parsley stems and cloves of garlic to the hot oil. "Not in authentic restaurants, they aren't." He stirred the stems and garlic with a metal spoon.

I went for my wine glass, needing something to do other than stare at this infuriating and beautiful man. "Well, here in America, we like chicken parm and spaghetti and meatballs."

"You will like this better." He added a fistful of spaghetti to the boiling water, then returned to the sauté pan. He removed the garlic pieces and stems, tossed them in the trash, then reached for two more garlic cloves and a grater. Like it was the easiest thing in the world, he grated the garlic into the warm oil.

I drank and watched, fascinated. Grating garlic? What magic was this?

He added chopped parsley, red pepper flakes, and a ladle of pasta water, then mixed it all around. "Do you have cheese? *Real* cheese, not the powdered kind."

"Yes, we have *real* cheese."

"*Va bene.* Bring me pecorino. Or Parmigiano-Reggiano."

"I have hunks of parmesan."

From his sigh of disappointment, you'd have thought I said we use a non-meat substitute in our meatballs. I'd better not mention that the parmesan came from a big-box discount chain.

I delivered the cheese to him and leaned against the counter. "You're a food snob. And a wine snob."

"You say this like it is a bad thing." He removed the pasta with tongs and added it all to the sauté pan. "But you will taste this and learn why simple quality ingredients are best."

Another ladle of pasta water, then he reached for the cheese and the grater. I enjoyed more forearm muscle porn as he grated the cheese atop the noodles. "Find me two plates," he said.

Taking the handle of the pan, he lifted it and began tossing the noodles in the sauce with little flicks of his wrists. I stood there, frozen, watching. Not a splash or a drop spilled. He worked the pasta around, his strong hands both capable and sexy, and I knew without a doubt those hands would be just as capable and strong on a woman's body. My heart was racing in my chest just thinking about it.

"Plates, Valentina," he repeated, and I realized I'd been staring at him for far too long.

I grabbed two plates from the overhead shelf, then Luca twirled two heaping servings onto the plates, making sure to add more sauce. He grated more cheese on top, then lifted both of the plates. "Bring our wine and follow me."

Another order. This man did not know the word *please.* I grabbed the wine glasses and bottle and trailed him into the empty dining room. He'd already placed the plates on a clean table and was removing the apron when I caught up. He held out a chair for me.

It felt weirdly intimate to be out here alone with him in a restaurant. Almost like a date.

No, he's just old school. Gentlemanly. He feels sorry for me.

"Thank you," I said as I sat down.

Luca lowered himself into the seat opposite and placed the napkin on his lap. "*Buon appetito.*"

"It smells amazing."

"It will taste amazing, as well."

He topped off our wine as I took my first bite. The sauce was a tad spicy but creamy, silky smooth in my mouth. The garlic flavor was the perfect amount. I quickly took another bite. "Oh, god. This is so fucking good."

Luca hadn't touched his plate. Instead, he reclined in his chair, wine glass in hand, and studied me as I ate. "I'm glad you think so."

"No, seriously," I said around another mouthful of food. "How can you produce something this good, this flavorful in five minutes? It's not fair."

"More like fifteen, no? And this dish would be better with the right cheese and real peppers."

I was too hungry to argue. After a few more bites, I asked, "How did you learn to cook? Did you go to culinary school?"

He sipped his wine. "I learned by watching. Food is very important in a family in my country."

"Do you have a big family?"

"Yes. I have three brothers, but I'm the oldest. They have always been my responsibility."

"Where are you from in Italy?"

"Catanzaro. Do you know where that is?"

"No. Is it near Rome?"

"Not even close. If you think of Italia like a boot, Catanzaro is the instep."

"That makes sense. I think my father's side is from near Naples, but I'm not entirely sure."

He didn't say anything, merely drank his wine, but I could feel his eyes on me as I continued to eat. When I finished my pasta, he swapped out my empty plate with his untouched one. I frowned at him. "Aren't you hungry?"

"No, signorina. You eat it." He waved his hand then poured himself more wine.

I wasn't shy, not about food. If he didn't want it, then the pasta was fair game. And it was too good to let it go to waste.

23

Digging in, I twirled another forkful. "Why are you in Paesano? Do you have family here?"

"I'm here for business."

Now the suit made sense. "What kind of business?" I kept eating, trying to appear casual, like I wasn't fishing for information when I totally was.

"Meetings." He waved his hand again, the silver watch on his wrist gleaming in the soft overhead lighting. "Nothing exciting, I'm afraid."

"Where are you staying?"

"I rented a house on the river."

"Wow, that must be cool. There are some really nice houses up there. I suppose that's better than staying at Anne's Bed and Breakfast in town."

"I prefer my privacy."

Something about the way he said it, a low husky, suggestive tone, caused me to glance up at him. Our eyes met and I swore a little arc of heat jumped between us. My breath caught and I couldn't look away from his intense dark stare. At this particular moment, he was watching me like I was *his* plate of delicious pasta. My mouth went dry and I could feel my pulse racing.

Was he hitting on me?

The idea seemed ludicrous. But that stare . . . it could melt ice from across the room.

Because I had zero chill, I blurted the first thing that came to mind. "I'm not going home with you tonight."

Chapter Four

Luca

Valentina Montella was a fucking knockout.

Dark glossy hair swirled past her shoulders, and her tits filled out the white silk blouse she wore. A long pencil skirt and heels showcased her long legs. She had a wide mouth with plush lips, and flawless features that needed little to no makeup. This was the kind of woman you both wanted to show off in public *and* never let leave your bed.

I hadn't expected it. Based on what I remember of Flavio Segreto, I assumed his daughter would be . . . less attractive than this.

And the way she looked at me? Curious. Interested. Most women in my country knew enough to recognize a dangerous man, but Valentina was letting me serve her wine and get her alone. Ma dai, these Americans. No sense. If she were my woman, a man like me wouldn't get within five meters of her.

Did I want to take her home tonight? Fuck, yes.

But for many reasons, I couldn't. So I needed to stop fantasizing about all the ways I'd like to defile this beautiful girl.

"This is not why I stayed and made you dinner," I said calmly.

"Oh." She looked down and twirled another forkful of pasta.

"And you are too young for me," I added. More for myself than for her, to be honest.

"Why, how old are you?"

"Too old."

Thirty-eight, but a number meant nothing when it came to age. What mattered was life experience, and I'd lived a hundred years as Don Benetti. I was a murderer, a drug trafficker. The head of a criminal empire that stretched across Italia and Europe. The things I've done and seen would horrify most regular people. I didn't want to answer to a wife, and I didn't want to put anyone at risk. It was why I hadn't married, why I *wouldn't* marry.

"Yeah, I feel that way some days," she said, wiping her mouth with the napkin. The haunted look in her eyes, the sadness in the set of her mouth? It pulled at something deep in my chest—exactly like when I watched her employees walk out on her earlier. I sensed this young woman was lost at sea, holding onto a very thin rope and trying to keep afloat.

I remembered often feeling that way when I took over the family after my father's death. My brothers had been there to help, thank Christ. So, who was helping Valentina Montella?

After another sip of wine, I studied her. "A girl your age should be in school. At parties. Having fun."

She snorted. "Sure. I'll get right on that in all my spare time."

This made me even angrier at her father. Even indirectly, Segreto could fix this. He could hire others to run this shit hole, allowing Val to live a life of her own. "You said your mother is sick."

She reached for her wine and drank. Her voice was soft and tight with pain when she said, "She was diagnosed with ovarian cancer when I was sixteen." She shrugged, a small lift of her shoulders. "She died two years later."

"I am sorry, *bella*."

And I was. My own mother had been my father's puppet, always choosing him over her children. I learned from a young age not to count on her for anything, including love. But I knew many good mothers, including the women who gave birth to Gabriele and Leonardo. I hadn't married either former mistress, but my boys experienced excellent childhoods, well loved by both parents.

"Thank you," she said. "I still miss her a lot, but having the restaurant helps me feel connected to her."

"And your father?"

The expression on her face shuttered. "He isn't in the picture much." She drained the wine in her glass. "He's pretty much an absentee father. Just blows into town for a day or two, then leaves again for half a decade." Reaching for the bottle, she almost knocked over a water glass. "Shit!"

We both reached out to steady the empty glass. I ended up wrapping my fingers around hers, and tingles singed my thighs. She kept her eyes on our hands, but I noticed her quick intake of breath.

We stayed like that, our hands touching, for a few seconds, like neither one of us wanted to move. Then she finally slid her fingers out from under mine and put her hands in her lap. I lifted my wine glass to my lips, suddenly wishing for something stronger than wine. I needed to get my head on straight.

The kitchen door swung open. "Val?"

A young man stood there, a ball cap on his head and a dirty apron around his waist. His gaze swept the room and landed on the table where I sat with Valentina. Then he looked at me, his eyes narrowing ever so slightly. Though I didn't know him, I didn't back down. I returned his stare evenly, calmly. Like I had the right to be here.

"John!" Val said, angling in her chair to see behind her. "How's it going back there?"

"I just finished up. But maybe I should stay a little longer. Until you're done eating."

"Oh, I'm done." She leaned back and held up her hands. "I can't eat any more."

John came over to the table and began clearing our plates. "I'll take these dishes back. Do you need a ride home?"

Val touched his arm—and my jaw clenched. Who was this man to her? Not a boyfriend, because there would not be a question as to how she got home. A boyfriend would take her home and fuck her all night long.

"You don't have to do that," she was saying. "I'll clean this up."

"It's no bother," he said, stacking dishes and silverware. "I don't mind. I'll wash these, then I can drive you home."

The implication was clear—he didn't trust me around her. While I could hardly blame him, I didn't like it. I noted the tattoos marking his arms and neck, some crude, as if inked by hand. So, prison then. I wondered what he'd done to earn time behind bars. He didn't strike me as a hardened criminal. Like me.

"John, is it?" I said, relaxing in my chair. "How long have you worked here?"

He didn't immediately answer, so Val filled the silence by saying, "John, this is Luca DiMarco. Luca, this is John Natale. He's been my dishwasher for the last year and a half."

Natale. Italian descent, then. I would have my men run a check on him. "*Piacere*, John Natale," I murmured. *Nice to meet you, motherfucker.*

He nodded his head once, then took the stack of dishes in his hands into the kitchen. When we were alone again, Val said, "Did you need to intimidate him like that? He's a good employee."

"Intimidate? I was very friendly."

"Friendly, sure. Look . . ." She blew out a long breath and leaned in slightly. Her fingers toyed with the stem of her wine glass as she stared at the table. "You here in Paesano, in my restaurant. Like, you're Italian and it's making me wonder . . . Are you here because of something to do with my father?"

She was smart, this girl. It was a good question—the right question—to ask.

The lies I'd prepared sat heavily on my tongue. I intended to

28

make up a story to get her on a plane quickly, then turn her over to Palmieri. What happened next was not my problem. If she or Segreto died, so be it. I had my own problems. I needed to get Niccolò out of prison before he toppled my entire empire.

But this was before I saw her holding onto this place by her fingernails. Before I heard her stomach growl because she took care of everyone else before herself. Before I noted a weariness in her eyes that made me want to help in whatever way possible . . .

And she'd just confessed that Segreto shows up here every now and again. That meant he was close, keeping tabs on his daughter, as I'd suspected.

Maybe I could give Flavio Segreto directly to Palmieri without using Valentina.

I needed to consider this.

Meeting her gaze squarely, I lied. "No. I am here for business."

"Oh, good," she said softly, almost dreamily, then her cheeks warmed and she bit her lip in the most adorable way. "I mean, good that it's not about my father. I really don't know much about him and I don't want to, either."

"When was the last time you saw him?"

"I think I caught a glimpse of him at my mom's funeral." She dragged a polished fingernail over the white tablecloth. Her nails were a deep red, a color I happened to find very sexy. "But he didn't speak to me."

Because Segreto knew it was dangerous to be seen with her. But I would bet anything he's close by, or at least keeping tabs on her.

Before I could comment, she asked, "Do you have family back in Italy? A wife? Kids?"

Was she fishing? "I have never been married, but I have two sons. They are sixteen and eighteen."

Her brows lifted. "You weren't in love with their mother?"

I almost laughed. Not because I thought loving a mistress was impossible, but because I didn't believe myself capable of the emotion. I hadn't experienced romantic love once since I started fucking at thirteen years old. And children outside of wedlock were common in the 'Ndrangheta. Every don I knew had at least one child from a woman who was not his wife. "Mothers, plural, and neither one was interested in marriage with me."

"I find that hard to believe. Having kids is a lot of work."

"Not when you have money. I gave both as much help as they needed and my sons had the best of everything."

A flash of something—disappointment?—crossed her face, but it was too quick for me to decipher. "So you weren't around."

Ah. She was comparing me to her own father. "I helped raise them. Hardly a day has gone by since they were born when I haven't seen both of them." Leo and Gabriele were my heirs, my legacy. Benetti through and through. It was my responsibility to see them shaped properly for what their future would bring. There could be no weakness or hesitation when it came time to take over.

My mobile buzzed again in my pocket, but I ignored it. Probably my men outside checking in. I brought seven guards with me to Paesano, though my brothers had argued for more. I overruled them, thinking I wouldn't be here long. Now that seemed foolish on my part.

Valentina propped her elbow on the table and rested her chin in her palm. Her lips curved into a smirk. "Are you telling me you changed diapers in your bespoke suit?"

"I hired a nanny to change diapers."

"Of course you did." She rolled her eyes heavenward.

"Gabriele vomited on me twice. Does this make you feel better?"

"It does, actually."

I found myself smiling at her. "I make you dinner and this is how little you think of me, eh? Ma dai, signorina."

She stared at me, her gaze slightly cloudy. I couldn't tell if it was lust or the wine, but I hoped it was the drink. I was already trying to resist her. If she encouraged me, I was lost and fucking her was a bad idea. My dick had already caused enough trouble. She wasn't much older than Leo, for fuck's sake.

The kitchen door opened again, disrupting the moment, and we both looked away. I willed my cock to calm down as John approached with my suit coat dangling from one finger. Had he checked the pockets for clues about me? If so, I was pleased to disappoint him. I wasn't as stupid as that.

I pushed back in my chair and rose to my full height. I had at least three inches on the dishwasher, which I wasn't afraid to use to intimidate him. I held out my hand for the jacket and he passed it over. "*Grazie*, John."

He ignored me. "You ready to go home, Val?"

"Yes, I think so." She stood up out of her chair. "Let me turn off all the lights and lock up."

"I will say good night, then," I said, hanging my coat over my arm. Then I went around the table to Val. Bending, I kissed both of her cheeks, making sure to inhale her sweet perfume while I had the chance. "A pleasure, signorina."

"Thank you for dinner, Luca. I can't remember the last time someone cooked for me like this."

A shame. This beautiful creature deserved to be pampered and taken care of.

Before I could make promises I had no business making, I said simply, "*Prego*, bella." And I forced myself to walk out the front door.

Chapter Five

Valentina

I overslept the next morning.

Plus, I started my period, which meant cramps all day on top of a failing restaurant. Why was the universe piling it on right now? Haven't I endured enough?

Around nine o'clock I dragged my ass into the Leaning Tower of Pastries, my usual stop on the way to the restaurant. There were a few people occupying tables at the cafe, typing on laptops, but the counter was free. This meant that Bev, the owner, saw me as soon as I walked in. "Hey, Val," she called. "What's up?"

I propped my sunglasses on my head and approached the counter. Bev's granddaughter, Sam, one of my good friends, helped Bev run the bakery. They were both staring at me curiously as I approached. "Morning. Can I get the usual?"

Sam's eyebrows raised as she looked me over. "You okay? You're looking a little rough this morning, girl."

"Bad night, bad morning. I'll be fine."

Sam turned to start making my double-shot oat milk iced mocha latte, but Bev lingered, her mouth pinched. "Does this have anything to do with the handsome gentleman handing out money like it was mints in your place last night?"

Shit. Has everyone heard about that?

"Yes, everyone's heard about it," Sam called over the noise of the espresso machine. "You know how Paesano is."

Yes, I did. I rubbed the bridge of my nose between my thumb and index finger. My abdomen was killing me. "Then you also heard everyone quit on me."

Bev waved her hand. "You're better off. Tony's food was terrible, honey. You'll find someone else."

I wished I shared her optimism. "Know any Italian chefs you can recommend?"

"What about Mr. Hundred Dollar Bills? Is he a chef?"

"Not a chef, unfortunately." Though that pasta dish was amazing. And he'd managed it so quickly.

Sam drizzled extra chocolate syrup on top of my drink, then put on a lid. "That's probably for the best. Anyone carrying that much money is bad news."

"He's Italian," I said, like it explained having that much cash.

Bev reached into the case and wrapped up a chocolate croissant for me. "Honey, we're all Italian."

"No, I mean he, like, lives in Italy. Thick accent. The whole thing."

"Ohhhh." Sam slid my drink over. "And did you spend a lot of time talking to Mr. Italy?"

Before I could answer, Bev put the croissant on the counter. "He must be the man who rented the Portofino McMansion."

I paused, the coffee drink halfway to my mouth. That house was the biggest in Paesano, owned by a family with reported mob ties. With seven or eight bedrooms, the place was straight out of a BBC Jane Austen adaptation dipped in gold leaf. "He said he rented a place on the river."

"Bingo." Bev rang up my total on the register. "I heard he made the Portofinos an offer they couldn't refuse."

"Stop. Next you'll say there was a horse's head in the bed." I paid with my phone and grabbed my croissant. "You're leaping to conclusions."

"Not a very big leap, Val. You should keep away from him. Your mom—"

When Bev bit off what she was about to say, I prompted, "My mom, what?"

Bev patted my free hand where it rested on the counter. "Your mom wouldn't want you messing around with those kinds of men."

Mom and Bev had been good friends, playing in a cutthroat mahjong group every week until Mom grew too sick. Since my mom died, Bev had watched over me, almost like a grandma.

Sam spoke up. "Gram, stop scaring her. You know Val doesn't have time for dating."

Guilt washed over Bev's expression. "I'm sorry, Val. I know you've had a lot on your plate these last few years."

An understatement. There hadn't been time for romance or even hookups. My mother got sick when I was sixteen, and all my time after that had been split between school, her care, and the restaurant. Now, five years later, I was an overworked, exhausted virgin, which was so embarrassing. Most girls my age were finishing college, having fun, while my nights were spent arguing with servers and chefs. And any man I'd even remotely tried to flirt with had quickly lost interest when they heard my schedule.

Sorry, I work every night. Maybe we could have a morning coffee date if it's before nine o'clock?

I was cursed. Sad and angry and cursed.

I finished paying and took my things. "Speaking of, I need to get over there. This situation isn't going to un-fuck itself."

"Wait," Sam said, heading for the edge of the counter. "I'll walk you out."

"Okay. Bye, Bev!" I lifted the hand holding the coffee in farewell and went to wait for Sam. When my friend joined me, we slowly made our way to the door.

"Don't let Bev scare you away," Sam said quietly. "She worries, that's all."

"I know. It's all right."

She elbowed me. "So, tell me about him. What happened after he handed out money and you closed up?"

"How do you know something happened?"

"I don't, but the way you're turning red right now is a pretty big clue. You look like that time in high school when our chemistry teacher told you to stop staring at Joey Brooks."

I bit my lip. "I swear, that boy was so fine."

"Agreed. Now, back to Mr. Hundred Dollar Bills, please."

"Not you, too. Ugh." Sometimes Sam and Bev were far too alike. "And there's not much to tell. He made me dinner and then—"

"He made you dinner?" Her voice was a screech that gained the attention of everyone in the room.

I wanted to crawl under a table. "Do you mind? I don't need the entire town to find out."

"Sorry. Oops, sorry." She took my elbow and led me outside onto the walk. "Wait, I need details."

I couldn't hold it in. I spilled about my stomach growling, the pasta dinner, how charming Luca had been.

"Oh, my god. You have a crush on him."

"Stop it. He's a stranger. And too old for me."

"How old is old?"

"Sam," I said with a heavy sigh. "Can this grilling wait? I haven't even had coffee yet."

"Too bad, Montella. Answer the question."

"He's late thirties, I think."

"That's not too old!" She clapped her hands. "I like this for you. I think you should make him some chicken parm as a thank you."

"You know I can't cook. And I have no staff. How am I supposed to make that happen?"

"I don't know, but I have some free time this afternoon."

"Thanks. I appreciate the offer." And I did. Sam was one of the kindest, big-hearted people I knew. She baked a custom cake for each of her friends on their birthday. Mine was a limoncello cake with mascarpone frosting and white chocolate shavings. I looked forward to it all year. "See you guys later."

The drive to the restaurant only took a few minutes. I'd kept the dependable blue minivan my mom bought years ago to drive me around to softball and soccer when I was a pimply faced tween. I could still picture her behind the wheel, making me listen to the boy bands of her youth. Maybe that was why I didn't want to get rid of it.

When I pulled up to Trattoria Rustico, there were two men waiting outside the front door. One was wearing a white chef's coat, holding a tiny case. The other man was wearing a nice double-breasted suit and carrying a leather portfolio.

What the hell?

I parked and got out, then walked around to the front instead of going in the back door. "Hello?" I called. "I'm sorry, but we're closed this week."

The men turned to face me. They both looked as tired as I felt. The one wearing a suit said, "We are here to apply for jobs, signorina."

Another Italian. What was in the water these days? "I haven't posted any job listings."

"May we come in and talk with you?"

This was weird, but also serendipitous? I mean, I did need to hire a chef. And at least one server. Were they here for those jobs? If so, I couldn't really afford to turn them away. "Sure. Let me unlock the door."

I put my key in and opened the door. I went through first and flicked on the lights, illuminating the empty dining room. No one else was here, which was eerie. Normally, the kitchen staff would already be in to prepare for lunch.

I didn't want to think about all the money I was losing.

"Have a seat." I gestured to the tables. "Let me put my things in the office and I'll be right back."

I flicked on the lights in the kitchen and went to the tiny office. The stacks of papers and bills awaiting me made my stomach hurt even worse. I put everything down except my coffee and returned to the dining room. The two men were seated at the same table. I could see resumes on the white linen.

Taking a seat, I placed my coffee on the table. "I'm Val Montella." I offered my hand to each of them.

"Signorina Montella, a pleasure. I am Roberto Ferrara," the man in the suit said, shaking my hand.

"Giovanni Peruzzi," chef coat said as he shook my hand. "Signorina."

The chef also spoke with an Italian accent. Alarm bells started going off in my head.

Roberto slid over the two resumes. "We are here to work at your restaurant, signorina. You will see we are very qualified."

"Yes, but how did you know of the openings?" Did Luca have something to do with this?

"A friend said you needed help with your restaurant," Roberto said by way of an answer.

Yep, definitely Luca. I sighed. Did I want to take more help from him? Could I afford not to? I was skating by as it was, and closing this week would seriously hurt my ability to stay afloat. The sooner I could reopen, the sooner we could earn revenue.

"I do need help," I admitted as I lifted the first resume. It was Giovanni's, and it wasn't very long. He'd worked in a total of one restaurant, but he was there for more than fifteen years. I kept reading. The restaurant was in Rome and had a Michelin star. Holy shit!

Jaw falling open, I glanced up at him. "Why in the world would you want to work *here*?"

"I was the sous chef. Working here would allow me to have my own kitchen."

I couldn't process this. My mind tripped over itself in disbelief.

"You realize where you are, right? A small town in New York State? We're not in Manhattan."

The edge of his mouth curled through his thin layer of scruff. "I understand, signorina."

I grabbed my coffee and sucked a big mouthful through the straw. Maybe I was still dreaming? I set Giovanni's resume aside and started reading Roberto's. His was longer, but as I started reading, I could tell he'd worked as a maître d' in some very prestigious restaurants. I recognized some of the names from social media. "You're a maître d'."

Roberto nodded once. "I am the front of the house, sì. But I can do almost anything you need, signorina. Balance books, oversee the staff, place food orders, greet customers. I am very experienced."

I didn't doubt it, based on his resume, but this was too good to be true. Employees like this didn't drop out of the sky, not in Paesano. There had to be a catch. "This friend, the one that told you to come here this morning. Do you have a way to reach him?"

The two men visibly paled as they exchanged a look. "Signorina," Roberto said. "We are happy to help. No one has forced us to come here."

What an odd thing to say.

Now I was even more eager to speak to Luca. "I'm sure that's true, but I'd like to speak with him anyway."

Roberto licked his lips. "I will call him for you. I will ask if he is available."

"Please do that."

Roberto stood from the table and walked a good distance away before pulling out his phone. He spoke quietly to whoever picked up on the other end. After a moment, he carried his phone over to me. "Mr. DiMarco, signorina."

I accepted the phone and put it to my ear. "Hello?"

"Ciao, Valentina."

Those two words, spoken in his deep-accented voice . . . holy Christmas. I stood up and walked to the other side of the room. "What have you done?"

"*Che cosa?* What do you mean?"

"Luca, these men are way overqualified to work here. I'm not sure I can even afford them. Did you force them to come?"

"Don't be ridiculous." I heard the clink of porcelain, like he was setting a cup down on a saucer. "You need employees and I found you the best. They jumped at the opportunity. Do not sell yourself short, bella."

I wasn't stupid. No one was jumping at the opportunity to work in my restaurant. "This is insane. You are insane. I mean, we just met. Why would you help me like this?"

"Because I can. I know people in the restaurant business looking for work, so I decided to help them and you. Do not make it more complicated than that."

I stared at the faded wallpaper behind the server station. Was I crazy for complaining? Luca was presenting me with a solution to my problems, so maybe I should accept it and stop looking for ulterior motives.

But I wasn't used to someone taking over like this. I supposed, if I dipped into Mom's life insurance fund, I could pay them a little more than their predecessors. And if we reopened quickly, maybe it wouldn't be so bad. "I don't know what to say."

"You don't need to say anything. I am happy to help."

"Out of the goodness of your heart."

He gave a soft chuckle that warmed my insides. "Sì, signorina. Out of the goodness of my heart."

I sighed, too hungover to think about this clearly. But I didn't want to accept, either. It felt wrong, like someone was taking away my choices.

"Valentina," he said quietly into the phone. "You have been doing this alone for a very long time. It is admirable. But there is no shame in accepting help from others when you need it. *Capisce?*"

I swallowed hard. He was right, of course. It had been forever since anyone offered any help. I knew it couldn't last, but maybe it would give me time to find proper replacements. "Okay. Thank you. I really appreciate this."

"You are welcome."

We sat there, seconds ticking by, neither of us speaking. It was weird, but not uncomfortable. I could hear the wind slightly on his end, so I assumed he was sitting outside. Suddenly, I wished I could see him. He was probably wearing silk pajamas, like some fancy designer brand I'd never heard of.

I blurted, "You'll come in for dinner when we reopen?"

There was a pause before he said, "Of course. I wouldn't miss it."

"Good. Then I guess I should officially hire my new employees."

"Va bene. *A presto*, Valentina." Then he hung up.

Chapter Six

Luca

Aldo strode into my office, an orange cradled in his thick hands. "Got a minute?"

"Are the cameras in place?"

"Yes." He lowered himself into the chair across from the desk and began peeling the orange. "Four at her house, six at the restaurant, just as you ordered. If Segreto shows up, we'll know it."

"Good. Any word on Niccolò?" Through our contacts, we were trying to learn where my cousin was being held by the police. With any luck we might be able to get him out from under the GDF's nose before he gave them any information.

"Sergio said nothing yet."

I stroked my jaw. This was unusual. We had police on the payroll and they gossiped worse than old women. A Benetti behind bars should be big news in Calabria. Something didn't add up. Were the police lying? Was Niccolò dead?

Aldo continued, saying, "Sergio is pissed you aren't putting her on a plane and coming right back."

My fingers twirled a pen, irritation gathering in the nape of my neck. I didn't answer to my younger brother, so I didn't give a fuck what he thought.

Besides, something was off. Ever since the meeting with Rossi, I'd been turning the situation over in my mind. Why had Segreto come out of hiding to kill Palmieri's daughter? And if Palmieri knew Segreto was guilty, why not find Segreto himself? Why trade my cousin away, when turning Niccolò against me would topple one of the biggest mafia empires in Italia?

Maybe Palmieri really did want to keep this quiet. But I had more questions than answers right now and that made me suspicious.

I tossed the pen onto the desk. "Sergio needs to do his job, which is to find our cousin, and leave Segreto to me."

Aldo didn't move, so I asked, "Was there something else?"

Before he could answer, my mobile buzzed. I checked the screen. Leonardo. We didn't talk business over the phone, so I knew this was a personal call. Holding up a finger to Aldo, I pushed the button to accept. "Pronto."

"Ciao, Papà," my oldest son said. "You didn't check in last night. Is everything all right?"

Leo was a worrier by nature, something he picked up from his mother. And he didn't like that I'd come on this trip myself. "Ciao, *figlio mio*. I'm fine. A late night."

"Do you need me there? Should I come?"

"No, that isn't necessary. I won't be here much longer."

"Thank fuck."

The relief in his tone concerned me. "Why? Che cosa?"

"I probably shouldn't tell you this, but Gabi wants to buy a new car. He went to drive it yesterday."

Mamma mia, another sports car. I scowled at the desk like it had offended me. "Your brother has enough cars—and he doesn't yet have a license to drive." I was too lenient with both boys, but Leo was cautious, responsible. Highly intelligent, but stubborn. Gabriele, on the other hand, was carefree and wild, more reckless. Like me at his age.

"You should talk to him," Leo said. "He won't listen to me."

"I will. Tell me, how are you doing? Anything I should know?"

"I'm fine," Leo said. "Finished work and I'm going to my mother's."

"Work" was following around one of his uncles and doing whatever was asked of him. "Tell Antonia I said hello," I said, referring to his mother. She married a few years ago, which was another reason I was glad Leo lived on the estate with me. I didn't want another man influencing my boys.

"How are the women there?" Leo asked.

Young. Beautiful, with dark eyes and dark hair. A little shy. Big tits. I shoved thoughts of Valentina away. "This is not that sort of trip."

"Dai, Papà. Every trip is that sort of trip."

"Is that what your Bianca would say?" Leo had been seeing the girl for almost six months. She was nice enough, but not who he would marry. I would make those decisions when the time came.

"Are you keeping the guards with you?" he asked, ignoring my question.

"I have been doing this a long time, figlio mio. You don't need to worry about me."

"You haven't been away like this in a long time. It's strange."

True, I hadn't been away much, especially not in the last few years. And I wouldn't be away now if my cousin wasn't sitting in jail. "I've only been gone a few days."

"When are you coming back?"

The words caught in my throat. I didn't have an answer. I could say soon, but I wasn't sure it was the truth.

I can't remember the last time someone cooked for me like this.

"Papà," Leo said in my ear. "Are you still there?"

"I'm coming back soon," I answered. "But you don't need to worry, capisce?"

"I can't help but worry. I feel as if something is going on, but no one is telling me shit."

I considered this. Maybe sheltering him wasn't necessary any longer. At some point I had to start trusting my boys with the problems I dealt with every day. "We'll discuss it when I'm back."

"Okay. I need to go. Mamma is expecting me. *Ti voglio bene.*"

"Ti voglio bene, figlio mio."

After we disconnected, Aldo smirked. "The boys say it's purple."

"What is?"

"The sports car Gabi wants to buy."

I rubbed my mouth, suddenly exhausted. "Madre di dio, that boy has no sense."

"Eh. No sixteen-year-old ever does."

I couldn't think about Gabriele right now. I had too many other things on my mind. "Tell Sergio to keep Gabriele in line." My brother was the only person my youngest son listened to. "What did you find out about this dishwasher?" I'd instructed my men to dig into John Natale's background. I didn't like how protective he'd been of Valentina.

"Nothing."

"Impossible."

"It's true. He's a ghost. No records of any kind. That's what I was waiting to tell you."

I sat a bit straighter. "No taxes, nothing online? No bank accounts?"

"No. It's like he doesn't exist. Identity must be fake."

Now this I did not expect. "Prison record? The ink on his arms was not professional."

"None that we could find."

Angry, I stabbed my index finger into the desk. "I want him followed. I want to know why a man with a fake identity is working in her restaurant."

"Of course, Don Benetti." Aldo pursed his lips and studied the table. "She is beautiful, no? Young women like her, they are like a wet dream for us old men, eh?"

The words lit my temper like a match to kindling. I didn't want anyone leering at her, including me. "Watch your mouth before I punch you."

"This would be unwise, considering she is here."

I paused, my muscles freezing in surprise. Valentina was here? "Why the fuck are you only telling me now?"

He lifted his hands in a helpless gesture. "Should I send her away?"

I should say yes. I shouldn't see her. No good could come of it. "What does she want?"

"She brought you dinner."

What the fuck?

Aldo's mouth curved into a smug smile at my obvious surprise. "But we know you don't eat food from strangers," he said. "So I'm happy to eat it on your behalf."

I stood and grabbed my mobile off the desk. "Where is she?"

"In the kitchen. I gave her a glass of sparkling water and told her to wait."

"Alone?"

He popped a slice of orange in his mouth. "I left one of the boys with her."

I hurried from the office. The air was crisp inside the mansion, the whir of the air conditioning the only sound in the cavernous rooms as I strode toward the kitchen. Though I didn't hear him, I knew Aldo was behind me. He was the quietest soldato I had, which made him the perfect guard for me.

In the kitchen I found Valentina on a stool, looking nervous and uncomfortable, while Carlo leaned against the counter and watched her. I scowled at him. "Get out."

Ducking his head, Carlo went through the back door, outside to where the boys congregated, while Aldo paused in the kitchen entrance. "Need anything from me?"

I shook my head. "I'm fine. We'll catch up later."

"I'll be close," he continued in our language. To Valentina, he said, "Ciao, signorina."

Shifting on the stool, she gave a little wave. A large brown paper bag sat on the marble counter in front of her. I walked over slowly. "Valentina. I wasn't expecting you."

"I know." She pulled her bottom lip between her teeth and squirmed in her seat—and I started picturing other ways I could make her squirm. Like if she sat on my face.

"I feel stupid," she said, distracting me from my dirty thoughts. "I had no idea there were so many people here. I assumed you were alone."

"Ignore them. What's in the bag?"

"I had Giovanni make you dinner. As a thank you. For helping me." She shook her head. "Sorry, I can string words together, I swear."

I kept my voice soft. Reassuring. "There is no reason to be nervous. I'm grateful. I can't remember the last time someone surprised me with dinner."

And I couldn't. I ordered what I wanted, with a hundred men available to carry out my every need and desire. Surprises weren't a good thing in my world.

Except from this woman, apparently.

I went to the cabinet and removed two plates. Then I found knives and forks and put everything on the island. "Would you like a glass of wine?"

"No, thanks. I have to drive back to the trattoria."

I took out another sparkling water and returned to the island, taking the seat next to hers. We were so close that our legs almost touched. She didn't move, so I finally asked, "Can I open it?"

That galvanized her into action. "God, sorry." Taking the bag, she pulled apart the staples keeping it closed then began unpacking the containers. "I needed to make sure Giovanni could cook my grandfather's chicken parm. And we had extra, so I thought I'd bring you some. I hope you like it—even though it's not Italian."

She said the last part with such an attitude that I couldn't help but smile. "I'm going to love it. Even if it isn't Italian."

Soon a plate filled with a cheese-covered chicken breast and spaghetti covered in tomato sauce stared up at me. It looked heavy and . . . unappetizing.

"You hate it."

"I haven't tasted it yet."

"I can tell from your face. You don't think it looks good."

I was usually better at hiding my reactions.

Wiping my face clean, I picked up the knife and fork. "I wasn't thinking anything of the sort," I lied and cut a small bite of chicken. Thick cheese shifted around atop the meat like a sloppy mess. I forced myself to balance the meat and cheese onto the fork and bring it to my mouth.

Exactly as I thought. Heavy. All wrong. Too much happening in one bite.

I swallowed and wiped my mouth with the paper napkin. "It's good."

She threw her head back and laughed. "You are the worst liar."

Wrong. I was an excellent liar. My life, my position, depended on it. Instead of commenting, I cut another bite and held the fork up to her mouth. "Now, you."

There was no need to feed her myself, but a dark craving settled in my veins. I wanted her mouth to touch where mine had been. Dutifully, she leaned forward and accepted the bite, her lips pulling across the tines. Her eyes nearly rolled back in her head as she chewed, a little moan of happiness rumbling in her throat. The sight was so erotic that my cock twitched, blood making its way south to my groin.

"So good," she said. "Even better than my grandfather's. Giovanni is a genius."

I worked on the spaghetti next, anything to keep from staring at her. "I'm surprised you were able to convince him to cook this."

"He wasn't happy about it. He told me the cheese ruined it, when everyone knows the cheese is the best part."

I didn't comment. The spaghetti wasn't terrible. Perfectly cooked, even if the sauce was a bit clumsy. I twirled up another bite.

She shifted again, her knee brushing my thigh. I was aware of her every movement, every breath, and it made me anxious, but in a good way. Could she feel this pull between us, too?

Suddenly, she cleared her throat. "Well, I should go. I just wanted to say thank you for, you know. Dinner the other night and for sending Roberto and Giovanni to me."

I didn't want her to leave. I wanted her to stay and keep me company. "Do you like them? Will they work out?"

"They're amazing. Roberto is making suggestions on how we can improve and grow. And Giovanni is a dynamo in the kitchen. I'm both impressed and terrified of him."

"He won't hurt you."

"No, I know that. I mean I'm terrified of getting in his way."

"It is your restaurant, signorina. Do not let anyone intimidate you."

"Not even you?"

I fought a smile and looked into her eyes. I held up a bite of pasta for her. "Do I intimidate you?"

Lowering her head, she accepted the bite. "Yes," she said through a mouthful of pasta.

"Why?" I was genuinely curious. I hadn't done anything but make her dinner and eat with her. She hadn't seen me at my worst, not even close.

"Your watch."

My head snapped up. "My *watch*?"

She covered her face with her hands. "That sounds so stupid. I can't believe I said that."

I glanced at the titanium watch on my wrist. A costly purchase, but I hardly ever thought about it. I used the accessory to tell time because I didn't always carry a phone. "Explain."

"It's expensive and sexy."

Sexy?

My mind tripped over this word. I didn't know what to do, speech deserting me, as the seconds ticked by. Women have been easily available to me since I was fourteen. There wasn't a time when I wanted one and couldn't have her.

Until now.

Fuck, it wasn't fair. I was drawn to this girl for some reason, even when I shouldn't be. And the feeling was reciprocated. In any other circumstance, I'd be angling to get her into a bed upstairs right now.

But I couldn't.

I took a long drink to clear my head. "You think my watch is sexy."

"Is that crazy? It's just metal and gears. But somehow it's elegant and mature. Like cuff links. Or reading glasses." She wrinkled her nose. "Ugh. Ignore me. I'm going to go."

My cuffs were rolled at the moment and my glasses were in my office, but I wore all those things.

She was out of her seat before I could stop her. "Again, thanks for your help, Luca. I really appreciate it."

There was so much I wanted to say, but my mind was a tangled mess. "You're welcome, Valentina."

She bumped into the stool, her arms flailing a bit as she lost her balance. I grabbed her wrist to steady her, and my fingers stroked her warm, soft skin for a few seconds before I let her go.

"Okay, bye." She gave me an awkward wave and headed for the back door.

"Ciao, bella," I said softly, not taking my eyes off her.

She left and I was alone. Dinner. She'd brought me food. I shook my head and studied my plate. She thought my watch was sexy.

What was it about her? She was too young, too innocent. American. A girl I was using to lure out her father. Pursuing her would be the height of stupidity.

And I wasn't stupid.

I can't remember the last time someone cooked for me like this.

She'd regarded me like a hero for such a simple act. And to thank me, she brought me food in return. When was the last time someone I wasn't paying had taken care of me like this?

I couldn't remember.

Cazzo, this girl. She knew all the right buttons to push.

I wasn't used to denying myself when I wanted something. I was the boss. The world bowed to my whims, not the other way around. As my father liked to say, *Chi nasce lupo, non muore agnello.* He who is born a wolf does not die a lamb.

I was tired of acting the part of a lamb with her.

Hoping wine might improve the taste of the food, I rose, poured a glass, then sat back down. My mind started churning, examining. Plotting.

This wasn't complicated. The business with Valentina's father and Palmieri was separate from any physical relationship I might have with her. We would monitor the camera feeds at her house and restaurant for any sign of Segreto, ready to grab him if he appeared. And there was a good chance we could get Niccolò out of prison before using her became necessary.

And if I eventually needed to get her on a plane to Italy, I would have an easier time of it if she trusted me.

There was nothing stopping me from having her. In fact, it might work to my advantage.

I needed to think. I returned my attention to the chicken dish. She wanted me to eat it? Then I would eat it. Even if it killed me.

Chapter Seven

Valentina

W e were busy. Roberto and I worked together on a plan to hire new staff, rearrange the dining room, and update the decor. I also met with Giovanni to discuss his vision for the menu. He deferred to me, though I could tell he was more than capable of doing this alone. Would probably do a better job, even.

But this place was mine. I wasn't letting anyone take over.

Like when Roberto wanted to remove my friend's wines from the wine list. Roberto argued New Yorkers could not produce a proper red table wine, but Maggie and I went to school together. Her family, the Fiorentinos, ran one of the biggest wineries in the Hudson Valley. We were leaving their wines on the wine list, period.

So when Roberto said that he had a surprise for me outside, I was instantly wary.

I wasn't a fan of surprises.

"Roberto, what's going on?"

"You will like this, signorina."

I wasn't so sure, but I followed him through the front door and out onto the walk. A large white delivery truck was parked at the curb. A guy was putting a ladder away in the back.

"What do you think?" Roberto asked, pointing up.

What the hell? No. Wait. I blinked several times.

The sign. The restaurant's sign had been replaced. Not only that, the name of the *restaurant* had been replaced.

Trattoria Rustica.

I didn't know what to say. This sign was elegant and beautiful. Eye-catching and classy, with black block serif letters on a white background.

But it wasn't the old sign.

The old sign had been there for as long as I could remember. It had a 1970s font and colors like the Italian flag. No doubt it went up when my grandfather opened the place.

My tongue felt thick, emotion strangling my throat. I couldn't cry. It was stupid, to be upset over a sign with its incorrect name and outdated font. God knew keeping the sign wouldn't bring my mother back. But I stood there, looking at this beautiful replacement, feeling like I'd failed. Like I'd disappointed her.

The ache in my chest multiplied, grief gathering like a wave, building and swirling inside me. I couldn't speak. I couldn't even move.

"Signorina," Roberto said, his eyes searching my face. "We thought you would like it."

I should. Any fool would be grateful for the upgrade. Anyone except me, apparently.

Wait, *we?*

Roberto hadn't made this decision alone. And immediately I knew who else was involved.

There is no shame in accepting help from others when you need it.

Damn it. Why did he do this? The old sign was perfectly fine, even if not technically correct. It was one little letter. Who really cared?

This restaurant was mine, my legacy. My link to my mother and her family, the generations of Montellas who'd lived in the Hudson Valley. And now it was transforming into something totally different, something unrecognizable. Something I hadn't approved.

Tears burned behind my eyelids. Jesus, was I going to cry over a sign? I dug my fingernails into my palms and tried to hold myself together. I felt brittle and helpless, a little girl trying to stay afloat in stormy waters.

"Signorina," Roberto tried again. "Say something."

I couldn't. If I spoke, I feared that I would crumble onto the asphalt.

A horn honked behind us, and I automatically turned. A familiar red pickup truck slowed at the curb, my friend Maggie behind the wheel. We'd chatted briefly last night as I caught her up on what was happening at the restaurant.

"Look at this!" She pointed to the new sign as she came around the front of her truck. She wore a tight Yeah, Yeah, Yeahs t-shirt, flared jeans and Chucks, her shoulder-length brown hair tucked under a baseball cap. This was her usual attire. I think I'd seen her in a dress only once, and that had been at my mother's funeral.

She came over to where Roberto and I stood and wrapped an arm around my shoulders. "Holy shit, Val! You're fancy."

I swallowed and tried to sound normal. "Is it too much? I mean, the old one was fine, right?"

"The old one went out with disco and key parties. This sign is really nice, babe."

"But . . ." I wasn't sure. "Does it fit?"

"Val." Maggie turned me to face her, hands holding onto my shoulders. "You like things to stay the same. I get it and I understand why. But you can't hold onto the past through signs and chicken parm."

I felt my eyes starting to burn again. I stared at Maggie helplessly, but my friend was rock steady. As always. "I'm being silly."

Her smile was kind. "No, but you are being given a gift that almost any restaurant owner would kill for, especially one who has worked as tirelessly as you have the past few years. Embrace it. Change can be good for you."

I sighed. "You're right."

"Of course I am. Now, introduce me to your bespoke friend."

Oh, I'd forgotten about Roberto. Wiping the edges of my eyes, I shifted to Maggie's side. "Roberto, meet a very good friend of mine, Maggie Fiorentino."

"Of the Fiorentino wines?"

"Yes."

He inclined his head. "Buongiorno, signorina. A pleasure."

Maggie didn't crack a smile. "You're the one who thinks my red table wine sucks."

"Margaret!" I hissed. "You promised."

Roberto seemed undaunted, his expression cool. "I mean no disrespect, Signorina Fiorentino."

"But you don't like it."

If I thought Roberto was too polite to quibble, I was dead wrong. He said, "There is no acidic backbone. Perhaps it is a personal preference." He shrugged, which somehow managed to come across as charming instead of asshole-ish.

"I'll show you no backbone," she muttered under her breath, then turned and started for the truck.

"Wait, where are you going?" I called. Was she leaving?

"I'm grabbing the wine for book club."

Oh, shit. I forgot about book club! That was tomorrow night.

"Book club?" Roberto asked.

"Yeah, it's the first Saturday night of every month. We always host it here. With everything going on, it totally slipped my mind."

"The restaurant is open on Saturday nights, no?"

"Yes, but we usually start around nine, after the dinner rush. Not that it matters tomorrow because we're still closed."

With his wrinkled brow and flat expression, his disapproval was evident. "Is this a good idea? The remodel is not yet complete."

"It'll be fine. We hardly ever break anything." Roberto's olive skin lost its pallor, his eyes going wide, so I hurried to say, "I'm kidding! It's six or seven women, sitting around gossiping and drinking wine. And after the sign surprise, you and my secret investor owe me."

He held up his palms. "I will return inside, signorina. There are more CVs to read through before our server interviews begin this afternoon."

Roberto strode to the front door and disappeared into the restaurant. I shifted to look at the sign again.

It wasn't terrible. It was actually nice.

But Investor Daddy and I needed to have a serious conversation. Too much was happening too fast. New chef, new kitchen staff. A maître d'. The restaurant my mother had loved and labored over, her legacy, my *grandfather's* legacy, was slipping away from me. I needed time to adjust.

"Stop freaking out and help me with this wine." Maggie shoved a crate into my arms.

I sighed and tried not to drop the crate. "I'm not freaking out."

"Please. I know you and I know that look on your face. Come on. I don't want this wine to overheat and lose its acidic backbone."

I laughed softly. "I'm learning that Italians are snobs when it comes to food and wine."

"Did Mr. Late Night Pasta teach you that?"

I'd confessed the entire story of Luca's visit to the restaurant to Maggie. Twice, because she made me repeat it. "Stop. Don't make up nicknames for him." Bad enough that I've already made up my own nicknames, and each one had the word "daddy" in it.

We walked inside and stopped, our eyes needing a minute to adjust. "Holy shit," Maggie exclaimed. "Is this really your place?"

I tried to see the changes through my friend's eyes. New coat of paint, new tall bar tables and chairs that Roberto found for a steal. The clutter was gone from the walls, and there were fewer dining tables, which made the place feel bigger, less cramped. "It's not finished," I said. "We've reached out to some local Hudson Valley artists for pieces to hang on the walls. And we hired guys to sand and stain the old wooden tables, so they'll look like farm tables."

"No more tablecloths?"

"No more tablecloths."

"Wow. This is major."

I set the crate on a chair. "It's too much, isn't it?"

"Are you kidding?" Maggie gaped as she looked around. "It's gorgeous. It's like a place you'd see in New York or Boston."

"But will people want to eat here?"

"Babe, the entire valley is talking about it. You're going to have lines around the block."

I tucked my hair behind my ears. I didn't like everyone gossiping about me, even if it benefitted the restaurant. "What are they saying?"

"At first it was about Tony and Christina. But now that the jobs are posted, some people think you sold the restaurant to an investor group."

That hit a little too close to home. "Why is he helping me?" I whispered, voicing my deepest fear to Maggie.

Maggie walked closer so we wouldn't be overheard. "Why don't you ask him?"

"Because I'm afraid of the answer."

"Maybe he thinks you're a hot piece of ass and he has money to burn." She shrugged. "I wish some gorgeous Italian fairy godfather would show up at the vineyard and make all my problems go away."

"What if he expected you to sleep with him in return?"

"Then I would count myself super fucking lucky."

The front door opened and daylight cut across the entryway. I couldn't see his face, but it was a tall man wearing a suit—and my heart jumped in my chest. Every part of me went on high alert.

Then the door closed and I exhaled the breath I'd been holding. Mayor Lombardi. Christina's father.

Shit.

The mayor looked around, his gaze taking in the restaurant, before finding me. The smile he gave didn't reach his eyes as he drew closer. His suit coat was unbuttoned, which meant I could see the way his too-small dress shirt stretched across his middle. He wasn't heavy, but he wasn't trim, either. I knew he liked to eat, though, because he usually came in once a week when Christina was working. He never paid—"It's a privilege for you to have the mayor eat here, honey," he told me the first time I brought him a check—but always tipped his daughter with a few hundred dollar bills.

Regardless, I hated how he stared at me over his chicken piccata.

He walked in like he had the right. "Hello, Val. I see you've been busy."

"Hello, Mayor Lombardi. Sorry if you came for lunch, but we're closed."

"I'm not here to eat." He nodded once at Maggie, then returned his stare to me. "I'm here to talk about how you fired my daughter."

Technically, Christina quit. I don't bother to say it, though.

"And," he continued, "you let her get involved with a member of your staff." He paused. "I thought we were friends, Val."

I could feel Maggie edge closer to my side. She never liked the mayor, either.

"I'm not sure what you're talking about," I lied.

"It's the talk all over town. How you fired Christina and your chef because you discovered they'd been dating."

"Dating" was a stretch. Something told me Tony wasn't taking the girl out to dinners and movies.

"That's not true," I offered. "If something was going on between them, I didn't know."

He slipped his hands into his trouser pockets. "Margaret, do you mind if I speak to Val alone?"

Maggie didn't budge. "Val?"

The mayor stared at me pointedly.

I could feel all the things my friend wanted to say, but she had a business, a livelihood here. Pissing off the four-time re-elected mayor wasn't wise, not if she wanted to keep afloat. "It's okay, Mags. Why don't you put the wine in the back?"

Maggie grabbed the crate of wine off the chair and walked it into the kitchen. When the swinging door shut behind her, Mayor Lombardi edged closer. "Val, my daughter is only seventeen. This employee of yours was twenty-six."

"The age of consent in New York is seventeen. No laws were broken."

The lines around his eyes deepened as he squinted at me. "You're right, of course. But I expected you to look after her when I asked for her to work here. You broke your promise to me."

"I'm sorry, I had no idea it was happening. If I had, I would've put a stop to it."

He studied me like he was looking for flaws, a police detective waiting for a suspect to crack. I held firm, though. He couldn't prove anything.

After an excruciating moment, he relaxed and chuckled. The laugh sounded forced. "Kids, I guess. What are you gonna do?"

I attempted a smile, but my face felt awkward. Stiff.

He took a tiny step back, but his gaze darted to my chest before he looked around the dining room. "Now, Val. I see you've been doing some remodeling, including a new sign outside. I assume you went through the proper channels and such forth with permits."

My stomach dropped. But I knew the laws.

"I didn't think we needed a permit. We aren't doing anything structural or moving any electrical or gas lines."

"Well, oftentimes these things are up to the discretion of City

Hall. I'll tell you what. I'll have someone from the Department of Buildings come down here tomorrow and we'll sort this all out."

This was because of his daughter. I was certain of it. "That isn't necessary. The building code—"

"Val." He moved in, closer than he was before. "There's no need to argue, honey. It might just be a small fine after we fill out some paperwork."

Paperwork took eons here. "I haven't done anything wrong."

"Well, that's not for me to say." He cocked his head. "But we could talk about it, if you like. At dinner tomorrow night, maybe? I know a great place over in Woodstock."

Woodstock was almost an hour away. Eating there meant he didn't want anyone—namely his wife—to see us together and this wasn't a business dinner. A wave of revulsion went through me.

Everything inside me wanted to say no.

But I thought about Roberto and Giovanni, Maggie and her wines. My mother, my grandfather. Book club. The stupid sign out front.

I couldn't afford for him to shut me down or fine me. My finances were stretched to the brink as it was, thanks to the renovations, new salaries, and being closed this week. I needed every penny left of my mother's life insurance.

One dinner. You can do it, if it means reopening on time.

I had to say yes.

Except the words wouldn't come. I willed my lips to work. *Say it, Val!* How hard was it to agree to one measly meal?

Still, the silence stretched.

I heard the slap of the kitchen door behind me. "Buongiorno, signore," Roberto called loudly—and relief flooded me. Had Maggie sent him out here?

Instantly, Mayor Lombardi took a step back, but his eyes remained locked with mine for another beat. Then he turned to enthusiastically greet Roberto, who joined us near the front. "Good morning. I'm Mayor Lombardi."

"Mayor!" Roberto offered his hand smoothly. "How nice to finally meet you. I am Signore Ferrara, the business manager for Signorina Montella." The two men shook hands.

I dragged in a deep breath, willing myself to calm down. I didn't like the feeling of being rescued, of not being able to handle the mayor on my own, but at least this bought me some time. I could figure out how to deal with the mayor's threats later.

"The place looks great," the mayor said to Roberto. "Very impressive."

"Grazie, signore. We are pleased with the results. You will come in when we reopen, no?"

"Of course, of course. I eat here all the time, don't I, Val?"

He glanced at me meaningfully, so I nodded. "Yep."

"Va bene," Roberto said. "Was there something we can help you with, signore? I could give you a tour of the place, if you like."

"No, that's not necessary. It seems like you have everything well in hand here. I need to get back to the office." He plucked his sunglasses out of his coat pocket. "We'll catch up later, Val, yes?"

"Of course."

He turned and walked out, disappearing out the front door. When the wood closed and we were alone, Roberto studied me carefully. "Was he giving you trouble, signorina?"

"His daughter used to work here. She was sleeping with my chef, which I didn't know until the night I fired him."

"Ah. He blames you?"

"How did you guess?" I raked my fingernails across my scalp, then adjusted my pony tail. "It's fine. I'll deal with him later."

"What does this mean, deal with him?"

"He says we need permits." I waved my hand. "Paperwork. But I can't let him delay the reopening or fine us. So I'll talk to him."

"Do not go near him alone, signorina. My mother would say he is *un lupo*, capisce? A wolf."

I didn't respond. I knew he was right, but what choice did I have? This was my problem and I would fix it.

60

"Is that creeper gone?" Maggie called from a crack in the kitchen door. "Is it safe to come out?"

"Yes," I said. "I assume you sent Roberto out here."

"Uh, yeah. You think I trust that man alone with you?"

I rubbed my eyes, despite my mascara. It was that kind of day. "Is it too early to start drinking?"

"No," Maggie said while Roberto said, "Yes," at the same time.

Maggie threw her arm around me. "Come on. Let's find our acidic backbone and open a bottle over lunch."

Chapter Eight

Luca

Pulling out a burner phone, I dialed Sergio. I needed an update. My brothers were sweating one of our informants tonight, trying to get information on Niccolò, and it was taking too fucking long.

Sergio answered my call right away. "Pronto."

"What have you learned?"

"Ciao, fratello," he said. "Nothing. This guy doesn't know anything."

"Cazzo!" I slapped a palm on the desk. "A Benetti does not disappear like this. Someone would be bragging about the arrest or the hit."

"I know, which is why it's strange. But there's no sign of him at all. If Niccolò is being held, no one is saying where."

"And he's still not picking up his mobile?"

"No."

I could hear my other brothers, Dante and Enrico, the youngest brothers, laughing in the background. I ground my back teeth together. Those two treated the mafia life like a big party. Murder, booze, drugs, women . . . they loved the money and the power. At least Sergio took things seriously.

"Allora, are you getting her on a plane?" Sergio asked. "Or are you still thinking her father shows up?"

"I want to give it a few days. If Segreto's close, he'll learn I'm here and show up."

"How do you know?"

"My gut." We took this very seriously in my world. Instinct kept up alive, so we'd learned to trust it.

"And if he doesn't, you'll get her on a plane."

"If we don't find Niccolò, then yes. But I'm still not certain we aren't being played."

"Just as long as you're prepared."

I swiveled my chair to stare through the window out to the river. The soothing view did nothing to ease the irritation I felt. "And why wouldn't I be prepared to do whatever is necessary for the family?"

"I'm not saying you won't." He paused. "I hear she brought you dinner."

Fuck, these gossiping men. I changed topics. "Did you speak to Gabriele?"

"I did. I told him women think men who drive cars like that have small dicks."

A grin tugged at my mouth. "And?"

"And he canceled the order with the dealership."

Thank Christ. "Grazie, Sergio. I appreciate all you're doing while I'm away."

"You'd do the same for any of us. And I love my nephews, the little fucks." He told me to hold on, then yelled, "You two, make yourselves useful. Go help with the cleanup."

Ah, so the informant was dead. We'd need to find another to replace him when I returned home.

"Anything else?" I asked my brother.

"Rossi called earlier. Wanted an update on the girl."

Interesting that he hadn't called me. "And what did you tell him?"

"I lied and said you hadn't found her yet."

"Good. Don't tell him shit until I figure all of this out."

"Okay, but turning over Segreto's daughter buys us time."

"Maybe. But I don't like helping the GDF on a *maybe*. I want facts."

Sergio didn't say anything, his silence weighted with judgment.

I gripped the burner phone tighter. "Do you have something to say, fratello?"

"Are you fucking her?"

"That is none of your fucking business."

"Luca, we need you here, not there. And it seems as if you're in no hurry. I have to wonder if she's the reason."

I can't remember the last time someone cooked for me like this.

From the moment I walked into that shit show of a restaurant, I was drawn to her. And the craving worsened with every second I spent in her presence. I could claim it was out of pity, that I wished to care for her as I would one of my boys. But there was nothing paternal about the way my dick responded to her, like it wanted to break her apart, split her open and completely wreck her.

And if I *did* decide to fuck her, no one had a right to say a word. I was the don, the head of our family. I didn't owe answers to anyone. "I don't need to explain myself to you."

"Come on, Luca. This is me. Stop trying to bullshit me."

Brother or not, he was pissing me off. "This is family business, fratello, and I am the head of the family. This means I make the rules. Leave the girl and New York to me. Capisce?"

"Is that how it is?"

"Sì, certo. If you learn anything, ring me right away." I disconnected, then broke the burner apart with my hands, plastic snapping as I destroyed it.

A knock sound.

"Prego!" I snarled. Aldo appeared and I could tell right away something was wrong. "What is it?"

"Roberto rang me. I guess the mayor stopped by the restaurant and scared the shit out of Valentina. Something about his daughter getting fired. He's taking it out on Valentina, claiming permits weren't filed for the renovations and saying he's going to shut her down. I guess she was really freaked."

"He, what?"

"Then the mayor suggested he and Valentina have dinner to discuss it."

There is a thing that happens when I get very angry. I get quiet. The complete opposite of our father, who would shout and scream his head off about every little thing. I always swore that when I took over I would never act like a raving madman.

So I absorbed the fury and let it sink in, let it fester inside me like an infected wound, corroding and destroying. I used it as fuel to make decisions, plot retribution that no normal person would dare to carry out.

The mayor was a dead man.

* * *

I waited in the dark.

The house was what one would expect, tasteless and full of its own importance. Americans had no sense of shame when it came to showing off their wealth. They didn't understand that true wealth was what you left behind for your family, your legacy, and living simply meant living longer.

Aldo argued against this errand, saying it was too risky for me to handle, but I insisted. This was personal to me. I would deal with the mayor myself, without a public display. And without killing him. Unfortunately. But I didn't need the hassle of the American police. So this meant I needed to get creative.

I wasn't worried. He would receive my message as clear as a fucking bell.

It wasn't long before the garage door began grinding open. I checked my watch and saw it was nine-thirty.

He was on his mobile as he entered the house, his voice full of arrogance as he disconnected the alarm system. "No, hold out on that a little longer. They can come up with more." A pause. "He's full of shit. Don't believe a word he says. Listen, I have to go. I just walked in and the wife'll kill me if I wake her up." He chuckled at whatever the person on the other end said. "Yeah, I don't want her finding out about that either. See you tomorrow morning. Tee time is six-fifteen. Don't be fuckin' late."

I heard him open the refrigerator, a sliver of light shining from the kitchen. Bottles rattled, then the door closed again. A metal cap hit the counter. A loud belch. Then his footsteps drew closer.

I switched on the lamp beside me.

His head snapped up. When he saw me, the glass bottle in his hand hit the floor with a thunk. "Fuck!" he hissed. "Who the hell are you? How did you get into my house?"

I was calm and quiet, in control, seated in the armchair with a heavy golf club draped across my lap. "I suggest you lower your voice." I rolled the driver in my fingers, twirling it. "And listen to every word I say."

He folded his arms across his chest. "Who are you?"

"I'm a friend of Valentina's. That is all you need to know."

The mayor's eyebrows flew up. "This is about Val?"

The fact that he used her nickname, as if they were close, caused a white-hot bolt of fury to rocket through me. "Signorina Montella to you, stronzo."

"Listen, I don't know who you think you are—"

"I am the man telling you to stay the fuck away from her."

He swallowed, but gathered his courage to say, "This is my town. You can't tell me what to do. I'm the mayor."

"I know who you are—you're a man who preys on vulnerable

women to get his dick wet. So listen up, because I'm only going to tell you this once."

I rose slowly, my hand tightening on the club handle. Then, in one smooth and quick motion, I stepped forward and swung the club. It landed directly between the mayor's legs—the wooden head smacking into his balls. Instantly, the mayor crumpled to the ground with a groan and a long curse.

Bending, I grabbed a fistful of his hair and pulled his face up to see mine. "Do not say her name. Do not stop by her restaurant. She does not exist for you. Am I making myself understood?"

The mayor's face was pale, his eyes glazed with pain, but he was wise enough to nod.

Letting him go, I straightened and snapped the club in half, then threw the pieces on the carpet. "She doesn't need any fucking permits. And she won't pay any fines or suck your tiny pathetic dick. If you try that shit again, I'll do more than break your balls. Capisce?"

I started for the front door. Just as I reached the hall, the mayor wheezed, "How did you . . . get past my alarm system?"

I snorted. Did he honestly think a cheap alarm system would stop someone like me? "I'm like a ghost. And I'm always watching."

Without another word, I opened the front door and disappeared into the night.

Chapter Nine

Valentina

"**S**ignorina," Roberto said quietly after he pulled me aside. "I don't like this."

I looked around to see what was wrong. At the moment young men crowded the bar to order beers and well drinks, and my book club ladies were under control. For the first time in a few days, the trattoria had money coming in. "What is it? What's the problem?"

"We are understaffed and I'm not sure letting in all these young men was wise. With everyone drinking and no food being served . . . "

He trailed off, but I understood. And I didn't mind. It was nice to have someone looking out for me and my friends. "It's okay. We can order cars for anyone who seems intoxicated."

Roberto's face made it clear I had misunderstood. "These men are hanging around and waiting, and I am concerned about the reason for it."

Ah. Now I got it. "Well, book club night has become a little bit of a pick-up spot in Paesano. There aren't many in this town, so everyone has learned to make the most of it."

"Mamma mia." He dragged a hand down his face and muttered to himself in Italian.

"What did you say?" I asked.

"I wish I had hired more staff to help. I don't like feeling responsible for you and your friends."

"You're not responsible. And I've known these guys my entire life. They're harmless. Everyone will behave themselves."

"Still." He frowned in the direction of the crowded bar. "I would feel better if we asked the gentlemen to leave."

"No, you can't! We need the bar revenue. And if the guys leave, my friends will want to leave, too."

"Valentina," he said along with a heavy sigh. "This is asking for trouble."

"It'll be fine. We'll order cars for everyone at the end of the night so no one drives home. Please, Roberto. This is the first book club where I've been able to sit and hang out. Normally, I'm running around during dinner service. Let me enjoy just one."

He threw up his hands and returned to the bar, where he was helping our one bartender serve drinks. Yes, we probably should've hired more staff, but I wanted to keep the overhead low tonight. Our finances needed all the help they could get.

When I returned to the table, Sam leaned over. "What is Mr. Fancy Pants upset about?"

"He doesn't like all the guys hanging out in the bar, drinking and waiting for book club to end."

"Did you explain how it's the only time some of us get laid in this town?"

"In a roundabout way, yes. Don't worry, I didn't take away your dick parade."

She snickered and sipped more wine. "If only. Can you imagine? Wrapped with little streamers and balloons?"

"Yes, I can only imagine," I grumbled. Most women my age had loads of sexual experience, but I felt like I was miles behind everyone else.

"Oh, Val. I'm sorry. I forgot." She bumped my shoulder. "Look at them over there. It's easy. Just pick one and start talking to him. The rest will take care of itself."

Maggie, who sat on my other side, turned at Sam's advice. "Are we trying to get Val some action tonight?"

"Yes," Sam said at the same time I said, "No."

"It's a waste of time, Sam," Maggie said. "These guys aren't *old* enough or *Italian* enough."

"Oh, fuck off," I said and tried to hide my smile behind another sip of wine.

"Why are you *grinning*?" Sam asked. "What happened?"

I couldn't hold it in any longer. I'd been dying to tell them. "I took dinner up to the Portofino mansion," I whispered.

"No, you did not!" Sam exclaimed, while Maggie said, "Holy shit!"

This got the attention of the entire table. I didn't want to share this story wide, so I led the conversation in a different direction. When everyone ignored us again, I said, "I took Luca chicken parm. And it was your idea," I said accusingly to Sam.

Maggie held out her fist to Sam and the two fist-bumped. "So then what happened?"

"Did he profess his love after he tasted it?" Sam asked. "Because I swear I would marry that dish if it were socially acceptable."

"No, he did not. I don't think he even liked it."

Maggie's mouth fell open. "Bullshit. I don't believe it. Everyone loves that chicken parm."

I went to drink more wine, then realized my glass was empty. Was this my second or third glass? I couldn't be sure, so I refilled it with some Fiorentino rosé. "Well, he didn't. He shared a few bites of it with me."

Sam clasped her hands together and put them under her chin. "Like *Lady and the Tramp* style?"

"What?"

"You know, with the spaghetti. Come on, everyone has seen that movie."

"Yeah, when they were *five*," Maggie said. "Let's get back to this intimate dinner." She ignored the roll of my eyes and kept going. "What happened next?"

"Nothing. I made up an excuse and left."

Silence followed my statement and they both stared at me in disbelief. "You left," Maggie repeated. "As in, like, left."

"I know." I dropped my face in my hands. "I'm hopeless. But I didn't know what to do. I told him his watch was sexy. It was so embarrassing."

"Did he try anything or give you any hints that he's interested?"

Sam picked up a napkin and threw it at Maggie. "Of course he's interested! He's Investor Daddy."

Maggie batted the napkin away. "I know, but I would think a guy that old at least has some game. I can't believe he let you leave, Val."

This conversation was making my head spin. "Do not call him Investor Daddy. It's bad enough I call him that in my head."

"I need to get a look at this man," Sam said. "Maybe I should drop off some pastries from the café one morning."

"Good luck." I set my wine glass on the table. "His security probably won't let you in."

"Security?"

"The estate is crawling with young guys who look like serious badasses. I had to show ID before they'd let me in."

"Damn, I want to be that rich," Maggie said.

"Me too," Sam echoed. "But a rich Italian man, living on that particular estate with a bunch of security? The Portifinos were connected. So what does Luca do for a living?"

The three of us stared at each other. "No, it couldn't be," I said. "You've been listening to your grandmother too much."

But the seeds of doubt were planted and started to thrive. Luca did carry a lot of cash. And there was Roberto and Giovanni's sudden appearance in Paesano. All the men in Luca's orbit seemed to defer to him as if he were the . . . .

"It doesn't matter," I told both of them. "I'm not going to see him again."

"Sure you won't," Maggie said dismissively. "How was the tension? Thick with sexual chemistry?"

"So fucking thick." They both clapped their hands and gave little squeals of delight. I could feel my skin heating, a blush working its way to my toes, so I rushed to say, "Stop. I just told you I'm not going to see him again."

Maggie topped off my wine. "Listen, whether he's connected or not doesn't matter. He's not husband material. Just have some casual fun for once in your life with someone you won't see at the grocery store for the next forty years." Maggie had dated a lot of guys in Paesano. She said she couldn't go anywhere here without running into at least two of her exes.

Sam nodded. "Yes, good point. And I bet he's *very* experienced. We need to find a way to manifest this for you. You deserve a temporary fuck buddy, Val."

"You're both insane. And I don't want to think about that tonight." I lifted my glass again. "Tonight I just want to drink and hang out with all of you."

"Okay, but don't think we're dropping this." Maggie lifted her glass in a toast. "To manifesting!"

We all touched glasses, with Sam giving Maggie a wink. "To manifesting!"

* * *

Luca

The computer screen blurred, so I took off my glasses and rubbed my eyes. Though I was tired, I couldn't relax. An hour had passed since my visit to the mayor, but I was still pissed. I kept picturing Val forced to fuck that piece of shit . . . and I wanted to hit something.

I'd tried to take my mind off everything by staying busy. I showered, then concentrated on work, moving money and reviewing financial reports. I even checked in with some of our distributors in the Netherlands.

But I couldn't concentrate, I was so wired. Maybe some food would help.

In the kitchen Aldo was sitting at the island, laughing at something on his phone. He didn't look up as I went to the refrigerator.

"Let me guess? Hamster videos." Aldo was obsessed with watching animal videos, usually hamsters.

"They are adorable. Per favore, can we get one?"

I shook my head as I searched for something to eat. I'd once watched Aldo pop a man's eyeballs from his skull, and he could dismember a body faster than anyone else on my payroll. And he wanted a tiny little ball of fur?

"Pronto," I heard him say, answering his phone.

I took the mortadella and cheese from the fridge. I missed my housekeeper in Catanzaro. She made the best sandwiches. Living with a bunch of guards and fending for our own meals was starting to wear on me.

"No shit?" Aldo said, snickering. "How many? Yeah, I'll tell him. A presto."

"What is it?" I asked, slicing open ciabatta for a sandwich.

"She say anything to you about her book club?"

I was too tired and irritated to play guessing games. "Spit it out, stronzo."

"Tonight is book club night at the restaurant. A bunch of hot girls get together and drink wine."

"And?"

"And all the single guys in town know to hang out in the bar on book club nights."

I froze, a piece of mortadella dangling in my fingers. "I thought the restaurant was closed."

"Restaurant, yes. Bar, no. Valentina insisted on opening it tonight, so they could recoup some of the lost revenue. It's one of her biggest money-making nights of the month, she told Roberto."

I fucking bet. *Hot girls. Wine. Single guys.*

No doubt the men were hoping to take one of the drunk women home. I pictured Valentina, helpless, trapped in a car with some man who didn't care if she were willing or not. My gut cramped and a red mist coated my brain like a thick layer of paint.

"Cazzo!" I dropped the meat on the counter. "I need to get over there."

"Do you want to change first?" Aldo asked, getting off his stool.

I wore a t-shirt and jeans, not my usual public attire. This was what I wore around the house. "There's no time. *Andiamo.*"

Aldo grabbed the keys from a bowl near the garage door. Soon we were speeding toward town in one of the two cars I'd rented. During the ride, I called Roberto and told him under no circumstances was Valentina allowed to leave before I arrived. There was a lot of noise in the background, but he said he understood.

The drive seemed to take forever. The restaurant's parking lot was full of pickup trucks and SUVs, but we didn't bother looking for a space. Aldo parked in the fire lane right in front of the restaurant.

I got out and strode toward the door. Voices carried out onto the sidewalk, mostly feminine laughter. A siren's song for every horny college-aged boy in town.

What in the hell was she thinking? Throwing open the door, I went in. My gaze surveyed the place in one sweep. At a large round table sat ten beautiful young women, all dressed up, laughing and drinking. The bar was crammed with over a dozen men of all ages, beer bottles in hand, lurking and talking quietly. A sporting event was on the screens, but the men were more interested in the table of women.

I found her and my heart stopped. *Che figa che lei mamma mia.* So fucking hot.

Her dark hair was slicked back and pulled back into a high pony-tail, accenting her face. The dramatic makeup she wore made her look older, more sophisticated, and her lips were painted a bright red. My dick twitched as I thought about those red lips nibbling on the head of my cock.

Why such effort? Was she hoping to take a man home?

It didn't matter. I wasn't letting anyone take advantage of her, not while I could prevent it.

I walked over to the bar. There was no use making a scene and disrupting the girls' fun, which would piss Valentina off. I would handle this quietly.

I went to the cluster of young men at the end of the bar. Three of the four wore baseball caps turned backwards. Several curious gazes met mine. I spoke softly, so they had to lean in to hear. "Get the fuck out. The bar is now closed."

They didn't speak for a long second, each sizing me up. Then one grew brave enough to say, "We're not leaving, bro. It's book club night."

I put my hand on his shoulder and squeezed. Hard. When he winced and tried to pull away, I only gripped harder, forcing my thumb behind his collar bone. "You are leaving now and you are taking your friends with you. Because if you don't, I'm going to knock out every single one of your teeth. *Bro.*"

"Jesus, okay. Let me fucking go!"

I released him and gestured to the door. "Leave. Now."

"I'm not paying my tab, asshole," one of them grumbled as he put his beer bottle on the bar.

Did he think I cared? "Get the fuck out."

The group shuffled out the front door. I continued working my way down the bar, through the other clusters of men, telling each the same thing. Nothing overly dramatic or violent, but I made it clear that leaving was in their best interest. They complained, clearly disappointed to miss out on drunk pussy, but the groups steadily trickled outside.

Only one man gave me resistance. So I bent his pinky finger back until it almost broke—and he quickly left.

"Hey, what the fuck?" The bartender watched the last group of customers disappear. "They still owe money on their tabs."

"How much?"

"A grand, at least. And you let them leave without paying!"

I withdrew a money clip from my pocket and peeled off two thousand dollars. "There. Now, get out. You're done for the night."

"But I'm supposed to—"

I put my hands on the bar, leaned over, and gave him a look that had caused grown men to piss themselves. "Fuck off before I remember that you were helping these assholes prey on drunk women. Because if I remember, I might be tempted to slam your face into the mirror behind you. Capisce?"

Paling, he untied his apron, took the money and disappeared into the kitchen.

I exhaled, turned, and leaned my back against the bar. The room had gone deathly silent. All the book club ladies were staring at me with their mouths agape, including Valentina.

"Holy . . . shit," one of the women said under her breath.

I tilted my head in greeting. "Buona sera, signorine."

"Luca." Valentina stood and I got a full view of her. She wore a tight sweater that showed off her tits and black pants that hugged her hips. I was momentarily distracted until she tried to take a step forward and stumbled.

"Whoa," she chuckled, putting her hand on the table to steady herself.

In a flash I was by her side, taking her elbow and helping her back into her chair. "Valentina, sit down."

"Did he just call Val Valentina?" one of the women loudly whispered to another.

"My god, that accent."

"Uh, Val, shouldn't you introduce us?"

I ignored all the voices and concentrated on Valentina. There were a dozen bottles of wine on the table, but no food. Or books. "Here, drink this." I handed her a glass of water. "No more wine."

She rolled her eyes. "Yes, *Luca.*"

Dio, that attitude. It made me want to fuck her and spank her and bend her to my will.

"Val, this isn't . . ." Two of the young women exchanged worried glances. "Is this your father?"

"No!" Val sounded horrified. "God, no. This is Mr. DiMarco."

"Ooooh, now I get it," said a woman, who looked at Valentina and mouthed, *Investor Daddy.*

Madre di dio. I dragged a hand over my jaw and willed my body to calm down. My dick would be half-hard if I let this continue. "Get your things," I told Val. "I'm taking you home."

"No, I have to stay and lock up." She was weaving in her chair. "Shit, the room is spinning."

I didn't hesitate. I needed to get her out of here and help sober her up. Bending, I slipped my arm under her knees and put the other behind her back. I lifted her easily and she threw her arms around my neck.

"Oh, my god," one of the women said, but I was focused on Valentina.

"Luca, what are you doing? Put me down." She contrasted this order by resting her head in the crook of my neck. "Mmmm, you smell so good."

Some of the women laughed—and I'd heard enough. We didn't need an audience any longer.

Roberto was hurrying across the dining room. We began a rapid exchange of Italian, with me telling him to hire cars to see the other women home. He apologized for calling me, but I reassured him it had been the right thing to do. I promised to talk to him tomorrow.

While this was going on, Valentina passed out in my arms.

I carried her outside and went to my car. Aldo opened the door for me and I placed Valentina in the back. When I straightened, Aldo closed the door and gestured toward the parking lot. "We have a problem."

I looked over. Pinky and Collarbone were standing beside a shit truck, the only two remaining schoolboys after I dismissed the class. Pinky was slowly slapping a stick into his palm, in a futile attempt to look menacing. A *stick*. I nearly laughed.

"Want me to send them home?" asked Aldo.

I looked at Valentina once more to be sure she was okay. She was still asleep, somehow as sexy as ever, even after too much wine. "No, I'll handle this myself. I'm in the mood."

"Are you sure that's wise? It might not be a good idea to attract too much attention—especially in front of her restaurant."

"Stay here," I said, ignoring Aldo's warning. I walked over to my two new friends but said nothing.

"Who do you think you are, asshole?" said Collarbone. "You come into our town and cockblock us? Then threaten us like you're some bullshit dago mobster? You're about to learn how we deal with outsiders here."

I couldn't help but smile. I was going to enjoy this. "What makes you think it's bullshit?"

Collarbone smirked and looked at Pinky. "Bro, can you believe this asshole?"

Before he could even look again in my direction, I punched him in the face with everything I had. It felt good. Collarbone's head rocked back and struck his truck with as much force as my fist applied to his face, and he crumpled into a heap on the pavement.

I knelt over him as he struggled to breathe and asked him one question. "Dago?"

Looking at me through his rapidly swelling eye, he appeared confused. No doubt because my question may not have been specific enough for him to understand.

I grabbed him by the hair and pulled him closer to me, so I was sure he could see me. I spoke to him quietly, but did nothing to hide the fury that I felt. "You think you are powerful, *coglione?* You don't know the first thing about real power."

I hit him in his other eye because I like symmetry, and then a few more times simply because it pleased me. I needed the exercise. His nose snapped and his skin split open with the force of my punches. I finally stopped when I realized that I might get blood on my clothes.

I glanced over at Pinky who was wide-eyed and pale and holding his arms up in a show of surrender, yet he still had that ridiculous stick in his hand. Following my gaze, he seemed surprised to see the stick and dropped it as if it was on fire.

"Take this piece of shit home," I said, "and don't come back. And if you mention this to anyone, I'm finishing what I started. With *both* of you."

Returning to the car, I found Valentina sleeping peacefully and my anger drained away. As I got into the back seat and laid her head in my lap, Aldo got in behind the wheel. "Where to?"

"Let's take her to the house."

Chapter Ten

Valentina

As I came awake, I instantly regretted all my life choices. Fuck, my head hurt.

And my stomach . . . Oh, no. No, no, no.

I rolled into a ball, hoping to prevent myself from puking. Why did I drink so much wine at book club?

My stomach twisted and I had to do some deep breathing. *Ugh. Stop thinking about wine.*

I must've fallen back asleep for a few minutes. When I came to, I felt slightly better. At least the nausea had passed. The headache had eased slightly, too.

I rubbed my feet into my sheets. The soft fabric felt amazing on my skin. Too amazing. Wait, were these my—

In a blink it all came rushing back. Book club, the restaurant, wine. *Luca.* Holy shit, Luca. He'd carried me out of the restaurant.

My eyes flew open.

A strange room filled my vision. A ceiling that was too high, too white. Gold fixtures. Large windows. A huge bed with gray sheets and a gray duvet. A divan was in the corner with a folded pile of what looked like *my clothes* on top.

I clutched the sheet around me. I was wearing only a bra and panties. Did Luca see me like this? God, please no. How much lower could I sink in that man's eyes? Between the troubles at the restaurant, then finding me drunk at book club, he must really think I'm a mature and responsible adult. Jesus.

At least he put me in a guest bedroom alone.

Please let this be a guest bedroom.

I lifted my head off the pillow slightly. *Shit!* There was a head-shaped indent on the pillow next to mine. Did he sleep next to me?

Flashes of last night stabbed through my aching head.

Me, falling onto his bed. "Wow, this place is nice."

Luca, handing me two pills and a glass of water. "Take these."

"Why?"

"Because I said so, fiore mio."

"Does 'fiore mio' mean 'pain in my ass?'"

"No, bella. It does not. Get under the covers."

"This sweater is too hot," I said, whipping it off and throwing it onto the floor.

"I will leave you now," he said, turning to go.

"Noooo, Luca. You have to stay." I lunged for his arm. "Please. Don't leave me."

Oh, God. I'd begged him to get into bed with me. He'd protested, but I pushed. *"What if I get sick in the middle of the night and no one is here to help me?"*

"Then you will call and I will hear you."

"No, Luca. I need you in bed with me. I won't feel safe without you."

He'd stared at me for a long time after that, but finally relented. He'd stripped out of his clothing and I really, *really* wished I remembered every single detail about those few minutes. But it was fuzzy, like my brain was telling me that I couldn't handle the full memory.

Wide shoulders, narrow hips. Chest hair. And . . . had I asked the brand of his boxer briefs?

"*I don't know,*" he answered, looking at me like I was crazy. "*A personal shopper in Roma takes care of my clothes.*"

I closed my eyes in humiliation. Finally, I went home with a man —except it was to sleep off too much wine. I was so lame, while he was handsome and sophisticated. And older. And possibly in the mafia.

Yikes. I had to escape.

I pushed up onto my elbows, then did some more deep breathing. Fuck, I felt awful. Where was my phone? The only thing on the bedside table was the half-finished glass of water. Did I bring my purse with me? Damn—my phone and purse were still at the restaurant. I left them in my office during book club.

Great job, Val. Mom would be so proud.

Crawling out of bed, I grabbed my clothes and hurried into the bathroom. There were way too many mirrors and bright gold fixtures for my liking, but I made the best of it and tried to get presentable. There was a new toothbrush waiting for me, which made me feel even worse. This was obviously something Luca did a lot, while this was my first time going home with a man.

And I could hardly remember any of it.

Had we . . . ?

No, I instantly knew nothing had happened. There were no marks on me, no aches or pains. I was fairly certain I would feel something if I had sex for the first time last night.

But wait, hadn't I asked him about it?

"*Do you want to have sex with me, Luca?*"

"*No more talking. Try to sleep.*"

"*Please, say yes. I'm tired of wondering what it's like.*"

There was a great pause from his side of the bed. "*A man like me would ruin a woman like you. Stay far away from me, fiore mio.*"

Oh, god. Just when I thought I couldn't feel worse.

I placed my palms on the marble countertop and closed my eyes. He must think I'm a complete idiot. I had to get out of here, *now*.

A minute later I was back in the bedroom, searching for my shoes. I couldn't find them. Maybe they were downstairs? I ventured along the upstairs hall, desperate to find someone to give me a ride home. I checked all the rooms, but the second floor was empty.

I went downstairs, but the house was deathly silent, not a soul around. Where were all those security guards from the other night?

"Ciao, signorina."

I jumped at the deep voice and spun around to find Luca's guard. I remembered him from the night I brought over dinner. Relief filled me. Now I could leave and never see this place or any of its inhabitants ever again. "Oh, hey. I'm so glad to see you. Can I trouble you for a ride home?"

He frowned. "Come. Signore DiMarco awaits."

"No, that's not necessary. I'm sure he's busy. I'd rather—"

Waving me toward a pair of French doors, he began speaking in rapid Italian, which I didn't understand. Did this man not speak much English? I tried again. "No, please. I need to get home."

He kept gesturing toward me, walking backward, and I knew a lost cause when I saw one. This man worked for Luca, so there'd be no getting around seeing his boss.

Resigned, I followed. "Okay, but just for a minute. I really have to go."

"Va bene, va bene. Andiamo!" He led me through the dining room and out through another set of doors, where we ended up on a gorgeous terrace. Just beyond was a rolling green lawn and the river moving slowly in the distance. It was the perfect view.

Except for someone with a hangover.

I shielded my eyes and tried to breathe through the pain in my head.

A chair scraped on stone. "Ah, there you are."

Luca came toward me, a black t-shirt stretched across his chest. Light loose pajama bottoms covered his lower half, and his feet were bare. I couldn't help but study his long feet, which were the same olive skin tone as the rest of him. In general, feet were gross. But Luca's feet? Totally sexy.

Do you want to have sex with me, Luca?

I looked away. This man did not want me, probably because I was constantly making a fool of myself in his presence. Now I was ogling him like I had the right? I needed to pull it together.

"I apologize for being undressed." He lifted my face in his hands and kissed my cheeks. He smelled like coffee and mint. Softly, he said, "Buongiorno, Valentina."

God, that accent. If I weren't so miserable, I would've melted into a puddle on the floor. "Um, hi."

"Come, sit. Have something to eat."

"Oh, I shouldn't. Really, I should go. You've already done far, far too much."

"Nonsense. Come, have caffè and a roll."

He took my elbow and began leading me to the table. Short of digging in my heels like a small child, I didn't have much of a choice but to follow him.

He pulled out a chair for me, so I plopped down awkwardly. Luca walked over to his seat and gracefully lowered himself down. "Aldo will bring you a cappuccino. Until then, there are pastries and juice."

I don't know what I expected, but this was no casual breakfast with a box of donuts and a carton of juice. There were china plates, tiny juice glasses, and sterling silver flatware. A crystal pitcher of orange juice rested on the table next to Luca's electronic tablet. Was this how he spent every morning?

He filled up my juice glass. "How do you feel?"

"Shitty."

"I'm not surprised. Eat something. It will help."

A cup and saucer appeared at my elbow. I glanced up and found Aldo there. "Allora, signorina," he said and put a cappuccino down in front of me.

"Thank you." Normally, I would dump some sugar into my coffee and savor it, but this wasn't that kind of morning. I had to get through this quickly. The sooner I finished, the sooner I could leave.

"Here."

Luca placed my phone next to my plate. I exhaled in relief and set down my cappuccino. "Thank you. I felt totally lost without it." I picked up the device and unlocked it. "How did you get it from the restaurant?"

"I had Roberto bring your things over last night."

I paused, my finger hovering on the glass. Roberto? "Wasn't he busy closing up the restaurant?"

Luca made a noise that sounded close to a snort and lifted his tiny espresso cup to his mouth. He should've looked ridiculous drinking from something so small, but somehow didn't.

He didn't answer and I couldn't let it go. "Wait, did you snort because he wasn't closing the restaurant?"

"First, I never snort." He threw back the rest of his espresso and set the demitasse cup down. "Second, I don't have any idea what he was doing. People usually do what I ask, bella."

A rush of hot and cold shivers went through me, like a mixture of both fear and attraction. It was a strange reaction. Thrilling, but unnerving, as well.

I should have known better, though. If Luca was a mobster, I needed to stay far away from him. My mother never spoke about what my father did for a living, but it was obviously something shady. He had money, lots of it, and tried to give her some over the years, but she refused to take it. She said money comes with strings, and she didn't want him in my life in any capacity.

Stay away from men who want to control you, Val.

Mom said this so often that I should have it cross-stitched onto a pillow. But I couldn't think about any of that now, not when I was so hungover.

Glancing at my phone, I found a bunch of texts from Sam waiting for me. They started not long after Luca drove me here last night.

ARE YOU OKAY

PLS CHECK IN

HE CARRIED YOU OUT OMG

OFFICER & A GENTLEMAN STYLE

I frowned. What was she talking about? Was that a book?

I looked up at Luca, only to find him staring at me intently. My mouth turned dry under his intense stare, which probably caused me to blurt, "What does officer & a gentleman mean?"

His lips twitched. "A movie. Richard Gere. Debra Winger. From the 1980s. A romance. You would like it."

A romance? What the fuck, Sam!

I went back to my other texts. These were from Maggie.

GIRRRRRRRL

I NEED TO HEAR FROM YOU

IF HE HURT YOU

ROBERTO SAID LUCA'S SOLID BUT

FR ... TEXT ME NOW

I texted them both back.

I'M OK. HUNGOVER BUT OK

Sam was no doubt busy at the café, so I didn't expect a response. But three dots appeared immediately in my thread with Maggie.

JFC YOU SCARED ME

ARE YOU HOME

NO, I'M AT LUCA'S

OH SHIT

CALL ME WHEN YOU GET HOME

I WANT ALL THE TEA

There was no tea. Unless you count me making a total fool of myself.

I gave her a thumbs up then set my phone down. "I really should get going. Are my shoes by the front door?"

"Your shoes are being washed." He began buttering a delicious-looking round pastry, which he set on my plate. "*Mangia*, Valentina."

I had to admit, I was a sucker for a good pastry. I picked up the roll and took a bite. Tender and delicious, it tasted of vanilla and a hint of citrus. The top had a light dusting of sugar. "Is this brioche?" I asked through a bite.

He was frozen, gaze locked on my mouth. "Sì," he said absently. "*Brioche à tête.*"

Did I have food on my face? I wiped my mouth with a napkin and tried to get us back on track. "Wait, why are my shoes being washed?"

"Because you vomited on them last night."

The roll fell from my hand and landed on the plate with a thud. *Oh, my god.* Closing my eyes, I muttered, "I'm so sorry. I'm giving up wine, I swear."

"Nonsense. Wine is one of life's greatest pleasures. But you need to drink less of it at one time."

I couldn't look him in the eye. This elegant gorgeous man had watched me vomit last night. On my shoes. And I had no memory of it whatsoever. I sent up a prayer that the terrace would open up and swallow me whole. "Please tell me I didn't puke in your house."

"No, you vomited outside. As I was helping you out of the car."

The way he said it caused my head to snap up. I studied him, but his handsome face gave nothing away. *No, dear god. No.* "If you tell me I puked on you, I will literally jump into that river and disappear."

"Then I guess I won't tell you."

I propped my elbows on the table and dropped my head into my hands. Holy shit. How could I ever look at him again? *I puked on him*. It was mortifying.

He chuckled. "Do not look so ashamed, bella. Now you *and* Gabriele have vomited on me. It's an honor."

Honor?

I scooted back and stood. "I really need to go. I have to get to the restaurant, but I need to shower first."

He waved his hand. "I informed Roberto that you would not be in today. So, relax. Finish your breakfast."

"No, I really . . ." I exhaled heavily. "Thank you for all of this, but I need to get home." I reached for my phone. I'd order a car to come and pick me up.

"I'll drive you." He placed his napkin on the table and rose out of his chair. "Let me dress first."

"It's okay. I'll order a car."

His hand suddenly covered my phone, lowering it. "Valentina."

He waited, still and quiet, so I glanced up at him. His intense dark stare sucked me in, trapped me. He stood so close that I could see his morning scruff, the long lashes framing his eyelids, and I had no desire to move away. Instead, every beat of my heart urged me closer.

His fingers swept across my jaw, then brushed the hair back off my face. It was done so tenderly, so sweetly, that I actually felt my insides quiver.

Then his big hand cupped the back of my neck to hold me in place, and the heat from his large body sank into my bones. It was like we were in our own little bubble, and the resistance melted clean out of my body. I probably would've agreed to anything right then, as long as he kept staring at me like this.

His deep voice turned soft. Seductive. "Let me take care of you. Let me drive you home. Va bene?"

"Okay," I whispered.

He didn't release me right away. Instead, his fingers pressed into my skin, tightening. It wasn't painful or intimidating.

No, this had the opposite effect.

I felt safe. Precious. Like I mattered. It almost seemed as if he was holding onto me because he didn't want to let go.

Then it was over.

He blinked and the moment was broken. Releasing me, he stepped back, his face wiped clean of any emotion. "Aldo will bring you more cappuccino," he said on his way to the terrace doors. "I'll only be a minute."

* * *

Luca

I was fucked.

As we drove back to the mansion after dropping Val off, I knew this like I knew my own name.

I need you in bed with me. I won't feel safe without you.

She'd begged so sweetly that I broke one of my rules for her. I never slept overnight in the same bed as a woman. It was both dangerous and too intimate. Yet I'd climbed into bed with Val and actually slept.

Do you want to have sex with me, Luca? Please, say yes. I'm tired of wondering what it's like.

Madre di dio, a virgin. I should be strung up and shot for the things I wanted to do to her.

"Check your phone." Aldo's eyes met mine in the rearview mirror. "Leo is trying to reach you."

I unlocked my phone and didn't bother reading the messages. I hit a button and rang my oldest son.

He picked up right away. "Papà, he's missing."

I could hear the worry in Leonardo's voice. "Who?"

"Gabi."

I froze, phone to my ear. "Explain."

"We've been looking for him all day. He disappeared overnight."

How could Gabriele disappear? The boys were never alone, guarded almost at all times. "Have you checked—"

"Papà," he interrupted. "I've checked everywhere. No one has seen him. And his cars are here."

My chest squeezed so hard that I couldn't breathe. Was this something to do with Segreto? Had Palmieri taken my youngest boy?

Or, was it one of my countless enemies?

The edges of my vision wavered, my mind reeling. It was my greatest fear as a father, that I would fail to keep one of my children safe. But the guards were supposed to keep an eye on both boys. So, what the fuck happened?

I would skin someone alive for this.

I heard talking. It was Aldo, so I glared at him, but he was grinning into the mirror, speaking to someone on his mobile. What did he have to be so fucking happy about?

I returned my attention to Leonardo. "Who was the last person to see him?"

"He was at the club with some of the boys. Cameras show him leaving with a guard around midnight."

I wasn't surprised Leonardo had pulled security footage. My boy was so smart. My mind raced as we pulled up to the gate. I would need to get on a plane immediately. There was no time to lose.

Instead of waving us through, one of the guards approached the car. That was odd. Aldo lowered the car window and rested an arm on the frame. "Che cosa?" he asked the guard.

"Papà, are you still there?" Leonardo asked in my ear.

"Yes," I answered. "I'll be on the jet within the hour."

The guard was saying to Aldo, "They just showed up. We didn't know what to do."

Someone was here? "Who showed up?" I barked.

"What is going on there?" Leonardo said in my ear.

"Gabriele is here, Don Benetti," the guard said, peeking into the back seat at me. "Inside. He arrived about ten minutes ago."

"What the fuck!" Leonardo shouted, obviously overhearing.

I clenched my jaw, hard. Cazzo madre di dio! Gabriele was here in New York. Relief and anger warred inside me. My fingers squeezed the glass and metal rectangle in my hand. "Gabriele has been found," I gritted out as Aldo started up the drive. "He's here with me, apparently."

"That stronzo!" my oldest son hissed. "I thought he was dead."

"He might still be, when I get through with him," I said softly. "We will speak later."

I rang off, then tapped my mobile absently on my leg. The stupidity, the sheer recklessness. If I had done something like this, my father would've beat the shit out of me.

"He brought a guard with him," Aldo said from the front seat. "They flew private under an assumed name. He did it smart."

"You knew?"

"I found out a minute before you did. Don't be too hard on him. You know how sixteen-year-old boys are."

No, I didn't. Because at sixteen I did everything my father told me, never daring to take a step out of line. He'd been cruel and ruthless, determined to mold his oldest boy into a powerful don.

I locked all that away as the car pulled up to the front door. I got out and tore up the steps. The entry was empty, just the usual dry fountain surrounded by gold cherubs.

"Gabriele!" I called. "Where the fuck are you?"

"Ciao, Papà!" My youngest son appeared at the top of the stairs, a wide smile on his face. One of the soldiers was with him and his downcast expression told me he was smart enough to be worried.

I pointed at the soldier. "I will deal with you later." To my son, I said, "Get in my office. Now."

"Papà," Gabriele said with a heavy sigh as he came down the steps. "Don't be angry with Totò. I didn't give him a choice."

I didn't want to hear it. At the very least this soldier should've informed Sergio with what was going on.

"Follow me," I said and started for my office. I was furious. At a time when I already had too much to deal with, now Gabriele had to act out, too? Didn't he realize the danger in leaving home, let alone coming here with only one man to protect him?

I could practically hear my father's voice, berating me for my failings with my sons.

You're too soft on them. They'll never be able to handle the responsibility after you're gone.

I held open the office door. Gabriele strode through, his sullen expression telling me he was unhappy with how this was playing out. Which was too fucking bad.

He was young and immature. He didn't understand the responsibility of being a Benetti.

But he would.

I watched him settle into a chair. Whereas Leonardo looked more like his mother, my younger son was exactly like me at that age, tall and lanky. His wavy hair flopped over his forehead and down into his eyes. He was a pussy magnet, and he knew it. The guards often complained about Gabriele's prolific sex life, saying he fucked anything with a pair of tits. I kept hoping he would find a mistress or a girl, like Leonardo, but Gabriele seemed determined to fuck the entire region.

I walked across the room and took my rightful seat behind the desk. "Explain yourself."

"Don't be mad. I came here because I know Niccolò is missing. I want to help find him."

No one should be discussing Niccolò in the presence of my sons. I was trying to distance them from this. "What are you talking about?"

"Allora, Papà. I am not stupid. Leo and I both know what is going on."

Merda! My boys were close with Niccolò and I didn't want them involved. Because if Niccolò did talk to the GDF, there was only one way I could deal with such betrayal. "Who told you?"

My son lifted his chin. "I'm not saying. I don't want them in trouble."

Resting my elbows on the desk, I steepled my fingers and took a few breaths. "Our cousin is missing, but likely still in Italia. How is coming here helping to find him?"

"Because the uncles aren't listening to me. They claim Niccolò is fine, just on holiday. But I know you'll believe me when I say I can help."

"And how can you help?"

"I have spent more time with him than Leo or anyone else. And he isn't on holiday."

I leaned back in my chair. I hadn't wanted him to know, but now I felt as if there was no option but to tell him. "Word is Niccolò has been arrested. He was delivering product to Belgium. The GDF is hoping to turn him against the family."

His face lost its color. "No. Impossible."

Remaining quiet, I let him sit with the information. We all knew what this could mean.

"Papà, Niccolò would never. He's loyal."

"It's all too easy to force a man against his will, especially when his life is threatened."

"Not Niccolò. He wouldn't do that."

I wasn't so sure. I'd broken the spirit of too many men to think it impossible.

Gabriele took his phone out of his pocket and began scrolling. "When was he arrested?"

"The night before I left."

"Here's his last text to me. This is how I know he's not on holiday." He handed his mobile to me.

I scanned the texts, which were about making plans to go club-bing that next night. There were a lot of peach emojis. Then Gabriele made repeated attempts to reach Niccolò in the days that followed, but there was no answer.

"So he could be in prison," I allowed. "Which would mean he doesn't have access to his phone."

"Except he turned his location services off. So I think he has his phone with him."

"What?" I handed Gabriele his mobile. "Show me. And please tell me you aren't stupid enough to have your location turned on for the world to see."

"Dai, Papà. I'm not so stupid. Niccolò and I use this app and we have our locations turned on only for each other." His thumbs moved rapidly, then he showed me the screen. "See this? He switched it to ghost mode."

I didn't know what that meant, but I believed what Gabriele was saying. "When?"

"I don't know, but he was last active the morning you left. Which means he wasn't in prison."

I would need to call Sergio right away. But first, I owed Gabriele an apology. "I'm sorry I doubted you. This is helpful, figlio mio."

He sat back, a grin splitting his face. "So does this mean I can stay with you here in New York?"

"I'm afraid if I tell you no that you will hire another plane to bring you back."

"Probably. Grazie, Papà."

I held up my hand. "It's not up to only me. You must ring your mother and ask her permission. If she says yes, then you can stay."

"I will."

"And ring your brother. You scared him half to death by disap-pearing."

"Yes, Papà. I'll do whatever you say, whenever you say it. I won't cause a bit of trouble."

"You'll do whatever I say? Even if I confine you to the house and grounds?"

His enthusiasm dimmed considerably. "But why would you, when no one knows who we are in this town? They told me you are going by the name DiMarco."

"Because it's safer. And you don't question my orders, figlio mio."

"Will you tell me why you are here?"

"No—but not because I don't trust you. I need to sort some things out first."

"Okay, but I'm here to help. I'm worried about Niccolò, too."

I sent him off to ring his mother and brother, then I stared through the window, thinking. If Niccolò wasn't in prison, then why had Rossi lied about it? It was possible Rossi had been given false information from Palmieri, but the more likely scenario was that Rossi lied to me. But why? Just to find Flavio Segreto?

I didn't like being used. I liked being lied to even less.

I needed to find out how these pieces were connected. And something told me Flavio Segreto was the key.

Chapter Eleven

Valentina

There was too much to do to take a sick day.

After Luca dropped me off, I forced myself to get ready for work, nibbling on crackers and sipping ginger ale the entire time. Of course I looked up what "fiore mio" meant as soon as I got home. It translated to *my flower*, an endearment in Italian.

My flower.

It was both beautiful and sweet and totally disconcerting. We weren't really at the endearment stage, were we? He must be humoring me. Maybe "flower" in Italian meant a foolish girl who drank too much and vomited on you?

"Wow, you look . . . " Roberto pressed his lips together as I walked into the trattoria around one o'clock.

"I know," I said. "I look like shit."

"I was going to say ill."

Giovanni's brow creased as he examined me. I had learned he wasn't overly talkative, despite my efforts to engage him in conversation. "Too much wine," my new chef said. "I will make you something."

"I couldn't possibly trouble you for that." I placed a hand on my stomach. "Besides, I'm not sure I can keep it down."

"Nonsense. Food is the remedy for most of life's ailments." He was already heating a sauté pan, his heavily-tattooed arms moving rapidly. "Sit, signorina."

"Yes, sit. Per favore, Val," Roberto said, pulling over a stool for me. "We will talk while we wait."

I tossed my bag onto the clean prep station, then lowered myself onto the stool and crossed my legs. "I'm sorry I drank so much last night and left you to lock up," I told Roberto. "Book club got a little out of hand."

"Ma dai," Roberto said, his brown eyes kind as they studied me. "That is what young women do. You deserve a little fun. Allora, I thought you would be mad at me for calling Signore DiMarco."

I remembered Luca coming into the restaurant, eyes wild until he spotted me. Then he circulated the bar area, speaking with each of the men there, and somehow convinced them all to leave. He hadn't raised his voice or caused a scene. Instead, he remained quiet and in control, yet forceful enough to clear the room. Normally, I had to threaten and yell to clear the bar on a book club night.

"I'm not mad at you," I said. "But I don't understand why you called him. Did something happen?"

Roberto shook his head. "Signorina, it was what could have happened. Those men in the bar were waiting, circling like hyenas. Young women who drink too much are at risk in such situations."

"But that's what we do every month. No one gets hurt and the bar makes a lot of money." Something occurred to me and my memory was too fuzzy. "Oh, shit—did the men pay their bar tabs?"

"Signore DiMarco paid the tab."

"For all of them?" Surprised, I swayed on the stool and had to put a hand on the stainless steel to steady myself. "That had to be more than a thousand dollars."

"Twelve hundred. And he gave Chase a gratuity, as well."

I shouldn't have been surprised, not after Luca gave each of my tables a hundred dollars the other night. He must always carry a lot of cash around. "I vomited on him last night," I blurted, needing to share my shame for some crazy reason.

A bark of laughter came from the direction of the stove, while Roberto glanced away, eyes dancing with laughter. "Go ahead," I told him. "I can tell you want to laugh at me, too."

"I am not laughing at you, signorina," he said kindly. "More at the idea of Signore DiMarco being vomited on."

"Hello?" a voice called from the kitchen entrance.

I glanced over my shoulder and saw Bev stepping through the back door. In her hand was a frozen coffee with chocolate swirled on top. *Dear Lord, please let that be for me.*

"Hi," I said. "What are you doing here? It's not even one o'clock." Her café stayed open until three.

"I came to check on you." She slid her sunglasses up into her short gray hair. "And bring you a treat since you didn't stop by this morning."

"Oh, god. I love you." I reached for the cup eagerly.

"Are you sure that won't make you feel worse?" Roberto muttered, his lip curled in distaste.

"It's oak milk," Bev explained.

I took a sip and the cold sweetness was pure heaven. "That is so good."

"Where is my treat, signorina?" Roberto asked Bev, a small smile playing at the edge of his mouth.

"Your espresso, you mean?" Bev's cheeks were slightly red as she turned to me. "I've never seen a human being gulp a hot drink so quickly. You'd think the café was on fire every morning."

Wait, was something happening between these two? Their reactions to one another was very telling, and Roberto was obviously spending a lot of time at Bev's cafe. "Every morning?" I asked him, lifting my eyebrow meaningfully.

He tilted his head in the direction of the dining room. "Just until the men install the new espresso machine."

"Speaking of, how are the renovations going?" Bev asked, regaining my attention.

I hesitated. With Mayor Lombardi threatening to drown me in paperwork, I had no idea how long this could take. No one from the Buildings Department had shown up yet, but the possibility was still there. I needed to deal with him soon—and the thought caused my stomach to turn over.

Setting my coffee drink on the pass, I said, "There may be some issue with permits."

Roberto made a dismissive sound. "There will be no issue, signorina."

The confidence in his tone gave me pause. "How do you know? Did the mayor say something to you?"

"Of course not." He waved his hand. "Ignore me."

How could I, when it seemed as if he knew more than I did? "What aren't you telling me?"

"Nothing! But I know how these men full of self-importance are, signorina. They are bullies. He will back down, *te lo prometto*."

Roberto's gaze was shifty, evasive. I was about to press him for information when Bev said, "Well, the mayor won't be bothering you today. I hear he called in a security company from Albany this morning to come down and replace his current alarm system. There are four or five vans outside his house."

"I wonder why?" I reached for my coffee drink. "It's not like anyone would dare to break into the mayor's house."

"I couldn't say." Bev shrugged. "But you can bet I'll find out."

I didn't doubt it. No one was better connected in town. Bev knew all the good gossip. "Let me know what you learn." The aroma from whatever Giovanni was cooking filled the kitchen and my stomach rumbled. "That smells amazing," I called over to him.

"I know," he said simply. "It will be the best asparagus risotto you have ever tasted."

I didn't doubt it. I felt very spoiled lately, from Luca making me pasta and looking after me last night, to Roberto and Giovanni assisting me in the restaurant. What had I done to deserve any of this?

There is no shame in accepting help from others when you need it.

Yes, but there had to be limits. I needed to rely on myself. My father never bothered to stick around, and cancer stole my mother from me. Becoming dependent on others led to heartbreak and failure.

"I should get back to the café," Bev said, reaching over to pat my hand. "I'll see you later, Val."

"Thanks again. I'll see you tomorrow."

She turned to go, then paused. "Incidentally, I heard about what happened at book club. I think it sounds romantic. Just like *An Officer and A Gentleman*."

"Ugh," I said, dropping my head onto the stainless counter. "Great."

"A classic movie," Roberto added unhelpfully. "And I can see the comparison."

"There's no romance between me and Luca. And I don't want to hear anything else about it." The two of them exchanged a quick look that scraped across my nerves. "What? What was that look about?"

"I don't know what you're talking about," Bev replied, now hurrying toward the back door. "See you later!"

"Ciao!" Roberto called after her and I shifted to glare at him. The man had the audacity to wink at me.

"I can still fire you," I said grumpily, even though we both knew I wouldn't.

"True, but you need my help to reopen next week. Incidentally, we still must hire two bartenders."

"What happened to the guy we interviewed yesterday?"

"Failed his background check."

Background check? "I didn't realize we were running background checks on every employee. What is the cost of that?"

"It's not a formal process, signorina." He shifted on his feet and slipped his hands into his trouser pockets. "It's through a friend of mine."

Roberto's response was cagey—and telling. I spoke very clearly, saying, "Is this friend Luca?"

"Not exactly."

"Hmm." I didn't love it. The sign, covering bar tabs. Background checks. Not to mention whatever happened with Mayor Lombardi. I made a mental note to take all of this up with Luca at my first opportunity.

Except it would need to wait because Giovanni set the risotto in front of me. I scooped up a bite and blew on it to cool it down. When I put it in my mouth, I almost died. "Oh, my god. This is the best thing I've ever eaten. Thank you, Giovanni."

"Better than chicken parm," I heard him mutter under his breath.

"Except for chicken parm," I shot back.

He shook his head, but he was smiling as he returned to the stove.

Roberto stuck around as I ate, so I figured it was a good time to catch up. "Have we seen an invoice from the construction guys yet?" I needed to work on finances today. My mother's life insurance was covering these renovations, but I had to be careful. I didn't have much left. We needed to open soon.

"No," Roberto said. "I haven't received one."

"Is John out there?" I asked, referring to the head of the construction company. "I'll just go ask him." I put down my spoon and rose.

"Wait, signorina—" Roberto said, but I was already through the door. The workers were replacing light fixtures when I went into the dining room. "Hey! Is John around?"

They pointed to the bar. I peered over the top and saw John working on installing a new water line. "Hi, John. Have a minute?"

"Sure, Val." He screwed in some plumbing pieces, then dried off his hands. "What's up?"

"I'm wondering if you have an invoice ready for me. I'd like to pay some of what I owe now, rather than waiting until the end."

"I don't have one drawn up yet, but I think you owe five hundred."

"Five *hundred*? That doesn't make sense." The estimate was eight thousand dollars. Why was it so cheap?

"Uh, the prices went down."

"By seven-thousand and five-hundred dollars?" I looked over at Roberto. "Did you know about this?"

Roberto shook his head. "No, it's the first I'm hearing of it."

John rose and shifted on his feet. "Well, you've been doing this on your own for a long time, Val, with your mom dying and everything. Sometimes we all need a little help and there's no shame in accepting it."

The words . . . they were too close.

And the price drop was too drastic, too convenient. Alarm bells went off inside my head, my heart kicking hard in my chest.

I looked at my contractor. "John, on the life of your little brother, Daniel, who I used to babysit, tell me the truth. Is Mr. DiMarco paying the difference?"

There was a long pause. "Come on, Val. Don't make me swear on my brother."

That was enough confirmation for me.

"I'll be back," I told Roberto. "I have an errand to run."

* * *

Luca

"She's at the gate."

I looked up from my laptop. There was no need to ask who Aldo meant. Roberto called me the second an angry Valentina departed from the restaurant.

102

"Want me to turn her away?" Aldo asked, then took a bite of the apple in his hand.

"No. I might as well get it over with."

"Should I bring her in here?"

I considered this. Gabriele was somewhere on the estate and I preferred that my son not run into Valentina. Best to have this conversation in private. "Yes."

Aldo left and the numbers on my screen blurred in front of me, my concentration fucked. I'd been thinking about her all day, how she pressed up against me in bed last night with those soft and lush curves, her breath warming my skin. It had been a struggle to get up this morning, leaving her to sleep, when all I wanted to do was feed my cock into her pussy.

A knock sounded. "Dai, entra!" I called.

Aldo held open the door and Valentina sailed into the room. She was flushed, hair pulled into a high ponytail, her eyes wild and angry. She wore a dress that looked like a man's shirt and it pulled across her chest, as well as showed off long, tanned legs. Fuck, she was gorgeous. My heart raced in my chest, pumping like I'd been jogging, while my skin sizzled with awareness.

Aldo shut the door and left us alone. I tried to keep my voice even. "I hadn't expected to see you again so soon, fiore mio."

She pointed at me, gaze narrowing. "Do not call me that. I know what it means."

Now I was confused. "This upsets you, this endearment?"

"We are not at the endearment stage. I barely know you, which is why I'm here." She folded her arms across her chest, which only brought my attention to her spectacular tits. "Stop meddling with my restaurant."

"Meddling?"

"Don't play stupid, Luca. The sign and the background checks? Now I find out that you're covering the cost of the renovations!" She threw up her hands and let them fall. "This is ridiculous. I barely know you and you've taken over what's supposed to be *my* restaurant."

I should be furious with the way she was speaking to me—with so much attitude and disrespect—but I liked her sassy mouth. It made me want to kiss her and bite her until she melted against me. And her perfume? Christ, it was driving me crazy. It was the same scent still on my sheets upstairs.

Do you want to have sex with me, Luca? Please, say yes. I'm tired of wondering what it's like.

Lust clawed beneath my skin, sharp and demanding, making it hard to breathe. Valentina was a mixture of soft and vulnerable, but also tough as balls. Who else would dare to come here and give me such a scolding? It only made me want her more.

In a flash I made a decision.

I was tired of fighting this, which meant I was planning to fuck her. But I couldn't fuck her without telling her my real name and what I did for a living. I was a cruel man, but I wouldn't deceive Valentina about something so basic.

Decision made, I slowly stood and put my hands in my pockets. "Come here."

She huffed, a sound of outrage and disbelief. "No. I want answers, Luca. You're overstepping and I want to know why."

"That isn't happening. Now, come here."

"No. You're going to distract me with all of your . . ." She waved her hand in my general direction. "You-ness."

I had no idea what that meant, but I wanted her to follow simple directions. "Get your sexy ass over here right now."

She licked her lips, but didn't budge. "Why?"

"Because I'm going to kiss you, but I can't until we talk first. And I want my hands on your body while I do it."

Her gaze darkened and the skin of her throat turned a dull red. "You're supposed to ask first," she said in a breathy voice. "Haven't you heard about consent?"

Madre di dio, this girl got my dick hard. "Now, fiore mio."

"Wait." Shaking her head, she put up her palms. "This is all happening too fast."

No, it wasn't. This was taking fucking forever. I usually had the patience of a saint, but this girl was testing all of my limits.

I edged out from behind the desk and stalked toward her. She lifted her shoulders but didn't move, just watched my approach with hooded eyes that told me all I needed to know. She was nervous but excited. Curious but hesitant. Eager but shy. I vowed right then to make this so good for her.

As I closed the distance between us, the muffled thump of my shoes on the carpet was the only sound in the room. When I reached her I stopped and stared down at her. I could see the pulse throbbing on the side of her neck, my virginal little flower.

I dragged my hand up her arm and felt the tiny shiver that ran through her. I kept going, higher over her shoulder and then her throat, until I cupped her jaw in my palm. My other hand rested on her hip, my body surrounding her. "I want to kiss you. Do you want it, too?"

She nodded and swayed toward me ever so slightly.

I nearly smiled, the victory was so sweet. "You need to say the words. We need to be very clear on what you are consenting to."

"You're a dick." But she was smiling as she rested her hands on my chest. She was tall, but even taller in heels, her forehead reaching my mouth. Madonna, I couldn't wait to have her beneath me in every way.

"Yes, I am," I conceded. "But I want to hear you ask me for it."

She stared up at me and I could see the indecision swirling in her gaze. "I'm still mad at you."

"I want you mad, bella. I want you to claw and scratch and bite me. Because that makes my dick even harder, capisce?"

"You're impossible. I can't win with you, can I?"

"If I kiss you, we both win. Now ask me, Valentina."

She swallowed. "Please, will you kiss me, Luca?"

Satisfaction flooded me but I didn't pounce. It's what a boy half

105

my age would've done, slobbered and pawed all over her like an inexperienced puppy. But I wasn't a puppy and I needed to show her what it would be like between us, slow and satisfying, unlike anything she'd imagined. If it killed me, I would exhaust myself to wring every drop of pleasure from this virgin's body. I would take my time and do it right, until we were both satisfied.

Lowering my head, I edged closer, my fingertips pressing into her skin, letting her feel me. Then I skimmed my lips over hers in the lightest caress, closing my eyelids to concentrate on every millimeter of her flesh. I moved gently, learning the edges of her lips, mapping the delicate bow at the top. Inhaling her warm breath. So sweet, this girl. I wanted to lick her from head to toe.

Her arms wound around my neck, so I moved my hand to the small of her back. I let my fingers linger near the top of her ass cheeks, brushing her skin through the thin cotton of her dress, imagining all I would do if she were naked. *Soon.*

A sound of frustration erupted from her throat as I bent to kiss her jaw. "You're teasing me."

"I am making you wait for it," I said into her velvety skin.

"I don't want to wait for it."

"That is too bad, because you asked me to kiss you and I am taking my time." I kissed a line along her throat, her pulse pounding against my tongue. I liked feeling her every reaction to me. I would bet my empire that her pussy was soaking right now.

I licked the tender spot where her neck met her shoulder. "I can't wait to bite you right here."

"Oh, god," she breathed, her fingers sliding into my hair. "Luca, please."

I didn't waste another second. Lifting my head, I slammed my mouth down onto hers. Soft and wet lips met mine and she kissed me eagerly, hungrily, as if she'd been dying for it. I didn't hold back, letting her feel exactly how much I wanted her with every pull and sweep of my mouth. Then I adjusted the angle and flicked my tongue against her lips, and she instantly let me inside. Hot and slick, her tongue met mine and I growled in satisfaction. Cazzo, she was perfect.

I held her face in my hands and let the kiss drag on. I couldn't remember when I'd kissed a woman for such a long time like this, with my full effort and attention, not intending to do anything more.

I can make her come, though.

Would she let me?

I pulled back, but didn't let her go. "I want to taste your pussy." She moaned and tried to kiss me again, but I held her firm. "Valentina. I'm serious."

She was panting, her big eyes blinking up at me. "Right now?"

"Right now."

"But . . ." She attempted to shake her head in my grip. "It's the middle of the day and someone might walk in."

"No one enters without my permission, and what? You think I can't give you an orgasm in the daylight?"

"It's embarrassing."

I smoothed her hair off her face, pushing the silken strands over her shoulder. "A man like me, on his knees for you, solely focused on your pleasure? How is that embarrassing, fiore mio?"

"I came here to yell at you, not have sex."

"We are not having sex. You are grinding your clit on my tongue until you come."

Her eyelids squeezed shut. "My god, the way you talk. You don't hold anything back."

Wrong, I definitely did. But before I confessed all of my secrets, I needed her to be relaxed and satisfied. I slapped her ass with my palm. "Do yourself a favor and get on the desk, Valentina."

She pressed her lips together and cast a suspicious glance at the desk. "If we do this, nothing changes. I still don't want you involved in my restaurant."

I slapped her ass again and she let out the softest, most arousing moan. "I make the rules, bella. Now, go lie down and spread your legs for me."

Chapter Twelve

Valentina

There were a hundred reasons why this was a bad idea.

For starters I needed to get back to the restaurant, and it was the middle of the day. Also, I was still slightly hung over. Luca and I were practically strangers. Oh, and no one had ever performed oral sex on me before.

I wanted to say no. But the words wouldn't pass my lips. My insides were on fire, my skin crawling with need. The way he kissed? The way he touched me? It was with absolute focus and concentration, like I was the only person on earth who mattered. So different from any of my previous experiences, limited as they were. Luca was unexpectedly gentle, too. I thought he'd be rough, impatient, but he was the exact opposite.

Safety—that's what he felt like.

I wasn't one to act impulsively, but didn't I deserve a treat after busting my ass for the last three years? After setting aside so much to care for my mom? After giving up dreams of traveling and parties to take over a family restaurant?

And I was certain I could trust Luca. He wouldn't hurt me and I bet he knew his way around a woman's body.

I walked over to the desk. Then I moved his things, climbed up, and waited. He stared at me intently, his deep brown eyes almost black, the hint of a smile curving his lips. I felt drunk on his attention, the most beautiful and sexy woman in the world, not an inexperienced twenty-one-year-old. The front of his trousers revealed the erection pushing at the cloth and I loved seeing the proof of his desire for me. This gorgeous man *wanted* me.

He ran a palm over the ridge in his trousers. "Do you like seeing how hard you get me, fiore mio?"

I licked my lips. "Yes. It's very sexy."

Dropping his arm, he started toward me. "My dick is sexy, or the torture you are putting me through?"

I gripped the edge of the desk, nerves and excitement at war in my chest. "Both?"

"My dick is exceptionally sexy," he said arrogantly, then leaned over me to put his mouth near my ear. "Soon I will show it to you and we will see if you agree."

My lips parted and I was panting, nearly vibrating with need. Between my thighs was already pooling with arousal and he hadn't even touched me yet. "Today?"

"No, not today." He straightened, only to drop to his knees. Large hands pushed my thighs apart and he glanced down to examine me. "Look at that wet spot all for me. Mamma mia, I am going to eat this pussy until you scream."

"Oh, god."

He dragged the back of his knuckles along the thin strip of soaked cloth between my legs, brushing over my clit. Shivering, I bit my lip to keep from begging him to hurry up. He hummed in his throat, a sound of male satisfaction, as he peeled my panties off my hips and down my legs. Then I was bare in front of him. "You wax all of your hair off," he said with a deep rumble. "I like it."

"You do?"

"I do. Cazzo, you are gorgeous."

He lightly traced the edges of my labia with a fingertip, a string of mumbled Italian falling from his lips. This teasing was too much. I was ready to crawl out of my skin. "Luca, please."

"Lie back, Valentina. Let me take care of this pussy."

I eased down onto the wide desk, nervous about being on display, but Luca began a soft press of his lips to my flesh, quickly erasing all my doubts. I expected him to go quickly, but then I remembered our kiss. Was he going to torture me again? The man had the patience of a saint, apparently.

His dark head looked positively indecent between my legs, his eyes closed as he explored my labia with his mouth. Damn, this man was fucking hot. That, and the combination of his warm breath and gentle touch on my most sensitive skin caused me to tremble with anticipation.

The tip of his tongue flicked at my entrance. He groaned. "Mmmm. So sweet." He tasted me again, then spread me wide with his hands. "Look at my girl, so wet and slippery. *Madonna*, the things I'm going to do to you."

I was so turned on that I barely registered the "my girl" comment. I squirmed, unsure of what I needed but desperate for something more. "Luca, please."

He dragged his tongue through my slit, then again. "Keep squirming, bella. I like it."

I didn't know what that meant, but he was licking me like an ice cream cone and pleasure streaked through every part of my body, little ripples of lust that twisted inside me. It was amazing. If he continued to do this, I might come after twenty minutes or so—

His tongue met my clit and I nearly shot up off the desk. My body jolted like I'd been shocked and a moan fell from my throat. Wait, was this what oral sex was all about?

"Relax, Valentina," he whispered, his hands pressing on my inner thighs to hold me open. "I'm going to take care of you."

Then he began in earnest, his attention focused solely on my clit.

Tongue, teeth, lips—he used all three, a mixture of pleasure and pain, varying his speed and suction as he feasted on me. My back arched as my muscles tightened, his mouth all I could feel, wave after wave of bliss driving me higher. I wasn't sure if it had been minutes or hours, but I never wanted this to end.

I was shaking, quivering, my body strung as tight as a bow. Close, so close. The orgasm was right there, building in my lower half.

"Take out your tits," Luca ordered against my skin. "I want to see them."

As if I were in some kind of haze, I unbuttoned the top of my dress and spread the edges apart to reveal my bra and cleavage. Luca's hand reached up, jerked one of the bra cups down, then palmed one bare breast. He growled—an actual, honest to god growl —and then resumed lashing his tongue over my clit. At the same time he shaped and molded my breast, squeezing, pinching my nipple. I gasped and my inner walls clenched. "More," I whispered. "I'm so close."

Luca's clever fingers tugged, tweaking on my nipple, as he sucked on my clit. The combination was a revelation, an uncontrollable high that shook me to my very core. I was at his mercy, on his desk, taut with lust, unable to do anything but lie here and let him do as he pleased with my body. *His play thing.*

That did it. An unstoppable rush of electricity started in my toes and raced to my clit. "Oh god!" I threw my head back, a shout ripping from my throat as my pussy convulsed, the orgasm blinding me to everything except Luca's tongue. It went on and on, my vision turning white for several beats.

When it finally ended I slumped onto the desk and tried to catch my breath. He eased up then, his mouth turning gentle as he nuzzled his way to my entrance. There he lapped at my arousal, gathered it on his tongue. "Fuck," he breathed. "That's what I need right there. So fucking delicious."

Then he pushed up to his feet and lunged for my breast, drawing my nipple into his mouth. I floated happily, blissfully, threading my fingers through his hair as he suckled on me. Letting me go, he bared the other breast, then held them in his hands. "Bellissima. They are better than I imagined."

"Thank you," I murmured.

"You like when I play with them, no?" I nodded, and he hummed in his throat. "Good, because I will be touching them a lot."

"You will?" Did he mean today?

"Sì, fiore mio. We will have a lot of fun together."

"We will?" My brain wasn't working right.

"Of course." He straightened and pulled the cups of my bra back over my breasts, covering me.

Were we done?

"Wait," I said as he started to button my dress. "I want to reciprocate."

He paused, like maybe he was considering it, but eventually exhaled heavily. "I want this as well, but not today." His fingers moved along each button, briskly and efficiently closing the two sides and smoothing the fabric.

"Why not?"

"I like that you are eager for my cock, piccolina. But we need to talk first."

"I didn't say—" I closed my mouth tight. Whatever I'd been about to say was a lie. I *did* want him. At least I was pretty sure I did. But maybe that was the orgasm talking. "About what?"

"Do you always ask so many questions?" Taking my hand, he helped me sit up. He smoothed the loose strands of hair off my face, stroking my hair, and I felt like a newborn kitten, soaking in the attention shamelessly. When was the last time someone gave me this much affection?

And wasn't it sad such affection came from a man I barely knew?

"Allora," he said softly, his voice husky and rough. "I need to tell you something. It is about who I am."

"Oh?" My eyelids drifted shut as he continued to run his fingers through my hair. God, that felt divine.

"My surname is not DiMarco. It's Benetti."

He said this as if it should mean something to me. I lifted a shoulder, but didn't open my eyes. "Okay."

"And the way I earn a living? I am not a simple businessman as I first told you."

"So, what are you?"

"I'm the head of a Calabrian criminal family."

I wasn't surprised. I hadn't expected him to admit it, but I wasn't surprised. "The mafia."

"The 'Ndrangheta, but yes."

I didn't know what to say. A myriad of emotions churned inside me—anger, fear, regret, curiosity . . . and yes, hurt. He'd lied to me.

But deep down, I'd known it all along. Or at least suspected it, as had Maggie and Sam. But I wasn't thrilled about having my suspicions confirmed.

I just let a mafia boss give me head.

My mother would be so proud.

When I didn't react, Luca said, "You don't seem surprised."

"That's because I knew. Or heavily suspected."

"This changes nothing between us, but I wanted you to know. I try to be up front with all of my mistresses."

Oh, wow. This was . . . wow. We just jumped from him eating me out on a desk to me living in an apartment that he paid for. "We should probably talk about this later." Jumping down from the desk, I scrubbed my face with my hands, not giving a damn about ruining my makeup. "I have to go."

"Tell me what you are thinking."

"That this is a fucking lot right now!" I eased away from him and put some distance between us. "You've blown into town and taken over my life. I'm not ready to be a mistress or whatever else you're thinking. Because if that's why you're helping me, then stop!"

"Valentina, I'm not helping you in exchange for anything. I never expected you to find out about the contractors or the background checks."

"Or the mayor?"

He grew very still, not even blinking. Ah, so I'd caught the great Luca DiMarco—make that Benetti—off guard. "Yeah, I know about that, too," I said.

"I won't apologize for scaring that motherfucker. So don't expect it."

I pressed my hands together and prayed for patience. "Luca, this is a small town. *My* town. We aren't used to thugs coming in and terrorizing everyone."

The planes of his face sharpened, hardened, his chest expanding. "This is what you think of me, that I'm a thug?"

"Is it the word you object to, or the definition? Because I can find another word, if you prefer."

"How about you thank me instead?" he snapped.

I rocked on my heels, the fury so swift and fierce that I wanted to throw something at him. "First of all, I have thanked you. And you can fuck off if you think I'll let you take over my life without putting up a fight."

Luca closed the distance between us and I began backing up. I wasn't afraid of him, but I hadn't argued with a mobster before. They weren't known for being reasonable.

Then my spine hit the hard surface of his office door.

Luca kept coming, his muscular frame even larger as he caged me against the wood, pinning me like a bug. His hot breath ghosted along my ear as he whispered darkly, "Fight me all you like, fiore mio. But you slept in my bed and came on my tongue. You're mine now and you will do as I fucking say. Capisce?"

Chapter Thirteen

Valentina

I should've been terrified. Scared out of my wits and begging for mercy.

I wasn't.

Deep down, I knew he wouldn't hurt me. Not the man who'd taken such care of me when I was drunk. Who'd cleaned up my *vomit*. If he were going to do something terrible, I couldn't have stopped him that night.

There are rules about women and children, my mother used to say about my father's violent world. I was scared of him as a child, terrified at night that he would return to kill her or me, but her reassurances always made me feel better.

I had to believe Luca ascribed to those same rules.

I stilled, waiting, the sound of my heartbeat thundering in my ears. I didn't move, but I could feel his heat and strength surrounding me. The slabs of muscle and long limbs. I was trapped—and it was like my body didn't mind in the least. I recalled the desk, his rough touch, and the bliss of his mouth between my legs. I softened against him. Acquiescing.

"That's it," he said, quieter now. Seductive. He pressed his hips forward and I could feel every inch of his very thick erection against my stomach. "Molto bene, piccolina."

Very good, baby.

My lower half clenched, desire sliding through me again. One big palm landed on my hip, while the other rested flat on the door above my head. Bending slightly, he rocked his hips once, his shaft sliding against my mound.

Holy shit.

Heat sparkled in my veins and my swollen clit pulsed. Suddenly, it was like I hadn't just come my brains out on his desk. A moan fell from my lips as I tilted my hips to feel more of him.

He hummed in his throat. "See? We will be so good together, bella. You are going to let me fuck you, to let me be the first cock inside that gorgeous pussy."

I grasped at my few functioning brain cells to say, "Are you going to stop interfering?"

"Never."

Asshole. "Then tell me why you're in New York."

"Business."

"Mafia business."

"There is no other type of business for a man like me."

I grabbed his tie and held on tight. "Be more specific. What mafia business do you have in Paesano?"

"You can't think I will truly tell you. There are rules, fiore mio." He ground his dick into my body again, causing me to suck in a sharp breath. "And trust me, it is better if you don't know."

This is why my mother never married my father, why she wanted nothing to do with him. Lies, deceit, evasions. And Luca *murdered* people for a living. I made a quick decision, even as my hips rocked to get closer to him. "We can't see each other again. And I don't want you involved in my restaurant."

"You think this is over? I would not believe you even if you weren't grinding on my dick right now." Embarrassed, I tried to pull away, but there was nowhere to go. He had me trapped.

His hand shifted to my thigh, where he pushed the hem of my dress higher. I hadn't bothered to put on my panties—those were somewhere in Luca's office—so his fingers found my bare skin easily. He dragged two blunt fingers through my slit, while his lips coasted along the back of my neck. Between my legs was a slick mess, arousal pooling at my entrance, and Luca mumbled Italian words in a deep husky voice against my skin.

It was too much.

"Stop. Speaking. Italian," I panted, my knees trembling with the force of my desire. I was dizzy with it, blind to anything but the magic he wove around me.

"Should I tell you in English, then? I said this is the prettiest pussy I've ever seen, so ripe and pure, tight like a fist. She has been waiting so patiently for my cock to come along and fill her up with all of my come."

God, that was worse. I should've been ashamed. I was putty in this man's hands, all of my independence and backbone melting into the floor at his touch. "This won't change my mind," I managed.

"No? Then let's try this again."

In a blink he dropped to his knees. He lifted one of my legs up and over his shoulder, spreading me, before his mouth latched onto my clit. There was no time to protest before he was sucking and lashing, rolling the bundle of nerves on his tongue. I was sensitive and swollen from earlier, so it was like picking up where we left off, my body already halfway up the peak.

"Oh, shit," I whispered.

A fingertip teased my entrance, then slid inside ever so slowly, invading. The pressure, oh god. My mouth parted and I panted, needing more. Craving him with every beat of my racing heart. I hadn't ever felt so frantic, so crazed before. No thought, only sensation. Finally, he filled me with one finger, stretching me, and I rocked my hips, eager for more. I had inserted small vibrators before, but this felt different. Luca was warm and solid, so deep inside me.

The orgasm was right there, coiling in my muscles. Ready to explode.

He released my clit with a wet sound. "You're going to be good for me, Valentina." A lick. "You're going to let me lick you, fuck you, pleasure you out of your goddamn mind." Another lick. "Say it, fiore mio."

"Luca," I whined.

He gave my clit a hard suck that caused my eyes to nearly roll back in my head. "Dimmi, piccolina. Tell me, baby, and I'll let you come."

I thrashed my head, my body strung tight. "Why do you care? There are plenty of women in this town."

Instead of answering, he went back to sucking my clit. It felt unbelievably good.

He withdrew his finger slightly, then pushed deep inside. Over my loud moan, he said, "The words. I need to hear them."

I was too far gone, too mindless. What had he wanted me to say?

His lips nibbled my clit, but the touch was too light to send me soaring. I blurted, "I'll be so good for you, Luca."

He grunted, then began eating me out with abandon. Wildly, like a man possessed—and the orgasm slammed into me like a train. I tried to stay upright as I shook against the door, my body shuddering, convulsing, my muscles turning liquid. It was more powerful than the one on his desk, with waves that went on and on, until I finally sagged. Strong arms kept me from collapsing on the floor.

Luca pulled me into his broad chest, holding me close. Hugging me. *A mafia boss who hugs. Who would've guessed?*

I clung to him like a wet noodle. Whatever cologne he wore smelled amazing. He was solid and big and I burrowed into his body, my face nestled in his throat. I should've been embarrassed, but I wasn't. There was something so comforting about Luca, but I couldn't put my finger on it.

After a long minute he eased back to see my face. His dark eyes were soft as he searched my features. "Are you alright?"

He could've gloated, but I was relieved he didn't. I gave him a half smile. "Yes. Thank you for that. Again."

"Do we understand each other now?"

I didn't pretend to misunderstand. "On this, yes."

If I thought he would be mad at my response, I was dead wrong. He threw his head back and laughed, the strong muscles of his throat working. "Oh, piccolina. We are going to have so much fun together."

He released me and stepped back, then reached down to adjust himself in his trousers. "Cazzo, you get me so hard. It's very distracting."

It seemed surreal that this older, sophisticated man wanted me. He could have nearly any woman on the planet. And while I wanted to sleep with him—god yes, please—I didn't want him micromanaging Trattoria Rustica. "Luca, I'm serious about the restaurant. Stop interfering."

He slipped his hands into his trouser pockets. "You work long hours and closely with other people. Then there are the strangers hanging out in the bar while you're drinking. People looking to take advantage of you." He shook his head. "I only wish for you to remain safe."

When he put it that way, it almost sounded sweet. "I don't need you paying my contractors or investigating my employees. I've been on my own for a long time and I'm doing just fine."

The lines around his eyes deepened as he narrowed his gaze on me. "Were you doing fine the night I broke up a fight in your kitchen?"

Now he was pissing me off. "Yes, I was handling it. Women don't always need a big strong man to come and rescue them."

The side of his mouth curled in a way that sent my pulse leaping again. "Big and strong?"

"Oh, god." I turned and grabbed the door knob. "I'm serious, Luca. Stop interfering."

He said nothing, just let me leave. I closed the door behind me with a snap. Irritating man. Sexy, but irritating. *Extremely* talented with his mouth, but irritating.

Had I really agreed to sleep with him? What was I thinking?

He was a mob boss. I should be running away from him, not agreeing to fuck him. Maybe he'd forget about me. No doubt he had a thousand illegal things to do everyday, all of which were far more important than chasing me down. I mean, the idea of Luca pining over me was ludicrous. He'd have no problem finding someone to take my place in his bed.

I should keep going and never look back. And if I felt a tiny twinge of disappointment at what might have been, I'd never tell a soul.

The entryway was quiet. Late afternoon shadows streaked across the smooth marble floor as I approached the front door. When I went out onto the stoop, a sedan pulled to a stop in the drive. It was a gorgeous dark blue Maserati with two men inside it. Because I wasn't anxious to run into any of Luca's "employees," I took my fob out of my pocket, put my head down, and hurried to my mom van.

"Ho! Beautiful! Hold up!" The deep voice was thick with an Italian accent.

No way was I reacting to that compliment. I was already fending off one Italian. I didn't need to deal with two.

My hand had just reached the door handle when someone grabbed my arm. "Wait a minute," he said, angling me toward him. "What is the hurry, bella?"

I could feel my jaw drop. *Oh, my god.* A younger version of Luca stood in front of me. Equally handsome, the same chiseled features, olive skin, dark hair. His eyes held a confidence only found in incredibly attractive people, like they knew everyone was staring at them. "You're his son," I blurted.

The young man blinked a few times. "I am. My name is Gabriele."

Of course. The one who vomited on his father. "I've heard about you."

"Then you have me at a disadvantage. Tell me your name, bambina."

"I'm Val."

Confusion marred his perfect face, but only for a second before he was grinning at me. "Ah. Va bene, va bene. You are her, the one from the restaurant. Valentina."

Had Luca mentioned me to his son? I would need to consider this later. "Yes, that's me. Now, if you'll excuse me, I need to return to the trattoria."

He chuckled and took a step back. "You were here to see my father. This explains why you look—" he gestured to his face "—so flushed."

Damn it! Did I look like a woman who'd just orgasmed twice? I dipped to look into the car's side mirror, which only caused Gabriele to laugh harder. "Don't worry," he said. "No one will know by the time you drive into town."

I straightened and sighed. Maybe I should run home first to clean up, before going back to work. "Nice to meet you. See you around, Gabriele."

"Everyone calls me Gabi." He snatched my hand and brought it to his lips, kissing the back. "And I look forward to seeing you again, Val."

The charming yet knowing twinkle in his eyes grated on my nerves. "We won't be seeing each other again. So enjoy your time in New York."

I opened the car door and got in. But not before I heard him say, "Dai, bella. I would not be so sure."

* * *

Luca

I frowned as my son entered the house. After Valentina left my office, I followed her quietly to make sure she departed safely, which meant I caught Gabriele arriving outside.

He left the house when I specifically told him not to.

Not even here a full day and already my son was causing trouble.

"Where the fuck were you?" I barked when he stepped inside.

He jerked, clearly startled, but then composed himself and closed the door. "I went out to grab a bite to eat."

"I told you not to leave."

"Except there's no food here."

Was he arguing with me? I ground my back teeth together, struggling for calm. "The kitchen is not bare. You want something, you prepare it."

Gabriele tossed the Maserati keys onto the entry table. "You mean cook, like on the stove? Dai, Papà. You know I can't do that."

Unfortunately, I did know this. Both of my boys were spoiled this way, thanks to my housekeeper and cook in Catanzaro. "I suggest you learn. I won't have you running around in town, putting yourself at risk and alerting everyone to your presence."

"There's no risk here. No one knows who we are."

There was always a risk for a Benetti. "That isn't the point. The point is I told you to stay here and you disobeyed me. And stop arguing with me."

He held up his palms. "Mi dispiace, Papà. But please, can we hire someone to cook for us? I need food—good food. You wouldn't believe what people eat here. It's disgusting."

"This is not a vacation, Gabriele. I'm here for business. And if you don't like it, then I suggest you return home."

"Business?" He smirked at me, the expression reminding me of my brother Sergio. "I saw how Valentina looked when she left. That didn't seem like business."

"Watch your mouth." I turned and started back toward my office. I was the boss—I wouldn't answer to anyone about my actions. Also, I could still smell her pussy on my face and I wanted to jerk off while the memory of her taste was fresh in my mind.

"Oh, now I know why you're so mad," Gabriele called behind me. "You saw me talking to her outside."

I couldn't let him think this had a grain of truth to it. I was his father, as well as his boss. "Do you honestly believe I am jealous of you?" I scoffed. "Be serious, figlio mio."

"No, you are." I heard him following me. "That's why you were waiting at the door, snarling at me. You didn't like me flirting with her."

I tried to be logical about it, to rely on cool intellect rather than emotion. I had no right to be jealous, and Gabriele was closer to Valentina's age. They made more sense together.

I'll be so good for you, Luca.

Fuck sense. She was mine—no one else's.

I stopped at the office door. "If that is what you call flirting, then I'm surprised you get any pussy at all."

He threw his head back and laughed. "You like her."

The denial sprang to my lips, but I couldn't force it out. And that infuriated me. I couldn't have feelings for *any* girl, but especially this one. I was using her to draw out her father.

Aldo emerged from the direction of the kitchen. He popped a slice of pear in his mouth. "Why are you two arguing?"

Gabriele spoke first. "I met Valentina."

Aldo grinned. "He didn't like it, did he?"

"I am angry because I told my son to stay on the property, yet my guards let him leave."

Before Aldo could answer for this lapse in judgment, my mobile buzzed in my pocket. I checked the caller. Unknown number. "Pronto."

There was a lot of noise in the background. A male voice spoke quietly, as if trying to not be overheard. "Luca? It's me."

I froze, every muscle in my body on high alert. "Niccolò?"

"Luca, I'm sorry."

"Tell me where you are, right fucking now," I said very carefully into the phone.

A sliding door slammed shut in the background before he said, "I did my best. Forgive me."

Then he disconnected.

Motherfucker! I took a deep breath and tried the number back, but it didn't go through. Niccolò probably used a burner to place the call.

Aldo was already speaking on his phone. He handed it to me and I heard Sergio's anxious voice. "Niccolò called you?"

"Just now, yes. He apologized. Said, 'I did my best. Forgive me.' Then he hung up."

"His best? What is that supposed to mean?"

"I don't know," I admitted. "But it can't be good."

"Any idea where he was calling from?"

I considered this. "A lot of noise in the background. A sliding door slammed shut, like a car door. Maybe on a van."

"Was he in a car?"

"No. The background noise was too loud. He was definitely outside."

"An airport, maybe. A bus station."

"Maybe."

We were both silent for a long second. I said, "Sounds like he's on the run, which means the police don't have him. Just like Gabi said."

"That's good news," my brother said. "But why call to apologize? Why not come to Catanzaro, where we can hide him?"

"I don't know, but we need to find him. Get CCTV footage from every airport in the EU. Have the boys check around this time for any sign of Niccolò."

"That will take forever. We need a way to search quickly."

I considered this. I knew someone who could help expedite the process. "Call our friend in Napoli. Ask him to get his computer guys on it. They can find answers faster than we can."

Enzo D'Agostino was the head of the Napoli 'ndrina and he

made most of his money through computer fraud. We'd traded favors over the years and he was currently in my debt. His hackers should be able to find Niccolò; after all, they successfully hid D'Agostino from the world for four years.

Sergio hummed his approval. "D'Agostino? Good idea. I'll ring you back with his answer." My brother ended the call.

I tossed Aldo's mobile back to him, then dragged a hand through my hair and stared at the wall.

"I told you Niccolò wouldn't turn on the family," Gabriele exclaimed. "Where did it sound like he was calling from?"

"I'm not sure. But if he's on the run, then he'll likely pass through an airport."

My son shook his head. "Niccolò gets sick on airplanes. He'll go by bus or car."

Ah. This was helpful. "Go with Aldo. Make a shopping list of what you want and I'll have it delivered. I need to ring Sergio again."

The two of them left the entry and I returned to my office, where I sat behind my desk. Instantly, my mobile buzzed. It was Sergio. "Pronto."

"He wants a face-to-face," my brother said.

"Fuck that. I don't have time to fly to Napoli."

"He's in New York. His woman has a show at Fashion Week tomorrow. He said you can come there to talk."

I rubbed my bottom lip between my thumb and forefinger. New York was two hours away. "Cristo, he's a pain in the ass."

"He said he wouldn't do it without talking to you first."

A negotiation, then. I needed his help, so I would have to find out what he wanted. "Fine, I'll go. By the way, Gabriele said Niccolò gets airsick, so he won't travel by plane. We need to have D'Agostino's people check bus terminals and car rentals."

"Okay, but D'Agostino has another condition. And you're not going to like it."

I sighed. What now? "Spit it out."

"He said this can't look like business. His woman will be pissed if he's working during her show."

"What does that mean?"

"He said you should bring a date. Make it look like you're coming to Fashion Week. He'll meet with you after."

My eyes instantly went to the office door where I ate Valentina's pussy not even thirty minutes ago. Would she come with me to Manhattan? I sure as fuck didn't want to take anyone else.

If she agreed, I would have her all to myself for one night, maybe two. My groin grew thick again as images of the filthy things I wanted to do to her gorgeous body flipped through my brain. Her tits, her pussy . . . her ass. Madre di dio, I wanted to bite and lick and slap that ass.

I wouldn't accept a refusal.

"I'll bring Valentina."

Sergio chuckled. "I thought you might say that."

"Call the hotel I like, stronzo. Book the nicest room they have available."

"Okay, but what if she doesn't agree to come with you?"

I thought of the woman who'd melted like butter in my hands. "Don't worry. She will agree."

Chapter Fourteen

Valentina

"Val, the toilet in the first bathroom is stopped up."

I glanced up from the order list I was working on for Roberto. Anne Marie stood in the office doorway, her expression full of regret at delivering me this news. We'd rehired my former server a few days ago, but this was her first day back since quitting. She'd agreed to return when I told her we had a new chef and that Tony was banned from the restaurant.

"It's stopped up *again?*" I asked, my voice rising in annoyance.

"It wasn't me," she quickly added. "Have the workmen been using it?"

"Probably." I closed my eyes and exhaled. I hated our old pipes. "Okay, I'll go plunge."

"Want me to do it, honey? You've got a lot on your plate."

Plunging toilets was a dirty, thankless job. One I wouldn't wish on anyone. And I never asked employees to do anything I wasn't willing to do myself. After all, I was the boss. It was my responsibility. "That's nice of you to offer, but I'll do it. I'm used to it."

"You might want to change first."

Right. I'd worn a cute outfit today, wanting to look my best in case a handsome older Italian gentleman stopped by. Which was stupid, because Luca had far better things to do than drive over here.

Like running a criminal mafia organization.

I tried not to think about our hookup when I was lying in bed last night. Or this morning. Or in the shower. Or on the drive into work. Or as I stopped for coffee.

Okay, I was obviously failing at forgetting it. I felt like the information was tattooed across my forehead for all to see: *I hooked up with a mob boss.*

"Damn it," I said to Anne Marie. "I don't have a change of clothing here."

"Then let me do it." She gestured to her jeans and t-shirt. "I'm dressed for dirty work."

I stood up. "No, that's all right. God knows it's not the first time I've plunged while wearing a dress."

"If you're sure, then I'll go back to unpacking the new glassware with Roberto. Good luck."

In the bathroom, I caught my reflection in the mirror. This dress really was cute. I discovered it while scrolling on a social media app late one night. The sleeveless wine-colored sheath dress had a tiny bit of ruching on the side, and I looked sophisticated in it. A woman in charge, like my mother. Not like a silly twenty-one-year-old virgin.

Bottom line? Nothing was going to ruin this dress. I locked the bathroom door, then carefully unzipped my dress and stepped out of it. I carefully hung it on the side of a wall sconce, far out of the way.

I stared down at myself and tried not to laugh. I now wore only heels, a thong, and a lace bra. It was ridiculous, but what choice did I have? Besides, this would be over soon and no one would ever know.

A long curse crossed my lips. At some point I really needed to get these old pipes dealt with. No matter how many signs you put up asking people not to flush paper towels or feminine products, rude assholes still did it anyway.

Just as I turned to the small supply cabinet for the tools needed to tackle the job ahead of me, a frightening bang on the door was accompanied by an equally frightening shout.

"What the *fuck?*"

I froze. That wasn't Anne Marie.

It was a man. A man I'd hooked up with yesterday in his office.

And he sounded *pissed.*

"Luca?"

"Valentina," he growled. "Open this door!"

"I'm right in the middle of something—and stop shouting at me!"

"Open up right now or I will break this door down!"

Oh, hell no. Where did he get off ordering me around? And what the fuck did he have to be so mad about? "Don't talk to me that way, and you are not coming in here."

"Allora . . . I will break the door down."

His footsteps came closer and I panicked. "No! Don't do that. Jesus. Then I'll have to replace the door." I turned the lock, cracked the door, and peeked through the sliver of space, as worried about who might see me as Luca's anger. "Stop right there!"

The planes of his face were sharp, eyes narrowed dangerously, as he thrust his hands on his hips. He was wearing a dark navy suit, and even as foolish as I felt right then, I couldn't help myself. My god, he looked fucking hot. The white dress shirt showed off his olive skin, and the dark blue tie that contrasted the color of his eyes. His wavy dark hair fell effortlessly in elegant sweeps, like it had been styled by a professional.

As I was studying him, I forgot that he was also studying me.

He looked slightly calmer, but no less intense as he said, "Stand back, I'm coming in."

"Why?"

"Because I said. *Andiamo*, Valentina."

"Not a good enough reason, Luca. I'm busy with something in here."

Leaning in, his voice went soft. "You need to learn your place, fiore. I'm coming in right now, capisce?"

My place? The fuck?

Now I was pissed. That asshole wanted to see me? Okay, fine! I hoped he enjoyed the show. Because that was all this high-handed fucker was *ever* getting out of me.

I stepped back and he took full advantage, barging into the bathroom. "Happy?"

I felt foolish, nearly naked, but then Luca's gaze performed an excruciatingly slow sweep of my body. I could feel his regard like a caress over my bare skin, the heat of his stare burning me. My nipples tightened and tingles spread along my thighs. He looked at me like I was something to be savored, a cold treat on a blistering hot day.

"Cazzo madre di dio," he whispered. "It's even better than I remember."

He wasted no time locking the bathroom door behind him. The click of the metal echoed in the tiny space like a gunshot and my mouth dried out. My breath came shallow and fast in the mask, my muscles trembling with anticipation. I had no idea what was about to happen, but I certainly wasn't angry any longer.

I was something else altogether.

His long stride ate up the distance between us. He captured my face in his hands and leaned in close. "You are mine now, fiore mio," he said quietly. "And my woman does not plunge toilets or clean bathrooms. Ever. Are we clear?"

A tremble rolled through me, but I couldn't tell if it was from his words or his touch. "Luca—"

"Are we clear, Valentina?"

"I'm not yours," I whispered.

A muscle clenched in his jaw. "Did I eat your pussy yesterday —*twice?*"

"Yes, but—"

"There is no but, piccolina. You promised to be good for me. Or do I need to force that promise from you again, right now?"

The amount of slickness gathering between my legs should've embarrassed me. God, I was shameless for this man. "No."

"Are you sure? Because I have no problem tonguing your clit in this bathroom for all to hear."

I could see it . . . Me, leaning on the sink, with Luca's dark head shoved between my thighs . . . .

I swayed toward him, teetering from the lust rushing through my veins. He chuckled. "You want that, don't you?" He pressed his lips to my forehead. "Soon. I'm going to give you everything you need very soon."

Then he surprised me by stepping away. "Get dressed. I'm taking you to New York City."

"Wait, what?" Now my head was spinning for a different reason. "I can't go to the city. We're opening in two days."

"Yes, you can. Get ready to leave. You have five minutes." He unlocked the door and reached for the handle.

"Five minutes? What the hell are you talking about?"

"Valentina." His voice was stern and he looked over his shoulder, expression unyielding. "Your sexy ass will be in my car in five minutes, even if I have to carry you out like that." He tilted his chin toward my mostly naked body. "Though I'll have to kill any man who looks at you. Is that what you want, fiore mio? A blood bath?"

I couldn't tell whether he was serious or not. Luca generally meant what he said . . . but would he really kill someone who saw me in my bra and panties? "No, but can you please explain?"

"There's no time. I'll explain on the drive."

* * *

Luca

I stepped out of the toilet, hoping my dick would calm down soon. I wasn't sure I could drive a car in my current state. Mamma mia, her body was a fucking crime. If we weren't already behind schedule, I would've taken off that flimsy bra and sucked on her tits for a few hours.

Later. I had a hotel suite waiting where I could have her all to myself.

As I entered the restaurant, I searched for Roberto. I found him at the bar, unpacking glasses with a woman I recognized from my first night here. She was the waitress who'd quit on Valentina. "Signora," I greeted coolly.

"Table Seven," she said with a smirk. "Nice to see you again."

I ignored her and pointed to Roberto. "A word." Then I strode to the front door, where he and I could speak privately.

He soon joined me. "Is there something wrong, signore?"

I pointed to the toilets. "She doesn't plunge and she doesn't clean. Get plumbers in here today to fix whatever the fuck is happening with those pipes. I don't care if they need to be ripped out and replaced with solid gold. See that it's done and send me the bill. Are we clear?"

"Sì, Don Benetti. Of course. I didn't realize what she was doing. I'll see that it's taken care of."

"Good. I'm taking her to New York overnight. I expect you to handle things here and not trouble her with drains and paperwork and glasses, capisce?"

"Understood. No problem."

"What are you two talking about?" Valentina was close enough to hear us, but we spoke in our language, not hers.

"Nothing," Roberto said confidently in English. "Luca informed me that he's taking you to New York and I said that wasn't a problem."

I wrapped my arm around her waist. "Come. Let's get on the road."

"Wait," she said, putting her hand on my chest. "Roberto, I was nearly finished with the ordering list for you. It's on my desk. And Giovanni wanted to talk about—"

"That's enough," I said and began towing her toward the door. "Roberto has run some of the finest restaurants in Italia. He can handle your little trattoria."

She bristled against me. "My *little* trattoria? It's my whole life, Luca. And I don't appreciate you being so bossy and condescending."

She continued to argue with me as we went outside, but I ignored her. As long as she kept moving to the car, she could yell at me all she liked. D'Agostino wouldn't wait around, so I needed to ensure we arrived at the show on time.

I let Valentina settle in the passenger seat and I closed her door. Then I hurried to the driver's side. Before I got in, I nodded at Aldo and another guard, who were following behind in a second car.

I slid into the smooth leather seat, buckled in, and started the engine. When I pulled away from the curb I noticed she was quiet. "Is something wrong?" I asked.

"Are you kidnapping me?"

The accusation was an unwelcome reminder of my purpose in this country. "No. You're free to stay here, though you might want to hear what I have planned first."

"Then am I at least allowed to stop by my house and pack?"

"I already did that for you."

She made a choking sound and glared at me in disbelief. "You broke into my house and went through my things?"

"Yes."

"Luca, what the fuck?"

I shifted gears and dodged around a slow truck. "First, you need better security. It was embarrassingly easy to break in. Next, would you rather Aldo packed for you? I assumed you would want me to choose your sexy panties."

"I'd rather choose my own sexy panties," she snapped. "And you are really grating on my nerves."

"Piccolina, you keep talking like that and I will find a better use for your mouth on this drive."

"You wish!" She folded her arms.

Cazzo, the idea of her lips wrapped around my dick . . . "I do. And we have already established that you cannot resist me."

"God, your ego . . . Do Italian women get off on your domineering arrogant attitude?"

"Yes, they do. Almost as much as American women."

"Have you—"

She closed her mouth abruptly, but I knew what she was going to ask. I said, "Not on this trip. But yes, years ago."

Silent, she mulled that over for a long second. Then she said, "I thought mafia bosses were always in hiding."

"Smart mafia bosses go wherever they like. It is the stupid ones who get caught." Frowning, I tapped my fingers on the steering wheel. Because I'd fucked Palmieri's wife, everything was now at risk. Who was the stupid one now?

She was busy exploring the car, and for once I was glad she wasn't paying attention to me. I didn't want to talk any more about mafia bosses.

After she investigated the contents of the Maserati's glove box, she closed the front. "So tell me why you're dragging me to the city."

"I have a meeting there."

From the side of my eye I watched her angle toward me. "You are dragging me two and a half hours away to attend a meeting with you?"

I took the ramp onto the motorway. "Yes."

"Luca, are you insane? I can't go to a mafia meeting! I'm a restaurant owner. I don't want to be a part of your illegal activities."

I sighed heavily. I supposed I owed her an explanation, but I wasn't used to someone yelling at me. The men in my life would never dare. "There will be nothing illegal about this meeting. I need a favor from someone else, another don. He's at his woman's show and refuses to meet with me unless I bring a date."

"Why?"

"Because it can't look like work."

"So I'm your date."

"Maybe. But only if you stop asking so many questions."

She wrinkled her nose and stared through the windshield. "You said he's at a show. Broadway?"

"Fashion week. She's a fashion designer."

"We're going to a *fashion* show?"

The way her voice rose in volume had me looking over. "This is a problem?"

"Oh, I don't know, Luca. Maybe because I was at work, *about to plunge a toilet* fifteen minutes ago? I feel gross, and now I have to attend a New York fashion show."

I put my free hand on her bare knee and slid my palm along her skin, moving higher until I reached her inner thigh. "You are not gross. You're hot as fuck, piccolina. Every man there will want to fuck you when they see you in this dress."

"Thank you," she said." There was a slight edge to her voice, but nothing like a moment ago.

"You're not thinking about what's important. Let me focus your attention."

I dipped my fingers into her panties. Smooth, hot skin met my fingertips. I brushed through the wetness gathering in her slit and nearly ran off the road. "You feel so good," I murmured. "I can't wait to eat this pussy again."

She shifted in her seat, making more room for my hand. "What if a truck drives by? They will know what you're doing."

"My hand is under your dress, which is all they will see."

"Still, it's obvious what's happening."

"Do you care?"

"Yes."

I adjusted my angle and thrust one finger deep inside her. "What about now?"

She threw her head back and closed her eyes. Her slim throat worked as she swallowed. "Maybe?"

"Va bene, fiore mio."

Fuck, she was tight. I couldn't wait to feel this virgin cunt strangle my bare cock later tonight. I knew she was on birth control because I'd found her pills earlier in her bathroom.

I pumped my finger a few times and she began panting, her hands clutching the leather upholstery. "Keep talking. In Italian."

"Take your panties off first."

After she wriggled out of her panties, I put my hand back between her legs. I continued to drive, my finger sliding in and out of her, and began speaking in my native language, words they don't teach in any translation app. Dirty, filthy things. Every depraved act I wanted to do to her body. What I thought of her tits and her pussy. Her hair, her face . . . How I shouldn't have touched her in my office, but now that I had I didn't want to stop . . .

She was close. I could feel her thighs trembling and the way her inner muscles were clamping down. I withdrew my finger and brought it up to my mouth. I sucked her juices off my skin, relishing the flavor on my tongue. "Madre di dio," I groaned. "So fucking delicious."

"Luca," she whined. "I'm so close."

I put my hand between her legs and rested two fingers on her clit. I held perfectly still, eyes on the road. "Are you going to be good for me?"

"Yes, yes. *Please*."

She rolled her hips, trying to chase my fingers, but I eased them away, teasing. "You're going to play the *mantenuta*, the woman in my life today?"

"Yes."

I circled her clit twice, then stopped. "You won't complain or cause trouble?"

"No. Now stop being a dick and stop teasing me!"

"And you're going to let me fuck you and spoil you?"

She hung her head and dragged in deep breaths. "Yes. Just make me come, please."

I moved my fingers vigorously, back and forth, circling, working her clit, and it only took a few seconds before she was climaxing, moaning and shaking, drenching my fingers. I hated that I couldn't see every moment, that my eyes needed to watch the road as much as they could watch her. But the next time this woman came would be underneath me, with my cock deep inside her.

When she sagged into the seat I lifted my fingers to her mouth. "Clean them, piccolina."

Her tongue swiped my skin before she sucked my two fingers past her lips and into her hot mouth. I snuck a glance at her, unable to resist the sight. Cazzo, that was hot. She was flushed, her expression dazed, almost trance-like as she followed my instructions. This girl . . .

I had to look away. I was too keyed up, my dick too hard. If I wasn't careful, I would pull over and do something stupid on the side of the motorway.

I put both hands on the steering wheel and tried to calm down. The meeting with D'Agostino was too important and whatever was happening with Val could wait.

For the next few minutes, Val put herself back together quietly, fixing her dress and her hair. I stared at the road. I ran through the meeting with D'Agostino, what I thought he might ask for—

I jolted as fingers jabbed at the pocket of my trousers. Instinct had me grabbing her wrist, stopping her. "What is this?"

Val held up her panties, the ones she'd taken off moments ago. "I'm trying to give these to you. Don't you want to keep them?"

My heart thumped erratically, surprise and desire a dangerous cocktail in my bloodstream. She was unexpected, both innocent and filthy, an intoxicating combination. I released her and relaxed. "Fuck yes, I do."

She tucked the used panties in my pocket, then patted my thigh. "Now you can think about those all day."

I'd be hard-pressed to do anything else. "Where did a virgin learn about giving a man her dirty panties?"

Leaning over, she put her mouth as close to my ear as she could manage. "I've read a *lot* of books." A second later she flicked on the car's stereo and music filled the sedan.

For the next hour and a half I contemplated those books and what else Valentina might have learned.

Chapter Fifteen

Valentina

Sitting next to Luca in the car was torture. Smelling his fancy cologne, watching his strong and capable hand work the gear shift . . . Everything about this man was sexy. Even the way he scowled at the other drivers was incredibly hot.

I was in big trouble. Not only was he dangerous and a criminal, he had this weird ability to rob me of my free will.

The reasons for that would need to be examined later when I was alone. For now I would just enjoy whatever the day brought. Luca said he wanted to spoil me and I was ready for spoiling. I couldn't remember when I last took any extended time away from the restaurant. My mother's funeral, maybe? And I hadn't been to the city since sophomore year of high school, when we took a class trip to Lincoln Center. It was right before my mother's diagnosis, before we knew how sick she was.

Right before everything changed.

Once we were through the tunnel, Luca navigated the streets with ease, almost as if he were a New Yorker. He waited impatiently for pedestrians and dodged taxi cabs. Finally, we eased into a parking garage. The daily price made my head spin, but Luca didn't blink as he turned over the car's fob. Then he took my hand and led me onto the sidewalk. "How do you know where you're going?" I asked, trying to keep up with his long legs.

"It isn't difficult. Most of Manhattan is a grid—north, south, east, west."

"How many times have you been here?"

"Twice."

That was as many times as I'd been here, and I wasn't nearly as familiar with the streets.

We passed an old building with people milling about out front taking photos. A red canopy hung over the door and a black carpet spread out on the ground. Luca continued past the entrance, though. "Was that it?"

"We're going in a different way."

Oh. Was he trying to avoid the crowd? He led me to a steel door farther up the block, where he pressed a buzzer. When the door opened Luca gave his name and we were admitted into a long hallway.

"Stairs are at the end of the hall. Go right and you'll see them. At the top, go left." the security guard said.

We followed his instructions and soon found ourselves backstage. There was no way it was anything else, with the number of people rushing about, hair and makeup chairs, and half-naked gorgeous men. I'd expected female models, but clearly the show was for menswear.

Hooray for me.

"I think I'm going to like this show," I said to Luca with a wide grin.

He wrapped his arm around my waist. "I thought you might. Try not to drool, bambina."

There was so much activity, it reminded me of the kitchen during the dinner rush. Controlled chaos was what my mother always called it. Everyone was busy, focused on their responsibilities yet working as a team, and I found it soothing in a way.

"Ah, there they are," Luca said, looking above the crowd. "Come with me."

Luca took my hand and led me through the chairs and racks of clothing. We finally arrived at an area with more space, where a gorgeous woman was adjusting a pair of trousers. The wearer of said trousers, a beautiful male model with caramel skin and lean muscles, stood perfectly still while the woman worked, and I noticed another man lounging in a chair nearby. He was also handsome, a bit older, and power radiated off him in waves. No one spoke to him and he watched the woman fiddling with the pants with an intense concentration that bordered on creepy.

This had to be the other don.

He wasn't what I expected, but then I hadn't thought Luca was a don either. These two could've passed for wealthy businessmen, not international criminals.

Luca edged around the woman and the model, walking directly toward the man in the chair. At our approach, the don glanced over, his eyes wary and sharp. He looked at Luca carefully, then gave me a quick once over.

"D'Agostino," Luca said in a friendly but soft tone. "Come stai?"

D'Agostino stood, expression unchanging, and the two men shook hands. Then Luca placed his hand on the small of my back. "Signore D'Agostino, this is Signorina Montella."

When he went to shake my hand, I said, "It's nice to meet you, Mr. D'Agostino."

His grip was firm. "Signorina. Glad you could make it." His voice was deep and thickly accented, the sounds slightly different than the way Luca spoke. A different dialect, which meant he wasn't from where Luca lived.

"Hi." The woman who'd been adjusting the pants joined us. She edged in between D'Agostino and Luca, her gaze locked on Luca's face. "Who's this, babe?"

D'Agostino softened considerably, pulling the woman close to his side and kissing the top of her head. She was unbelievably gorgeous, tall and thin, with her makeup done to perfection. I was instantly jealous of her superior eye liner skills. She wore a low-cut, loose, patterned dress that was tighter on top and flowed around her legs, paired with a cool pair of low boots and funky jewelry on her wrists and around her neck. Her style was both elegant and edgy, and I couldn't help but admire her.

"Gianna," D'Agostino said. "This is Signore Benetti and Signorina Montella."

Gianna continued to stare at Luca, then her smile dropped as she whirled toward D'Agostino. "You promised. Goddamn it, Enzo."

I moved closer to Luca's side, not sure what was happening. He ran his hand up and down my back, and I arched into his simple, soothing touch, seeking more. It was bizarre how my body responded to him.

D'Agostino bent and began whispering to Gianna. She pushed at his chest, interrupting him. "Stop. I don't have time for this. We'll discuss it later. Go away." She returned to her model, bent down, and ignored us.

D'Agostino sighed and shook his head. "I am not leaving."

Gianna said nothing, just continued to work on the trousers. Someone came over and told her of a problem with one of the jackets, and Gianna gave instructions to an assistant on what to do with the trousers. Then she stood up and darted off into the crowd.

"We'll find our seats," Luca said to D'Agostino, who was watching the spot where Gianna disappeared.

D'Agostino responded in Italian and Luca nodded. Then he led me away, following the signs marked for the stage. We went out into the main area, but I was surprised not to find a runway or stage. Instead chairs were lined up around the perimeter of the white room, with big black boxes scattered throughout the middle, sort of like a maze. Nearly all the seats were taken, with more people filtering in from the back, but Luca led me to a reserved section.

We sat and Luca draped his arm around the back of my chair and crossed his legs. I leaned into him, which I seemed to be doing a lot lately. I wasn't sure why, but I'd think about it later. For now I just wanted to enjoy the day with this incredibly handsome man. "What did Mr. D'Agostino say in Italian before we left?"

"Nothing important."

Which meant he didn't want to tell me. "Was he pissed?"

"That is one way of putting it," Luca drawled. "It's nothing you should worry about." He picked up my hand, kissed it, then brought it over to his thigh and curled our fingers together.

We fell into silence and I watched the crowd settle. There were several celebrities I recognized, a few actors and sports stars. I tried not to stare, but it was hard. Almost everyone in the room was incredibly good-looking. And the women my age seemed so together and sophisticated—not like they'd been dealing with plumbing problems earlier today.

If mom hadn't died, maybe that could've been me. I might've gone away to school, traveled and become cultured, experienced the world. Instead, I was stuck in Paesano, running the family restaurant and trying to keep my head above water.

Luca put his lips near my ear. "What is it? Why do you keep looking at that group of young girls?"

They were around my age, but I didn't bother correcting him. "No reason. Just curious."

"Valentina, there is nothing wrong with staying home, close to family."

"I know," I snapped, annoyed that he'd read me so easily.

"Good." He kissed my hand again. "And so we are clear, you are more beautiful than all of them put together."

He was being very generous, but I took the compliment anyway. "Thank you."

The entire room went dark and music filled the space. I sat straighter, eager to see what Gianna's designs looked like. Lights flickered overhead, illuminating a pathway between the giant boxes on the floor. Models began appearing from backstage one after the other, their walk smooth and steady, and their flat, almost angry gazes focused straight ahead. The clothes were so cool, more androgynous than traditional men's clothing. I would definitely wear some of the shirts and sweaters.

At the end Gianna emerged and everyone clapped wildly. She waved and smiled, following the models in a long train around the room once more. Then it was over and the house lights came up, and the crowd began talking and moving toward the exits. Luca didn't stand. He kept hold of my hand and remained seated.

"Should we go?" I asked.

"No, we will wait here for a moment. What did you think of the show?"

"It was so good. She's mad talented."

He smiled at me in a strange way—soft and affectionate, yet also amused. He tucked my hair behind my ear. "Yes, I think so too."

I shivered at his gentle touch. "You're laughing at me."

"No, I promise I'm not. I think you are adorable. And also mad sexy." Then he lowered his head and gave me a deep kiss that was definitely not appropriate in public.

I couldn't bring myself to complain, though.

When he pulled away I was dizzy and breathing hard. "Was that really necessary?"

"Of course. I want you ready for later tonight."

My nipples tightened in my bra just thinking about it. Thanks to what happened in the car, I still wore no panties and if he kept kissing me like that, I was going to have problems. As it was, I could already feel sticky wetness on my thighs.

Luca's phone buzzed. He read the screen, then typed something back quickly. Then he put his phone away and pulled me to my feet. "Come."

I stood and straightened my dress. "Are we going backstage again?"

"No. We are going to dinner with them."

* * *

We arrived first.

Luca held a chair out for me as we sat down. The restaurant was Italian, naturally, and smack in the middle of Mulberry Street's Little Italy. The place was quaint and on the small side, not as touristy as the others we'd passed, and the staff spoke to Luca in Italian when we walked in, which he returned in kind. I struggled for classy nonchalance, but hearing him speak his own language was hotter than hell. No doubt my lust was written all over my face.

Needing a distraction, I looked around. I rarely ate out, especially at other Italian restaurants, so I took it all in. A white tablecloth covered the table, a small vase of flowers in the middle. Oil plates and wine glasses were already down, which Roberto hated. He maintained the less on the table to start, the better. I had to admit, the setting did feel cluttered.

The black and white photographs on the walls were reminiscent of my restaurant before the remodel. Roberto had insisted we find local Hudson Valley artists and use their art instead of the photographs. It had worked nicely to brighten the space and the artists were grateful for the exposure. These photographs were dark and dated.

The menu was an eight-page heavy book with plastic sheets. Exactly the menus Roberto had tossed in the trash his first day at Trattoria Rustica. He said simpler was better and Giovanni agreed. The new menu would have limited choices, all fresh ingredients, and printed daily depending on what was in season.

I could see now what they meant, but this was what I knew. What I had grown up with. Cluttered tables, photographs, and plastic menus. The new restaurant was a big change from the old way. What if the valley wasn't ready for it?

Luca ordered a bottle of wine from the server, gaining my attention. When we were alone I said, "Maybe I didn't want wine."

He reached over and placed a hand on my thigh. The warm

weight of it was possessive and delicious, like he had the right to touch me. I didn't hate it. At all.

"You will like this wine," he said. "It's produced in Calabria by a man I know. Besides, we have already established that your taste in wine is terrible."

"No, you're just a wine snob."

Luca moved closer, his lips near my ear as he said huskily, "Are you even old enough to drink wine, piccolina?"

"Barely." I grabbed his dark blue tie and turned to face him. "Does that make you feel like a dirty old man?"

He hummed in the back of his throat, then angled his head to meld his lips with mine. When he parted my lips, I opened for him eagerly, desperate to feel his tongue once more. I lost all sense of time and space when Luca kissed me, like my mind was a sieve, incapable of holding onto the simplest thought.

"I see the party has already started."

The dry female voice startled me and I broke off, letting go of Luca's tie. Gianna and D'Agostino had arrived. We said hello and the mob boss settled the designer in the seat next to me. As D'Agostino lowered himself into a chair, the hostess tried to hand him a menu, only to have D'Agostino sneer at it. He snapped something in Italian and the hostess scurried off.

Gianna bent toward me and whispered, "I force him to eat in Little Italy every time we're in New York." She snickered. "It makes him *crazy*."

"He doesn't appreciate the reminders of home?"

"This is nothing like my home," D'Agostino said. "It's an affront to my country. And she does this merely to irritate me."

Gianna shook out her napkin and placed it on her lap. "How can I resist? You make it so easy, il pazzo."

D'Agostino picked up Gianna's free hand and brought it to his mouth. I expected him to kiss her hand, but he bit her fingers instead. She just laughed and flipped open her menu. "What are we ordering? I'm fucking starving."

The server returned with the wine and presented the bottle to Luca. D'Agostino's brows lowered menacingly and he said something in Italian to Luca. I didn't understand it, but D'Agostino was not happy. Luca merely smiled and directed the server to pour for the table.

"Oh, good choice," Gianna said. "I love the Ravazzani wines. It's nice to support the family business."

"Your family has a winery?" I asked her.

"My sister's husband." Then she asked the server to bring an Italian beer for D'Agostino. "Enzo would rather die of thirst than drink this wine," she explained to me.

"Your show was amazing," I blurted when the server left. "I know nothing about fashion, but I loved every piece."

"Aw, thank you. That is nice of you to say." Gianna smiled wistfully, her eyes a bit sad. "It's always a letdown when the show is over, like I'm letting go of my little babies. Meanwhile, I'm already designing three shows ahead. The fun never stops."

"Yet you're doing very well," Luca said. "I saw you were picked up by several stores recently."

"Yes, and I've been asked by a European chain to design some pieces. So I'm definitely busy." She picked up her wine and regarded Luca. "I'm sorry I was so rude before, Mr. Benetti. But I have a clear No Work policy when it comes to Fashion Week, which Enzo is more than aware of."

"Mi dispiace, signorina," Luca said, hand on his heart like he was making a pledge. "If this were not an urgent matter, I never would've intruded."

"How did you know?" I couldn't help but ask her. "We could've been at the show for a totally different reason."

Gianna rolled her eyes. "Girl, when you grow up in the life, you learn how to spot these guys a mile away."

"And yet," Enzo said smoothly, leaning over to kiss her temple. "You did not spot me, micina."

Gianna's olive skin flushed as she pushed Enzo back to his side of the table. "I'm still mad at you. Go away." Enzo smirked and sat back, his hand resting on Gianna's forearm on the tablecloth.

The server returned and I couldn't help myself. I had to order chicken parmigiana to see if it was better than mine. Luca asked the server a bunch of questions about the fish—where it had been caught, how long ago, was it ever frozen? He then ordered a pasta dish, apparently not liking the news regarding the fish. I couldn't blame him. Getting decent fish was tricky in the restaurant business.

Enzo and Gianna ordered, then we were alone again.

"So, what's your story?" Gianna angled toward me. "Let me guess? You're a student at NYU and you met this one—" she gestured to Luca "—in a coffee shop while you were doing homework."

"Not even close. I own a restaurant in the Hudson Valley. It's been in my family forever. Luca came in to eat one night." I shrugged. "That's pretty much it."

"You own a restaurant? Damn, I wouldn't have guessed it. Is it Italian?" She blew out a breath. "What am I saying? Of course it's Italian."

I laughed. "Yes, it's Italian. Best chicken parm in the state."

"Which is not Italian," Luca muttered under his breath.

I considered kicking him under the table. "Stop. Our Italian-American culture has become something that is ours, not yours. I'm sorry if that offends you, but take it up with the millions of immigrants who moved to this country in the 19th and 20th centuries."

Gianna began chuckling. "Oh, I like her. I have to remember that the next time I get a craving for spaghetti and meatballs."

"Also not Italian," I mimicked in a deep Italian-accented voice.

Gianna laughed loudly and even Enzo cracked a smile. Luca didn't smile, but the warmth in his eyes wrapped around me like a soft blanket. I tried not to blush under his attention and wished that I could kiss him again.

The conversation flowed easily from there. I learned that Gianna was from Toronto, but split her time between Naples and New York. She had a sister who lived in Sicily and another in Siderno, and a pack of nieces and nephews. And there was now a large diamond ring and wedding band on her ring finger, which I hadn't noticed before.

"Were you wearing your rings earlier? I feel like I would have noticed them."

She wiggled her fingers, admiring the giant stone. "No, I never wear them when I'm working. The stone gets caught on the fabric."

"It's absolutely gorgeous. But aren't you worried you'll, I don't know, lose them or something?" I kept all my mom's jewelry in a safety deposit box at the bank. My house was way too messy and I was never home to organize it.

Gianna shrugged. "If I did, I'd make him buy me another one, I guess. I never really worry about it."

Oh. Wow, I felt stupid. Of course she wouldn't worry. A man like Enzo could no doubt afford a hundred diamonds just like that one. This was a woman who *definitely* didn't buy her clothes from social media ads or live off ramen so she could afford to pay her staff during a lean week. She was gorgeous and stylish and rich—the complete opposite of me. What the hell was I even doing here?

Our food arrived, thank god, so at least I could focus on chicken parm instead of me. The portion was decent, though I could've used a bit more melted cheese on top. I tasted the sauce first. It was good, but a little sweet. I cut up a bit of chicken and ate it. It was the right thickness, but the breading was a tad soggy. My next bite I put all the components together and it wasn't bad. Nowhere near as good as my grandfather's recipe, though.

"Allora, Valentina," Luca said, gesturing to my plate. "What is the verdict?"

I realized everyone was watching me and I tried for a careless shrug I definitely didn't feel. "Nice. I wouldn't order it again, but it's not terrible. Mine is better."

That made Gianna and Luca laugh, then Luca forked up a bite of pasta and held it up to me. "Try this."

I opened my mouth and eased forward, scraping the tines with my teeth. Heat and spices exploded on my tongue. "Wow, that's really good."

"Of course it is."

"Not as good as the pasta dish you make, though."

Gianna set down her wine glass with a thud. "Wait a minute. Luca *cooks?*" She glanced over at D'Agostino. "Wow. You better step up your game, marito."

"My *game*," D'Agostino replied smugly, "seemed to satisfy you enough on the ride down."

Gianna laughed, then leaned over to kiss his cheek. These two were adorable, in a weird enemies-to-lovers kind of way. They probably fought all the time, but made up just as passionately.

I gave all my attention to my dinner. Gianna did the same, which made sense after the rings conversation. She probably thought I was a small-town bumpkin with no business on the arm of a man like Luca. The opinion wasn't altogether wrong, either.

When I couldn't eat any more, I decided to escape to the ladies' room. I scooted my chair back. "Excuse me."

Luca, because he was classy and older, also stood and helped me out of my chair. "Everything all right?"

"Yes. I just need to visit the ladies' room."

"Oh, good idea." Gianna eased out of her chair, as well. "I'll come with."

I couldn't very well refuse, so I started toward the back of the restaurant. I found the ladies' room and went inside, then held the door for Gianna. We both used the toilet, flushed, and came out to wash our hands. Then she leaned against one of the sinks. "Okay, spill."

"About what?"

"You and Luca. I need details. How long have you been together?"

I paused, paper towel in my hand. I wasn't sure if I was supposed to tell anyone the truth, but Luca hadn't told me to lie, either. Besides, my lying skills were terrible. If Luca didn't like it, too bad.

"We're not together. It's true what I said. He came into the restaurant to eat a few nights ago. I've seen him a few times, but it's not serious."

Gianna's perfectly sculpted eyebrows rose. "Please. That kiss when we first walked in? That was a we-are-very-serious type kiss."

Heat crawled across the back of my neck. "Still, it's true. He brought me today to pose as his girlfriend so you wouldn't think this was business. He said I was his manten-something."

"Mantenuta?"

"Yes, that."

She blew out a breath and leaned in like we were having a heart-to-heart. "Valentina. Honey. *Mantenuta* does not mean girlfriend. It means mistress. Kept woman, specifically." She shook her head. "Girl, you've been mafiosoed."

I blinked a few times, my brain scrambling to catch up. This was the second time the word mistress had popped out of Luca's mouth. "Mafiosoed? What does that mean?"

Lipstick in hand, Gianna angled to the mirror, our eyes meeting in the reflection. "These men, these mafiosos. They are crafty sons of bitches. They'll lie to get what they want from you. You have to keep on your toes with them—or next thing you know you'll find yourself kidnapped and trapped on a yacht with one. Don't believe a goddamn word he says."

All of this hit way too close to home. Luca's lies and evasions, the fact that he'd dragged me out of the restaurant this morning with no notice whatsoever. Gianna was right—I did need to be careful. No matter how many orgasms Luca gave me, he was a dangerous man.

Exactly like my father.

"Oh, shit." Gianna capped her lipstick and whirled to grab my shoulders. "I can tell you're spiraling. I'm sorry if I've scared you. My sisters always say I'm too blunt."

"No, I'm glad you told me. I needed to hear this."

She let me go but didn't move away. "Look, you seem like a sweet girl. And I get it. Men like this? They fuck like gods. Charisma off the fucking charts. Believe me, I tried to resist, but that crazy, sexy man out there pulled me in and didn't let go. So if you want Luca, then sleep with him. Be a mantenuta or not. But do it with your eyes wide open. Have it be on your terms instead of his, you know?"

"Thank you. I will."

"Good. Now, you are slaying in that dress, girl. Where did you buy it from?"

No way was I telling this fashion designer where I found this dress. "Oh, it's nowhere fancy." Undeterred, Gianna wiggled her fingers at me, ordering me to give up my source, so I said, "You're going to think it's stupid."

"Doubtful. I've shopped everywhere. Thrift stores, department stores, warehouse clubs. I once pulled a jacket out of a trash bin in Barcelona. Tell me."

"A social media app," I whispered the words like they were dirty. "You know, they show those ads and—"

She was already unlocking her phone. "Oh my god, yes. Which one was it?"

Chapter Sixteen

Luca

When the women left the table, I swirled the wine in my glass and regarded the man across from me. "I apologize if I caused trouble between you and your woman."

D'Agostino lifted one shoulder. "Don't worry. I like when she's pissed at me. You told Vito you needed help with your cousin?"

"Niccolò has disappeared and I need him found. I'm hoping your computer experts can look at CCTV footage for me."

"What reason could he have for disappearing?"

"I don't know, but I'm being told he's in custody. I don't believe it."

"If it's true, this would be very bad for you," D'Agostino said.

"It would, which is why I need to find him. Your people can use facial recognition software on video of the trains, parking lots, whatever. He can't be that hard to find."

"This takes time." He met my gaze pointedly. "And money."

"I have plenty of the second, but not much of the first."

D'Agostino stared off into space and I wondered what he was

153

thinking about. We didn't know one another well, but I'd heard of his troubles with Ravazzani, the torture he'd endured. Many men wouldn't emerge sane from such an ordeal, so I respected D'Agostino.

"I don't want your money," he finally said. "I want a marina. The big one."

"Roccolletta?" I gaped at him. "Fuck off. No way am I giving up control of that marina. And why do you need a port? You're already on the water."

"Ravazzani controls most of the marinas on the eastern coast, save yours. It's only a matter of time before he approaches you with a deal." His smile turned predatory. "I would like him to negotiate with me instead."

"What makes you think I would ever give up any of my marinas, let alone the biggest?"

"Ravazzani's empire grows larger with each passing day. Which is bad for the rest of us."

"If he tries, then I'll reject his deal. You think I am unaware of his efforts to put a stranglehold on everyone else?"

"No, but you can't withstand him alone. You'll need allies."

"An ally like you."

D'Agostino rolled his hand meaningfully. "There are worse friends to have, Don Benetti."

"You can't have the entire marina."

"Then I don't know why we're here."

I sipped my wine and then carefully wiped my mouth. "Name something else."

"There is nothing else I want."

"I have a son close in age to your daughter."

His brow wrinkled with disapproval. "Gia would have my balls if I agreed to an arranged marriage. She is very fond of my children. No, I want the marina."

I didn't think Gabriele would be fond of the idea either, so I didn't push it. "I have construction contracts, business contacts. Members of the Italian government. Name it."

"I have already named it."

Merda! I curled my hand into a fist, my mind racing. The marina was used for both illegal and legal imports, and every vessel paid a fee to me. Giving it to D'Agostino would be a huge loss. "It's hardly a fair trade. Your men find my cousin, but I lose the marina for good? You ask too much. But we can compromise."

"Meaning?"

"You can use it freely. My men will continue to oversee the traffic there, except for your business."

He rubbed his jaw, long fingers stroking over his rough skin. A fingertip was missing from one of his fingers. "I'll agree if there's no time limit—and if you promise to come to me first if Ravazzani ever offers you a deal."

"Agreed." I offered my hand and we shook. "I'll have my brother call Vito to work out the details."

"Va bene."

Just then the women emerged from the washroom and walked toward our table. I leaned toward D'Agostino and lowered my voice. "You hate him, don't you?"

"More than you can ever know. But I also respect him, which is how I know he won't be satisfied until we're all out of business."

We both rose and helped the women into their seats. Valentina remained quiet for the rest of the dinner. Even during dessert, she pushed the tiramisu around on her plate, not participating in the conversation. What happened in the washroom to sour her mood?

I paid for dinner and the group of us gathered on the walk to say goodbye. Surprisingly, Gianna hugged Valentina. "Remember what I said," D'Agostino's woman whispered in Valentina's ear.

I frowned. Had Gianna said something about me?

I shook D'Agostino's hand. "Sergio will be in touch."

"Good. I'll tell my brother to expect his call."

They got into the limo and drove off. I considered my options and went with the simplest. Aldo and Carlo were talking at the curb, so I caught their attention and pointed north. Aldo nodded and I took

Valentina's hand and began leading her up the block. She glanced over at me. "Have they been here the whole time?"

"Yes."

"How did I not notice?"

"It is their job to make sure no one notices them."

"Where are we going?"

"You didn't like your tiramisu, so I thought we would try gelato."

"You know a gelato place here?"

I needed her closer. Letting go of her hand, I put my arm around her waist. "There must be one nearby, no?"

We soon found a gelato shop and they served the treat the true way—in a cup with a spoon. Not a cone in sight. Valentina chose chocolate, while I got blood orange. After I paid, we walked and ate silently, letting the sights and sounds of New York City surround us. I sensed she was working something through in her mind and I didn't want to push.

Besides, she knew where I stood on the issue of her and me. My plans for the night hadn't changed one bit.

"I like Gianna," she said.

"I thought you might. She's a ball-buster, like you."

"Did you and Enzo work out whatever the issues were?"

"Yes." D'Agostino hadn't made it easy on me. I needed to warn Sergio of what we'd promised in exchange for D'Agostino's help. "Which means you have my attention for the rest of the trip."

"She said not to believe a word you say."

I didn't like it, but it was decent advice, considering her history with D'Agostino. "Have I lied to you?"

"Yes."

"About my name, but I told you why I need secrecy. And you've already agreed to be mine. You cannot take it back."

"Of course I can. I can change my mind anytime I like. I'm not going to be your mistress."

Ah. Now her attitude shift made sense. This was what Gianna

had warned her about. "I have a mistress back in Catanzaro. I don't need another."

Valentina gasped, then hit me in the arm with her gelato spoon. "Luca! What the fuck!"

"Did you think I was celibate?"

"No, but I'm not getting involved with you when you're already involved with someone else."

"I am not *involved* with her. I fuck her when it's convenient for me."

"Oh, my god," she muttered around a mouthful of gelato. "Do you pay her?"

"It doesn't work like that."

"Then explain how it works, please."

"I'm a busy man. My free time is infrequent and unpredictable. I don't have the energy to find a woman every time the mood strikes. So Chiara is available when I need her. And yes, I pay for her villa."

"What does she do the rest of the time when you're not around?"

"I don't know and I don't care. We do not talk about our lives."

"This is unbelievable. How did you meet her?"

"She was fucking one of my men. Then she came onto me."

"And he didn't care?"

"Of course not. He introduced us."

"I don't understand your world at all." She dug into her cup for another bite of gelato. "How do you know she isn't still sleeping with him or with another one of your men? Or anyone else, for that matter?"

I snorted. "Because I am the boss."

"Which means, what? You don't share?"

"Exactly." I put my free arm around her and kissed the side of her head. "I don't share, bella. Ever."

"But I'm expected to share?"

"Why would you care?"

"Because it's gross. And wrong. And misogynistic."

"I don't understand. She is back in Catanzaro. What does this have to do with what is happening here?"

"It just does," she snapped. "Are you planning to break it off with her?"

"No."

She stopped in the middle of the walk, her jaw falling open. "You have got to be shitting me. You expect me to be okay with that?"

This was enough. I didn't need to explain myself on the street. If Valentina wanted to have this conversation, we would do it privately. I tossed my half-full gelato cup in the trash. Then I took her elbow and led her to the car where Aldo and Carlo were standing. I opened the door. "Get in."

"Aren't we going to finish this conversation?"

"Yes, but I'm not going to do it on the street. Climb in, or I'll put your sexy ass in there myself."

She sighed but did as I asked. "Give us a minute," I told my men.

They both nodded and put their backs to the car, allowing me privacy and also blocking us from pedestrians. I went around to the other side and got in next to Valentina.

Taking her empty gelato cup, I put it in a cup holder. "Tell me why this matters to you."

"Does she think you're still in Italy? Is she waiting around for you?"

The suggestion was ridiculous. "I don't answer to her. Part of being the boss means everyone answers to *me*."

She folded her arms and stared through the car window. "Well, I don't answer to you."

I put my hand on her thigh and slid it high under her dress. "Yes, you do, fiore mio. You've already agreed to be mine. And this means that I now make the rules."

She tried to push my hand away, but I didn't budge. I was stronger and needed to make a point.

"Stop it," she said. "We're fighting and I don't want you to distract me."

Ignoring her protest, I let my fingers creep higher and higher, relishing the softness of her skin. I wanted to bite her inner thigh, mark her as mine. Finally, I brushed the tip of my finger across her seam and we both inhaled a surprised breath. *Dio mio.* No panties. "Who makes the rules, Valentina?"

"Not you, if your rules include sleeping with me and other women at the same time."

I pressed my lips to the spot behind her ear, then kissed down her jaw. "Dimmi, bella. Who makes the rules?" I whispered, caging her in with my body.

She clutched my tie in her fist, a good sign of her willingness. "What if I said we both do?"

I bit her throat lightly. "Then I would give you a demonstration to prove otherwise. Is that what you want? Right here on the street?"

"No."

The single word was nothing more than a gust of air. Not very believable as far as protests went. I gave her slit another swipe with my fingertip. "Are you sure?"

She tugged me closer by my tie. "Kiss me."

It was barely audible, little more than a breath, but I was more than happy to oblige. I tilted my head and slid my lips over hers. Her mouth was soft and welcoming and receptive, and she kissed me back with no hesitation. I let myself sink into her, blissfully unaware of everything around me as I flicked her tongue with mine. How long had it been since I'd last really kissed her? Not even twenty-four hours, yet it felt like decades. I'd missed the little sighs she made in the back of her throat and the way she turned soft.

She chased my lips whenever I readjusted, her grip on the tie almost strangling me. I petted her clit with the slightest of touches, edging her with a hint of what was to come. Her hips rocked, seeking, but I didn't give her enough to satisfy either of us. That would wait until we were alone in the hotel and I could make her scream with pleasure.

I moved my mouth near her ear. "Who makes the rules?"

"Luca. I'm serious. Don't sleep with her again, not until you and I are finished."

"Okay."

"Grazie, baby."

My chest tightened—a strange and unfamiliar reaction. I ignored it and gave her slit another brush with my fingertip. "Now, who makes the rules?"

"You do, Luca."

The sexiest three words I'd ever heard. I kissed her temple, then knocked on the window to signal the boys to get in the car. "Va bene, fiore. Now I will take you to the hotel and fuck you."

Chapter Seventeen

Valentina

T he suite was like something out of a movie set.

A long entryway opened into a luxurious living room. Sofas and chairs surrounded a coffee table, while a grand piano rested in the corner. There was a crystal chandelier, for god's sake, while floor-to-ceiling windows provided a spectacular view of Central Park.

The furniture looked like antiques—expensive antiques. So expensive that I was afraid to put my old knock-off purse down anywhere. I held the cheap leather in my arms and walked around, not quite knowing what to do with myself. Did he expect me to go straight to the bedroom? Start stripping off my clothes?

More nervous than I wanted to admit, I wandered to the windows. The park stretched out below, the best view in the entire city, one I'd never seen except online. In person it was far more impressive.

The room was silent. Why wasn't he saying anything? Were we waiting on something? "Are they bringing our bags up?" I asked.

"That happened earlier, when Carlo checked us in."

"Who's Carlo?"

"My other guard."

Right. Luca traveled with guards because he was a mob boss and people might try to kill him. I couldn't think about that right now. I caught his reflection in the mirror. He was watching me, his hands in his trouser pockets, appearing calm and confident as always. But his gaze was anything but calm. Even in the glass the intensity of his dark stare made me shiver. *Who makes the rules?*

I licked my lips, moistening them. "What are you thinking about right now?"

"How I'd like to fuck you up against that glass."

Mouth dropping open, I spun around. Tingles ran all up and down my body, and I really hoped it was from horror. "But you won't. Right? All those people would see."

"Put your bag down on the chair and come here."

I examined the closest chair. It belonged in a museum, not a hotel room. And it had no business holding my raggedy purse. I put my bag on the floor and walked over to Luca, who was watching me carefully. "Why did you put your bag on the floor?"

"Because it's old and costs probably as much as a bar of soap in this place."

He shook his head and slid his hands onto my hips. "The chair can handle it, but we'll deal with that tomorrow. Right now, I have plans for you."

"Are these naked plans?"

"Yes." He wrapped one hand around the back of my neck. "Relax. You will like them very much."

Without waiting for me to comment, Luca dipped his head and sealed his mouth to mine. This was a much different kiss than the car. That had been coaxing, teasing, almost like a game between us. This was fierce and relentless, and I could sense his determination with every swipe of his lips, every flick of his tongue. His heat and strength wrapped around me, bolstering me, chasing away my fears, and I leaned into him, letting him hold my weight.

He broke off, and I was happy to hear his breathing was as labored as mine. "Go find the bed, piccolina."

Arguing or refusing never even occurred to me. I was going to have sex with this gorgeous and sophisticated older man tonight. I'd deal with everything else tomorrow.

My head swam with so much desire that my limbs shook with it. I nearly tripped as I made my way into the bedroom. Luca was right behind me, silent, with not even his feet making noise on the floor. But I knew he was there because my skin prickled the way it did whenever he was in the same room. Something about this man felt inevitable, a temptation I'd never been able to resist. A reward for so much loss and heartache.

I deserved this in a very temporary, non-mistress kind of way.

In the bedroom was a perfectly made king-sized bed. White sheets, fluffy pillows. Classy, exactly like Luca. I sat on the edge of the mattress as instructed and waited for whatever happened next.

He stopped a few feet away, his mouth curving wickedly as he removed his suit jacket. God, that tie did crazy things to me. Actually, any time he wore a tie. Something about the power and confidence of it made me want to wrap that long silk strip around my fingers and never let go.

His shoulders shifted as he removed his cufflinks and slipped them in his trouser pockets. Did any man my age even own a pair of cufflinks? Certainly none I'd met. Luca's hands went to his throat and he loosened the tie, then slid it off his neck in a whisper of silk. He tossed it on the bed near my hip. "Just in case," he said, his eyes glittering. "We might need it later."

Before I could spend too much time thinking about that, he pulled his shirt tails from his trousers and started smoothly unfastening each button. I could feel his eyes on me the entire time, but I couldn't look away from his hands—his large, capable sexy fingers that had been teasing my clit about twenty minutes ago. I pressed my thighs together as more and more of his chest was revealed.

Then his stomach came into view and I forgot to breathe. If there was ever a doubt as to whether a man in his late thirties could have abs, I could say that yes, yes they definitely could. It wasn't an eight pack like a fitness model, but a solid four. Luca was in *shape*. You could tell he took care of himself and cared about his appearance.

The shirt fluttered to the ground. I rolled my lips and inhaled a deep breath as I looked him over. My god. This was a *man*, not a boy. He had wide shoulders and toned arms, not to mention a chest with hair on it. His muscles moved beneath the skin, veins popping in all the best places, and I wondered if he'd unlocked some kind of forearm kink in me.

His hands went to his belt.

I sat up straighter.

He unbuckled the ends and pulled the leather from the loops of his trousers in one smooth motion. He tossed the belt on the floor. When his fingers went to his trousers, I couldn't miss the large bulge behind the fabric. I edged forward. This was the best, most erotic striptease I'd ever seen in my life, and I was dying to see the rest of him.

"The way you are watching me," he whispered as stepped out of his shoes. "So eager and attentive. It gets me so hard, piccolina."

"I thought—" My voice caught, so I cleared my throat. "I thought I would be stripping for you."

"You will, don't worry. But let me show you everything I have for you first."

The rasp of the zipper lowering was like teeth scraping across my nipples, which were now pulled taut, aching. I gripped the soft bedspread with both hands, panting slightly. Jesus. He'd barely touched me tonight and I felt drugged. Drunk on his pheromones and manliness.

He pushed the trousers past his hips and stepped out of them, his socks quickly following. When he straightened, he wore designer boxer briefs that hugged every ridge and bulge like the fabric was tailored just for him.

"Wow," I said, unable to help myself.

"Dai, it gets better," he said with a cocky smile, then stripped off the boxer briefs.

Holy shit.

He wasn't kidding. It did get better. A lot better. A lot, a lot better.

Granted, my experience with dicks was limited to the virtual kind, but I'd seen enough to know that Luca was gifted. His dick was long and thick, the type that women whispered about behind their hands when they got together.

I never thought to actually see one of these in person.

Luca gave himself a long, slow stroke, almost as if he was showing off. Which was totally unnecessary, in my opinion. This dick spoke for itself.

"Allora, piccolina. Take that dress off."

I started to wriggle the garment off, more than eager to get started. But he held out a hand. "I want you on your feet. Show me— but slowly."

As I stood up Luca walked to the bed and stretched out. He put his arms behind his head, his naked body presented like a feast, with his cock resting proudly on his stomach. He even had nice balls, his pubic hair neatly trimmed—

"Valentina," he said sharply. "Focus."

I dragged my gaze off his groin and unzipped my dress. Then I lifted the hem and began lifting the cloth higher and higher, teasing him, until the dress rested just below my crotch. He was watching me intently, his dark stare liquid fire across my skin, while his chest rose and fell with labored breaths, and a rush of power went through me. This man wanted me, desired me, and the knowledge cranked my lust up several notches. I moved slowly, seductively, dragging the cloth up past my pussy, letting him see the bare folds.

He groaned, his expression twisting into one of pain. "Madre di dio, you are so fucking hot. I've been fantasizing about that pussy all day."

He had? God, the things that came out of his mouth. I expected to feel awkward, but Luca had a way of making me feel sexy and worldly, capable of seducing anyone. I didn't wait to reveal the rest of my body. I removed my arms from the dress, first one side, then the other. Then I shoved the fabric past my boobs and down my hips, all the way off my legs.

I straightened and started to remove my bra.

"Leave it on. Get over here." Luca's voice sounded strangled, like he was barely keeping it together.

I let my arms fall and came over to the bed. Before I could lay down, he grabbed my wrist and pulled me on top of him. I sat on his stomach, with my legs on either side of him. He smoothed his palms up and down my thighs. "Fuck, that bra. It is a gift from God, piccolina."

"Thank you. It was a splurge." I bought the bra in an actual store rather than from an app. Maggie had been with me and she practically forced me to buy it.

"Take it off."

I pulled the loops off my shoulders and down my arms first. Then I reached back and opened the fastening. It took some dexterity, because I wasn't a dainty bra girl, not with these boobs. I flung the bra onto the ground and Luca was already reaching for me. He palmed my tits, molded them, and squeezed my nipples, no fumbling or uncertainty. He touched me like a man who knew exactly what I needed.

"Come here." He grabbed my arm and pulled me toward him. I placed my hands on the pillow to brace my fall, which left my boobs directly over his face. "Perfetto," he crooned, his hands cupping my breasts. "You have the perfect tits. So fuckable."

He flicked my nipple with his tongue, then drew it into his mouth and sucked with delicious pressure. Guys had been interested in my boobs since I turned thirteen, and my limited high school hookups had squeezed them too hard. Luca was firm, yet gentle, and every pull of his mouth answered deep in my belly, like there was a direct line between my nipples and my clit. Lust-drunk, I hardly noticed when he switched to the other side, and I started grinding my hips against his stomach, desperate for friction.

"Up." He patted my ass. "Sit on my face."

"Wait, what?" I couldn't see how this was a good idea. I'd read about it in books, but assumed it was fiction, like nice billionaires and down-to-earth celebrities.

"Trust me, you will like this." Luca seemed very sure, and he guided me forward until I straddled his head. "Sit, fiore. Let me taste you."

"But you won't be able to breathe."

"Yes, this is the point. And after you make yourself come on my tongue, then you will ride my dick."

"How—?"

He didn't let me finish that thought. He pulled on my hips and I dropped onto his face, smothering him. I was worried for half a beat, until I heard him groan like he'd just tasted tiramisu for the first time. His mouth began to move, his tongue swiping my flesh, encouraging me. His big hands circled my waist and I had to admit, it felt good. Better than good. Holy shit, he was everywhere, hitting all the best spots. I started rocking, grinding, the pleasure coiling inside me. "Oh, god," I breathed. "Luca."

He growled and continued to use his tongue, sucking in air occasionally, as I chased the high. He reached up to hold both of my breasts and pulled on my nipples, and my thighs began to shake. I could feel the climax building, the release getting closer and closer. I held onto the wall, anchoring myself, and built up a rhythm with my hips. Then I exploded, just tiny particles of light and sensation that flew apart as I convulsed atop him.

When I sagged against the wall, he gave me one final lick and eased me off of him. I shouldn't have worried about hurting him. He looked so fucking hot. His face was flushed, his jaw taut with desire, and his mouth was wet with my juices. "Cazzo, that was nice," he rasped and patted my thigh. "Sink down on my cock."

"I need a minute, I think," I mumbled, unsure about my coordination after that orgasm.

Holding my hips, he lifted me like I weighed nothing and put me on his stomach. "Now, piccolina. Your pussy is soft and wet, and I need to feel it strangling my dick in the next ten seconds."

I knew what to do, but I hadn't expected to be on top my first time. "Wouldn't it be easier if you did this?"

"Not for you. This way you set the pace, capisce?" He reached between my legs and grabbed his shaft, then maneuvered me until the tip of his dick met my entrance. "Take me inside, let me show you how good it can be."

"Wait." The post-orgasm high receded enough for some of my intelligence to return. "You're going in bare? What the hell?"

"I'm clean and you're on the pill. Andiamo, Valentina." He lifted his hips and then he was inside me. Not a lot, but enough for me to feel it.

"Luca." Pausing, I dug my fingernails into his chest. "How did you know I'm on the pill?"

"I saw them in your bathroom." He swiped my hair off my face. "Okay? You are ready to do this?"

My chest pulled tight. A mafia boss concerned with consent? My heart might not survive it.

Instead of answering, I let myself drop a bit more, taking another inch or so inside me. I closed my eyes at the rush of pleasure, and Luca exhaled sharply as his fingertips pressed into my skin. "That's it. Take more, bella. Take it all."

It wasn't easy, but I was determined. Luca's patience surprised me. His muscles bulged, but he let me go at my own pace. Luca watched me wriggle and pant, shift and bounce until our hips met.

Finally, he was completely inside me and I felt so *full*.

His chest heaved as he stared at where we were joined. "Va bene, va bene. *Guardati*, fiore mio. *Sei tutta mia*."

I didn't know what he was saying, but it sounded so sexy coming out of his mouth. "I thought it would hurt, but it doesn't. You're so thick, stretching me out. But there's no pain."

He hummed in his throat as he cupped my breasts again. "Virgin no more. You belong to me now."

If sex always felt this amazing, then yes. I could belong to him for as long as he was in New York.

"Ride me," he directed, his voice thick. "Bounce on my dick and grind that clit on me."

I gave him what I hoped was a sexy smile. "You make the rules."

"Fucking right I do." He slapped my ass. "Move, Valentina."

I began slowly, rolling my hips, dragging him barely in and out. Learning how far I could go, what felt best for me. Luca let this go on for a few minutes, but then he grabbed my hips. "Up and down. I want to watch your tits bounce while you fuck me. And go fast."

He guided me, showing me what he wanted, and I was up for all the experimentation we could handle tonight. I wasn't sure I'd like this, but I gave it one-hundred percent, using my thigh muscles and glutes to ride him over and over. Luca folded his hands behind his head and watched, absolutely absorbed, his gaze darting between my face, my chest, and my lower half.

"You are killing me," he said in a tortured whisper. "I am so close to filling you up. Fuck!" He grimaced and closed his eyes briefly. "Do you think you can come again?"

I was close, but not that close. "I don't know."

He licked his thumb and brought it between us. Then he began rubbing my swollen clit and speaking a stream of Italian I didn't understand. But I didn't need to. It was the long vowels and lyrical quality of the words that got me every time. Like some ancestral part of my brain recognized it and longed for remnants of the past.

I came barely a minute later.

My walls were still convulsing around his length when Luca flipped us over. Then he was pushing in again, his body stretched out over mine. His hips thrust fast and hard, driving into me, our bodies slapping. This was like another level of fucking, the more advanced version I'd expected earlier. And his weight on top of me? Absolutely delicious.

I held him close as his breath started to stutter. His muscles tightened and I knew he was about to climax. I put my lips by his ear. "Have you ever come inside a virgin before?"

The response was instant.

"Merda!" He pressed deep and threw his head back, his hips locked to mine. I could feel him thicken as he shuddered, his big body twitching and jerking while he came. Several seconds later he pulled out, flopped onto the bed and then dragged me to his side.

I curled into him and closed my eyes. His hand stroked my back in long sweeps and my brain floated happily, unable to catch a thought. When was the last time I was this relaxed? I couldn't remember.

"Where did you learn to say those things?" he asked. "About coming inside a virgin?"

"Books."

He grunted. "I am increasing your book allowance."

I smiled into his skin. "I thought you might like it."

"Dio mio, Valentina." He rubbed his eyes with his free hand. "If I had liked it any more, you might have killed me."

"That would give me a lot of explaining to do," I said with a snicker. "I don't think your men would believe me that I killed you with words."

"No, but they would believe you killed me with this body of yours."

I could feel my cheeks heat. Luca probably encountered beautiful women every day, so his compliments were flattering. Energized and giddy, I rubbed my feet against his calves. "Now, what?"

He cracked open an eye and focused it on me. "What do you mean?"

"What are we going to do now?"

He rolled to face me. His hand wrapped my throat, turning my head so he could kiss along my jaw. Then he bit me gently. "Sleep," he whispered. "That is what we are going to do."

"No, come on." I pushed on his shoulder so I could see him. "It's too early to sleep."

"I can't fuck you again so soon."

"No, I don't mean sex. I want to shower and order room service. Maybe watch a movie."

The edges of his mouth turned down at the suggestion. "Valentina," he started in a grumpy, boss-like tone.

"No way, Luca." I slipped out of his grasp and stood up, then turned toward him. "I gave you my virginity. That means I get to make the rules for the rest of the night."

"That is not how this works."

"It is tonight. You owe me."

He stared at my boobs for a long beat before his gaze returned to my face. The edge of his mouth lifted slightly. "Tonight, fiore mio. That's all you get."

Chapter Eighteen

Luca

She was *una nottambula*, a night owl.

I should've known this about Valentina, considering her profession. Most everyone in the restaurant business kept odd hours. But I wasn't prepared for how much energy this girl had at one o'clock in the morning. I didn't dare suggest going to a club for the fear that she would agree.

Though I was exhausted, I didn't complain. Yes, I was jaded, a hardened criminal, but how could I not indulge her? It was clear she hadn't stayed in a hotel this luxurious before, nor had she ever ordered room service. Her delight at the ability to summon a grilled chicken sandwich, french fries, and a hot fudge sundae in the middle of the night had been adorable.

Now I was wearing a hotel robe, eating greasy food and watching a mindless reality show on the television—all because she wanted me to.

She licked her spoon, then pointed it at me. "Admit it, you like this show."

"It's terrible." A bunch of young and dumb people were on an island together, and the only point I could see was that they were trying to fuck each other. "They need to go on a tv show to get laid? Dai, Valentina."

Her foot pushed against my leg. "It's not about getting laid. They're looking for *love*."

I rolled my eyes and withheld my opinions.

"Would you go on one of these shows?" Her eyebrows rose dramatically. "What if it was Mafia Island, where they put a bunch of mob bosses together? You could compete in challenges like racketeering and blackmailing. Or who has the prettiest mistress."

I shook my head. "Your imagination, it is incredible."

Her attention returned to her sundae, but her brow wrinkled as her mood seemed to darken. What was she thinking about? "What is it?" I asked gently.

"Do you hurt people, Luca?"

"Yes." There was no use lying about it, and she deserved as much truth as I could give her.

"Do you feel bad about it when you do?"

"We all make choices, Valentina. I've learned to live with mine. There is no other life for me than this one."

"But . . . the people you hurt, they deserve it, right?"

I knew what she was doing, but I could not have her romanticizing me or my life. "I do what needs to be done to get what I want. Always."

She peeked over at me. "That's harsh."

"The world is harsh, no?"

"Aren't you worried you'll be killed? Or one of your sons?"

"If that is meant to be, then I can't stop it. I have prepared my sons, raised them to be strong men. But no one escapes this world without pain and sorrow." I'd lost family members, friends, and Valentina lost her mother to a terrible disease. Yet we kept going. Life was not for the weak.

The metal spoon scraped on the ice cream dish as she finished her dessert. She peeked over at me. "My father is in the mafia."

I hid my surprise. It was a fact I already knew, but I was shocked she was confiding in me. "Here in New York?"

"No, in Italy."

"Oh? I don't recall any Montellas."

"He has a different last name. Segreto." She studied me. "Flavio Segreto. Do you know him?"

While I hadn't encountered Segreto personally, I certainly knew of him long before Rossi forced me into this mess. I kept my voice even as I answered, "I have never met him, but there are many of us spread out over Europe. It's not as if there is a Mafia Island where we drink and party together."

She gave me an adorable half smile that twisted something in my chest. "Maybe not, but you kind of wish there was, don't you?"

I took the ice cream bowl from her and put it on the tray resting on the bed. Then I leaned over her, my body half covering hers. Bending, I nibbled at her lush lips. "If there was, I know who would win the prettiest mistress competition."

Her arms twined around my neck. "I'm not your mistress, Luca."

I kissed her throat, making sure to cover every millimeter of her soft skin. Then I bit her earlobe. "Are you sure?"

"Y-yes," she said, her voice wavering.

"You might want to rethink your answer. There are perks to being a mistress, fiore mio."

"Sex is not a perk."

We would need to disagree on that. I spread open her robe and ran my hand along her side, over her ribs, and up to her breast. I cupped her and massaged the plump mound. Blood pulsed in my groin, then along the length of my shaft, getting me harder with each heartbeat. I didn't know what it was about this girl, but she made me feel like a fucking teenager, desperate and horny.

I dipped my head and tongued her nipple. The little whimper

174

she gave made me even harder, and my skin began burning as I heated up. The damn robe had to go.

Rising up on my knees, I shrugged out of the heavy piece and tossed it to the ground, leaving me naked. Valentina dragged her hands over my chest, exploring. "Hmmm. You are so sexy. You know, for an old guy." The teasing smirk she wore instantly made me think evil thoughts about her mouth.

"Old, is it?" I straddled her body and dragged my dick through the valley of her breasts. "Push them together," I ordered. "Smother my cock with your tits."

Using both hands, she pressed the mounds in to surround my dick, and I rocked my hips gently, shoving my cock between her breasts. Cazzo, that was fucking hot.

"Open," I said, shuffling my knees forward. I aimed the head of my cock at her lips. "Get me wet."

She opened her mouth and I rubbed my crown over her slippery tongue. "More." I don't know which one of us said it, but I slid in deeper, feeding her my length, until she was sucking me down eagerly. The sight of her pretty lips wrapped around me, not to mention the tight suction . . . madre di dio. It was perfect.

I kept going until she gagged. Saliva pooled over my shaft and my balls squeezed. I eased back slightly. "That is what I want. Nice and wet, piccolina. Again."

We repeated this a few times until I was coated in spit. When I pulled out and moved away, she whimpered and clawed at my thigh. "No, Luca. Come back."

It was tempting. I liked a girl who was eager to suck on my dick. "In a minute. I'm going to fuck your tits first." I put my drenched cock between her breasts. "Squeeze me."

Biting her lip suggestively, she pushed the mounds together, and warm, soft flesh encased my cock. Fuck, that was nice. I started moving, dragging my length through the slick channel. It didn't feel as good as fucking a woman's pussy, but there was something about the visual of this woman's tits swallowing me up that got me off. "Pinch your nipples," I ordered as I moved my hips. "Make yourself feel good."

She did as I asked and her eyelids fluttered, a moan rumbling in her throat. I answered with a groan of my own. This girl was so beautiful, so responsive. I was crazed, feverish to have her again. I braced my hands on the headboard and rocked, the underside of my shaft rubbing her sternum, my foreskin and her spit allowing me to slide easily.

Then she lifted her head and stuck out her tongue, giving my crown a swipe every time I moved forward. My gut cramped as pleasure arced through me. Merda! How did she know exactly how to drive me fucking out of my mind?

I moved faster, a man possessed. "Are you eager to taste my come, bella? Keep licking me. Show me how much you want it in your mouth."

Her eyes flicked to mine. "Please, Luca."

I couldn't wait. The orgasm was building, undeniably close. Rising up, I angled toward her lips. "Circle the root in your fist. I want to fuck your mouth."

She wrapped her fingers around my base and I slid my shaft into her hot wet mouth. I didn't hold back, thrusting into her face, my balls slapping her fist. Her hand kept me from hurting her at this angle. Next time I would show her how to take me all the way in, deep into her throat.

Her free hand cupped my ass, guiding me, and her fingernails dug into my skin. The sting arrowed through my balls and I rocked faster, fierce need coiling inside me. Then her fingers wandered into the crevice between my cheeks and the idea that she might play with my ass was like a shot of white-hot lightning to my groin. I was lost. Come shot out my dick, my hips stuttering as my muscles tightened. She sucked me, moaning as I poured into her mouth, and I nearly blacked out. This girl, *madonna*.

When I was drained, I withdrew and dropped onto the bed beside her. "Fuck, Valentina."

"That was fun." She cuddled up next to me. "Do you think I'd win the Whose Mistress Gives the Best Blow Job competition on Mafia Island?"

My mouth twitched at her choice of words. She was coming around to the idea, which pleased me very much. "Without a doubt, piccolina."

"That's good. Do you know which competition I'd like to see?"

"Which one?"

"Which mafia boss gives the best head."

Without missing a beat, I rolled her over and settled between her legs. "If there is still any doubt, then I had better show you right now."

* * *

Valentina

"Let's go shopping."

I finished applying a second coat of mascara and glanced over my shoulder. Luca stood there, already dressed in a dark suit and looking good enough to eat. I was tempted to climb him like a tree and never let go.

But the restaurant was reopening tomorrow. It was my responsibility to see that everything was ready. "I need to get home, Luca."

"This afternoon. First, I am taking you shopping."

"You don't need to do that. And I really need to get to the restaurant as soon as possible."

He came toward me, his eyes never leaving mine in the mirror as he approached. His big body sealed to my back, while the marble counter pressed into my hip bones. My mouth went dry. Even though we had sex again in the shower this morning, I still craved him. Would I ever get enough?

His hand wrapped around my throat and he leaned down to kiss the soft spot behind my ear. "Who makes the rules, fiore mio?"

The words in his deep voice? Pure sin.

A full body shiver went through me. "You do, Luca," I whispered.

"That is my girl. Now, finish getting ready so I can take you shopping and spoil the fuck out of you."

"How long will it take?" I needed to let Roberto know when I would return.

He eased back and slapped my ass. "As long as I fucking say. Hurry up, woman."

Biting my lip to keep from grinning, I reached for my phone. "I'll text—"

The phone suddenly disappeared from my fingers and Luca slipped it into the pocket of his suit coat. "I have already let Roberto know of your schedule. Andiamo, Valentina. You have five more minutes before I drag you out of here." He walked out and shut the door.

Bossy mafia boss.

I finished getting ready, packed up my things, and stepped out of the palatial bathroom. When I did I found Luca on his phone, speaking in Italian. Though he sounded sexy, he also sounded annoyed and the little divot between his eyebrows was much deeper than usual. Still, it was hot.

When he hung up he started texting rapidly, his mouth turned into a frown. I zipped up my suitcase, asking, "Who are you mad at?"

I didn't expect him to answer, so I was surprised when he said, "Gabriele. He is a pain in my ass."

"He looks exactly like you."

"I know." Luca put his phone in his pocket and came closer. "He's nothing like how I was at his age, though."

"How so?"

He took my hand and we started for the door. "Let's go. The boys will bring your things to the car."

"Wait, my purse!"

"You will not need it."

"But—"

"Basta, Valentina." Luca opened the door and tugged me through. We went to the elevator, which was being held open by Aldo.

"Good morning," I said to Luca's man.

Aldo gave me a polite nod. "Buongiorno, signorina."

All three of us stepped into the elevator and it began descending. In the silence I peeked at Luca, who was frowning at the doors. Was he still mad at his son? "What were you like at Gabriele's age?" I asked him, returning to our earlier conversation.

"Serious."

"Like, you never went out and had fun?"

"No."

I stared at his hard profile. He was angry, and maybe before last night I would've kept quiet. But honestly, who was this man fooling? I poked his ribs. "Come on. You've had two kids by two different women. I think you had a *little* bit of fun."

Aldo made a sound like he was trying not to laugh, while Luca turned toward me. The side of his mouth lifted arrogantly as he slid his hand over my hip to cup my waist. "And last night I was doing my best to make it three."

I couldn't help but chuckle. Thank god for birth control. "Don't forget this morning."

He leaned down and gave me a quick kiss. "I will never forget this morning. It's my new favorite way to shower."

My face heated. Did he always talk like this in front of his men?

Luckily, the elevator stopped and the doors opened. Luca took my hand and we strode through the hotel lobby and onto the street. A big SUV waited at the curb. Aldo opened the rear door and Luca helped me inside.

When Luca came around and got in next to me, I asked, "Why aren't we taking your car?"

"This one is safer. It also has more room."

We pulled into traffic. I watched the people hurrying on the side-walk, everyone moving with a sense of purpose. I used to think, before my mom got sick, that I would move here. I imagined having an important nine-to-five job where I made lots of money and lived in a fabulous apartment.

But when mom was diagnosed I learned what really mattered in life. Like family and roots. I started to appreciate feeding people and running the restaurant. Money was nice, but it wasn't the end all, be all.

The car turned a corner and slowed. Luca finished texting on his phone and put it away. "We're here."

I looked past him and saw where we were going. The Hermès store. My eyes grew wide. This was one of the most famous brands on earth.

He opened the door and got out, then reached for me. I slid across and took his hand. Once on the ground I adjusted the dress Luca had packed for me. "Are we buying scarves?"

"Do you need scarves?"

"No."

We walked toward the entrance. "Then, no. We aren't buying scarves."

"Ties?"

He sighed heavily and opened the door for me. "Get inside, bella."

The second we walked in the air in the store shifted. It was like every sales person paused to size Luca up, then went on high alert. It was the same way some bartenders claimed they could sense a big tipper from a mile away.

Luca pointed to a young man hovering near the ties. "You."

The young man dropped the ties and came over. He nodded at me first. "Hello, ma'am. Sir. How may I help you?"

"I called earlier to arrange to buy some purses."

Was he crazy? Purses here were a bazillion dollars. "Oh, Luca. I don't need—"

"The ones you don't keep out on the floor," he said to the salesman.

The man nodded his head. "Of course. You probably spoke to Ms. Dumas, the manager. Follow me."

Luca put his hand on the small of my back and guided me forward. I lowered my voice and moved closer to him. "What are you doing? This is insane."

He didn't respond, and then I lost the chance to argue because we were shown into a back room where a woman waited behind a small counter. She was polished from head-to-toe, the kind of elegant lady who could contour like a pro and never, ever plunged toilets. "Mr. Benetti," she greeted. "Miss. Welcome. I'm Ms. Dumas, the manager, and I'll be happy to assist you this morning."

"Thank you," Luca said. "We appreciate it."

We? I wasn't on board with this outing.

Ms. Dumas slipped on a pair of white gloves before reaching into a locked cabinet. She pulled out the most exquisite beige leather handbag, the kind you heard whispered about on social media but never saw in person. Ms. Dumas set the tote on a cloth in front of me and I couldn't look away. It was gorgeous. With a simple design, the bag was a decent-sized rectangle with small handles.

The other woman flicked the gold clasp on the front and the top flap opened. "Each Birkin bag is made from rare heritage leather and has unique character." She continued on about the saddle stitching, but I zoned out, my brain trying to wrap itself around what was happening. Who carried a bag like this? I'd splurged on a one-hundred dollar purse once and the guilt drove me to return it the next day.

"Do you like it, Valentina?" Luca was asking me.

I licked my dry lips and saw Ms. Dumas watching me carefully. No doubt she was wondering what I was doing here, too.

Lady, I don't have a clue.

I didn't want to seem stupid, so I said, "It's lovely. Really. But—"

"We'll take it," Luca blurted. "What other colors do you have?"

My jaw fell open. This handbag cost over twenty thousand dollars. "No, wait! That's not necessary."

Luca put a hand on my back, the alpha male signal for, *I'm handling this.* But I couldn't let him buy me even one of these handbags, let alone other colors. It was outrageous.

Ms. Dumas carried on like I hadn't said a word. "We don't have any others in the store. In fact, I was actually saving this one for myself."

"Oh, then I couldn't possibly—"

Luca squeezed my waist and I quieted. He said, "Which is why we are paying double for it. Show us smaller handbags, then. Clutches, everyday bags."

With a nod, Ms. Dumas left and I clutched Luca's arm. My voice was a desperate whisper. "What the fuck? Have you lost your mind? This is too much."

He shifted toward me and cupped my face in one hand, the other resting on my waist. "I told you I was going to spoil you. What did you think that meant?"

I put my hands on his chest, his dress shirt smooth and soft beneath my fingers. "Honestly? A mochaccino and a chocolate croissant. Maybe some French toast if we were feeling especially wild."

The scowl he usually wore disappeared and I could feel his big body relax. "You think a lot about food."

"Doesn't everyone?"

"Not around you. I'm too busy thinking of ways to defile your sexy body."

A rush of lust tightened my nipples into painful points and I edged closer to him. "And when you do, I'll need my strength. Which means I need food. See how that works?"

Luca's chest shook as he chuckled. "I will buy you french toast, fiore mio, as soon as we finish with the handbags."

Ms. Dumas returned and I jumped away from Luca guiltily, like we'd been caught planning a robbery and not discussing brunch. He didn't let go of me, just continued to look amused. Over the next ten minutes he picked out a black clutch, a white coin purse, and a leather and canvas navy tote. I stopped protesting after a while. It did no good because he wasn't listening.

Finally, he handed Ms. Dumas a credit card and she disappeared. I stared at the row of handbags, my mind spinning. While I loved math, I was scared to calculate the final bill. "This is too much."

He lifted a shoulder in a casual, yet arrogant way. "I'm rich, Valentina. It's something you need to accept, capisce?"

It wasn't only that he was rich. Luca's money was *mafia* money. It wasn't exactly clean. And what did he expect in exchange for all this? I tucked a strand of hair behind my ear and lowered my voice. "My mother spent her whole life refusing my father's financial help. She said his money came with strings."

Luca slipped his hands in his trouser pockets and cocked his head. "You've seen my 'strings.' Are you telling me you hated all the orgasms I gave you?"

"No," I said quickly, glancing over my shoulder for Ms. Dumas. "But I don't want there to be debts between us. You're already doing too much for the restaurant."

"There are no debts or expectations that accompany my gifts. When I first helped you we weren't sleeping together, so you should believe me when I say I do it because I can. All you need to do is to say *grazie* once in a while."

What else was there to say? I could protest, but I sounded ungrateful. If he wanted to drop a mint on handbags for me, then okay. "Grazie, Luca."

Oh, he liked that a lot. His eyes darkened just like earlier when he pinned me against the shower wall before sliding his dick inside me. He dragged the backs of his knuckles along my collarbone. "See? This pleases me, piccolina."

"Here you are, Mr. Benetti."

Ms. Dumas placed a slip on the counter for Luca to sign. I closed my eyes. If I saw the total, I might throw up.

When Luca finished he told the manager to have the handbags

boxed up and someone would come by to pick them up. Then he took my hand and strode into the main part of the store. "Now, we go for French toast," he declared as he held open the front door for me.

"Good—and it's my treat."

He ushered me toward the SUV. "I will allow you to buy breakfast." Then he put his mouth near my ear. "Because maybe then you will not complain when I take you to the jewelry store."

Chapter Nineteen

Luca

She was quiet on the drive back to Paesano. We were in the SUV, with Aldo behind the wheel, while Carlo drove my Maserati back. I held her hand, perfectly content to sit in the silence and watch the scenery.

Valentina had been a pleasant surprise today.

I wasn't used to a woman being so frugal around me. Or this funny. Or affectionate. Valentina touched me *a lot*. Little brushes of her hand. Grabbing my arm to make a point. Rubbing her foot against my leg under the table at breakfast. I liked it.

We had a nice day together, shopping and eating in the city. I couldn't remember the last time I stayed off my phone for so long, but work had been the furthest thing from my mind today. It was refreshing to get lost in the crowds, a nobody with zero responsibilities. This allowed me to experience the city with Valentina.

My girl obviously didn't travel much. As we walked after breakfast, she marveled at everything from the horse and carriages for hire, to the street vendors, to the different accents and cultures on every corner. At our last stop I bought her a pair of diamond earrings, though she refused to let me get the matching bracelet.

I bought it anyway.

I hadn't spent this much money on a woman in a long time, not since Carlotta was pregnant with Gabriele. But I liked doing it for Valentina. She deserved it. This girl busted her ass all day long, even cleaning bathrooms, to keep her family's legacy alive. I could relate.

Yawning, Valentina put her fancy juice drink in the cup holder. "God, I'm so tired."

"Come here." I tugged her down so she was lying across the seat. "Put your head in my lap."

She didn't argue, just flipped her hair out of the way as she settled on my thigh. "Why am I always sleeping on you?"

My chest expanded on a deep breath and I smoothed her hair, letting the long strands run between my fingers. The night of her book club she'd begged me to sleep next to her. *I won't feel safe without you.* What demons haunted her? Segreto? Or had something happened in her childhood?

I vowed to find out.

Now that I have secured D'Agostino's help, I might be able to locate my cousin quickly. This would keep Valentina out of this mess. Because no way was I letting Palmieri or the GDF get their hands on this woman.

Minutes passed and Valentina's breathing evened out. I stared down at her profile while my fingers continued to stroke her head. Part of me didn't want to return to Paesano. I didn't want her in that tiny home all the way across town. The place wasn't safe, not to mention that I wanted her with me. Could I move her into the mansion?

"Never thought I would see it," Aldo murmured in Italian from the front seat. I glanced up and met his gaze in the mirror. "Like a teenager."

"Fuck off," I said quietly.

"She's a good kid. Works hard. Cares about people."

I knew this about her. It was part of the reason I like spoiling her. Ungrateful, entitled people thought the world owed them everything. But this world didn't owe any of us shit. Valentina knew this and she was a fighter, tough like me. Yet she was also sweet and innocent, and that twisted me up inside.

"I want her things moved into the mansion," I ordered. "See that it's done."

Aldo shook his head. "She won't like that. The house belonged to her dead mother. You've seen it. The mother might as well still be living there. Your girl is not ready to let go of the past."

I sighed. I would need to handle this carefully. But after our stay in New York, I was confident that I could convince her.

My phone buzzed with more messages. I eased the rectangle out of my pocket and spent the rest of the ride answering questions and checking in with my brothers. Then I texted Leo, as he'd been quiet the past few days. That wasn't uncommon for my first born. He was responsible, more serious and independent than his brother. Leo answered immediately, saying he'd booked a trip to Sardinia for a few days. I told him to have fun at the beach with his girlfriend and ring me when he returned to Catanzaro.

Valentina stirred when we were a few minutes out of town. I rubbed her back and continued to read a quarterly report from one of our legitimate businesses.

"Where are we?" she murmured sleepily.

"Just outside Paesano."

"Damn. I hadn't expected to sleep that long. Why didn't you wake me up?"

"Because you're obviously fucking tired."

She pushed herself up. "More like I'm tired because of fucking."

A huff of laughter escaped my lips. "Madonna, that mouth of yours."

"Are you saying you don't like it?"

The devilish glint in her eye called to me like a cape to a bull. I leaned in and gave her a deep kiss. "I like it very much," I said when we broke apart.

She patted my chest then glanced down at her watch. "I really should get to the restaurant. Aldo, can you drop me at the trattoria?"

He looked at me in the rear view mirror for confirmation. I supposed it was only fair. I'd monopolized her time enough for today and I knew she was reopening tomorrow. I gave Aldo a subtle nod.

"Of course, miss." Aldo began pressing buttons on the car's navigation.

I pulled her close to my side and kissed the side of her head. "I'll take your packages to my house."

"Or you could drop them at mine, seeing as how locks are no issue for you."

Ignoring that, I said, "Come to the mansion when you're finished today. We'll have dinner together."

"Just dinner?"

A grin tugged at the corners of my mouth. "Maybe more."

When we pulled up to the trattoria, she tried to open the car door herself. I grabbed her arm. "Wait, piccolina. I'll come around and help you."

"That's not necessary. And I need to hurry."

I gave her a look, one that had intimidated dangerous men across Europe. Valentina just rolled her eyes. "Fine. But hurry up, Luca."

I got out of the car and buttoned my suit coat. Then I came around and helped her to the ground. Instead of letting her go, I grabbed her hand and started walking her inside.

"You're annoying," she said under her breath.

"Are you saying you don't like it?" I asked, throwing her words back at her.

She bumped her shoulder against mine. "I might like it a little."

"Good." I opened the trattoria's door and held it for her. "We'll talk later about where you're sleeping tonight."

"I'm sleeping at home." She tugged on my tie as she walked past. "We're reopening tomorrow. I need to be on my game."

I followed her inside, then stopped in my tracks. Gabriele stood behind the bar, using a knife to cut something.

Che cazzo? What was my son doing here?

Dropping Valentina's elbow, I strode directly to the bar until I was standing in front of him. He had the nerve to keep slicing lemons instead of addressing me. I spoke in our language so no one would understand how furious I was. "What the fuck are you doing?"

"Ciao, Papà. How was New York?"

I grabbed the knife out of his hand. "I asked you a question, figlio."

He shrugged. "I asked to be a bartender. I thought it might be fun —and I'll get to eat here for free. Have you tasted Giovanni's food? It's so fucking good."

"You are not working here."

I sensed her a second before Valentina appeared at my side. She reached across the bar to offer her hand to Gabriele. "Hey, Gabi. I see you've convinced Roberto to give you a job."

"Ciao, Signorina Montella." Gabriele shook her hand.

"Have you bartended before?" she asked.

"He's not bartending here." I pointed at Gabriele. "Get your shit. I'm taking you back to the house."

"Luca, wait." Valentina put her hand on my arm. "Why can't he work here?"

"My son is not a bartender. He has far more important duties than pouring drinks for frat boys and lonely old women."

She drew herself up and gave me a withering stare. "Oh, so you think he's too good to work here." Before I could explain myself, she faced Gabriele again. "Welcome aboard. We're happy to have you, Gabriele."

My son grinned and leaned toward her, too close, almost flirtatiously. "You can call me Gabi."

Turning, I spotted a young man polishing forks. "Find Roberto. *Now.*" He got up and sprinted for the kitchen.

I drummed my fingers on the bar, waiting, seething. Valentina and Gabriele were chatting, ignoring me. Apparently there were laws in New York about alcohol, and Gabriele was too young to serve drinks. I didn't give a fuck, because he wasn't staying.

From the second he landed in New York Gabriele had done his best to piss me off. I'd instructed him not to leave the house, yet he ran here as soon as my back was turned. I should send him back to Catanzaro tonight.

"Papà."

I looked over at my son. Valentina had stepped away to deal with one of the construction workers, so we were alone.

Gabriele leaned across the bar and though no one understood our language, he lowered his voice. "I'm here to keep an eye on her. I know you have cameras here and at her house. Aldo said the former dishwasher used a fake name, too. I don't know what's going on, but I want to help you. So let me help you."

I was surprised. I hadn't expected him to pick up on any of this, but it was a good idea. He could watch over Valentina when I wasn't around, as well as keep an eye out for Segreto.

And hadn't I told Valentina there was no shame in accepting help?

My anger dissipated and a flare of pride welled up in my chest. "You're right. This is smart. Thank you."

The edge of his mouth curled like he was fighting a smile. "So you'll fill me in later?"

"Yes, I will. Nice work, figlio."

The kitchen door swung open and a very pale Roberto entered the dining room. He came straight over. "Signore DiMarco. Welcome back."

I put my hand on his shoulder. "Look after him, capisce?"

"Mi dispiace, signore," he said quietly. "He asked and I didn't know what to tell him."

"It's okay. He's here to keep an eye on things for me. Treat him as you'd treat me."

A small, curvy body wedged between me and the manager, forcing distance between us. "Roberto, don't listen to Luca. We're happy to have Gabi on staff."

She pulled me away and I didn't resist. Finally, she maneuvered me into a small area away from the dining room. "Will you quit it?" Her fingers smoothed my tie. "You're overreacting."

"How so?"

"Scowling at everyone and scaring poor Gabi. Don't ruin our perfect day. If Gabi wants to work here, then let him."

"Okay."

Her gaze cut to mine abruptly. "Okay?"

"That is what I just said, no?"

She hooked her fingers into the waistband of my trousers, under my belt. "You are being very agreeable today."

I dragged Valentina to my chest, then put my nose in her hair and inhaled, letting the flowery scent roll through me. "Thank you for coming with me to the city. I hope you had a nice time."

"I did. Thank you for taking me." She snuggled into my body, her arms winding around my neck. She tilted her head and kissed my chin. "Are you coming for the opening tomorrow?"

"Of course. We will have dinner together."

"Luca!" Moving away, she frowned at me. "I can't sit down for dinner during the reopening. I'll be too busy."

"No, *Roberto* will be busy. You will be having dinner with me."

Valentina threw her hands up, her expression filled with exasperation. "Ugh! You're the worst. Get out of here. I have things to do."

She turned to walk away, but I grabbed her waist and pulled her back against my chest. I ground my hips into her ass, letting her feel me, then I put my mouth to her ear. "You will come to me when you finish tonight. Capisce?"

She swayed, then softened, almost letting me support her weight. "Okay."

"Va bene, piccolina." I let her go, then slapped her ass. "Go and do your things."

I watched her hurry away, enjoying the view of her body in the skirt and heels she wore. Fuck, she was hot. I couldn't wait to bury my dick inside her again.

Once I was back in the car, I asked Aldo, "Did you know Gabriele went to the trattoria for a job?"

His eyes flew to mine in the mirror. "No! He did?"

My mobile buzzed, so I took it out of my pocket. "He wants to be our eyes and ears inside the restaurant." Glancing down, I saw the call was an unknown number. Not unusual in my world, so I hit the button to accept. "Pronto."

A strange voice began cursing at me in my language. "Chi cazzo credi di essere?" *Who the fuck do you think you are?* "You dare to fuck my daughter? You parade her around the city like your mantenuta? You fucking pig, Benetti."

Flavio Segreto.

I gripped the glass and metal rectangle in my hand, yet my voice was calm. "Segreto. It's nice to hear from you. Maybe we could meet in person and discuss your issues with me."

"Are you so eager to die, then? The only reason I didn't put a bullet in your head today was because my daughter was with you."

I snorted. "Don't act like you care about her. You've ignored her for years."

"You don't know shit, Benetti. Stay the fuck away from her."

"Do you think I'm afraid of you? A coward who stole money and then disappeared? Ma dai, stronzo."

"Again, you don't know shit. If you don't leave Val alone, you'd better watch your back. Because I'm coming for you."

He disconnected.

Aldo spoke up in the front seat. "Was that Segreto? What did he want?"

I nodded. "He's obviously nearby, watching her. He followed us to the city." Thinking, I tapped my mobile on my leg. If I could get my hands on Segreto, I could find out why Rossi wanted him and what that had to do with Palmieri.

I rang my brother. Sergio picked up on the first ring. Before he said a word, I ordered, "Get your ass to New York and bring two dozen men with you."

Chapter Twenty

Valentina

I was barely awake when Luca lifted my leg and pushed his very hard cock inside me. I was wet but not entirely ready, so it took him three thrusts to get all the way inside. "Oh, yes," he whispered in my ear, his warm chest tight to my back. "This is what I need. Your pussy, strangling my dick."

He didn't move, just stayed still, letting me adjust. His hand cupped my breast and strong fingers plucked at my nipple, rolling it. We were in his bed at the mansion, because he'd won the argument about where I would sleep last night.

At the moment I wasn't regretting that decision in the least.

Ribbons of pleasure unfurled in my belly, my senses overloaded with the way he surrounded me both inside and out. Like how his breath heated my skin, the coarse hair from his chest and legs rubbing against me. I could feel myself growing wetter, my need building, so I arched and wrapped an arm around his neck. "Baby," I breathed, incapable of saying more.

He groaned and rocked his hips. "Fuck, amore."

I knew that word. *Love.* Italians used it as an endearment, but Luca hadn't said it to me before. And hearing him utter it in his sexy bedroom voice? I melted like warm butter. "I need you," I said over my shoulder.

"Get on your knees. I'm going to fuck you hard."

As if in a daze, I got up on my hands and knees, and he positioned me where he wanted me. Then he was pushing inside again and I moaned loudly into the sheets. The pressure, the heat . . . god, it was so good. He was taking up all the space inside me until there wasn't room for anything else, no thoughts or worries. No responsibilities. I was focused solely on him and me and the way we fit together.

This was the best stress relief ever created.

He started moving then, hips slamming into me repeatedly as his cock sawed in and out of my channel. It was brutal, punishing, with each thrust rattling my bones . . . and I loved it. "Don't stop," I demanded. "Oh god, Luca."

He drove deep and hit the perfect spot every time. I floated, lost in the rhythm, with each stroke better than the last. All I could do was dig my fingers into the mattress and hold on, muscles tightening as I climbed higher. Were there people who thought older men didn't have stamina? *Jesus.* Luca could prove them wrong.

"Reach down," he said between thrusts. "Play with your clit and come on my cock."

I balanced on one forearm, then put my fingers between my legs. My flesh was swollen, slick, so sensitive, and I rolled my clit in tight circles. The tips of my fingers brushed his shaft and he grunted. "That's it. Pull it out of me. I have so much come stored up for you and I'm going to give it to you, every drop." I brushed his balls this time and the response was instant. His hips stuttered as he shouted, "Fuck! You need to hurry!"

I swirled faster, rubbing my clit, gasping as the pleasure doubled, tripled. I was moaning the whole time, Luca's dick hammering into me, and then I felt his hand between my ass cheeks, his thumb tracing my rear hole. Tingles rippled through my entire body, a mixture of fear and excitement. Was he going to touch me there? I wasn't sure if I was going to—

Without warning, the tip of his thumb slipped inside, breaching the tight ring of muscle, and the orgasm hit me like a wall. Euphoria surged through me. I began trembling, shaking, my voice echoing off the high ceiling in Luca's bedroom. "Oh my god! Luca, *fuck!*"

He grabbed a fistful of my hair and tugged, holding on as he ground his hips into me. I could feel his cock thicken as he started to come. "Cazzo madre di dio," he growled. "So fucking good."

Then it was over and we both slumped onto the mattress. I was face down, unable to move, while Luca rolled onto his back, chest heaving, an arm over his eyes. I felt wrecked in the very best way, but energized. Like I could start all over again.

After several moments I shifted onto my back. "I'm seriously obsessed with your dick."

He made a pleased sound in his throat. "Good, because it is seriously obsessed with you."

I stretched and considered round two. "What time is it?"

"Around nine-thirty, I think."

Oh, I had time before—wait, no I didn't. It was opening night. *Shit!* I had to get moving.

I started to get up and a big hand caught my arm. "Where do you think you are going?"

"I need to get up and shower. I have to get to the trattoria."

He hummed and yanked me down onto his chest. "You can spare me ten minutes. I want to hold you and think about how much I love to fuck you."

My restaurant was reopening in a few hours and he wanted to cuddle? "Luca," I protested, trying to push against him. "I have to go."

"Ten minutes, amore."

Goddamn it. That word was my downfall. I had no defenses against it.

I learned during our overnight in the city that Luca was a cuddler

196

—who would've guessed?—but we would need to discuss his bossiness. Later, when he wasn't being so sweet. And comfortable.

I relaxed and closed my eyes, forcing my thoughts away and emptying my mind. He was warm and solid against me, our legs tangled together on the world's most comfortable sheets. Admittedly, it was nice. Neither one of us spoke. Ten minutes of post-orgasmic bliss passed in silence, as the sounds of the river and chirping birds filtered in through the windows.

This might be heaven.

"Va bene," he said, kissing the top of my head. "Now, we shower."

"I'm not sure I can get up." I was heavy with relaxation, the kind of sluggishness that required binge-watching a show on my couch for a full day.

Luca pinched my right butt cheek. "What of your opening tonight?"

That did it. I forced myself off him and stood up. Luca's eyes did a quick sweep of my naked body, his gaze hot and possessive. "I have everything set up for you in the adjoining bathroom. Use that one."

I grabbed his dress shirt off the floor and slipped it over my head. Then I walked over to the nightstand and picked up my phone. "So we aren't showering together?"

Muscles and tendons shifted as he sat up. "I thought you needed to hurry to the restaurant."

"I do! I was just wondering why."

"Get moving, fiore mio, or I'm going to eat your pussy in my shower and make you very, very late."

Everything inside me squeezed and, for half a second, I considered it. Damn, that sounded nice. But I really did need to get to the restaurant. "Any other day I would take you up on that," I said on my way out the door.

The second bathroom was as big as Luca's, decorated in a similar over-the-top style. I used the toilet as the shower heated and then hurried under the spray. The bath products were familiar, the same shampoo, conditioner, and face wash I used at home. There was even a razor like mine. Had Luca peeked inside my bathroom yesterday? Sweet, but strange.

I took as long as I dared, then got out and dried off. Someone must've unpacked my suitcase from the trip because my makeup bag was on the counter. I tried not to be too mad. I'm sure Luca was trying to be helpful, but I could unpack my own damn suitcase.

So I didn't freeze, I slipped Luca's dress shirt back on, then took out all my beauty products and got busy. After I finished with my makeup, I dried my hair with a fancy hair dryer that was definitely out of my price range. Now I just needed to run home and change into clean clothes.

I found him in a blue dress shirt and navy trousers, buckling his leather belt in his big walk-in closet. "Hey," I said. "I need to go home to change. Can you drive me or should I order a car?"

His upper lip curled, like the suggestion offended him. "I don't want you riding in cars with strangers. I will have Aldo drive you whenever I'm busy."

"Okay, so are you busy?"

"You don't need to go home. Check the closet in the adjoining bedroom."

I narrowed my eyes suspiciously. "Did you buy me clothes, too? I told you, I don't need you buying me things."

"Just go and look, bella."

Turning, I marched out of his bedroom and into the adjoining one. He really needed to stop. The handbags yesterday cost a mint. Now he'd bought me clothes? Probably designer shit that I had no business wearing around town. Everyone was going to think I'd lost my mind.

I stopped in my tracks. The huge walk-in closet was filled with .. . my things. My dresses, my pants, my sweaters. Everything. All neatly arranged on hangers and folded on shelves. My shoes were stacked on one wall. He'd, what? Moved me in?

I blinked, sure I was mistaken. He wouldn't do that. Would he?

There were drawers, so I opened those, hoping to not find more. *Please, god. Let me be wrong.*

Nope, there they were—my panties and bras all neatly arranged. What. The. Fuck.

I usually tried to control my temper. But I came from a long line of loud Italian-American women who took no shit from anyone. And this was absolutely too much.

"Luca!" I shouted. "Get the fuck in here!"

"Problem, bella?" he answered instantly in an even tone.

I whirled and found him casually leaning against the door frame, his hands in his pockets. Had he been standing there this whole time? "Yes, there is a fucking problem!" I waved my arm toward the hangers. "You moved all of my shit here. Are you *insane*?"

"Your house isn't safe. I told you earlier how easy it was for me to break in. Anyone could come in there and hurt you."

I put my palms together and prayed for patience. "Luca, no one in this town is going to hurt me. I grew up here. I've been here my whole life and we have, like, zero crime. But forgetting all that, you can't just move me in here without at least asking me first!"

"I knew you would say no." He lifted a shoulder, his demeanor so calm and arrogant that I wanted to throw something at him. "And so I made the decision for you."

Holy shit. I had been *mafiosoed*, just like Gia warned me might happen.

My skin grew hot, fury gathering steam in my chest as I glared at him. "I want my stuff moved back. Now. You had no right to this."

He pushed off from the door frame and strolled toward me. I straightened my spine and braced my feet for a fight. I knew he was going to try to work some mob boss mojo on me, and I wasn't having it.

Once we were close enough, he placed his hands on either side of my throat and brushed his thumbs over my jaw. "Amore, there are still things in your house. I didn't move you out and you may go back there anytime. I thought you might like having some of your things here for when you sleep over."

"Okay. Phew." I relaxed, feeling foolish for overreacting. "I was worried there for a minute."

"But," he continued, more forcefully. "I would prefer it if you stayed here with me. Where I can keep you safe."

"So you want me to stay here all the time? Or occasionally?"

The edge of his mouth curved, secrets dancing in the depths of his espresso-colored eyes. "Do you want me to answer honestly?"

I shoved him away. "Ugh. Get out of here, you overbearing man. I need to get dressed and I don't have time for this conversation. We'll finish it tonight over dinner."

I expected him to leave, but he walked over to the hangers and began flipping through them. "Wear this," he said, pulling out a low-cut black dress. I bought it a year ago for one of Maggie's winery parties.

"Luca, that isn't a daytime dress appropriate for a restaurant owner. It's tight and my boobs practically fall out of the neckline."

"Which is why I want to sit across from you at dinner while you are wearing it." He took the dress off the hanger and handed it to me. Then, while I was trying to wrap my head around this turn of events, he snatched up a pair of black heels and the new burgundy handbag. "These too."

I frowned as he handed the accessories to me. "You're pissing me off."

"Then it's too bad you are seriously obsessed with my dick. Because it is attached to me." He leaned down and kissed me briefly. "You look beautiful in whatever you wear, piccolina. But do this once for me, okay?"

Fuck, he was hard to resist.

"Fine. This one time." I bit my lip and moved in closer. "But if you're picking out my clothes, can I pick out your tie?"

"Of course. Get dressed and come back to our bedroom." He rubbed the pad of his thumb over my lips then walked out.

Our bedroom.

What in the fresh hell?

And why was I smiling as I finished getting ready?

Chapter Twenty-One

Luca

I held Valentina's hand as we descended the stairs. She was as gorgeous in the black wrap dress as I'd imagined, maybe more so. Long smooth legs, small waist and generous hips, and tits for days. I was already anticipating peeling the dress off her later.

Loud voices echoed in the direction of the kitchen, which meant the Benettis had arrived this morning. Good. It was time to find Segreto and put an end to all this.

I started toward the back of the house, but Valentina tugged on my hand. "Luca, I really need to go."

"Come." I kept walking, bringing her with me. "I want you to meet my brothers."

Her jaw fell open. "What? Your brothers are here? When? Why?"

The edge of my mouth lifted. "Because I told them to. They flew overnight."

"I can't meet your brothers. I'm . . . " She huffed in the most adorable way. "This is weird. They're going to know that we, you know."

"That we were fucking upstairs, yes. And anyone who sees you in this dress would kill to trade places with me."

There wasn't time to say more. I put my hand on the small of her back and escorted her inside the kitchen. Enrico and Dante were sitting on stools at the counter, while Sergio was standing next to Aldo, demitasse cups in their hands.

Conversation stopped as every eye turned toward us. "This is Valentina Montella," I announced. "Bella, these are my brothers. Dante, Enrico, and Sergio."

"Hello," she said shyly. "It's nice to meet all of you."

No one else spoke, and I could sense my brothers trying to make sense of what they were seeing. Our world revolved around trust, and I didn't have much to give. Consequently, I didn't invite women to my home. I took them to a hotel or their house, never mine. So Valentina being here was surprising.

But that didn't excuse rudeness.

I lifted a menacing brow at Sergio. Jolting, he immediately put down his demitasse cup and came forward. "Signorina, come stai?" He leaned down to kiss both of her cheeks. "It is nice to finally meet you."

"Finally?" she asked, with a quick glance up at me. "You've told them about me?"

"Of course." I pulled her closer to my side. "There are no secrets in my family."

Dante and Rico were next, greeting Valentina properly, then returning to their seats. They shared an amused, knowing glance that set my teeth on edge, but I ignored it. For now.

Before I could get to the espresso machine, a bleary-eyed Gabriele strolled in, shirtless and wearing striped pajama bottoms. "Ciao, *zii*! I can't believe you're all here." My son went over to say hello to his uncles.

"Gabi, buongiorno." Sergio kissed my son's cheeks. "How is my favorite nephew?"

"Fucking tired," was Gabi's answer. "Someone woke me up early."

"Sorry if we were too loud," Dante said, slapping Gabi's back.

"Oh, it wasn't you. Someone else was loud upstairs about an hour ago."

My brothers had the audacity to laugh, but I frowned. Even though Gabriele spoke in Italian, I didn't appreciate the joke. "Gabriele," I snapped. "Show some fucking respect."

He put his hands up apologetically. "Mi dispiace, Papà." He nodded at Valentina. "Buongiorno, Val."

"Hi, Gabi."

"You look beautiful." He whistled. "The customers are going to swallow their tongues when they see you in that dress."

"It's too much, isn't it?" She bit her lip and looked up at me, her expression full of doubt. "I told you I shouldn't wear this."

"No, signorina," everyone said almost at once. "You should definitely wear that," Rico finished with.

"Yes, I agree," Dante added. "You look bellissima."

"Thank you, but I think I'll go and grab a sweater." She gave me her handbag. "Be right back."

Her heels clicked on the tile as she left the kitchen and went into the hall. My teeth ground together as I carefully placed her handbag on the marble island. Then I wasted no time in closing the distance to my youngest son, my hands curled into fists. Wisely, Gabriele started backing away from me when he saw the look on my face.

"Papà, I was kidding with her." He darted behind Sergio, putting my brother between us.

Sergio held up a hand to stop me. "Let's stay calm."

Reaching over Sergio, I grabbed my son's shoulder and squeezed hard. "Do not comment on her, capisce? Not on what she's wearing, not on how she sounds. You are polite and respectful at all times. Am I clear, figlio mio?"

Gabriele winced but didn't try to pull away. "I understand. I'm sorry."

"Easy." Sergio peeled my fingers off Gabriele. "He didn't mean any harm, Luca."

I took a step back and straightened the cuffs of my dress shirt. "I'm taking her to work. The three of you, be ready. We will get to work when I return."

Gabriele grabbed a breakfast roll and his phone, then hurried out of the kitchen. Dante and Rico were quiet, but Sergio said, "Don't be so hard on him. He's only sixteen, Luca. He's a dumb kid and desperate for your approval."

"I never acted like that at sixteen. Can you imagine if I spoke to one of our father's girls like that?" My father would've had my balls strung up and displayed for the entire town.

"To be fair, you've never had a woman sleep over before. We were all caught off guard this morning."

The clack of a woman's heels grew louder and we stopped speaking. After I grabbed a breakfast roll off the counter for her, Aldo handed me two travel mugs. "Grazie," I told him. "Start the car. You're driving us."

He nodded and headed for the back door. Valentina came in, a black cardigan sweater pulled over her arms and chest, buttoned high. A crime against humanity, that sweater. "I'm ready," she told me, taking her new handbag off the counter.

Each of my brothers bade her a polite goodbye and we went out to the car. Once we were settled in the back seat, she took the cappuccino from me. "Why are you mad?"

"I'm not mad."

She took a sip from the travel mug. "Luca, I have eyes. Gabi said something you didn't like. What was it?"

I set my jaw and stared out the window. "Don't worry about it."

Her small hand landed on my thigh and she smoothed my trousers, almost petting me. "Baby, tell me. I know it was something about me." She was quiet for a beat and I could almost hear her thinking. "Does he hate the idea of me sleeping over? Is it because of his mom?"

Needing to touch her, I grabbed her hand and threaded our fingers together. "No, nothing like that. But I don't want to repeat what he said. It doesn't matter."

"Did he hear us arguing this morning?"

I didn't move a muscle, didn't breathe, because she was so close to the truth.

It turned out she didn't need any help from me. She was smart and arrived at the answer all on her own.

Her eyes grew wide. "Oh, my god. He heard us . . . oh, my god. That's it, isn't it?" Leaning forward, she rubbed her forehead with her one hand. "Holy shit. I want to crawl into a gigantic hole and die."

I needed my hands free. Cursing my son, I took the mug from her and set it in the holder, along with mine. "Valentina." I cupped her face in my palms and brushed my thumbs over the velvety skin of her jaw. "I want you passionate and loud. I want you to scream your pleasure so the entire town hears it. And I wasn't quiet, either. So who gives a fuck?"

"I do," she said, frowning. "It's humiliating. We're not having sex in your house again."

No way would I agree to that. I gentled my voice. "Piccolina, I'll fuck you in every room of that house, if I choose. And I won't care who hears it."

"Well, I do. And we can stay at my—"

I cut her off. "Don't say it. I'll move Gabriele to a hotel before I agree to sleep at your house."

"There's nothing wrong with my house. Beef up the security if you want. Make it safer, I don't care. But we'd be totally alone there."

No, this wasn't happening. I wanted her in my house, which was more secure than most prisons. Therefore, this discussion was over.

I unbuckled her seat belt and lifted her up onto my lap. Her ass settled on my thigh and her side pressed against my chest. I kissed her throat, my hand drifting up to cover her tit. The smell of her body wash—which I now knew was melon—invaded my senses and my dick started plumping. Fuck, I was insatiable for this woman.

She arched her neck to give me better access, while her hands gripped my suit coat. I nibbled and licked, then bit her gently and she gasped—a tiny intake of breath that had me wanting to lay her down in the back seat, remove her panties, and eat her pussy for breakfast.

"We're not done . . . discussing this," she said between breaths.

"Amore, who makes the rules?" I whispered, plucking at the buttons on her sweater, opening them.

"*Luca.*" It came out more like a whine.

I dragged my knuckles along her cleavage, wishing there was time to suck on her nipples. "I should take you into the restaurant, lock us into your office, and fuck you again. Then you could feel my come inside you all day long."

Her fingers tightened. "Everyone would know."

"Yes, that's true. Everyone in the restaurant would know how greedy this pussy is, how much you need my cock."

"Oh, god." She slumped against me, pliant and soft. "Stop talking. Aldo can hear you, and I have a restaurant to reopen."

"Then stop arguing with me. Trust me to take care of you."

She smoothed my silk tie, the one she picked out earlier. "No one has taken care of me in a long time."

"I know." I kissed the top of her head. "Which is why I want to do it. No one is more deserving than you."

"That is very sweet." She played with the knot of my tie. "So who takes care of you?"

I frowned, almost insulted at the question. I was raised to be strong, a man who needed no one. There hadn't been any compassion or understanding in the Benetti household. My father's love had been wrapped up in cruelty and responsibility, and my mother always sided with him, even after he treated her like shit. I did what I could to shelter my brothers from him, but it hadn't been easy.

My father discussed a marriage for me many times, but died before seeing it through. Then as the years passed, I resisted bringing a woman into my world. What need was there to marry? I had two sons already and I fucked whomever I pleased. The staff oversaw the house. And I wouldn't love a wife, so why would bother?

"Luca?"

Blinking, I glanced out the window. I was so lost in my own thoughts that I hadn't realized we'd arrived at the trattoria. "Andiamo," I said, setting her on the leather. "I'll walk you inside."

She put her hand on my shoulder and her keen brown gaze searched my face. "Are you okay?"

"Of course."

Her expression didn't change. Leaning in, she placed her lips on mine and kissed me sweetly. Unhurriedly. Like we had all the time in the world. I heard the door close, which meant Aldo was giving us privacy. So I deepened the kiss, needing to prolong it. I wasn't ready to turn her over to the busy day ahead. Being with her was a tiny respite, a slice of happiness in a brutal and terrible world. It was like Valentina washed away all my sins, a benediction of kisses that made me feel whole.

The air in the car turned humid, so I pulled away. We were both panting. "You ruined my lipstick," she whispered. "And now it's all over your mouth."

"I don't give a shit. You're still beautiful." I wiped the edges of her now-swollen lips. "And everyone will know I kissed you goodbye before work."

She bent down and reached into her new handbag. When she straightened she held a tissue in her hand. "Hold still." She proceeded to wipe the lipstick off my face, her touch firm as she cleaned me. I didn't move. No woman had taken such care with me. No one would have dared. Or maybe I wouldn't have allowed it. It was hard to say why I was allowing it now, except that I didn't want to hurt Valentina's feelings.

And maybe I liked her attention.

"There." She sat back and sighed. "God, you're disgustingly handsome. I could swoon just looking at you."

The edge of my mouth lifted in a half grin. "Swoon?"

"Shut up. Let's go. I need to get inside."

After I walked Valentina into the trattoria, I returned to the car and Aldo headed for home. I scrolled on my phone, waiting for him to say something.

It didn't take long.

"You should keep her."

There was no use pretending to misunderstand. I glanced up. "She's not a kitten, Aldo. She has a life here."

He waved his hand as he turned a corner. "Dai, these things can be worked out, if both people want to try."

I grunted and said nothing. Aldo didn't know what he was talking about. Valentina had a long future ahead of her, one that didn't include me.

"Are you planning to tell her? You know, about Palmieri and her father? She might be pissed."

"I don't see a reason to tell her. If I can find Segreto and get answers, then all of this goes away."

"And you'll, what? Return to Catanzaro and leave her here?"

I hadn't thought much about it, but wasn't it obvious? "Yes."

"What if you don't find Segreto? What if you have to turn her over to Palmieri?"

A dark, sick feeling bloomed behind my sternum, a cancer that slowly infected my bloodstream with dread. I stared at my phone but didn't see it, my mind stuck on my sweet girl at the mercy of Palmieri and the GDF. She was too trusting, from a small town where no crime occurred, according to her. She didn't even speak Italian. I couldn't let Palmieri get his hands on her.

But what happens if I refused?

"I will do what needs to be done as the head of this family," I said, my voice flat.

"That is what I'm afraid of," Aldo muttered. Then he turned up the music in the car, drowning us both out.

* * *

My brothers were waiting in the kitchen when I returned. They immediately quieted and waited, watching me as I set my travel mug on the marble countertop. Aldo walked in behind me. "Another cappuccino, Luca?"

"Sì, grazie."

Before I could address the three men staring intently at me, my mobile buzzed. Grateful for the reprieve, I answered. "Pronto."

"It's Rossi. Your brothers have left town, I'm told. Does this mean you've found her?"

I rubbed my eyes. Rossi was the last person I wanted to deal with right now. "No, I haven't. There's another complication here."

"What complication?"

"Dai, you know I won't answer that." Not on my mobile, when anyone could be listening.

"This has dragged on too long, Luca. Our friend in Roma grows impatient."

"That is too fucking bad. I don't answer to him."

"True, but you answer to *me*. And I want this business concluded."

I seethed, too angry to speak, my fingers strangling the metal and glass in my hand.

"Allora," he continued. "When you find her, bring her to me first. Then we'll decide how to deal with Roma, capisce?"

Allow Rossi to get his hands on Valentina? Absolutely fucking not. And why would he want to intervene, if getting Valentina to Palmieri was so imperative?

Again, more fucking questions.

"I need to go," I told him. "We'll keep you updated." Then I disconnected.

"Rossi?" Sergio asked.

Nodding, I folded my arms and leaned against the far counter where I could see all my brothers. Their gazes were filled with hesitation and worry. I addressed the Valentina issue head-on. "Don't bother trying to talk me out of it. She's with me and that's all you need to know. And I won't turn her over to Rossi or Palmieri, so that is off the table."

"Are you willing to risk prison for her?" Sergio asked. "To destroy everything we've built?"

It was a fair question, so I smothered my irritation. "It won't come to that. First, I don't believe Palmieri ever had Niccolò. So if the GDF is building a case against me, it's bullshit. Second, I know where Flavio Segreto is."

Rico paused with his cup halfway to his mouth. "You found him?"

"He found me. He's here, watching her. Watching *us*."

"Porca puttana," Sergio muttered. "I thought she hadn't talked to him in years."

"She hasn't." I accepted the cappuccino from Aldo and took a sip. "He's staying close but not interacting with her. She has no relationship with him."

"Did he approach you?" Dante asked. "What did he say?"

"He called me," I said. "Not sure how he got my number, but he knew I took her to Manhattan. He warned me away from her."

"This is a small town," Aldo said from the coffee machine. "How has he gone unnoticed?"

I shrugged. "I don't know. Why didn't you notice that we were being followed in the city?"

He had no response for that.

Sergio put down his cup and leaned on the counter. "By all accounts, Segreto was crafty. Smart. Did a lot of dirty work. No one had any idea he was skimming money until it was too late."

"He has to know that no one ever forgets," Rico said. "He'll never be safe, no matter where he goes."

I'd been thinking a lot about this. "He's too smart to live openly. My guess is that he's in hiding, but nearby, and he has someone watching her and reporting back."

Sergio nodded. "Someone in town. That makes sense. Didn't you say the mayor was too close to her?"

"The mayor is a coglione and too stupid to be a spy. She would notice him right away. No, it has to be a person she trusts."

"The woman from the coffee shop," Aldo suggested as he sliced open a brioche roll. "Or one of the girls from her book club."

I considered this. "They're not around enough. And I'm not sure a woman would work with Segreto."

"Maybe she doesn't have a choice," Dante said. "Maybe he's blackmailing her."

"Maybe," I allowed, still thinking. It didn't feel right, though. Segreto was a hardened criminal. How would he get close enough to any of those women to blackmail them? The town was small and people talked. An association like this would be hard to keep secret.

"So if it's not a woman, then a man." Sergio asked. "Who is she close to? Male friends?"

"There are none." My tone was brittle, like cut glass.

My brother put up his hands. "Calm down, I mean no offense. It could be someone at the restaurant."

"We ran background checks on all of them," Aldo said. "Even the ones she fired. They all checked out."

"Except one." I lifted my head, suspicion nagging at the back of my neck. It was like when I knew someone was lying to me, or when they had more to tell. My intuition was rarely wrong. "One employee failed the background check."

"Cazzo, I forgot about him," Aldo said. "The former dishwasher. John Natale."

Sergio stared at me like he'd never seen me before. "You let a man who failed a background check work in her restaurant? Ma che cazzo?"

I lifted an eyebrow at his tone. "The restaurant closed immediately after we learned about him. He hasn't been around."

"Not to mention we were busy with other things," Aldo added.

Everyone in the room knew he meant me and Valentina. And I

had no defense—I'd let her distract me. I ground my back teeth together. John Natale was a loose end, and I never left loose ends. "We need to find him. He'll lead us to Segreto, I'm sure of it."

"What do you know about him?" Sergio asked.

I dragged a hand over my jaw. "Late twenties, so not Segreto's age. But he has tattoos that look done by hand, not a needle."

"So prison?" Dante asked.

Rico slapped the back of his brother's head. "Yes, prison. Pay attention, *idiota*."

"Quiet," Sergio told them, then turned to me. "What else?"

"I got the sense he felt protective of her. He didn't like me eating dinner with her that first night. He offered to drive her home."

"And you couldn't find anything on him?"

I shook my head at Sergio's question. "No records of any kind. No driver's license. It's a fake name."

"Is he back at the restaurant?" Aldo asked and took a bite of his breakfast roll.

"Let's find out." Within a minute, I called Roberto at the trattoria and got my answer. I told my brothers, "Natale never returned for a dishwashing job. Roberto has no idea who we're talking about, and all the current employees have passed background checks."

"He has to be around," Sergio said. "If he's helping Segreto, he hasn't left town."

I could kick myself for forgetting about Natale. I slapped my palm on the countertop. "We need to fucking find him—*today*."

Aldo reached for a second breakfast roll. "The easiest way to find him is to follow Val."

This was true—and she needed security now that she was mine. "Let's put two guards on her when she's not with me," I told Sergio. "Tell them to stay hidden and be fucking vigilant. I also want her house checked for bugs. Rico, you and Dante do that now." If there were listening devices, my brothers would find them. All of us had been raised from birth to guard against being eaves-dropped on.

"I'll text you the address," Aldo said as he found his mobile on the counter. "Key fobs are on the table."

"We're on it." Rico finished his cappuccino and set the empty cup down. "Let's go, D."

My youngest two brothers left through the back door and silence descended. Aldo was busy chewing, while Sergio regarded me through his lashes. I scrolled on my phone and waited. Sergio would have his say sooner or later.

My brother stirred his cappuccino slowly, the spoon clanging lightly against the porcelain. When he set the spoon down, he said, "She's beautiful."

I slipped my mobile back in my pocket. "And?"

"And what happens after we find her father?"

"We get answers."

"And?"

"And if I find out Rossi has lied to me, we take him out."

"You're going to kill the head of the region. Ma sei pazzo?"

"No, I'm not crazy. If it brings war with the other clans, so be it. I won't be made a fool, left to dance on Rossi's string."

He nodded, like this was what he expected me to say. "And Valentina? Are you moving her to Catanzaro?"

"I think he should," Aldo put in, but we ignored him.

I stared at Sergio, unsure why he was pressing on this. Was he worried she would disrupt my life? As I told Aldo in the car, I would return to Catanzaro alone. Valentina had the restaurant and her friends here, and my work consumed all of my time. I didn't have time for dinners and dates.

So who takes care of you?

The answer was simple. I took care of myself, as I'd been doing my whole life. My mother never made her children a priority and my father had raised killers, not sons. The housekeepers over the years had shown us more affection than our own parents. And still we thrived, the four of us boys, like a pack of wild dogs that stuck together.

So, no. I wouldn't take her to Catanzaro, even if this burning sensation in my stomach, this inexplicable craving for her, never abated. I would learn to live with the ache.

Family came first.

"No."

Sergio's shoulders relaxed, like a weight had been lifted, and he exhaled toward the ceiling. "Thank fuck."

"Why do you care?"

Sergio leaned down on his elbows. "Do you really believe she'll forgive you after she learns why you're here? To use her to find her father. Not to mention you were originally prepared to kidnap her and turn her over to the GDF. Think about it, Luca."

"She will never find out."

"Dai, Luca. You can't be this naive."

My voice turned hard. "Do you have a death wish, fratello?"

"I am looking out for you!" He straightened and faced me. "For the family. We are all in jeopardy right now because of this woman and your decisions. I've been holding everything together in Catanzaro since you left, then you order me here at a moment's notice. I barely slept on the plane and arrived here to learn you've moved her into your house. What the *fuck*?"

"There is no jeopardy, stronzo." I stalked over to the island and stared him in the eye. "We are going to find Segreto and get answers. Whatever happens outside of that doesn't concern you."

"*Anything* related to you concerns me. You are don of this family and every decision you make affects all of us."

"You think I don't know this? I have lived with the responsibility longer than you've been alive. And it won't change until I'm dead."

"Which could happen at any moment now." He dragged a hand through his hair and began pacing, which was unusual for my normally calm brother. "You are completely exposed here in the middle of nowhere. The house and grounds aren't nearly as secure as back home, and you don't have enough men. And why are you risking your life? For a woman who won't speak to you after she learns that truth."

"I understand that you are worried—"

"Of course I'm worried!" He stopped moving and pinched the bridge of his nose with a thumb and forefinger. "First you fucked Palmieri's wife, now this woman . . . You know it's dangerous to move her in, yet you did it anyway. It's like you have a death wish."

My upper lip curled into a sneer as I considered it. "I'm not scared of Segreto. And it's safer for Valentina to live here until this business is sorted out."

"Safer . . . or just more convenient for you?"

Fury flooded my veins and my muscles bunched in preparation for violence. I'd never hit him, not once even when we were young, but I wanted to hit him now. I wanted to punch him until these disrespectful words stopped coming out of his mouth.

But I couldn't. This was my brother, my closest confidant. My family.

Through sheer force of will, I remained calm. "Stay out of my relationship with Valentina. She's here until I say otherwise and that's all you need to fucking know." Sergio's jaw tightened and he stared at the wall, but I didn't care. I turned to Aldo. "Gabriele moves out to the pool house today. See that it's taken care of."

I didn't wait for his response. I walked out of the room and headed for the office. I needed to be alone.

Chapter Twenty-Two

Valentina

Roberto and I double-checked the reservation list one more time. The day had flown by and we were three hours from the reopening. "I still can't believe it," I said. "We're completely booked all weekend. Not an open table to be found."

"Why are you surprised, signorina? This is the most exciting thing to happen in this town since Bev added pumpkin spice lattes to the menu."

My head snapped up as I laughed in surprise. "You are turning into a real local, Roberto."

He shrugged. "I like it here. And I like flirting with Bev."

"So I've gathered." Roberto visited the Leaning Tower of Pastries daily, even after the trattoria's espresso machine was installed. "And everything is ready?"

"Of course, signorina. You don't need to worry. We have this covered."

"Okay." I blew out a long breath. "Will you get Giovanni? I want to talk to you both before we get too busy this afternoon."

"Is something wrong?"

"No, nothing like that. It's all good, I promise. Meet me in the alcove in the back, okay?"

Roberto strode to the kitchen and disappeared. I went to the server station, where I'd hidden a bottle of champagne earlier. Taking three flutes, I filled them as I waited for the men. It wasn't long. The sleeves on Giovanni's chef coat were rolled up to show off his tattoos, and his face was etched with his usual scowl. Roberto walked behind him, and soon they were crowding into the small alcove with me.

"I'll make it quick." I handed both of them glasses of champagne. Then I lifted mine for a toast. "I don't know how Luca managed to get both of you here, but I'm so, so grateful that he did. I never could've done this on my own. Roberto, you've transformed this stuck-in-the-past relic into something chic and modern. And Giovanni, you're a genius with flavors. You've designed a menu that will amaze and impress, but will still have a familiar feel to the locals. Whatever happens after tonight, I want you both to know how much I appreciate everything you've done." My voice cracked as emotion clogged my throat. "You feel like family."

"Do not cry, signorina." Roberto pulled me in for a one-arm hug. "You will ruin your makeup."

"And look like a raccoon on opening night," Giovanni added, patting my shoulder.

I chuckled and my mood instantly lightened. "Thanks, guys. I pour my heart out and you're worried about how I look."

"Aww, you're beautiful." Roberto kissed the side of my head. "It's obvious how much you care about this place and your family's legacy. They would be so proud of you, signorina."

My chest tightened again and the urge to cry returned. Giovanni must've seen it on my face, because he quickly added, "I still do not think we need the chicken parmigiana."

That got me to laugh. "You will never win that fight, sir." I lifted my glass. "To the new Trattoria Rustica."

They touched their flutes to mine. "*Cin cin,*" they each said, and I repeated the toast as well.

We drank and Giovanni returned to the kitchen. Roberto said, "Come with me. I want to talk about some of the guests."

"Sure. Let me clean this up first." I took the champagne and empty glasses to the bar. I handed them to Gabriele, who looked incredibly hot in his crisp white shirt and black tie. Even though he wasn't twenty-one, Gabriele had produced an Italian birth certificate claiming he was of age. Roberto had argued it was best to let Luca's son do as he pleased.

Just like his father, I was coming to find out.

"Thanks, Gabi," I said when he took everything from my hands.

"You are welcome," he replied, exaggerating the enunciation. "How does my fancy English sound?"

"Like the ladies are going to die over your accent. Don't worry, they'll be throwing money at you right and left."

"I don't need money, bella. But I will take phone numbers."

"Oh, god." It became clear why Gabi wanted to work here. "Do not hit on my customers."

Gabi lifted up his hands and adopted an adorable mischievous expression. Though he looked like Luca, they were complete opposites in personality. "I promise I won't, but I can't help it if they hit on me."

And they would, too. "I'm glad you're here, Gabi."

"Me too." He grew serious and put his hands on the bar, leaning closer. "And I apologize for this morning. I was out of line."

"Thank you. I appreciate that." Pausing, I decided to fish for information. "Was your father mad at you about it?"

Gabi grunted and rolled his shoulder. "That is one way of putting it."

"What happened?"

"Nothing." He waved his hand. "But I've never seen him so mad over a woman before. He is making me move into the pool house."

"Oh, my god. I'm sorry. I shouldn't have slept over."

"No, no. You don't understand. My father has never allowed a woman to sleep over before. Not once. It is a big deal."

My toes curled inside my heels as my stomach dipped. "Never?" I croaked.

"Never. He didn't try to hide his mistresses, of course, but he didn't bring them to the house. And he didn't move them in. Capisce?"

I nodded like I understood, but I really didn't. Luca didn't bring women home? That didn't make sense. He'd practically moved me in after one night together. "I'm not his mistress," I mumbled.

"True." Gabi didn't look up from where he was slicing limes. "You're his girlfriend."

I gripped the edge of the bar as the words echoed in my head. Girlfriend? Really? Did that mean Luca was my boyfriend?

"Signorina!" Roberto called from across the room.

Shaking myself out of my thoughts, I left the bar and went to the reservation desk. Roberto took in my face. "What's wrong? Why are you so pale?"

"It's nothing. Who did you want to talk about?"

Roberto asked me questions about some of the reservations, townspeople he didn't know, and we discussed who needed VIP treatment. I pointed to the mayor's reservation. "You saw this, right? He won't pay, but we should treat him well."

"He will pay," Roberto said. "No one gets a free meal here."

"But the mayor—"

"Will pay his bill, signorina. Don't worry. Now, this person here." Roberto gestured to a name I didn't know. "He is a food influencer with over a million followers."

"What? Oh, my god. How did he find out about us?"

"The new social media account." Roberto had started it a few days ago, mostly posting pictures of Giovanni and his food, and we had over twenty thousand followers.

"Should I say hi? Bring him a free drink?"

"I'll take care of that. You should enjoy yourself this evening.

Leave the little things to me, including this person." He pointed to another name. "This is a food critic from the *Times*."

I felt dizzy, so I grabbed the wooden stand. "The *Times,* as in *The New York Times*?"

"Sì, signorina."

"What the fuck? On opening night?"

"They generally come more than once before writing the review, so don't worry."

Strangely, this did not make me feel better. "Does Giovanni know all this?"

"Yes, he does. I'll remind him and the waitstaff as the tables are seated, however."

I placed a hand on my stomach, hoping to settle it down. "Okay. Any other news I should know?"

"Mr. DiMarco has requested a table with you at nine-thirty. I blocked it here," he said and tapped a reservation marked with the initials LDVM.

"You know his name isn't DiMarco," I said quietly. Roberto was well aware of Luca's identity and profession.

"True, but appearances are important. Especially in a small town such as this."

I bit the inside of my cheek, suddenly nervous. Roberto had become like an uncle to me since we started working together. I respected his opinion and trusted his guidance. He was very smart and good with people. So I needed to ask. "Do you think I'm crazy for getting involved with him?"

He placed his forearm on the stand and met my gaze. "He will not hurt you, if that is what you're asking."

"That isn't what I mean. I'm not worried he'll hurt me physically. I'm worried about everything else. He's a lot older than me—and not exactly on the right side of the law."

"I think," Roberto said after a beat, "that life is short and you should do what makes you happy. But you must remember a tiger is still a tiger, no matter where he resides."

"And Luca is a tiger."

"Sì, and he will never change. And his life is there, not here."

Which was fine. Whatever was going on between us was temporary. A hot, yet brief, fling. Because when Luca's business in New York concluded, he'd head back to Italy and we would never see each other again. The idea sat like a stone in my throat, but I needed to go into this with my eyes wide open, just as Gia had warned.

"No one has taken care of me in a long time."

"I know. Which is why I want to do it. No one is more deserving than you."

Ugh. If only he weren't so damn sweet. But I couldn't allow myself to fall for him. No matter what else happened, I had to guard my heart around him because he'd break it without thinking twice.

I bumped his shoulder with mine. "Thanks, Roberto. You're pretty wise."

"Many years of experience, signorina. I hope you avoid some of the bad choices I made along the way."

This was new. He hadn't opened up about his past before, despite my repeated attempts to get information out of him. "Like?"

"No, those are conversations for another day. We'll sit down with a bottle of wine and I'll tell you all my dark secrets."

"I'm holding you to that promise. Though I think one of them is how you secretly like Maggie's red table wine."

He made a sound in his throat that resembled a scoff. "That is definitely not one of my secrets."

Two lines on the phone lit up at the same time. "Time to go to work," Roberto said.

I patted his shoulder. "I'll take line two from the office."

* * *

Luca

Bodies were packed tightly into the trattoria's entrance. I had to squeeze past several couples to reach the hostess stand. When I did, I found a young woman there. "Buona sera," I said. "I am—"

"Mr. DiMarco. I know. I remember you from book club night."

Ah, so a friend of Valentina's. "I am here to have dinner with—"

"Val, I know. Roberto has your table reserved. Follow me."

The girl talked fast and clearly liked to finish sentences. I didn't mind, if it got me closer to Valentina any quicker. I trailed the hostess through the dining room, which was full of diners and busy wait staff. A few people had their phones out, taking photos of Giovanni's cuisine. Good. The more publicity for the trattoria, the better.

Wisely, Roberto had given me a table against the wall. It was my habit never to sit with my back to a crowded room, which was even more important with Segreto lurking around. My brothers were still searching for signs of the former underboss, as well as John Natale.

I lowered myself into a chair where I could see the entire dining room. "How is she doing?"

"Hovering like a nervous mother. It will be good to get her out of the kitchen and into a chair. While I tell her you're here, what may we bring you to drink?"

"A bottle of the Ravazzani cirò, I think."

"Good choice. And Giovanni is making something special for you both, so no menus."

That was fine with me. I nodded my head and relaxed, taking in the room. Valentina and Roberto had outdone themselves. The trattoria was now much more mature and modern, simple, without all the cliché knick-knacks from before. It could be any upscale restaurant in Napoli or Roma. I was so fucking proud of her.

My son was behind the bar, pouring drinks and smiling at a bunch of young ladies. My father was very likely rolling over in his grave at the moment. A powerful heir to the Benetti kingdom, a bartender? But I liked knowing he was here. It gave me one more person looking out for Valentina.

A server came over and blocked my view of the bar as she

presented the bottle of cirò. After I tasted the wine, she poured two glasses and left me alone. I was about to take out my mobile and ring Leo when the most gorgeous woman in the world came into view.

Valentina.

Madre di dio, I couldn't take my eyes off her. She came toward me, the heels making her long legs even longer, wearing that wrap dress that hugged every curve. Dark brown hair swirled around her shoulders in waves. She'd removed the sweater, showing off her olive skin, the mounds of her tits, and everything inside me clenched with protective instinct. It was like I needed to put my name on her forehead, claim her as mine.

Cazzo, this girl. I was in trouble.

Heads turned as she walked by. I couldn't blame them. She was fucking beautiful.

I stood as she neared. Like we'd been together all our lives, she came right to me and tilted her face toward mine, letting me kiss her lips. "Hey, baby," she whispered. "You look good tonight."

I didn't bother speaking in English, because I didn't know enough words for what I needed to say. So I told her in my language what I was thinking and feeling inside, an outpouring of emotion I should've been embarrassed by. Except I wasn't. It felt necessary to tell her, even if she couldn't understand.

"Stop," she said, smoothing my tie. "I didn't understand that, but it sounded very sweet and I need to look professional tonight. I can't melt into a puddle at your feet."

I pulled out her chair. "Congratulations. The place is a success."

"Tonight's gone well." She placed her napkin on her lap as I sat down. "A few snafus in the kitchen, but Giovanni has handled it all beautifully. And Roberto?" She blew out a breath. "He's a genius. So smooth with people and anticipates their needs. I don't know how you convinced both of them to come here, but I'm very grateful, Luca."

A lot of money and my last name usually did the trick. "You are welcome, piccolina. Let's toast."

224

We both raised our glasses. "To proper wine," I said with a smirk.

She rolled her eyes, but laughed. "Still a wine snob. Fine, I'll give a toast. To you, investor daddy. You helped me to see that I can be more, do more than just live in the past. I'll always be thankful you walked in and insulted my restaurant."

That nickname again. I should've been embarrassed by the way it affected me, the dirty thoughts my brain conjured up because of it. "Investor daddy?"

Shrugging, she touched her glass to mine. "You have to live with it. The nickname's already stuck."

Live with it? I could hardly think of anything else. I had a strong urge to drag her out of here, take her home, and fuck her all night long while hearing that word on her lips.

She started to drink, but I put a hand on her arm. "I haven't given my toast yet."

"Oh, you have a real one? Let's hear it."

I held her gaze steadily as I leaned in with my glass raised. "It has been my honor and privilege to watch you bloom, fiore mio. Thank you for trusting me. And no matter what happens in the future, know that I have enjoyed our time together more than any other time in my life." I lifted her hand and pressed my lips to the back of it. "I am drowning in you, Valentina."

Her eyes grew glassy, moisture pooling at the edges. "Oh, god. Luca. You . . ." She dabbed at her eyelids with her fingers. "You can't say things like that when I can't kiss you."

"Come here." I tugged her closer and pressed my lips to hers. It was chaste in comparison to how I usually kissed her, but I hoped she could feel the truth, the honesty behind my feelings for her. And I didn't care who saw.

"Wow," she whispered when we parted, her fingers clutching my forearm on the table. "If we haven't started a scandal in town before tonight, that kiss definitely did it."

"Who cares what anyone thinks? Don't let other people hold you back, amore mio."

She bit her lip and straightened, settling in her chair. "Easy for you to say. You'll leave here soon and I'll just be the girl who once dated a handsome older Italian man."

I frowned. I didn't like the idea of that. The next words were out of my mouth before I could stop them. "Or maybe you'll be the girl living in Catanzaro who used to own a restaurant in New York."

"Okay, now you're freaking me out." She adjusted her napkin on her lap and avoided my stare. "Stop talking crazy."

Was it crazy?

You should keep her.

Aldo's words ricocheted through my brain for the hundredth time. The more I considered it, the more I came to like the idea. What was holding her here? This restaurant? That wasn't a good enough reason to live here in my opinion. And I wasn't finished with whatever this was between us. "You will like Catanzaro. It's known as *Città tra due Mari*, city of the two seas. I have a private villa on the water—"

"Luca! I'm not leaving Paesano." She tucked a strand of hair behind her ear, the lines across her brow deepening. "But I don't know, maybe I could come visit sometime."

I didn't want to argue with her, not tonight. So I dropped the subject . . . temporarily. But I wasn't interested in a long-distance relationship. My schedule was too chaotic, too demanding for that. I needed someone available at a moment's notice. Not to mention that anyone in my life needed protection, even a mistress. Flying back and forth, living here alone, would only put her at risk. "We'll see," I said vaguely.

The dishes began arriving then, little bites for us to try. Oysters, beef tartare, fried anchovies. Each plate was beautifully arranged, a small mouthful packed with flavor. Better than the food, though, was watching Valentina eat. I loved how much she enjoyed food, the little noises of pleasure she made. The way she licked her lips . . . I could stare at her all night. "You tried these before the opening, no?"

"Some of it, yes. But once I realized how talented Giovanni was, I basically stayed out of his way." She reached over and stole my plate containing a scallop topped with prosciutto foam. "This is my favorite, though, so I'm stealing it. Sorry, not sorry." She ate the scallop in one bite, her eyes nearly rolling back in her head as she chewed.

"I like seeing you enjoy it." I sipped my wine, studying her mouth. "It makes me think of what I'm going to do to you later."

A flush spread over her cheeks, but she shook her head. "Don't get your hopes up. I don't know when I'll be finished, but it'll probably be late."

"Wrong. You're leaving with me after dinner. Roberto can finish up."

Her lips parted as her brows came together dangerously. "I'm not leaving early. It's not fair to the staff."

"Valentina," I said seriously. "You have to learn how to be the boss. Treat your people well, but in the end they work for you. And if you can't trust them to handle things in your absence, then you haven't hired the right people."

"I suppose next you'll tell me that I make the rules."

"At the restaurant, yes." Leaning over, I brushed my fingertips over the shell over her ear. I was pleased to see her shiver. "But with me? No."

"God, you're so predictable." She pushed her empty plate away. "Speaking of Catanzaro, how much longer do you think you'll be in the States?"

"Not much longer, I imagine."

"Oh." She looked down at her lap and adjusted her napkin carefully. "That's too bad. Your brothers seem nice."

I was still pissed at Sergio for the way he spoke to me this morning. Our interactions today had been terse and angry, especially when our efforts to quickly locate Segreto failed. "They can be, yes."

"Which one are you closest to?"

"Sergio. We are the two oldest and he is my advisor when required."

"And what did he advise you about me?"

I slid her a glance, surprised. "Why do you think he said something?"

"Because I'm practically half your age and you've moved me into your house with all of them. I don't have a brother, but it seems like this might be something worth discussing, considering who you are."

She was very smart, my woman. "I don't give a fuck what anyone thinks, Valentina. And you shouldn't either."

"Well, I do. And I don't want to cause trouble between you and your family. So I'll sleep at home for the next few nights."

"No, you won't. You don't need to worry about my brothers or my son."

"Gabi said you made him move out to the pool house."

Ah, so they'd been talking today. "What else did my son tell you?"

"He says that I'm your girlfriend."

Girlfriend? I paused, my mind tripping over the word. In all my life I'd never had a girlfriend. Mistress, yes—there had been plenty of those. But no woman I shared emotional ties with. I was currently obsessed with Valentina . . . but that would soon fade, no?

Silence descended and I played with the stem of my wine glass. I couldn't tell from her expression what reaction she was hoping for from me. Did she like the idea? Was she hoping I agreed? "And what did you say?"

"Nothing. It caught me off guard. I think I was too freaked out to respond."

"The idea upsets you?"

"It's pretty overwhelming. I mean, I've never had a boyfriend before, so I didn't know what to expect. But I wouldn't ever have imagined one like you."

"Older?"

She nodded. "And Italian. And a man with a very dangerous job."

I leaned closer and put my free hand on her thigh. "Normal jobs are boring. And Italian men are handsome and well dressed. We like good food and good wine. And I'm very rich, well-endowed. What's not to love, piccolina?"

Chuckling, she reached over and caressed my jaw with soft, gentle fingers. "Let's not forget arrogant."

A throat cleared, catching our attention. I eased back in my chair but didn't remove my hand from her leg. Our server was there, two plates in her hands. "I apologize, but I have your next course."

"That's fine, Lizzie," Valentina told the girl. "We're ready."

Two plates were set before us, and conversations about our relationship were quickly forgotten.

Chapter Twenty-Three

Valentina

I could feel the stares of nearly everyone in the room. They were watching me with Luca, wondering, speculating. The gossip would spread like wildfire across all of Paesano by tomorrow.

I tried not to let it bother me.

Tonight wasn't about me; it was about celebrating the reopening and Giovanni's brilliance. I didn't know if an upscale Italian bistro would work in this small town, but I was willing to try. The social media posts were getting good results, and everyone seemed encouraged. There were a large number of tourists in the Hudson Valley, especially in the summer and fall, so maybe they would come here.

But I couldn't worry about all that, not right now.

I finished my small plate of saffron risotto, which was absurdly delicious. Luca had a linguini and shrimp dish, and he said it was the best he'd ever tasted. No doubt this was a lie for my benefit, but I'd take it. I needed all the positivity I could get.

Luca topped off my wine, then refilled his glass. His hands were sexy and strong, the veins shifting along with bones and tendons. He had clean, manicured nails. There was something appealing about a man who took care of himself, who liked for the world to notice him.

"Are you done inspecting me?"

I looked up and found him smirking at me. "I like your hands."

"This is good because they will be all over you in a short while."

I rolled my eyes. Relentless, this man. But I wasn't leaving early tonight. How would it look if I left before everyone else? This was my restaurant. I had to stay and congratulate everyone, not to mention close out the receipts. I reached for my water, not the wine. I needed to keep my wits around Luca.

Lizzie returned with our next course and when she set the plate in front of me, I smiled. Chicken parmigiana. "Tell him thank you," I told Lizzie. "I know he wanted to send out something else."

As she gave Luca an order of the stuffed chicken, Lizzie said, "I think it's growing on him. And it's one of the most popular orders tonight."

"I'm not surprised. It's a classic for a reason." I loved the way Giovanni prepared my grandfather's chicken parm. It was the same Montella sauce, but Giovanni used tomatoes canned in Italy and fresh herbs instead of dried. He also sprinkled a blend of cheeses atop the breaded chicken instead of just mozzarella. In my humble opinion, more cheese makes most things taste better.

I waved my hand toward the magnificence that was my plate and asked Luca, "Would you like another taste?"

"No, thank you. Once was enough."

I studied him as he cut his stuffed chicken. "Did you finish it or throw it away that night? Be honest."

"I ate it. Every bite."

"Admit it. You loved it."

"I most definitely did not."

I shrugged and cut a tiny bite of chicken and cheese. "Fine. That just means more for me."

The first bite was heaven, the second even better. I couldn't remember the last time I was this happy. Good food, good company.

The restaurant was bustling, just like I remembered from my child-hood. My mother would be so proud right now.

"I love to see you like this," Luca said. "You're practically glowing."

I didn't know how to put it into words. "This is what my family intended for the restaurant, to provide a welcoming place for people to gather by serving really good food. And when I was younger we used to be this busy every night. So it's very gratifying to experience it again, even if it's only tonight."

"It won't only be tonight, bella. I wouldn't have brought Giovanni here if I didn't believe in his talent. The reviewers are going to love it and word will spread."

"I hope so," I said around a bite of chicken parm.

Over the next thirty minutes Roberto and our server stopped by to check in. But mainly, Luca and I talked over dinner, the conversation flowing easily. Giovanni then came out to personally serve our dessert, which was a hard chocolate ball covering a scoop of pistachio stracciatella gelato. He poured hot espresso over the top, which melted the chocolate onto the gelato. The result was like a sundae flavored with chocolate and coffee. I nearly climaxed when I tasted it.

"Holy shit, this is good," I muttered as I scooped up another bite. Luca merely watched me, sipping on an espresso, and I couldn't understand why he wasn't digging in. "Don't you want to try it?"

"And miss the little noises you're making, licking your lips for me? No, you eat it, amore."

"Stop making everything dirty."

"I can't help it when I'm around you. Everything you do makes me want to get you naked."

Holding his gaze, I lifted the spoon to my lips and slowly slipped it into my mouth. The creamy sweetness hit my tongue and I cleaned the metal dramatically, letting out a little moan to torture him.

Luca put his arm on the back of my chair and angled toward me. My skin broke out in goosebumps as his mouth found my ear.

"Unless you want to get fucked in the bathroom, say your goodbyes. I'm taking you home."

Heat gathered between my legs, an undeniable wave of arousal, and I was fully on board for whatever Luca had in mind. But I wasn't sure I could leave yet. "Later, baby. I need—"

"No." He reached into his pocket and took out a grip of money. I watched, mesmerized, as he peeled off five hundred dollars and dropped it onto the table. "Let's go," he said, his jaw tight and hard, his demeanor in full boss mode.

It was probably wise not to test the bathroom threat.

"Okay, but let me say goodbye to the kitchen staff and Roberto. Ten minutes, okay?"

"Five," he said, his voice deep and almost menacing.

But I wasn't scared. Far, far from it. There must be something wrong with me, because I suddenly craved all of that aggression and domination focused solely on me.

I pushed away from the table and hurried to the kitchen. As I crossed the dining room, friends and acquaintances offered up their congratulations, so the journey took longer than I anticipated.

Inside, the kitchen was winding down. They were still busy, but not slammed, so I gushed to Giovanni over his food, then gave my sincerest thanks to the entire crew. I apologized for leaving early, but no one seemed to care. Huh. Maybe Luca had been right about that.

My bag was back in the office, so I went to the rear of the kitchen to get it. No way was I leaving a twenty-thousand dollar handbag here overnight. I'd locked it in my desk drawer earlier, terrified someone would steal it.

I unlocked the office door, then removed my bag from the drawer. I left Roberto a note, telling him thank you and that we'd catch up tomorrow. Just as I was leaving, one of the kitchen staff came in from a smoke break in the alley. These were common, so I didn't think twice about it, until he said, "Miss Valentina? A man was asking for you outside."

A man? I was instantly on edge. "Who?"

The line cook pointed to the alley behind him. "He said to tell you only if you were alone. It's your father."

Every muscle in my body went rigid. My father? Here? What the actual fuck? Why would he come here tonight of all nights?

I hesitated, my mind debating what to do. I wasn't eager to talk to Flavio Segreto, but I didn't want him interacting with any of my staff members—or Luca. That could be a total shitshow. No, my father needed to go away and stay gone.

I took a deep breath and stormed out into the alley, ready for battle.

It was dark. Only the light over the door provided any illumination, so I peered into the gloom. "Where are you?" I hissed.

"Over here," an accented male voice said by the dumpster.

I marched over, my heels clicking on the cement. Sure enough, my father was waiting there, cleverly concealed. God forbid he actually acted like a normal father.

He looked the same, with a little more gray in his closely cropped hair. Maybe a little more round through his middle. But the haggard face, the dark suspicious eyes? I'd recognize them anywhere.

"What do you want, Flavio?" I snapped. "I'm a little busy."

"Luca Benetti is a dangerous man. You need to stay away from him."

I exhaled heavily and looked to the sky for support. "Seriously? That's what you came here to tell me? You have no right to comment on anything regarding my life. Now, if that's all, see you in five years or so."

I started to turn, but he grabbed my arm to hold me. "Valentina, don't be stupid. He is a murderer, a torturer. He is not a nice man. Even if he weren't too old for you—"

I ripped my arm out of his grip. "God, stop it. I know exactly who Luca is, and none of it is your business. If this is your attempt at protecting me or acting like a real father, it's too little, too late. I don't want to hear anything you have to say."

"You need to listen to me! I know you hate me, but you do not want to get mixed up with him or his family. He would kill you without a moment's thought."

"No, he wouldn't. You don't know him like I do. And you don't have a leg to stand on, Flavio. You come from the exact same world."

"Yes, which is why I am warning you away from him, *figlia*. This will only end badly for you."

Maybe, but I didn't want to hear it. Not from this man. He'd ignored me nearly all my life, letting my mother raise me alone, then letting her die with only me at her side. Letting me struggle with the restaurant, the mortgage. Fuck him. "Go away and don't come back. I don't need you or want you in my life."

"Don't be stubborn, Val. Not now. Your mother—"

"Do *not* speak of my mother. Get her name out of your mouth. You lost that right years ago."

"Mamma mia," he said, dragging a hand across the back of his neck. "I know you hate me, and I can't change that, but I'm telling you Benetti is the worst kind of man. I can't let you get mixed up with him."

"Can't let me?" God, the absolute nerve. I made a sound that was half between a scoff and a dark laugh. "You have no control or influence over my life, Flavio. None. Thanks for stopping by," I said sarcastically. "Don't do it again."

I started to walk away, but my father wasn't done.

"He's only here to use you to get to me."

I stopped in my tracks and looked over my shoulder. "What are you talking about?"

"Benetti. He's here in New York, getting close to you so he can find me."

"You're delusional." I put up my palms like I was warding off an evil spirit. "Seriously. Now you're trying to make me believe it's all about you? Jesus. Just when I thought you couldn't get any worse."

"Think about it, Valentina. Why did he come to your restaurant that first night? Why is he hanging around this shithole town? Why has he moved you into his house?" He shook his head. "Do you really think this is some love affair between the two of you? You can't be that naive."

A lump formed in my throat. I wanted to brush off the words, but these were all of my deep-seated fears. Not even my own father had loved me, so how could any other man? I'd worked through a lot of this with a therapist before my mom grew sick, so I knew it wasn't true. But inside my heart, buried in my soul, I always believed it.

I folded my arms. "Fine, let's say you're right. Why would Luca want to find you?"

"Because I'm a wanted man back in Italy. My enemies. They will put me to death. And Benetti means to make it happen."

My god, the drama. This was unbelievable. My limbs vibrated with anger as I pointed at him. "You're crazy. I get that you don't want me to date him, but to make this stuff up is ridiculous. Seriously, go away."

Turning on my heel, I hurried toward the kitchen. "You don't know him!" my father called.

I didn't stop. I needed to get back to the dining room. I didn't want Luca coming to look for me and finding Flavio. My father was an embarrassment, nothing more than an old fool spouting lies and trying to act like he gives a shit about me.

I wish I'd never gone outside.

Luca and Roberto were chatting at our table when I returned. Needing to calm down, I inhaled and let it out slowly, then I put a smile on my face. Like we were tethered by an invisible string, Luca glanced over as soon as I started toward him. His eyes roamed all the way down my body, the examination slow and thorough. When I grew closer I could see that the heat in his gaze was genuine, not faked for my benefit. And it caused a riot in my bloodstream, my pussy growing wetter with need.

My dad could fuck off. Luca was the best thing that had ever happened to me.

And I was more ready to show him.

"Ciao," Roberto greeted as I approached the table. "I was telling Mr. DiMarco of our success tonight."

"That's nice," I said and reached for my half-full wine glass.

Luca rose and buttoned his suit coat. "Are you ready to go?"

Holding up a finger, I drained my remaining wine in two large swallows. "I am now." I bid goodnight to Roberto and let Luca escort me from the dining room.

When we reached the front walk I threw myself into Luca's arms. He grunted, but held me close. "Okay, piccolina?"

"Did you drive yourself to the restaurant?"

"Yes. Why?"

"I'll show you on the way home. Hurry up."

Chapter Twenty-Four

Valentina

I lunged for his belt the minute we were alone in his car.
Luca adjusted his arms on the steering wheel, making room for me. "Che cosa? What is this?"

"Start driving and ignore me."

He pushed the start button and the engine purred. "I'm not sure that is possible."

After unfastening the clasp on his trousers, I unzipped his fly. The thick length of him was there, waiting like a present beneath his fancy briefs. He wasn't fully hard, but stiff enough to make my mouth water. I rubbed him through the soft fabric. "You're so fucking hot. You don't even know."

"Are you talking to me, or my dick?"

"Both."

I reached under the waistband and hot smooth skin met my fingertips. Luca began driving, but I hardly paid attention. I couldn't explain why I was so eager for this, but it felt necessary. Like I needed to drive him wild or die trying. There was no mistaking our connection, the feverish hunger burning under my skin every time he was near. I wanted to forget everything else but this man.

I pulled his cock out of his briefs and gave him a rough stroke, causing him to grunt. His free hand slid through my hair, brushing it to the side. "Do you need my cock in your mouth?"

"God, yes."

I lunged forward, but he kept my head still, not allowing me to move. "Slowly, fiore. Kiss it and lick it first. Get me nice and hard and wet. Worship it and maybe then I'll let you suck."

"I'm good at following rules," I whispered.

"I know, baby. You're so obedient, so perfect. Exactly what I like."

My pussy clenched at the words, slick building between my thighs. Jesus, this man. I craved his approval like a drug.

I shifted in my seat, angling my upper body across his lap, my face directly at his crotch. He helped me settle, widening his thighs and moving my hair out of the way, all while operating the car along the dark streets.

I let him feel my breath first. He wasn't cut and when I asked, he said his foreskin is very sensitive. So I blew air along his shaft, watching intensely as he grew harder and harder. He hummed in his throat, a deep rumbling sound. "That's nice, Valentina. Keep going. Use your lips."

We turned a corner. I held onto his leg to keep steady as I pressed featherlight kisses on his base. Then I slowly worked my way higher, the lightest of touches to his velvety skin, until I reached the crown. He was fully erect now, so I paid equal attention to the tip, kissing all around. It was nice, lavishing him with this attention, smelling him. There were no worries, no problems. I could zone out and concentrate on this, nothing more.

Exactly the distraction I needed.

I flicked my tongue across his slit. Luca jumped, like I startled him. "Did I tell you to lick me?" he growled, easing me off his cock.

"No."

"*Esattamente.* Now you must start all over again with your lips."

I didn't question it. I was in a trance, happily willing to follow his orders. *So obedient, so perfect.* I glided my lips over the root of his shaft, my eyes closed as I explored him once again. I couldn't wait to lick him, to suck on him. To make him shout and tremble, to shatter his precious control. For that, I would do this as long as he wished.

We stopped at a light. "That's it," he crooned, his hand stroking my head, petting me. "Prove it to me. Prove how much you are aching to suck my dick, little girl."

Little girl? Oh, this was new.

I peeked at him. His eyes were opaque, glittering, and his lids heavy with lust as he stared down at me. *It's working.* "I will do anything, Luca. *Please.*"

"Soon, baby, soon. Keep going."

The car began moving again, his attention back on the road.

Reverently, I brushed my lips over his taut skin until I reached the crown. I badly wanted to taste him, but I kept it light kisses all around and down the other side. I didn't use my hands, so I nuzzled him with my nose to get where I needed to go.

His fingers plucked at the belt holding the front of my dress together. Then the sides were open and he was lowering the cups of my bra to free my breasts. "Cazzo madre di dio," he muttered as he pinched my nipple. "It will be a miracle if I don't crash this car."

Pleasure streaked from my nipple to my clit, an electric charge that sent heat rolling through me. I panted and clutched his thigh. "Oh, god."

"*Lick,* little girl."

I hurried to obey his low command, thrilled with my victory. I used my tongue every way I knew how—long swipes, short flicks—to bathe his cock in my saliva. He tasted perfect, salty with a hint of something all Luca. I returned to the slit in the crown and found a drop of fluid waiting for me. "Yum," I said after I licked it up. "Give me more."

"Merda!" The car weaved as he jerked the wheel.

I nearly smiled. Thank goodness for spicy books. Not only had I discovered some of my own kinks, they helped me tap into some of Luca's, too.

He wrapped my hair in his fist as we turned another corner. "Suck. *Now*."

I opened my mouth and swallowed him down. It wasn't easy. My jaw went as wide as it could go, but I couldn't come close to fitting all of him. I worked up a quick rhythm using my lips and tongue, his fingers tight against my scalp, holding me.

Through labored breaths, he said, "Keep going. Suck hard. Show me what a dirty little girl you are, with your tits out and my cock in your mouth."

I moaned in response, the words causing moisture to pool between my legs. No doubt my panties were soaked. I couldn't wait until we got back to the mansion and he put his dick inside me.

The car slowed, turned, and went over a few bumps. I hardly noticed. All I could think about was making him come in my mouth.

Suddenly, the wheels stopped and Luca threw the gear shift into park. "Andiamo."

He lifted me off him and tucked his cock in his trousers, then I was being carried into the night. Freshly cut grass and dirt teased my nose and I looked around. "The cemetery? Really? Isn't this sacrilegious?"

"Would you rather I fucked you by the side of the road for everyone to see?"

I buried my face in his throat to hide my smile. A desperate, aggressive Luca was my favorite. "Maybe?"

His long stride didn't falter as he walked off the path, into the darkness of the graveyard. Without the streetlights it was hard to see, but we were quickly surrounded by headstones. I'd been to this cemetery before, but never at night. The high school kids often partied here, but those days passed me by, considering I'd been dealing with the restaurant and my mom's illness at the time.

The headstones grew larger, some with ornate angels and crosses, and finally Luca stopped by a waist-high headstone with a smooth flat top, almost like an altar. He set me down, his hand holding my jaw hard as he gave me a brutal kiss. "Get naked, little girl."

I didn't hesitate.

I threw off my open wrap dress and kicked off my heels, leaving me in a bra and panties. The soft glow of the moon bounced off Luca's taut face, highlighting every sharp angle, his big hands clenched at his sides. He made no move to disrobe, just watched as I unclasped my bra and tossed it to the ground. I shimmied out of my panties and stood before him bare in the warm summer air.

"This," he breathed. "This is how you should be fucked. Naked, in the moonlight. A pagan sacrifice."

I shivered under the weight of his stare. "Are you also going to get naked?"

He reached into his briefs and pulled out his cock, stroked it once. "Lie down on the stone. Offer yourself to me."

I rushed to do as he asked. The stone was cold and unforgiving on my back, my calves dangling off the end, and goose bumps broke out all over my skin. The night sky stretched out above me, a blanket of tiny stars winking down.

"Such obedience," Luca murmured as he drew closer. His hand swept up my thigh and over my stomach. "You like when I tell you what to do, no?"

"Yes, Luca."

He cupped a breast and squeezed. I arched at the pressure, seeking more. Instead of giving it to me, he released me—then slapped my breast. I gasped, the sting sending sparks between my legs. He did it again and I moaned shamelessly. Before I recovered, he pinched my nipple between his fingers, hard. I threw my head back, pain radiating throughout my body. When he released me heat replaced the pain and shot directly to my clit. I had to bite my lip to keep from shouting.

"There is no one to hear you, little girl." His voice was dark and coaxing, the devil offering up wicked temptation. "And I will keep going until you scream for me, capisce?"

Oh, god.

My eyelids fluttered closed as he squeezed my other nipple. I panted through the bright agony. Just when I thought I couldn't take anymore, he released me and I nearly levitated off the stone as pleasure chased away the pain. Sounds emerged from my throat, uncontrollable whimpers and moans that floated up to the heavens.

He smoothed his palm down my sternum, over my stomach, until he reached my mound. "Now I will pinch you here—and it will hurt like hell. But the reward will be worth it, te lo prometto. Ready?"

"No, Luca, wait—"

"You will do this for me. Take a deep breath."

Before I'd finished inhaling his fingers latched onto my clit and pressed hard, the tender flesh squeezed painfully in his strong grip. "Shit!" I hissed. "Ow, fuck!"

I tried to twist away, my nails scratching the stone, but he held me down with his other hand. "Stay still. Another few seconds. You can do it."

"No, please. God, Luca!"

"Breathe, Valentina."

His low command penetrated my haze and somehow I endured another second. Then it was over.

Liquid fire streaked through my veins and I shouted up to the sky. I was floating, my clit throbbing like my heart was centered between my legs, and I barely noticed when Luca arranged me closer to the edge of the stone. My mind was buzzing and light, my limbs heavy, with the air a cool caress over my hypersensitive skin. I felt drunk, even though I hadn't had much wine at dinner.

He rolled me to my stomach and the stone scraped over my swollen nipples. The rough pressure made me aware of my breasts in a very elemental way and I discovered that I liked the soreness. Then

Luca spread my legs wide and pushed inside, his cock stretching me open.

"Cazzo, your pussy is so wet and hot. I wish you could feel it." He slid deeper, his hands stroking my sides and back. "The things I want to do to you . . ."

His hips began churning, hard punches that rocked me into the stone altar. I held on, spread out beneath him, limp, ready for whatever punishment he dealt out as he fucked me. It was so good. The friction of his shaft at this angle was bliss and my eyes fell shut as pleasure built deep in my belly. "So good," I said dreamily, echoing my thoughts. "Don't stop."

The pace he set was brutal. Our hips slapped together, his big hands yanking me back into his pelvis. Soon it was too much and a climax tore through me, my limbs trembling, eyes rolling back in my head. My pussy contracted around him and he grunted. "What do you want, little girl? For me to come inside you or on your back?"

"Inside me, daddy." The word tumbled out without me even realizing, but it felt right. I had a feeling Luca would like it, based on whatever game we were playing.

"Fuck!" he shouted and his cock thickened inside me. His rhythm slipped as his deep groan cut through the darkness, his hips sealed tight to mine like he was trying to join us together, his body emptying into mine.

Air washed over me suddenly and he was gone. I glanced over my shoulder and saw him spread out on the ground, panting as if he'd run a race. His trousers were undone, cock glistening in the moonlight, but otherwise he was dressed. I gathered my strength and pushed off the headstone, then stumbled my way over to him, my legs unsteady. I dropped to the grass beside him and tried to gather my wits.

"I think you fucked me stupid," I muttered.

"I've never come so hard in my life. I think . . . I should be embarrassed."

Rolling my head, I studied his face. His brow was wrinkled. "Why? Because we had sex in a cemetery?"

"No, of course not. I'm not superstitious. If the dead are angry with me, they will need to get in line."

I pressed my lips together to keep from laughing. What else would he be embarrassed—

Oh.

Now I was grinning. "You liked it when I called you *daddy*."

He winced. "Why did you say it to me?"

"I suspected you might like it. After all, you were calling me *little girl*."

His hand reached for me. "Come here. I want to make sure you are okay."

I scooted closer. "I'm fine."

"I will see for myself." He rose up on one elbow and leaned over me. His fingers skimmed my right nipple, then the left. "Sore?"

"A little. A good sore, though."

Humming, he bent and pressed a soft kiss to each taut bud. "And here?" Moving lower, he inspected my clit. "Did I hurt you?"

"No. Maybe don't do that every day, but it was like fire when you let go."

He gave my clit a kiss, as well, then kept kissing my labia. "Fiore mio, *sei bella e dolce*." Then he straightened and ran his fingertips over my cheekbones, along my nose. "Nothing could compare to how beautiful you are right now. You make the moon weep with jealousy, the stars cower in shame. It's like you were born to be fucked outside."

Grabbing his tie, I yanked him down for a soft kiss. His lips moved over mine sweetly, reverently, and neither of us tried to deepen it, content to breathe each other in. Something had shifted between us tonight. This wasn't a casual fling—I felt so much more for this man than I'd intended—and I sensed that he may feel the same.

"Luca," I whispered against his mouth. "Is this crazy?"

Silent, he dragged his thumb across my bottom lip, a gentle sweep back and forth. Warm, adoring eyes stared down at me, a dark fathomless gaze that sucked me in and held me captive. I never wanted to look away.

Without warning, he pushed up and held out his hand. "Come. I want to fuck you again at home."

Chapter Twenty-Five

Luca

I woke slowly, my head struggling to free itself from the grip of a nightmare. In the dream I was with Valentina at my beach house, playing with her in the blue ocean water. Then the water around her turned red, her eyes becoming dull and lifeless, her body limp in my arms.

Cristo santo. I didn't have nightmares often, thankfully, but when I did they were never about the woman in my life. What in god's name had brought this on?

Opening my eyes, I stretched my arms. Last night was fun. After the cemetery, Val had been insatiable until around two o'clock, when we both fell into an exhausted sleep. I came twice, her five. My dick was worn out today, not even showing signs of morning wood.

I peeked over at her. She was on her side with her arms wrapped around a pillow. Tangled brown hair was thrown every which way, her naked back smooth and perfect. I had a strong urge to move over there and hold her tightly until she woke up. It wasn't sexual, either. It was an emotional need.

Luca, is this crazy?

It was clear what she had been asking. Were we crazy for indulging in each other, for developing feelings for someone we barely knew? Valentina was young, inexperienced. It stood to reason that she might grow attached to me.

But I knew better. There had been plenty of women—singles, doubles. A number of triples. We'd fuck for hours then fall asleep in an orgy of limbs. And I never had the urge to cuddle with any of them, not once.

But something about this girl brought out a different, gentler side of me and I wasn't sure what to make of it.

I grabbed my watch. Cazzo, it was already ten o'clock. I needed to get up. Deciding to let her sleep, I edged out of bed and found my mobile on the nightstand. I had to shower before I went downstairs, so I crept to the bathroom, not making a sound. I closed the bathroom door softly and turned on the water to let it heat up. Then I caught a glimpse of myself in the mirror and blinked.

My upper body was covered in scratch marks and . . . Were those hickeys on my neck? I chuckled as I stepped under the hot spray. My woman was aggressive in bed and I liked it.

Bracing my hands on the tile, I let the steam and heat work on my sore muscles as the water poured down on me. I needed a cappuccino, then I had to check in with my brothers about the search for Segreto. But all I could manage at the moment was to close my eyes and stand still.

The glass door opened. A soft pair of breasts met my back and arms wrapped around my waist. "Hey, baby," she mumbled sleepily into my skin.

"Amore mio. Buongiorno." I turned and brought her close to my chest, my face buried in her hair. "I was going to let you sleep."

"It's okay. I'm a light sleeper. I heard you get up."

A long minute passed and I relaxed, letting my mind go blank. She felt so good, the weight of her tits resting on me, her soft skin slippery and warm. My cock began to respond, thickening with every beat of my heart, pulsing, and before long I was half hard.

When I reached down to adjust myself, she mumbled, "There's no way I can handle you fucking me today. In fact, I might need to sit in a salt water bath later."

"I can't keep from getting hard when your naked body is clinging to mine." I cupped her tit and massaged the plump flesh with my fingers.

"Ignore it. I'm not sure I have the energy to fuck you right now anyway."

"Last night was fun." She nuzzled her face into my throat. "Didn't you think so?"

"It was very fun."

Her lips nibbled my jaw. "Maybe tonight we can have more fun."

I smiled and squeezed her ass in my hands. "You'd better believe it, piccolina."

She eased away from me—and gasped. "Oh, my god! Your chest. Your arms. Oh, shit. Did I do that?" Her gaze finally landed on my throat and she instantly covered her mouth with her hand. "No, no, no." Then she rubbed the skin of my throat like she was trying to wipe it clean. "I gave you hickeys!"

I took her wrist. "It's okay. Don't worry."

"This is so embarrassing." Her expression dropped. "Everyone will tease you. They'll think I'm immature, a silly teenager—"

"Stop." I took her face in my hands and kissed her mouth softly. "Every man who sees them will be jealous, amore. And if it makes you feel better, I promise to hurt whoever dares to comment."

"Well, damn. I don't want that either." She put her hands together between us. "Please, can we just stay in bed all day? We'll hide out in your bedroom and order our meals in."

I chuckled and let her go. "Benettis don't hide. And I have too much to do today."

"So do I, unfortunately. Ugh. I'll never be able to look your brothers in the eye." She put some body wash in her palms. "At least let me wash the scrapes."

I put my arms out at my sides and she rubbed the soap onto my chest, her hands working over my skin, gliding and skimming, and paying extra attention to the scrapes. "Do they sting?"

"No," I said. "And even if they did, I wouldn't stop you right now." I was fully hard now, my dick jabbing her stomach. I loved the feel of her hands on me, the soft caresses over my torso, even parts I never considered as erogenous. But Valentina paid attention to every millimeter of me, and that turned me on.

She was breathing faster as she reached for more soap. "Now I'll clean the lower half."

While that sounded nice, I needed to get my hands on her. Standing still while she touched me was the worst kind of torture. I nudged her hands away from the body wash. "No, it's my turn."

"You don't have to reciprocate."

"I know. I want to." I rubbed my hands together and knelt on the hard shower floor, water cascading around me. "Give me your foot."

Bracing herself on the wall, she lifted her foot and I began cleaning it, top and bottom, between every toe. She had pretty feet, with painted nails and soft skin. They were inexplicably sexy. Propping her heel on my thigh, I started to massage her feet. I swept my slick hands along the instep and dug my thumbs into the underside. Back and forth, back and forth, gently pressing.

"Holy shit," she breathed, her free hand gripping the top of my head. "You have no idea how good that feels after wearing heels all night."

I could only imagine. I kept at it, applying pressure to release the tension in her muscles. Tugging on her toes to loosen them up, pushing on the ball and the heel. Then I placed that foot on the ground, picked up the other one, and started all over again.

She moaned and swayed on her feet. "You're killing me."

I was certainly in more pain at the moment. My erection throbbed, each heartbeat echoing in my groin. Why was I so desperate for her? I came twice last night, so it made no sense. When would this fever abate?

When I finished with her feet, I washed her legs. Her calves were bunched, so I worked out the knots until she slumped against the tile. Water dripped down her beautiful face, her lashes dark spikes around her eyes. "Luca," she whined.

I smoothed my palms over her thighs. "What do you need, fiore mio?"

"A very quick orgasm, please and thank you."

Chuckling, I kissed her stomach. "I thought you were too sore."

"I am, but now you've got me feeling things and I can't go to work all horned up like this."

Horned up? Dio, the way this generation talked.

Rising, I angled her shoulders until her back was against the tile. Then I braced myself with one hand, leaning in so we were close, but not touching. "Later. I want you thinking about me all day."

"Pretty sure I'll be doing nothing but, especially when I drive by the cemetery." Valentina nipped at my throat. "God, that was hot. It makes me want to bite you some more."

Chuckling, I stepped back under the spray. "Are you part vampire?"

"Maybe. Would you let me turn you immortal so we could be together forever?"

"If it means I can keep fucking you, yes."

We finished in the shower and I dried her off with a towel. Then I wrapped one around my waist and headed for my closet. I expected her to do the same in the other bedroom, but she followed me. "Are you wearing a suit today?" she asked as I found a pair of briefs.

"Do you want me to?"

Using a band from her wrist, she fashioned her hair up into a wet ponytail. "I always want you to wear a suit. You look so hot in them. Though your pajama bottoms are pretty hot, too."

Pajama bottoms? Hot? "Then, yes, I'll wear a suit."

"Yay! I get to pick out your tie." Humming, she bounced over to the neat line of ties hanging and began sifting through them. I pulled on a dress shirt and absently did the buttons, my attention fully on

Valentina. The towel she wore barely covered her ass and her long, smooth legs were on full display. I loved her legs. They were strong, with velvety soft skin, and fit perfectly around my waist as I drove inside her warm, wet pussy.

"Wear another dress today," I said. "And heels."

She looked at me from over her shoulder, and there was a strange expression on her face, almost like panic or worry. "Why? Are you coming to the restaurant tonight?"

"Do you want me to come in?"

"No!" she said emphatically—and my eyebrows raised in surprise. Instantly, she smiled and waved her hand. "I mean, we'll both be busy, right? You should stay here and work on your things. I need to catch up with Roberto and Giovanni, then meet with the social media person we're trying to hire. Place orders and whatnot. You know, restaurant things. It'll be super boring and I won't have time to sit down."

My senses went on high alert. Valentina was babbling and trying to keep me away from the trattoria. Why?

"No problem, amore," I said casually, though my mind was racing. "I'll eat here and we'll see each other tonight."

She handed me a tie and kissed my cheek. "Perfect. I'll go get ready and you can drive me in."

Questions burned my tongue as I silently watched her go. I didn't know why she was acting this way, but I would definitely find out.

Chapter Twenty-Six

Luca

I texted my brothers as soon as I left the trattoria. I needed a full report on what happened last night. I also instructed Sergio to get all the camera footage from Valentina's office, the dining room, and the alley.

If something happened, I would discover it.

Aldo drove me back to the house, his hands tapping on the steering wheel along to the music he was enjoying. I put my mobile in my pocket and tried to stay calm. There was no use speculating on the reason for Valentina's behavior until I knew more. Maybe she was tired of me interfering with the restaurant. Or she didn't want people to gossip about us. I tried not to think it might be another man, because I would have to kill him.

She's only ever been with me. There is no other man.

Still, there was that nagging doubt. Any fool could see that she deserved to be with someone her age, someone from this town. Yet the idea of her with another caused my gut to cramp. I was *not* giving her up.

"Anyone see anything last night?" I asked.

"Where?"

"At the restaurant."

"Not that I know of. We were up the block watching the cars. Dante and Rico were on the doors."

Sergio had stayed back to watch the cameras, while a dozen men went out to search the area for Natale and Segreto. I texted with Gabriele earlier, who said all went smoothly at the bar with no sign of either man.

"Why?" Aldo met my gaze in the rear view mirror. "What are you thinking?"

"Something Valentina said this morning. It made me think she's trying to keep me away from the restaurant."

"Maybe she needs space. Women don't like to be smothered by their boyfriends."

Interesting advice coming from a man who'd never had a girl-friend or wife. "How would you know?"

"Women talk about it online. Don't you ever watch any of those clips on social media?"

No, I didn't. "I'm not her boyfriend."

Aldo snorted as he turned a corner sharply. "You moved her in, spent a fuck load of money on her. You're barely able to keep your hands off her, don't want any other women. You let her give you love bites. All due respect, Don Benetti, but you're her *ragazzo*."

I didn't bother to reply. This was the second time the title had been brought up, but I was too old to be a boyfriend.

When we returned to the house, I found Sergio in the office. He was connecting his laptop to the big flat screen on the wall. He looked up as I entered and did a double take when he spotted my neck. Smirking, he said, "Nice hickeys."

"Fuck off." I dragged two chairs to face the screen. "Where are Dante and Rico?"

"In bed. I didn't wake them yet."

Suddenly, the flat screen came to life and six squares of video feed appeared. Sergio clicked a button on his laptop, then sat down beside me as the video feeds began rolling.

"I have them synched up," he explained. "Is there something you're worried about? Did something happen last night?"

I repeated my worries over Valentina's comment.

Sergio knew me well enough not to dismiss my suspicions. My instincts were rarely wrong. So he remained silent and watched along with me.

It was hard to pay attention to all six squares at one time, especially when I didn't know what I was looking for, so I followed Valentina in every frame. She stayed busy, dealing with the staff, greeting customers, talking to the diners . . . going, going, going. She did a little bit of everything, always moving and smiling.

Sergio watched the screen as intently as I did. "I can't believe you allowed Gabi to bartend. Look at how much attention they are giving him."

I switched my focus to the bar camera. My son was leaning over, elbows on the wood, and giving a flirtatious grin to two middle-aged women. More women were circled around, either openly ogling him or watching him through their lashes. One customer pulled out her mobile and took a selfie with him, which caused my brother to sigh. "This is going to be a problem."

I rubbed my eyes with my fingers. "I'll talk to him today."

We continued studying the footage. Aldo brought us cappuccinos and rolls, and we had to stop the laptop several times when calls came in from Catanzaro. The whole process was slow and arduous. Nothing happened during the day as the entire restaurant prepped for opening. When we began the night footage, however, a familiar man walked into the restaurant and Valentina was there to greet him.

Mayor Lombardi.

My muscles clenched and I set my cup down carefully. "This man has a fucking death wish."

Sergio paused the footage. "Who?"

"The mayor." I gestured to the screen. "He came to eat at the restaurant last night."

"I thought you took care of him. What is he doing there?"

"I don't know." I couldn't believe the stronzo was stupid enough to show his face at the trattoria after I warned him away from Valentina.

"Maybe this is it. Maybe she didn't want you to fight with the mayor again."

No, I didn't think so. "Restart it. Let's see what happens."

The older woman with the mayor had to be his wife. She clung to his arm with an air of familiarity and comfort, her expression filled with self-importance. The mayor glanced around nervously as he smoothed his tie. Good. I hoped he was nervous. Lombardi had no business coming to the trattoria for any reason.

Then Valentina walked the couple to their table and exchanged a few words with the other woman. Valentina nodded to the mayor and strode away, and this camera angle showed how the mayor ogled Valentina's ass as she retreated.

Motherfucker.

"I'm going to kill him," I said quietly.

"How did he get a reservation? Roberto is usually very thorough."

This was not Roberto's fault. I hadn't said anything about barring the mayor, unfortunately. I'd obviously given Lombardi far more intelligence than the man actually possessed.

We continued to watch the footage. I was pleased to note that Lombardi and his wife ate quickly and left, with no more interaction with Valentina.

The office door opened and my two younger brothers entered. Sergio explained what we were doing, and Dante leaned against the wall and crossed his feet. "There was no issue at the front door. No sign of Segreto or the dishwasher."

"Or the back door," Rico added. "It was quiet back there."

Grunting, I didn't take my eyes off Valentina as she bustled throughout the busy crowd. She unlocked her office, went in, and removed her sweater. Then she put on fresh lipstick and fluffed her hair in the mirror on the wall.

"There you are, Luca," Rico said from over my shoulder. "Right on time at nine-thirty."

I knew what the entryway camera would show—me, speaking to the hostess and being shown to my table—but I stayed locked on Valentina. She checked her breath, then tugged the neckline of her dress higher, then lower. Higher again. Finally lower. Was she excited for our dinner? Nervous? There was no reason for her to be, but I found her uncertainty adorable.

"You have it bad," Sergio said.

"What is bad?" Dante asked.

"Luca's obsession with Valentina." Sergio angled toward my younger brothers. "He's grinning like an idiot at the screen every time she appears. And wait until you see his neck."

I ignored them. On the screen Valentina walked toward me, and I watched as she pressed tight and gave me her mouth. When we both finally sat, I could only see her profile from the camera angle. "Skip ahead," I told Sergio. "Find where she goes into the kitchen. See what happens then."

Sergio clicked on the laptop and the video footage sped up. Dinner progressed, we shared dessert. When Valentina got up from the table, Sergio let it play at normal speed. As Roberto came to speak to me at the table, Valentina went into the kitchen and talked to Giovanni and the kitchen staff. She looked excited and happy, and she made sure to hug each of the workers. Lucky for each man, he kept the contact brief and respectful. She went into her office, and I could see her from that camera.

She didn't spend long in there. It all seemed very routine until she left the office and reentered the kitchen. At the same time, one of the line cooks came in the back door.

"Dai, I remember that guy," Rico said. "He was out taking cigarette breaks all night."

On the screen, the line cook spoke to Valentina and hooked a thumb over his shoulder to indicate the alley. I straightened in my seat, the nape of my neck itching once again.

Valentina hesitated, then her spine lifted as if she were preparing herself. I held my breath. Who was in that alley? She wouldn't be stupid enough to go out there alone, would she?

Silence descended as my brothers and I watched Valentina slip out the back door into the alley.

My brain short-circuited as fury filled every vein, cell, and pore inside my body. "Motherfucker!" I snarled, then whirled on Rico. "You didn't think to mention this to me?"

He held up his palms. "Luca, I swear. I didn't see her come outside."

"Then explain how you missed it, stronzo."

Color lit his cheeks and he shifted on his feet. "The car alarm started going off—"

I slapped my palm on the armrest of the chair. "Porca di una puttana!"

"It was quick," he finished. "I went to shut it off and came directly back. There's no way Segreto got past me in that short amount of time."

"You had better fucking hope so, fratello. Sergio, enlarge it and play it," I barked.

The alley camera filled the television screen. Valentina glanced around, then marched over to the dumpster. Because of the camera position, we could only see her, not whoever was behind the dumpster.

But I knew. That was Segreto, getting Valentina alone in a place where he could still hide from me.

To keep from strangling my brother, I gripped the armrests and watched her. I couldn't see her face, but it was clear from her body language that she was telling Segreto off, arguing with him. *Good.*

Then she tried to leave and her father grabbed her arm, moving forward just enough where the side of his face was revealed to the camera for a split second. "There he is," I hissed. "That's Segreto. Touching her."

She ripped her arm out of Segreto's grip and continued arguing with him. I couldn't see her father any longer, but the two of them seemed to be going back and forth. She threw her head back, as if laughing, but I doubted this was amusement. Then she marched toward the kitchen once more.

Abruptly, she stopped and glanced over her shoulder. Segreto must have said something upsetting, because she whirled around and started gesturing with her hands, talking back to him. She folded her arms angrily and listened to whatever her father was saying. Was he trying to warn her about me? Forbid her from seeing me? Finally, she pointed in Segreto's direction as if telling him to go away, then hurried back inside the kitchen.

Once there, Valentina wasted no time in returning to our table, where she gulped wine and told me she was ready to go. The two of us walked out into the night.

Sergio shut off the video.

Very slowly, I turned toward Rico, the leather chair creaking beneath my weight. In any other situation I would collect my thoughts, give my emotions time to level out before speaking. But I was too fucking angry right now. There was no reason left inside me, no grace to be given. "Get out of my sight. Go back to Catanzaro. Immediately, *fratello*. Because if you stay, I'm going to beat the shit out of you."

Sergio and Dante remained quiet. Both of them knew better than to intervene.

Rico sighed heavily. "*Perdonami*, Luca."

"Go!" I roared.

I dragged both hands through my hair, then rested my elbows on my knees. Cristo santo, this was unbelievable. Segreto was right under our noses last night—and we missed him. Worse, he somehow got to my woman and upset her.

"Should we follow her?" Sergio asked quietly. "Maybe he will try to approach her again."

"No, he won't. She wasn't receptive to whatever he said last night. It's a waste of time for him. And by now he knows that we've seen him."

"So what will he do?"

The answer was obvious. It was exactly what I would do if I were in Segreto's shoes. "He'll try to kill me."

Sergio nodded his head in understanding. "You should stay here, safe, while we search for him. And we need to keep Valentina away from you, or else she's at risk."

"He won't hurt her. Last night was about warning her. He wants her to know who I am." Yet she still came to me, went home with me. Let me fuck her for hours. My chest pulled tight as a lump of emotion gathered behind my sternum. It was like a boulder sitting there, pressing down on me, weighing me down. I hadn't felt like this before, protective and grateful. Greedy for her. Never wanting to let her out of my sight.

Am I in love with her?

Was this what love felt like? Obsession with a dash of panic?

It seemed improbable. What would a man like me know about love? I loved my brothers, but we grew up together, took over the empire together. We banded together as boys to endure our father's ruthlessness.

But a woman? An outsider? An American? I couldn't possibly—

"What is that smell?" Sergio swiveled his head, inhaling.

I took in a deep lungful of air and realized the scent right away. Cazzo madre di dio! Shooting to my feet, I raced for the door. "That is smoke. "

Chapter Twenty-Seven

Valentina

Roberto and I were walking to Leaning Tower of Pastries, discussing last night's opening, when the city's two fire trucks roared by. They were headed out of downtown, toward the neighborhoods.

"That's weird," I said, shielding my eyes from the morning sun as the trucks disappeared. "They don't usually take both trucks for emergency calls."

"Maybe it's a fire."

"Maybe." But we rarely had fires. More than likely it was someone not feeling well or a gas leak. But I had to focus on Roberto. I needed to have a private conversation with him, which was why I'd asked him to walk with me. "Listen, I have to talk to you about something."

"Oh?"

I paused, not certain how to start. "It's about my father."

"You don't talk about him much. He left when you were young, no?"

"It's the opposite. He didn't know I existed until I was thirteen." I sighed as we crossed the street, lowering my voice. "He is in a similar line of work as Luca."

"Mamma mia," Roberto muttered. "I did not know this. Is he American?"

"No, Italian. My mother met him over there while studying abroad in college, but she didn't learn what he did for a living until a few months into their relationship. She immediately returned to New York and discovered a few weeks later that she was pregnant with me."

"She never told him?"

"No. She didn't want him involved in my life. But he found out anyway and has come here off and on since I turned thirteen. Every two or three years he pops up to see me."

"Why are you telling me this, signorina?"

"Because he was at the trattoria last night. In the alley."

Roberto stopped in his tracks and stared at me intently, his dark gaze filled with concern. "Did he hurt you?"

"No, he didn't hurt me. He wanted to talk to me. To warn me away from Luca."

Roberto slipped his hands into his trouser pockets and stared at the ground, the sunlight playing off the silver in his hair. "Does Mr. DiMarco know this?"

"God, no. And I don't want him to know, either." I grabbed his arm. "Please, please don't tell him, Roberto."

"Signorina, he should be told. Your father could be dangerous—if not to you, then to others around you."

"Flavio won't hurt anyone. He wanted to warn me, so I heard him out and told him to go away. But I needed to tell you because he might come back. He approached one of the line cooks on break to find me and tell me to go outside."

Oh, Roberto didn't like that. Not one bit. I'd never seen him angry, not once, his level-headed composure something I had relied on during the entire chaotic opening process.

But now? His jaw was clenched, every line of his face taut with fury. If I didn't know better, I would suspect that steam was coming out of his ears. "Which line cook, signorina?"

"I'm not telling you. He doesn't deserve to be fired—"

"Cazzata! He should not be putting you at risk, sending you outside alone to talk to a man in an alley! Which line cook?"

"It doesn't matter! I'm trying to warn you about my father, so he doesn't catch you by surprise."

He pressed his lips together and stared off into the distance. Finally, he gestured in the direction of Bev's. "Andiamo, signorina."

We started walking, but I wasn't finished with this conversation. "Do not tell Luca, Roberto. Do not break my trust by going against my wishes."

"There are bad people in this world, Valentina. You live here, in this small place, sheltered from most of the ugliness that surrounds us. And you are young, a good person. This is not a bad thing, but others will take advantage of you if they have the opportunity. Signore DiMarco, for all his faults, he will not let anyone hurt you."

"I don't need saving. I can handle my father."

"All due respect, bella, but you cannot. It takes a lion to fight another lion, capisce?"

"God save me from Italian patriarchy," I muttered as we approached the door of the pastry shop. "I'm serious. Take this to your grave. That's an order from your boss."

Roberto said nothing as we went in, his demeanor changing entirely as soon as he spotted Bev. "Ciao, ragazzi!" he called to the room, gaining the attention of everyone inside the café. Bev was cashing someone out at the register, but I saw the way her cheeks turned pink. Was she wearing *mascara*? Oh, this was getting interesting.

"Have you taken her on a date?" I asked Roberto under my breath as we waited in line.

"Do you think I should?"

"If you like her, then yes."

He stroked his jaw. "I haven't been on a date in a very long time."

"Why not?"

"Back home I was working. There wasn't time for a life outside of the restaurant."

I could feel myself frown as I thought about this. Roberto and I had been working constantly, him more than me, in getting the restaurant ready to reopen. I'd at least taken some time to be with Luca. When had Roberto taken time for himself?

"I'm giving you the weekend off," I said as we shuffled forward in line.

"This isn't necessary, signorina. The restaurant has barely reopened. I don't need time off."

"Nonsense. Saturday and Sunday, do not come in. If you do, I'll call Luca and have him send you home."

He glanced over at me, surprised. "You would do that to me?"

"In a heartbeat. Sometimes it takes a lion to fight another lion, capisce?"

Roberto threw his head back and laughed, the sound filling the small café. "Very true, very true. Allora . . . I will take time off soon, but not now. When this business with your father is concluded, okay?"

"Don't be silly, Roberto. I'm serious about time off. Giovanni, too. I want you both to stick around, not get burned out in the first month."

Roberto threw one arm around me and hugged me. "You have a good soul, Valentina."

Then Bev was ready for us. As soon as we stepped up to the register, Roberto turned on the charm and started chatting with her like we had all the time in the world. It was adorable.

"Sam," I said loudly to my friend, who was working on the espresso machine. "I meant to tell you. I can't go to the show with you. I hope you aren't mad."

Sam's eyebrows lifted. "Remind me, which show was this?"

"The one on Broadway. About the movie from the 1980s."

"Oh!" Bev perked up. "I've been dying to see it."

I was aware, which was why I'd mentioned it. "Well, you can have my ticket. You and Sam could go together."

Sam put a cup on the counter. Because she was smart, she played along. "But then who would watch the café? No, I think you should take a friend, Gram. Then the tickets won't go to waste."

I tried to sound casual as I scrolled on my phone. "Have you ever seen a Broadway show, Roberto?"

"No, I have not, signorina."

Sam pointed to the two of them. "You guys should totally go together, then."

There was an awkward beat of silence, and I wondered why Roberto wasn't pouncing on this opportunity. Wasn't this generation supposed to be better at in-person communication? These two were hopeless.

I nudged him gently. "What a good idea. Right?"

"Sì, certo. Would you like to go together, signora?"

"If you're sure," Bev said, also awkwardly. "That might be fun."

The bell above the door jangled. I glanced over and saw Mrs. Picarelli hurrying in. Mrs. P. had worked at the police station, answering phones and filing paperwork, for as long as I could remember. She wore bright colors and comfortable shoes and always had the best gossip in town. She wiped her forehead and then waved. "Whew! Bev, honey. I need an iced Americano, quick."

Sam turned to make the drink and Bev punched a few buttons on the tablet for the sale. "Gina, what on earth is going on?"

"I'm going to be up all night. Did you see the two trucks go by a few minutes ago?"

"The fire trucks? Of course. Did someone have a heart attack or break something?"

"Nope." Mrs. P handed her credit card to Bev. "There's a big fire out by the river. One of those mansions."

I froze and the room seemed to shrink along with my ability to breathe. No, it couldn't be. "I'm sorry, which house?"

"Oh." Mrs. P seemed to notice me there for the first time. Her expression turned sympathetic. "I'm sure everything is alright, sweetie."

"Is it Mr. DiMarco's house?"

She gently removed my fingers from her arm, which was weird. I hadn't even realized that I was holding onto her. "Well, now," she said. "I can't say, as I didn't take the 911 call. But I was told it was one of those Italian men we've been seeing around town and he reported a fire in his home."

I swayed on my feet as the edges of my vision wavered. Luca . . . fire. Was he okay? They sent *two* trucks. They never sent two trucks unless it was serious. "Oh, my god."

"Valentina." Roberto took my hand and patted it, like he was trying to keep me awake. "Let's stay calm. I'm sure everything is okay."

This was no time for calm. I needed to see with my own eyes that he was alright. I couldn't take it if something happened to him.

Did that mean . . . ? Was I in love with him? It seemed crazy, falling in love with someone in such a short amount of time, but I was physically sick at the thought of losing him.

Pulling away from Roberto, I started hurrying toward the door. "I have to get out there."

"Val!" Someone called, but I didn't stop. I had to get my van and drive out to Luca's.

"Wait!" Bev was right behind me. She grabbed my shoulder and thrust a set of keys at me. "Here, take my car. It'll be faster."

Roberto opened the shop door and held it for me. "I'll come with you, signorina."

Bev's car was behind the store, so it took no time at all to get in and set off for Luca's. My hands were shaking as I steered, panic fueling me as I punched the gas. Roberto grabbed the doorframe with one hand and the dashboard with the other. "Slow down, signorina. He would not want you risking yourself to get to him."

It was like all the worry and panic had rage babies inside me and words began rushing from my mouth. "Do *not* tell me what to do right now! The last thing I need is to be coddled and ordered around."

He quieted, though I could feel his anxiety leaching into the car interior. But I was a safe driver. I've been driving these roads since I was fifteen, even before I had a driver's license. I knew every turn, every bump. When to slow down, when to speed up. There wasn't anything I couldn't handle.

Then everything went wrong.

A loud pop sounded, and the tiny sedan began skidding and lurching wildly. I screamed as my fingers locked in a death grip on the steering wheel.

"Don't brake!" Roberto yelled. "It makes it worse."

I couldn't see how that was possible, but I trusted him. Taking my foot off the brake, I let the car slow down on its own. I instantly discovered he was right because the swerving stopped and it was easier to keep the car on the road. Finally, we rolled to a halt in a grassy patch off to the side.

Both of us gripped the interior of the car, panting, our adrenaline racing. "What the fuck?" I wheezed. "We almost died."

Roberto glanced behind us. "There was something in the road. We drove over it and the tire popped."

"Shit!" I slammed my palm into the steering wheel. "Bev is going to kill me. Let's get out and see how bad it is."

* * *

As soon as we got out of the car, I realized our mistake.

This hadn't been an accident. Whoever placed something in the road had put it there purposely.

And that person was my father.

Flavio materialized out of the woods, dressed in head to toe camouflage, a gun pointed at Roberto.

"You have got to be fucking kidding me," I said as my father eased closer. "Flavio, have you lost your mind? I could've been *killed*."

"It was only the front tires. I knew you would be okay." He gestured to me with his free hand. "Come with me, Valentina."

"Abso-fucking-lutely not. I need to get up to . . . " Pieces of information connected in my brain, the events of the morning coming together like ends of a magnet. "Oh, my god. The fire. Please tell me you aren't responsible. Did you do all this? Why?"

"I will explain everything later, figlia mia, when you and I are safely away. Now, let's go."

"You're crazy. And dangerous." I put up my palms and tried to get in front of Roberto. "I'm not going anywhere with you."

"Then I will kill your friend here. Is that what you want? For people to die, Valentina?"

"Don't do it, Val," Roberto said softly. "Don't believe him. Stay here."

"I-Is Luca okay?" My mouth was dry, my tongue thick with worry, but I had to know. "Did you kill him?"

"He is fine. No one was hurt. There, are you happy? The mob boss lives—for now. But I promise I will kill him and your restaurant man here if you do not follow me." Flavio aimed the gun at Roberto's leg and there was a puff of air.

Roberto went down, collapsing in a howl of pain.

Holy shit! My crazy father shot Roberto.

I knelt down, unsure what to do. I'd seen injuries in the kitchen, but never gunshots. "Are you okay? Oh, my god. Roberto, talk to me."

"Stings," he said from behind clenched teeth.

"Fuck." I straightened and discovered Flavio now standing much closer. "You psycho! I can't believe you just shot him!"

"It's nothing. A tiny scrape. But the next bullet is in his head unless you come with me. Andiamo, figlia."

"No, Val," Roberto said from behind clenched teeth, his hand gripping his leg to stem the bleeding. "Let him kill me. Don't go with him."

How could I allow that? Luca, his brothers, Roberto . . . How many people was Flavio willing to hurt to get to me? I cared about these people—*loved* one of these people. I couldn't let them come to more harm because of my stubbornness, not when I had the power to save them.

I inhaled deeply, then let it out slowly. "Okay, I'll come. Just let me call to get Roberto help."

"No. In fact, give me both of your phones." He waved the gun. "Toss them over on the ground. Hurry."

I glanced down at Roberto, who was watching me with a defiant expression. "It's okay," I told him. "He won't hurt me. Give him your phone."

"No, signorina—" Then he gasped and squeezed his eyes shut in pain.

I took my phone out of my pocket. "Yes, Roberto. Throw over your phone. It's okay. Someone will come along soon." The firemen, at the very least.

I threw my phone at my father. Reluctantly, Roberto did the same. "Stall him," Roberto said under his breath.

"Tell Luca where I went," I whispered back.

"Let's go," my father ordered as he slipped the two phones into his pants. "This way." He gestured toward the woods. I lifted my chin and forced my feet to move. It wasn't easy. I didn't want to leave Roberto, but I knew staying was certain death for my friend. I could only hope that someone would find him soon. Then paramedics could treat his wound and end his suffering.

"If Benetti comes for her, I will kill him," Flavio warned over his shoulder as we reached the tree line. "Tell him to stay the fuck away from my daughter."

Roberto said nothing and the forest quickly swallowed us up. It was quiet and shady, the canopy of trees concealing us from the world. "Go right," my father said behind me. "I have an ATV waiting not far from here."

My feet crunched on the leaves and sticks as I walked forward.

The trees grew denser, the air cool and musty, and a true bolt of fear went through me. Even if I managed to run away from him, I could get lost here. I wasn't the outdoorsy type. I could handle the restaurant like a champ, but my sense of direction was terrible and I had zero survival skills.

Thank goodness he wouldn't hurt me. At least, I didn't think he would.

I stepped over a rotted log. "What are you hoping to accomplish, Flavio?"

"You need someone to save you from yourself."

"Oh, and you're the best person to do that?" I made a scoffing noise in my throat. "Please. No wonder my mother wanted to keep you away from me."

"You think you know things, figlia, but you don't."

"Yeah, well, I want your promise that if I go with you that you won't hurt anyone, ever."

"I can't promise that."

"So, what? You are kidnapping me and never letting me go?"

"I'm not kidnapping you. I'm taking you until he leaves for Catanzaro."

"Are you listening to yourself? You can't keep me that long. I have a restaurant to run."

An ATV was waiting behind some long branches. Flavio moved the branches off and told me to get on. After I did, he threw his leg over and settled in front of me, then handed me a helmet. I put it on as the engine roared to life. Before I could brace myself, he revved and the wheels jolted forward. I cursed, grabbed his shoulders, and held on.

We drove for what felt like forever, through the brush and trees, swerving and dodging as we bounced along. I was worried about Roberto. I hoped he didn't suffer any permanent damage after that gunshot.

And Luca. I needed to see him, make sure he was okay. Flavio said Luca wasn't hurt, but I didn't trust my father. He might be lying to me.

I had to come up with a plan. As soon as Flavio had his say and let down his guard, I would disappear. Woods or not, I would get away and find someone to help me. No way was I staying with him until Luca went back to Italy, which could be weeks. Months. Who knew?

Finally, Flavio drove around the edge of an inlet and a small house came into view. Gray with only one story, the tiny building had a slip with a motor boat docked. There was nothing else around, no other boats or houses. No people.

Was this where he lived?

My question was soon answered when Flavio drove up behind the house and turned off the ATV. I didn't waste any time jumping to the ground and putting distance between us. Wrapping my arms around myself, I looked behind me and tried to memorize how we got here for when I made my escape.

"Don't bother," Flavio said. "I drove us around in circles."

"My sense of direction is amazing," I lied.

"Cazzata," he said and pocketed the ATV key. "You're like your mother. Can't navigate your way out of a box."

Unfortunately, it was true. But I wasn't sure how Flavio knew this. "Let's get this over with so I can return to town. Say whatever it is you need to say."

"Get inside, figlia."

I trudged up the back wooden stairs to the door and tried the knob. It was unlocked. I went in and expected to find the place empty.

John Natale was sitting at the kitchen table, eating.

I stopped, my hand still on the door as I stared at my former dish-washer. "John. What are you doing here?"

"Hi, Val."

My father nudged me into the house and I stumbled forward,

confused. "I don't understand." I shot my father a look. "Why is he here? How do you two even know each other?"

"Prison," my father said as he closed the door and locked it.

I blinked several times and looked at John. "So you were working for me and reporting back to my father?"

"I'm sorry, Val." John had the grace to appear sheepish. He stood and took his now empty plate to the sink. "I'll give you two some time alone."

What the fuck? My father had sent John to the trattoria as a spy? I rounded on Flavio in disbelief. "Why? Please, help me understand."

"Sit down, per favore. Sit down and I will explain everything."

Chapter Twenty-Eight

Luca

Firemen raced all over the estate like ants.

I stood in the street, leaning against a car and watching, all while contemplating the ways I planned to hurt Flavio Segreto when I found him. No one had been harmed in the fire, but I hated the idea of strangers in my personal space. Not that I left anything incriminating in the mansion for the firemen to find. That would have been incredibly stupid.

A man in a crisp blue uniform with the tag "chief" on it approached me. "You are very lucky, Mr. DiMarco."

"Am I?"

"Yes." He pushed his glasses further onto his nose. "You have minimal damage, mostly contained to the garage where the fire was started. There's some smoke damage on the ground floor of the house, though, so I would recommend leaving the windows open to air the place out."

"How was it started?"

"Rags with an accelerant in a bin. You're lucky none of the cars were parked inside. Otherwise, we might not be standing here talking to you."

Fucking Segreto. I was going to enjoy killing him.

"Grazie." I offered my hand for him to shake, which he took. "We appreciate you coming so quickly."

"It's our job. We're happy when the fires are this easy to contain. I'm going to recommend the Portofinos install a smart system throughout the property. The fire could've been detected earlier and saved you a lot of headache."

I thanked him again. "I'm going to have the trattoria send over some food to the station house later, as a way of showing my gratitude."

"Not necessary, but I'm sure they'd appreciate it, Mr. DiMarco. Thank you."

Slowly, the crew began leaving, and I made sure to thank each one and shake their hand. It was something we always did back home. A personal touch went a long way with people, something unmatched by texts and emails.

As the trucks rolled away, Aldo and my brothers circled around me. Even Rico, who I was still pissed at.

"Fucking crazy," Dante remarked. "The garage is a mess. It needs to be torn down and rebuilt."

"I'll speak to Portofino today," I said, rubbing my eyes. "I'll explain what happened and pay for the damage. How the fuck did Segreto get on and off the estate? What did the cameras see?"

"He snuck here last night when we were away. Came on a boat, docked down river and walked over. Then he set the fire on a timer so it would go off today. Guards didn't see or hear him."

"Why today?" Rico asked. "Why not burn it all down last night? And it was a nuisance fire, not a giant blaze meant to hurt anyone. It doesn't make sense."

A terrible feeling settled in my gut. "This was a distraction," I said, my heart beginning to pick up speed. I reached into my trouser pocket and pulled out my phone. "Call Roberto," I snapped at Sergio as I pressed the button to reach Valentina.

She'd better answer.

It went straight to voicemail. "Merda!" I tried to connect again.

When that failed I knew something was wrong. It could be nothing, but my intuition was screaming that a terrible thing had occurred. I rang her a third time and pinned Sergio with a harsh stare. "What did he say?"

Sergio shook his head. "He didn't pick up. Straight to voicemail."

"Call Giovanni. Call the trattoria. Find out if anyone has seen them." Valentina's phone went to voicemail again. "Cazzo!" Disconnecting, I left my brothers and hurried toward the car. "Aldo!"

"I'm here, Don Benetti," he said.

"The fob. I'm taking the Maserati."

"We are coming with you." Sergio jogged up alongside me. "You're not going alone with Segreto somewhere around. He's probably waiting for you to drive into town so he can ambush you."

I couldn't argue with that logic, but I wasn't slowing down. I would leave without them if they couldn't keep up. When we reached the car, Aldo unlocked it and slid into the driver's seat. Sergio got in the back with me, talking into the mobile at his ear. "Che cazzo? Hold on." He quickly put it on speaker. "Here, Luca. Listen. It's Giovanni."

"Don Benetti. The fire chief just called here. On the way back into town they found Roberto on the road. There was an accident and he has been shot in the leg."

"Valentina?" I croaked. "Was she with him?"

"According to Roberto, Valentina's father caused the car to crash by blowing out a tire. Then he took her away on an ATV."

All the air left my body in a rush. "Fuck!" I punched the back of the leather seat three times, my skin stretched tight with fear and anger. Segreto had Valentina. Had taken her away on an ATV. I was going to chop that motherfucker into tiny pieces when I found him. I punched the seat again.

"Calm down," my brother said under his breath. "Do not lose your shit. We need to find her."

"How badly is Roberto hurt?" I asked into the phone.

"Bullet went through his calf. He'll be fine according to the medics."

"Any other details? Anything else that could help us find her?"

"Her father took both of their phones. Said he would kill you if you tried to follow them."

I wasn't afraid of Flavio Segreto. The man was a coward, hiding out and sneaking around. I was not a coward; I dealt with my problems directly. When I killed someone, they knew exactly who was responsible before they took their last breath. And my face would be the last thing Segreto saw before he died.

"Anything else?" Sergio asked Giovanni.

"She reassured Roberto that her father wouldn't hurt her. Then they drove off into the woods."

I told Giovanni to deliver food to the firemen today, then we rang off. Sergio and I locked gazes. I saw the determination in his eyes, the blaze of fury and retribution, and no doubt he saw the same in mine. No one fucked with Benettis and lived.

"Find the crash site and stop," I said. "We'll get out there and start searching."

"They could be anywhere, Luca." Sergio gestured to the woods around us. "And Segreto knows how to hide."

The boat was the key. I knew it in my bones. Segreto had traveled by boat to my estate to start the fire, and it reasoned he was living either on the river or near an inlet. "He's near the water."

Sergio made a dismissive noise. "Everyone is near the water. Have you seen the length of the river? It's as bad as the woods."

"Look." Aldo pointed as we turned a corner. "There's the car."

A lone sedan had skidded into the grass, its two flat front tires lurching awkwardly. My stomach dropped. She must have been terrified. Two police cars were parked nearby, and a man was writing notes by the empty car.

"Pull over," I said. "Let's talk to them and then we'll begin searching."

Once we stopped, I walked toward the officers. Another car with my other brothers and two guards followed, and they parked behind Aldo. When I approached the officers I gave them a humble, non-threatening smile while letting my accent thicken. "Ciao, officers. Come stai?" I offered my hand, which they all accepted. "Do we know what happened here?"

An older officer shook his head and rested his hands on his utility belt. "Some nut put spikes in the middle of the road. Caused that car there to skid to a stop."

"That is terrible," I said sympathetically. "And the people inside the car?"

"We can't share those details yet," the younger officer said. "We're still looking for the suspect."

"I see. May I speak to the other officer, the one making notes? I live nearby and perhaps can offer some insight."

They looked skeptical, but they shrugged. "Go ahead. I think Detective Antonelli is almost finished."

I thanked them, then told my brother to wait. There was no need for both of us to approach the detective and scare him off.

"Signore," I said. "May I have a word?"

He looked up from his notebook, his eyes weary with a dash of suspicion. "Who are you?"

"I'm a man who will be very, very grateful for any information you can give me regarding what happened here."

"Listen, I don't have time for this. I need to get back—"

"You aren't listening." I moved closer and lowered my voice. "My name is Luca DiMarco and trust me, I am someone you should like to have on your side, detective. I'm very generous to those who help me."

He rose to his full height, and I was surprised to learn he was as tall as me. Young, in good shape, with a short dark beard covering his face. Definitely of Italian descent. "Are you bribing me?"

I shook my head and thrust my hands into pockets, trying to appear unthreatening. "I'm not that stupid. I am offering a favor, however. Any time you need it in the future. As I said, I'm resourceful in ways that are maybe considered old school in this country. But I know how to get things done. Capisce?"

"Ah." He sized me up. "You're the one I keep hearing about. The Italian businessman who rented the Portofino place. You're dating Val Montella."

I dipped my chin in confirmation. "You have an advantage, Detective Antonelli, as I've not heard of you before."

"I can't talk about an active investigation, Mr. DiMarco."

"Detective, Valentina was in this car when it crashed. Her father is responsible. And he drove away with her on an ATV. I need your help in finding her."

"That's the same story the other man in the car, the one who was shot, told us. It sounded pretty far-fetched, though, and there isn't any evidence of an ATV."

"His name is Flavio Segreto and he is a danger to her. The ATV was hidden in the woods. I believe he took her somewhere near the river or an inlet of some kind."

Staring at the ground, he toed a rock with his shoe. "A favor, you said?"

"Yes."

Antonelli pulled out his mobile and unlocked it. "I know of a few inlets that are fairly remote. We used to fish out here a lot as kids." He loaded a map and zoomed in with his fingers. "This is where we are," he said, showing me his screen. "Out here—" he slid over to the west and south "—there are three or four inlets."

"Houses?"

"Yes, on a few of them."

He gave me the coordinates and I entered them into my phone. "Grazie, detective." I put a hand on my heart. "I owe you a favor. *Sul mio onore.*"

"I'm coming with you." Antonelli closed his notebook and unclipped his sunglasses from his shirtfront. "We can look together."

"No offense, detective, but this is best handled by me and my brothers."

His lips thinned unhappily. "No offense, Mr. DiMarco, but I insist. We don't allow vigilante justice here. You aren't in Italy any longer."

I took offense to that.

"With all due respect, detective, no one will prevent me from doing what needs to be done when I find Segreto."

He let out a big sigh and stared off into the woods. "Shit. I really don't need this hassle today."

I lifted my palms out and put a few steps between us. "Let's pretend we never spoke."

"How about I give you a thirty-minute head start?"

I could live with that. I held out my hand again and we shook. When I turned to go, he said, "I'm holding you to that favor, Mr. DiMarco."

I nodded once then strode back to where my brothers were huddled together, far away from the police officers. Distrust of government authority ran deep in the Benettis, regardless of the country we found ourselves in.

"What did you learn?" Dante asked.

"He told me of a few remote inlets. I have the coordinates. Let's go."

"How are we getting there? By car?"

"On foot. It's not far and he won't hear us coming."

* * *

Valentina

I dropped into a chair at the kitchen table, my head reeling. The fire, the car accident, Flavio shooting Roberto . . . and now my former dishwasher conspiring with my father? My god. I wasn't sure if I could handle anything else.

Flavio set a glass of water on the table for me, then lowered himself into the chair opposite and drummed his fingers on the wood. I ignored the water. I didn't want one thing from this man other than an explanation. "Let's hear it. Then I need to get back and make sure Roberto and Luca are okay."

The lines around his eyes deepened, like he was irritated, but he didn't argue. "I grew up in a small town in Southern Italy—"

"I don't have time for your life story. Skip ahead already."

"Valentina." He slapped his palm on the table. "You will listen. It is relevant to why I am here."

I folded my arms and cocked my head, saying nothing. Flavio took this as his opportunity to continue. "Where I come from, figlia, there are no jobs. No opportunities for young men. Everyone is broke and the 'Ndrangheta? They suck you in as babies. I never had a hope of another life. And what did I care? I was able to feed my mother, my sisters. My father was dead and if joining the 'ndrina saved my sisters from being sold off to predatory men, I would gladly do it." He inhaled then let it out. "I was good at being a soldato, too. Kept my head down, did what was asked of me. Soon I rose higher and higher, until I was part of the Padrino, the five men who reported directly to the capobastone."

Was he trying to justify being in the mafia? Or impress me with his rank? I didn't care. I didn't want to know anything about him or his motivations. "Good for you," I said sarcastically.

"Then I met your mother." He paused and stared down at the tabletop for a moment before meeting my gaze again. His expression was sad, a strange light in his eyes reminiscent of bitter and happy memories. "She was . . . Well, you know. Abby was the prettiest, most beautiful woman I had seen. I was struck from the first second I saw her. Like Cupid's arrow, no? Smart, too. We met in the bar of a restaurant when she was out with friends. I worshipped at her feet like she was Mary and I was a sinner begging for salvation. Did I lie about my vocation? Of course I did. I couldn't tell this woman I was a killer, a demon among angels. I was stupid and selfish."

We could definitely agree on that.

"But I loved her," he continued, placing his hand on his chest. "If you believe nothing else, please figlia, believe this. Your mother was the other half of my soul, the pure half."

"So why didn't you stay with her? Why did you let her go?"

"Men in the 'ndrina don't leave. There isn't a way to get out other than death. Women join our world, not the other way around, and your mother wanted nothing to do with that life. It wasn't like I didn't try. Talked until I was out of breath, but Abby wouldn't bend. I had to let her go."

This matched with everything I knew about my mother. "She said to stay away from men who want to control me."

Surprisingly, this made him laugh. His weathered face transformed to make him look younger, more carefree. "I never wanted to control her. She was too tough for that."

My chest ached, the ever-present grief rising up to remind me that she was really gone. But even in this, I didn't want to share her memory with my father. He didn't deserve her. I lifted my chin, ready to move this along. "So you let her go and found out thirteen years later that I existed."

"I was sent to prison shortly after Abby left. I was young, angry that I'd lost her, and I did something stupid. For four years I couldn't get to her even if I had wanted to."

"What about when you were released?"

He tapped his fingers on the tabletop and stared through the window. "Men like me, we are a cancer, a poison to the decent and vulnerable. She was innocent. Why would I drag her down into the pits of Hell with me?"

Hard to argue with that. "How did you find out about me?"

"I came to Canada on business and had a moment of weakness. I decided to check up on her. I couldn't stop wondering about Abby, even all those years later. I never planned on speaking to her."

"But then you learned about me."

"I knew the instant I saw you. Your eyes are your mother's, but your nose and chin are from my side. You look like my mother."

A warmth spread through my chest, unbidden and surprising. "Is she still alive?"

"No, figlia mia. She died before I met your mother."

I tried not to be disappointed, but it was hard. This man was my only family—and he was a monster. "Okay, keep going. Let's finish this."

"I approached your mother and you might guess how such a conversation went. When I returned home I decided to get out. I didn't ask permission from the capo because I wouldn't receive it. So I went dark. To find me, they fabricated lies to turn everyone against me. Said I was a traitor. But it wasn't true. It took some time, but I finally settled here."

My jaw fell open. "You've been hiding in New York for *seven* years?"

"Five, but yes."

I couldn't wrap my head around it. "What the fuck? Did she know?"

He folded his hands, then placed them on the table. Then folded them again. It was clear he was stalling.

I sucked in a sharp breath, realization dawning. "She knew. You two were talking."

He dipped his chin in acknowledgment, but didn't meet my eyes. It was a red flag. My voice rose dramatically. "And more?"

"And more."

Holy shit. I felt . . . stunned. And betrayed. My parents had been sleeping together while I was at school. I couldn't believe it. Why didn't she tell me? How had I never noticed?

"We could not tell you," he said. "It was too dangerous. If I resurfaced, then you both were at risk."

"So you made an exception for her, but not for your daughter. Great. Thanks for clearing that up."

"There is no need for sarcasm, figlia. Your mother was an adult, you were not. There is a difference."

"Right. The difference is I needed a father. I needed help when she—"

I couldn't say it.

He drew in a shaky breath. "Perdonami, Val. But your mother insisted. She did not want you involved in my world. I had to respect her wishes."

"So you just stood around and watched her *die?*"

"No. She allowed me to help in the ways I could after she grew sick. Little things. Groceries, repairs. Laundry. You were at school, and this was important to her. She did not want you giving up your future to take care of her."

I thought back to that chaotic time. I'd spent so much of it scrambling between her, the trattoria and school. "She told me the neighbors were helping out."

"Sì." He pointed to his chest. "I was the neighbors. I fixed the kitchen sink. I made sure the fridge had food. I helped her shower."

It was too much. I pushed out of my chair and began walking around the kitchen. I gave the neighbors free food for months in gratitude. They must've been so confused.

But this was bigger than free meals. My head spun with what this meant. "You really loved her."

"With all my heart."

"Shit." I could feel my eyes welling, the sting of oncoming tears. "I want to hate you so badly right now."

"I know I have not been a good father to you. I never wanted you to be tainted by my past. Worse, I didn't want you to lose another parent. I thought it was better if I stayed away in case Don Rossi found me."

"Don Rossi?"

He waved his hand. "It's not worth explaining. But they can't allow me to live, Val. I know too much, especially now."

"It's been a long time. Why would they even care?"

"These men, they never forget. Now that they know where I am, I will need to go somewhere else to hide. I stayed here only to watch over you the past few years. I wanted to keep you away from men like Benetti."

I leaned against the kitchen counter and folded my arms. "He's not a terrible person. He cares about me."

"Dai, figlia mia. He is a violent monster, a cruel man. He only cares about himself, his family. And he will destroy your life, if you let him."

"You're wrong. He's sweet and very gentle with me."

"That is how they seem at first. Once you give in, he will do whatever he wants to you. He's already moved you in! You give these men an opening and—"

A floorboard creaked. My father fell silent, his body going rigid.

A half-second later, Luca walked into the kitchen. In his hand was a gun pointed at my father.

Luca was here. And he looked *terrifying*. Eyes hard, muscles taut. His face was etched in granite as menace leached from every pore. This was the mob boss, the killer. The man he hid underneath the naughty words and orgasms. I hardly recognized him, even though those hickeys were definitely mine.

How on earth did he find us?

Luca didn't spare me a glance. He kept his attention entirely on Flavio as he snarled something in Italian. My father didn't respond, which seemed to make Luca even *angrier*. He said more that I didn't understand, so I snapped, "English, Luca. I want to know what you're saying."

"I am saying," Luca responded, "that he needs to come with me and get away from you."

Flavio snorted derisively. "Tell her what you really said, Benetti.

Tell her how you promised to slice me open and remove my organs in punishment for kidnapping her."

I flinched. Had Luca really said that? "Gross and unnecessary, Luca."

"Yet this is the man you've chosen to align yourself with," my father reminded me. "Do you now see what I mean, figlia?"

"Shut your mouth." Luca edged closer. "Or I will shoot you in the face."

I wasn't a huge fan of my father, but I wasn't about to let him get murdered, either. "No, you're not. Put the gun down, Luca. We're having a civil conversation."

"He is incapable of a civil conversation," Flavio said unhelpfully.

One of Luca's brothers appeared in the doorway. Sergio said, "I would shut my mouth, Segreto, if I were you. Luca has had a shitty day. We wouldn't want him to take it out on you."

"Luca, please." I walked over to him and placed my palm on his arm. The heat nearly scorched my skin, even through cloth, and the muscle was locked tight.

"Go with Sergio, Valentina," he said quietly, his gaze on Flavio. The two seemed engaged in a silent battle of wills.

"So you can kill my father? No, I won't do that."

"Now, Valentina."

"No way, Luca. I'm not leaving. Please, put the gun away and let's talk."

"There is nothing to discuss. He caused you to crash and kidnapped you. Shot Roberto. Set fire to my home. For those reasons and many more he will die today."

"The fire was small," Flavio said with a hand gesture. "And I shot this man in a place I knew would not cause lasting harm. It's nothing."

Was my father for real right now? Justifying arson and shooting a man in the leg was not helpful. Luca's right eye began twitching, so I hurried to say, "I'm fine, though. You don't need to kill anyone today."

His head turned slowly and Luca met my eyes for the first time since he'd arrived. I could see remnants of panic there, the worry he'd been carrying, the anger over what my father had done. I put my hand on his cheek. "I'm okay. Really. And you can't hurt him." He stared at me, unmoving. I wasn't sure if he was breathing. The coldness in his dark irises sent a shiver through me. "Luca, please."

Slowly, muscle by muscle, he relaxed. The gun lowered to his side and I could see some of the man I knew—the one who cuddled with me, who laughed with me—resurface. "Thank you, baby," I whispered.

"You are only delaying the inevitable, fiore mio."

We would see about that.

I grabbed Luca's free hand and shifted to face my father. "Are we done here? Because I need to go check on Roberto."

My father's glance dipped to where Luca and I held hands and his upper lip curled into a sneer. "Have you asked him, figlia? Have you asked him about what I told you?"

"About your crazy ramblings in the alley? No, I haven't. And we're leaving."

"Ask him!" My father's voice rose. "Ask him why he came to New York. Ask him why he's so focused on you."

I felt Luca's body jolt next to mine, but I ignored it. "You're talking about conspiracy theories, Flavio. Save it for trolling scientists on social media, okay?"

"He knows it," my father said, indicating Luca. "Look at his face. The guilt is written all over it. You think he cares for you, maybe even loves you, but he's here for me and you are collateral damage, Valentina."

The words, coming from a man whose love I'd craved all these years, hurt more than I expected. "Because no one could really want me for me, right?"

"No!" Flavio shot to his feet, his weathered face twisting with impatience. "Per favore, figlia. I'm not letting you leave until you ask the questions. Because ignorance hurts you most of all."

Suddenly, it dawned on me that Luca hadn't said anything. His silence was weird, considering the man had an opinion on every situation. Why wasn't he telling Flavio to shut up? Or denying the claims as untrue?

"Fine." Dropping Luca's hand, I angled toward him. "Why New York? Why me? Was it only about my father?"

Chapter Twenty-Nine

Luca

I should lie.

She was asking questions I didn't wish to answer and the words of denial burned my tongue. I couldn't look at her. I focused on Segreto, promising retribution with every breath.

"He can't even say it," Segreto said, his mouth curving into a satisfied smile. "He knows and would rather lie to you, figlia."

"Fuck. Off," I growled. I wished we could have this conversation privately, in my own language, because I had all the words needed to threaten Segreto into silence.

"Luca, give me a straight answer." Valentina tugged on my arm. "Just shut him up by telling the truth."

"She will find out regardless," Segreto said to me. "Do you honestly think you can keep it a secret forever?"

Maybe not, but I'd hoped to keep Valentina ignorant of everything happening with Rossi and Palmieri. "You know nothing, old man."

"I know the don of a powerful family does not come across the ocean, put himself and his family at risk, for a simple reason. I know the 'Ndrangheta wants me dead and they have tasked you to bring me back. So why did you agree, Don Benetti?"

I didn't owe him explanations. My reasons were my own. But was Segreto trying to convince me he was blameless? "You killed Palmieri's daughter two years ago. Did you believe this would go unpunished? That he wouldn't seek retribution? If so, then you are a fool."

Segreto froze, his mouth parting slightly. I could see him thinking, but Valentina jumped into the silence. "You killed someone's daughter? That's terrible. How could you? Especially when you have a daughter of your own!"

Segreto still hadn't moved. "When did this supposed murder take place?"

"Two years ago."

"When my mom was *dying?*" Valentina asked her father. "You said you were here, taking care of her."

"I swear that I haven't left New York since I arrived, figlia mia. And I wouldn't have left your mother's side for anything in the world during her last months on earth."

"Look, someone is lying." Her head swiveled between the two of us. "Who is this Palmieri person and what does he have to do with you, Luca?"

It was Segreto who answered. "He's one of the top officers at the Guardia di Finanza. They oversee financial crimes in Italia, including policing the 'Ndrangheta and Cosa Nostra."

"Wait. Luca, are you in trouble?" she asked. "Is this about, like, money laundering?"

"Amore, why don't you go with my brother and I'll explain later? I need to speak to your father alone."

She took a step back, putting distance between us. "I want to hear whatever it is you need to discuss. Because it sounds like it involves me."

I didn't want to do this. I much preferred speaking to Segreto alone.

Looking over my shoulder, I tiled my chin at my brother. He immediately stepped forward. "Val, why don't you come with me back to the mansion."

Segreto was on his feet, his gun pointed at me. "Touch her and Benetti dies."

Valentina dragged her hands through her hair. "Everyone calm down! Luca, I want to know why you came to New York."

There was no avoiding it now. I went to the table and sat down across from Segreto. Ignoring Valentina for now, I said to the other man, "Rossi approached me. He said Palmieri learned you were responsible for the car bombing that claimed the life of his daughter. He wanted you found and brought back."

Segreto put his hand on his heart and began talking in our language. "In the silence of the night, under the light of the stars and under the splendor of the moon, I swear on my life. On our holy chain, on the holy society from which we all came, I did not kill that man's daughter."

It was a serious promise using parts of the oath we recited when inducted.

I believed him.

"What are you saying?" Valentina asked, her voice rising. "Speak in English, please."

I said to Segreto, "Rossi told me my cousin Niccolò had been arrested and Palmieri was willing to trade him for you. Once here, however, I suspected Niccolò wasn't in custody. And if that wasn't true, then how could I believe anything I'd been told?"

"Rossi is a snake," Segreto said. "He can't let me live because I know who was really stealing money from the other 'ndrine."

I rested my pistol on the table. "Are you saying Rossi was stealing from the other families?"

"Yes. Missing shipments, skimming payouts. Rossi has another

290

family in Longobardi. He needed more money for the kids' private school, capisce?"

"How did you discover this?"

Segreto waved his free hand. "I was the underboss. I used to handle the books. It wasn't hard to get answers, once I noticed things weren't adding up. But I kept quiet about it until . . . "

"Until you found out about your daughter and wanted to leave."

"I thought he would let me go."

"You tried to blackmail him."

He nodded once in confirmation and Valentina huffed. "That was incredibly risky. Why not just disappear?"

"Because this life never lets go, figlia mia." He stared at her for a long beat. "Never forget that."

"Wait." Confusion marred the perfectly smooth skin of her forehead. "Luca, you said you had to bring my father to Rossi. But how did you know Flavio was here when no one else did?"

This was the part I dreaded. Once I said it, there was no going back. "I didn't know he was here." I inhaled and let it out slowly. "I knew *you* were here."

"I don't understand. You were watching me in the hopes that Flavio was in the area?"

"Not at first."

"Figlia," Segreto snapped unkindly. "He was planning on using you. He was going to take you back to Italia to lure me out of hiding."

Valentina paused and I could see her brain working. Finally, her dark eyes studied my face. "Wait, is my father telling the truth?"

When I remained silent, her face dropped as her body recoiled. "You . . . You came here to kidnap me. This was about finding my father the entire time." Her hand shot out and she braced herself on the counter, shoulders hunching as if she were in pain. "Oh, my god. This wasn't real. It was exactly like he said."

I didn't know what she meant, but I could guess it was something Segreto said to her. "Valentina—"

"Oh, my god, Luca. You were going to *kidnap* me! What the actual fuck?" She stared at me like I was a monster, a bogeyman under her bed. "You're an asshole. You made me think . . . and then we . . . Oh, my god. I'm the business you came to New York for. What a fucking idiot I am!"

"Stop it," I barked. "And let me explain."

"What was going to happen once you took me back to Italy? Were you going to let the police keep me locked up until Flavio arrived?"

"They wouldn't have locked you up."

"But they would've kept me somewhere. My god, I am stupid."

"Fiore mio—"

"Do *not* call me that!"

"You need to calm down and hear me out."

"Fuck off! Do not tell me to calm down like I don't have a perfectly good reason for freaking out right now."

This was enough. I needed to get her alone where we could talk privately.

I started to rise, but found Segreto's pistol aimed at me once more. "Don't even think about it," he said in our language. "I will slice your balls off and force them down your throat."

"Get out of my way, old man, or I'm taking you out."

"Give me the key to the ATV," Valentina called. "Then you two can beat each other to death."

"Fratello," I said, knowing my brother would understand. I couldn't let Valentina leave without me.

"He touches her, you die," Segreto said softly, then he tossed a key to Valentina. "Do you know how to drive it?"

"Are you kidding? All the guys out here have them. I learned how in middle school."

"Do not leave," I said. "Per favore, amore. You must let me explain."

"There is no explanation for this." She grabbed the knob on the back door. "Other than I was a fool to believe a single word you said."

292

"I never lied to you."

Pulling on the door, she threw it wide open. "Sure, Mr. DiMarco. Keep telling yourself that." She paused and closed her eyes, chest heaving. I thought she might be willing to hear me out when she said, "Do not kill my father, Luca. Do not hurt him, either. If you have any shred of decency, any respect for me at all, you will not harm him. Give me your word on whatever honor you have left."

My muscles twitched with the violence lurking just under the surface of my skin. I wanted to make Segreto pay for ever involving himself in my relationship with Valentina. Now she hated me, and it was unclear whether I could ever gain her forgiveness.

He deserved to suffer for this.

"Valentina," I said, putting all my displeasure into the single word.

"No, don't *Valentina* me. Promise you won't hurt him. He said he didn't kill this man's daughter. That should be enough for you. The rest doesn't matter."

The rest? Did she mean the two of us? "If I agree, then you must listen to my explanation."

"Is that your promise?"

I ground my back teeth together and spat, "Yes, I promise not to hurt him if you hear me out."

"Okay, then. I'll listen to your explanation." She gave a bitter laugh. "Send me a text message and I promise to read it."

Before I could comment, she disappeared out the door, making sure to slam it behind her. Seconds later, the ATV roared to life. She gave it gas and we heard the whine of the engine as she rolled away.

Segreto took a few steps back but kept the gun on me. "She deserved to know."

I put my hands on my hips and pinned Valentina's father with a hard stare. "You know I care for her, yet you poisoned her against me. I should kill you for it."

"But you're a man of your word," he said. "So you won't. At least one of us has her best interests in mind."

293

"I have her best interests in mind. It's why I didn't kidnap her, why I've been helping the restaurant. I would do anything for your fucking daughter!"

Segreto lowered his gun slowly. "Which is why you're going to give her up. She deserves better than a life of prison and blood."

Chapter Thirty

Valentina

I found Maggie in the main tasting room.

In search of solitude, I fled to the Fiorentino Winery yesterday after leaving the tiny lake house. I knew Luca would approach me at the trattoria or my house—and I certainly wasn't returning to the mansion. Maggie had taken me in, no questions asked.

Women were the fucking best.

"There you are!" My friend waved from where she was standing with three men at a round table.

They all looked over at me, so I forced a smile. No doubt it was as brittle as my insides, cold and without feeling. As I drew closer, I saw they were tasting wine.

I reached for an empty glass and the open bottle. "Exactly what I needed. Thanks for breakfast, Mags."

She put a hand on the bottle, stopping me. "Let's start with coffee instead, okay? Adam, will you grab Val a cup of something strong and black?"

"Sure." Adam was a guy we went to high school with, and he'd been working at the winery for a few years. He walked toward the bar while Maggie asked the other men to give us a minute.

When we were alone, she said, "I know you're heartbroken, but let's wait until five o'clock before we start drinking."

"How about noon?"

My friend didn't laugh. "Val, he's not worth it. No man is worth it. But especially not a criminal who lies to you and wants to turn you over to the Italian police!"

I'd confessed everything to her yesterday in a blubbering mess as I demolished a box of tissues. "I know. I just . . . I need this feeling to go away." I rubbed my chest, which felt hollow and sore. "I'm so tired of being sad, Mags."

Maggie's expression softened as she squeezed my arm. "I know, babe. This is a lot on top of the grief you've been dealing with the past few years. It hardly seems fair. Which is why I'm going to kick that Italian in the nuts if I ever see him again."

"I'd like to see you do that, actually."

"Has he tried to contact you yet?"

"I don't know. I still haven't turned my phone back on."

Yesterday I used Maggie's phone to check in on Roberto's condition as well as to touch base with Giovanni. Roberto assured me that he was fine, but I insisted he take a few days off to rest. Giovanni seemed to have the trattoria well in hand and he told me not to come in last night. I decided that one evening off wouldn't hurt anything.

Two mugs of coffee arrived, one for me and one for Mags. Hers was light with cream, exactly as she preferred. We thanked Adam and he left the tasting room.

"He knows how you like your coffee," I said as I lifted the mug to my lips. "Interesting."

"Shut up." Maggie's lips curled like she was fighting a smile. "He's my employee."

"Which means you've thought about it." I sipped my coffee and the almond liqueur hit me immediately. God bless Adam. He'd spiked my coffee. "This is the best coffee I've ever had. I think you should marry him."

Her brow wrinkled as her eyes narrowed. "Don't be weird. And why are we talking about me? I want to talk about *you*."

"There's not much to say. We're done."

"Do you think he'll go back now?"

"I assume so. There's nothing keeping him here. My father didn't kill that girl and I'm certainly not getting on a plane bound for Italy. Luca can deal with his own problems from now on."

"Oh, shit." Maggie's eyes were focused on something behind me. "Don't look now, but here comes your wanna-be kidnapper."

Fuck.

My entire body clenched, muscles tightening in shock. "Do *not* leave me alone with him."

"Don't worry, girl, I'm one step ahead of you." Maggie darted around the table and put her back to mine, her front facing Luca. "We're closed, sir."

I could see his reflection in the glass, how he stopped halfway across the floor and slipped his hands in his pockets. "Signorina Fiorentino. I would like a moment with Valentina, per favore."

"There's no Valentina here."

I heard Luca sigh. "I have no time for games, signorina."

"This is my girlfriend," Maggie tried. "And she's not out, so if you don't mind? Skedaddle."

"Valentina, amore," he said in his deep, accented voice that I loved so much. "I need to speak with you."

There was no use dragging this out. I just needed him to go away. "I told you to text me."

"I tried, but your phone is off."

Which meant he'd tried calling. Not one to follow directions, this man.

I make the rules, Valentina.

Well, not anymore. Now I made the rules.

Spinning, I met his gaze over Maggie's shoulder. "You have five minutes, Luca."

"Alone."

"No way. Maggie stays."

A muscle jumped in his jaw. "You want her to overhear such a private conversation?"

"How about I stand over by the bar?" Facing me, Maggie pointed to where Adam was polishing glasses. "And I'll set a timer."

I nodded once. "Thanks, Mags."

Before she walked away, she smiled sweetly at Luca. "If you hurt her any more, Benetti, I'm going to kick your balls into your throat."

He didn't respond, his expression unreadable as she left us. I returned my attention toward the windows, giving him my back, but I could see as he approached me. He strode to the opposite side of the small table and stood there, silent. The hickeys on his neck mocked me, mottled bruises left by an innocent girl who thought she'd found a good man.

Was it only yesterday when I thought I might be in love with him? God, I was a fool. He'd deceived me from the moment we met.

"Clock's ticking," I said and sipped more coffee. "Better hurry."

He folded his hands on the table, his cufflinks tapping lightly on the wood. "If I wanted to kidnap you and take you to my country, it would've happened already. I changed my mind weeks ago."

"How fortunate for me," I drawled, the sarcasm thick.

"I know you are angry I lied to you, but—"

"There is no *but*, Luca. You were using me the entire time. If my father hadn't been nearby, you would've kidnapped me and given me over to the Italian government like some pawn!"

"You're wrong. I wasn't going to use you. In fact, I was doing everything in my power to prevent it. I've been dragging my feet since the night we met, looking for other solutions."

"Like what?"

"Like enlisting D'Agostino's help to find my missing cousin."

That business dinner in New York. "And did you find him?"

"No, not yet. But Valentina, I want to take you to Catanzaro, not for anything to do with Rossi or Palmieri. I want you to come for me. I want you to live with me and—"

I let out an incredulous bark of laughter. "You've got to be joking! Now you're trying to get me there by convincing me you care about me? Jesus, Luca. You are unbelievable."

"I do care about you." His voice was low and angry. "Have you not been paying attention? I would do anything for you, including risk my family, my empire. I should've returned by now, except I've been staying here. With you."

I shoved aside any tenderness his words elicited inside me. This man was a liar, through and through. Calmly, I sipped more coffee. "Well, I'm not going with you to Italy, so . . . " I lifted my shoulders in what I hoped was a casual shrug.

"Why not?"

"First, I don't believe you aren't still trying to use me as a bargaining chip. Second, I have a life here. A restaurant, friends. My mom's house. You're asking me to sign up for blood and crime in a country I've never visited."

"I'm asking you to sign up for only me. I swear to protect you from the blood and crime."

"This is a pointless discussion because I'm not going anywhere with you. I'll never believe another word that comes out of your mouth."

"Valentina." He rubbed his eyes with his fingers, then dropped his hands on the table again. "I was trying to find your father to make all of this go away. But I can't stay here. I must return home and deal with Rossi. If I don't do it soon, he will try to kill me—or your father. Maybe both."

"Five minutes!" Maggie called from the bar.

He dragged a hand through his hair, messing the thick strands. "Don't do this. I am crazy about you. I would rather cut off my own arm than hurt you. Te lo prometto, bella."

Maybe it was true. Maybe he wasn't lying *this time.*

But I couldn't risk my entire life on a maybe.

And he didn't love me—he just didn't want to lose me.

As I hesitated, he moved in, shifting closer until we were nearly touching. "When I learned that your father took you I nearly lost it. I've never been so scared in all my life. I promised a favor to an American police detective in exchange for information, for fuck's sake. I would have done anything to find you." He exhaled and dragged his knuckles along my cheek. His gentle touch sent a flight of butterflies loose in my chest. Softly, he said, "I need you, amore. I am nothing without you."

"Hands off!" Maggie yelled from across the room, and her sobering voice shook off whatever spell he was weaving on my heart and mind.

Clarity returned and I took a step back. "My answer is no. And we're done here."

Luca's hand fell to the wooden tabletop. "I'm leaving tonight. I hope you change your mind. But if you don't, you are always welcome in Catanzaro—even if it takes months. In the meantime, I'm leaving Gabriele here to look after you."

"You don't need to do that. I don't want your son spying on me for you."

"He is not a spy. He will keep you safe so that I don't worry. You hold my heart and my soul, fiore mio. Per sempre."

Forever.

When I didn't respond he rapped his knuckles twice on the table, like an exclamation point to his words. I watched him walk toward the exit in the reflection, his proud shoulders shifting with every step. My chest ached as anger and hurt and longing all battled inside me.

But I knew with a deep-down certainty I was doing the right thing. I had to distance myself from whatever mess my father and Luca were involved in. Their problems were not my problems. I had enough to deal with on my own.

And I would never forgive Luca for lying to me—no matter how much I missed him.

An arm wrapped around my shoulders. "I'm proud of you," Maggie said, resting her head against mine. "For a minute there I thought you were going to cave."

"Me too," I said shakily, my eyes welling up again. God, I was so tired of crying.

"Aw, don't cry, babe. We'll get through this, exactly like we've been doing for the last few years."

"He wanted me to come live with him in Italy."

She snorted and tightened her hold on me. "I guess we should be grateful he asked instead of kidnapping you."

I let out a wobbly laugh. "Yeah, I guess. Wow, my life is fucked up."

"No, *his* life is fucked up. He just dragged you into it for a few weeks. But now you've escaped, thank god. You dodged a bullet, Val. Maybe literally, considering his line of work."

I put my arm around her and we stared out at the vineyard stretching out across the landscape. "Thanks for everything, Mags. I don't know what I'd do without you."

"Probably drink really shitty wine and have a lot less fun."

"Can I hang out here for a few more hours?"

"Girl, we are day drinking starting at noon. You're not going anywhere."

Luca

A man like me was not inclined to hope. I dealt in cold, hard realities within a world that rewarded neither fairness nor forgiveness. I knew the cruelties man had to offer, as I was often the one doling them out. And I knew my end would not be gentle or banal. Such was the life I had chosen.

And yet, I'd hoped.

Waiting, I held onto her like a talisman, a beacon of light in my dreary and lonely existence. Praying she would arrive, forgive me, and stand proudly by my side.

I'm not going anywhere with you. I'll never believe another word that comes out of your mouth.

At least I had tried. No woman had received such declarations from me before, my heart and soul bared so vulnerably. Yet it hadn't worked. She wasn't coming.

I stared out the tiny window into the darkness, failure bitter on my tongue.

My mobile rang and my heart leapt into my throat. I looked at the screen. Gabriele. "Pronto."

"She's not coming."

My shoulders deflated, hope popping like a balloon. "Thank you for letting me know. We'll speak later—"

"Wait, Papà. Before you ring off, I want to tell you something."

"What is it, figlio mio?"

"I've been listening and researching. I think there's true opportunity here. No one is leading, and D'Agostino's brother is up in Toronto. He could be a partner. You should consider staying."

"And here I thought you were only tending bar."

"What can I say? People like to talk to me. You would not believe the things I learned working at the trattoria. Allora, this could be a way to expand."

I liked that he was thinking about the family. It showed maturity and foresight. "This is surprising, but a nice surprise. I'm impressed, Gabriele."

"You are? Does this mean you'll do it?"

Expanding into New York sounded exhausting, especially when there was much work to be done back home. But I didn't want to crush his confidence. "I'll consider it. Okay?"

"Grazie, Papà. A presto."

Putting down my phone, I pressed a button to connect me to the cockpit. "Andiamo, per favore."

The wheels began turning and I heard Dante mutter in the back, "Thank Christ."

My stomach cramped when we lifted off the ground, proof that it was truly over. I was leaving her behind, yet it felt like a piece of me was still there with her.

You're asking me to sign up for blood and crime . . .

Valentina's parting words raced through my mind. She was not wrong. I had no right to ask her to come with me, but I was a selfish man. I wasn't ready to let her go.

I poured another glass of whiskey and took a swallow.

My brother spoke quietly. "You should've kidnapped her and turned her over to the GDF."

"If you say it again, I will break your teeth."

Sergio sighed heavily. "We have bigger problems now. Your life is at risk. If Rossi doesn't decide to kill you, he will throw you to Palmieri."

"I'm not afraid of Rossi or Palmieri. I don't believe Niccolò gave the GDF any evidence against us."

"I hope you are right. I'm assuming you will go and visit Rossi right away."

"Seems foolish, if what Segreto said is true." And I was inclined to believe Valentina's father. "We need to prove that Rossi is the one who ordered the hit on Palmieri's daughter."

"Sure, sounds easy."

"Someone knows. Rossi is too stupid and lazy to plan a hit himself."

Sergio scrubbed his face with both hands. "What a fucking mess."

"A hit like that?" Aldo whistled from across the row. "Not many would accept the job. My guess is he would outsource it."

Sergio asked, "Russians? Serbians? Albanians?"

I nodded and reached for the half-empty glass of whiskey in front of me. "Seems likely." I took a sip, thinking as the liquor burned its way down to my stomach. "There is someone we can ask. Someone who might know."

Sergio helped himself to a glass of whiskey. "Who?"

"Remember Alessandro Ricci?"

"Of course," Sergio said.

Aldo let out a dismissive noise. "Ricci had a rule against taking out women and kids. It wasn't him."

I knew this. Almost everyone did. "I was thinking of his assistant, the one who handled all the jobs."

"Wasn't she former Russian intelligence?" Aldo asked.

"Yes, and if Rossi put the job out for hire, she would remember."

"Ah." Sergio put down his drink and took his mobile out of his pocket. When he unlocked it, I said, "Do you have her number?"

"No," Sergio answered. "To get to her, you need to go through Ricci. And you aren't getting to him without going through Giulio Ravazzani. And to get to Giulio Ravazzani . . . " He let that trail off.

"Fuck me." I finished the rest of my drink and set down the glass. We were lawless criminals, but we did have a code, one I tried to adhere by. "Ring him. Let's get this over with."

Sergio tapped on his phone quickly and handed it to me. As it rang, I stared at the sky surrounding the small plane.

"Pronto."

"It's Benetti," I told Marco Ravazzani. "Is he around?"

"Depends. We heard you were in New York."

I didn't respond. If Fausto Ravazzani's consiglieri thought I would explain myself to him, he was wrong. We were not equals, not even close.

Marco sighed. "Hold on."

The line quieted, no doubt muting his end as he checked with his cousin. But I knew Fausto would pick up, if only out of curiosity. It wasn't often we spoke.

"Benetti," a deep voice said. "This is unexpected."

"Ravazzani," I greeted. "Ciao, come stai? I hope you and the family are well."

"Everything is fine here. And you? How is the food in New York?"

"Improved, now that I brought a chef over." We both chuckled, then I got to the point. "I am calling because I need to speak with your son's ragazzo."

"Regarding?"

"It's not safe for me to say over the phone."

"I see. He is retired, capisce?"

"I'm aware," I said. "We are looking for information on something that occurred a few years ago. We hoped his assistant might remember."

"Ah. Does this have to do with why you were sent to New York?"

It was possible Ravazzani had learned of the GDF, Segreto, and Rossi. I saw no reason to lie. "Yes, it does."

"If I allow it," he said slowly, "and you solve this puzzle in which you've found yourself, you will not forget, capisce?"

Meaning I would owe him. "Of course."

"Va bene. I will have Alessio contact you shortly."

"Grazie. Give my best to your family."

I started to hang up, but he continued speaking. "You know, I went through a similar situation a few years ago with Mommo. But there is an African proverb, *When there is no enemy within, the enemies outside cannot hurt you.* Clean your house, Benetti." Then he disconnected.

So he had learned of Rossi and the GDF.

I blew out a breath and gave Sergio his mobile. "Ricci will be in touch soon."

"What else did he say?" my brother asked.

"That we have to kill Don Rossi."

"Minchia!" Sergio said at the same time Aldo muttered, "Mamma mia."

"He's right. I hoped to turn Palmieri and Rossi against one another, but that could take too long. Valentina is at risk every minute that Rossi lives because he won't hesitate to use her to get to Segreto."

"But killing the head of the region . . . Cristo, Luca." Sergio rubbed his jaw. "The other families could turn against us."

"Ravazzani managed it and survived. Grew stronger, even."

"You're missing one problem," Aldo said. "As your brother said, your life is at risk. When Rossi learns you've returned alone, he can't allow you to survive, let alone get close enough to kill him."

"And we have to clear this with the other families first," Sergio added. "You can't kill him without approval."

"I'm not leaving Valentina at risk while holding meetings with the other 'ndrine. We need to get creative." I angled out of my seat until I could see the back of the plane. "*Fratelli!*"

"What do we need them for?" Sergio asked.

"Because they see things differently than we do. We don't have much time before we land and I want to be ready the moment we touch down."

Chapter Thirty-One

Luca

I never thought I would walk in voluntarily.

Yet I was doing precisely that on a clear day, my hands and feet unrestrained as the sun beat down on my skin. There was every chance I would never feel the sun again. This was a gamble, and no one quite knew the outcome.

The building was brown and square, the footprint a full city block. The stories towered above the street like a sentry against the Roman sky. I carried no mobile, no identification. No Euros. I had nothing but the clothes on my back.

My heart beat slow and steady despite my trepidation. There was no changing my mind now—not that I would. I pulled open the door and approached the security checkpoint.

"Name and who are you here to see?" the guard asked me.

"Luca Benetti. I'm here to see Colonnello Palmieri."

The officer looked up from his computer, mouth slack. I didn't move a muscle. The cameras would've picked me up by now. No doubt some alarm was sounding amongst the officers.

Sure enough, the phones began ringing at the desk.

Out of the corner of my eye, I saw a dozen officers sprinting toward me. The urge to flee, ingrained since birth, was strong, but I remained still. In a blink they were on me, shoving me into the desk and dragging my arms behind my back. Hands ran up and down my legs, my waist. They even grabbed my balls, as if I had a pistol taped to my sac.

I didn't fight, didn't protest. They hauled me up and cuffed my wrists. Then they marched me through the metal detector. My belt set off the alarm, so that was quickly removed and I was sent through once again. When I cleared, they sneered at me, telling me of my stupidity, how I'd never see daylight ever again.

"I'm here to see Colonnello Palmieri," I repeated loudly enough for the cameras to hear.

They dragged me to an elevator and shoved me inside. Instead of going up to the offices, we went down. I wasn't surprised. They wouldn't trust me around others.

It was cool below ground. Under the fluorescent lighting, rows of doors stretched along the corridor. They opened one and took me inside, where I was handcuffed to the chair, my arms stretched painfully behind me. It was pointless to complain, however.

How long would he make me wait? If I were in his shoes, I wouldn't rush. I would keep the criminal miserable for as long as possible. But I suspected that many of Rossi's claims were false, including Palmieri's case against me in retaliation for his wife. If this was the case, Palmieri would be shocked and curious over my appearance today.

I'd soon find out.

The minutes crawled by. I tried to adjust my position, but there was no relief. Finally, my arms went numb. I counted the dots on the ceiling, a mindless task that prevented me from second-guessing myself.

Before we touched down in Catanzaro, we spoke to Alessandro Ricci's assistant, who said the hit hadn't been put on the open market.

This meant Rossi hadn't hired an assassin. I had to assume he'd handled the job himself, which might explain why it had gone to shit.

Just when I wondered if they were planning on keeping me like this all night, the door opened. An older man entered, a thick file folder in his hands. He wasn't very tall and a thin mustache graced his upper lip. The wrinkled suit he wore wasn't flashy, but it was quality.

I said nothing as he slapped the file folder on the table and lowered himself into the seat opposite me. "God must be smiling upon me today."

I smirked, hoping to annoy him. "Colonnello Palmieri. You are supposed to be intelligent. Haven't you stopped to ask yourself why I walked in?"

"It hardly matters." He gestured to the folder full of papers. "This ensures you won't ever walk out. So the reason for your visit is immaterial."

"Wrong. It is very material, Colonnello."

He pounded his fist on the tabletop, causing the file folder to jump. "You slept with my wife!"

Ah. So he was aware. "She approached me in a bar and gave me a fake name. If I knew she was your wife, I would've turned her down."

"I don't believe you."

Sighing, I rolled my lips together. "Don't be stubborn. I'm not here because of your wife."

"Illuminate me, then, Don Benetti. Tell me these reasons for why you have sought me out today."

"Is that all for me?" I asked, tipping my head toward the folder on the table.

"These are only the recent things I have discovered about you and your 'ndrina. There are six more folders upstairs."

"Six?" I whistled. "Impressive."

"Is this wise? Sarcasm from a man facing prison for the rest of his life?"

"And what is the charge?"

Palmieri stared at me flatly, his fingers drumming on the tabletop. "Are you here to cut a deal? To turn on your family and the 'Ndrangheta?"

"I would shoot myself in the head before I ever betrayed my family. I'm here to ask questions."

The way he stared at me would've shriveled the balls for a lesser man. "You are a criminal, a murderer. Why would I ever help you?"

"Because I have information on your daughter's murderer."

That got his attention. His back straightened and he leaned closer. "Did you find Flavio Segreto?"

I didn't say anything. I wasn't talking until I had my questions answered.

"Dimmi!" he snapped.

"Ma dai," I said calmly, "that is not how this works. You answer my questions first, then I'll tell you what I know."

Seconds ticked by as he seemed to consider this. Finally, he shoved the file folder to the side and propped his elbows on the table. "Fine. I agree."

"Turn off the cameras first." I tilted my head toward the corner, where I knew all the footage was being recorded. "I don't want anyone overhearing this."

He rose and went to the door, mumbled something to a person in the hall, then came around behind my chair. Grabbing my wrists, he deftly unlocked the handcuffs to free my hands.

"Grazie," I gritted out as blood painfully rushed back into my arms.

When he retook his seat, he said, "There. No cameras. Ask your question."

I shook out my shoulders. "Did you have my cousin in custody?"

"Who?"

"Niccolò Benetti."

"No."

"Did you have him at a safe house or any other facility?"

310

"How many different ways can I say no? We never had him in any capacity. I've never met him."

Ah. So Rossi had lied. I had no idea where Niccolò went and why he was no longer answering his mobile, but it had nothing to do with the GDF.

And Rossi would pay for using me.

"And," Palmieri added, "if I had one of your cousins in custody, you would be in prison already."

He was so smug, but Benettis didn't rat out our family. "No doubt."

"I've answered your question, so now you will tell me where to find Flavio Segreto."

"Not until I make a call first."

Palmieri's eyes widened and his nostrils flared. "Why should I let you use a phone, or do anything else, for that matter?"

I met his look of incredulity with one of steel. "Because that's the only way you'll find out what you need to know."

Palmieri considered my demand for another moment and then looked toward the door and held his hand to his face as if making a telephone call. Soon the door opened and a burner phone was placed on the table. "This had better be worth it, Benetti."

"Alone," I said when he didn't leave.

He frowned but disappeared into the hall, the lock engaging behind him.

I dialed a familiar number.

"Pronto," Don Rossi answered.

"You lied to me." I kept my voice smooth, like a snake just before it strikes. "About my cousin."

"I don't know what you're talking about."

"Yes, you do. The whole thing was a setup and I don't appreciate being used, stronzo."

"Are you threatening me? We are not equals, Benetti. You had better watch what you say."

"Fuck off. This isn't done."

I disconnected, broke the phone apart, and tossed it onto the desk.

A few seconds later Palmieri returned. "I've waited long enough. Where is Segreto? I know he killed my daughter."

"He didn't. Segreto has been in hiding the entire time."

"Impossible. The evidence points to Segreto."

I cocked my head. "Who gave you this evidence?"

"It doesn't matter. I know it was Segreto. Rumor is you went to find him. So where is he?"

Frustration began to build, but I squashed it. "Colonnello, Segreto did not kill your daughter. I suggest you start looking elsewhere."

"You say this as if you are certain, as if you know who is responsible." He tapped his fingers on the old table. "So tell me who, Benetti."

I couldn't rat out Don Rossi, even if I wished, because it would break our code and bring dishonor to my family. It could possibly start a war with the other 'ndrine. It went against everything I'd ever promised. "I can't tell you. But I can confirm Segreto is innocent. The information pointing to him was incorrect."

Palmieri shot up out of his chair and began pacing, his shoulders stiff and angry. "I want a name! I want to know who slaughtered my little girl. He deserves to stand trial and I deserve vengeance!"

"I understand, Colonnello. But I can't tell you any more than I already have. It would put my life and family in great danger."

Whipping around he pounded his fist on the table. "You should fear *me*, Benetti. Because if you don't tell me, you will live to regret it."

"Then we are at an impasse, because I will not say more." I pushed to my feet and pulled on my cuffs, straightening them. "Good luck, Colonnello."

He moved to block my path. "Where do you think you're going?"

"Home. Unless you're arresting me, but we both know you don't have cause."

"I have cause," he said, motioning to the folder. "I have ten years' worth of cause."

"No, you don't. Because if you did, you would've arrested me long before today."

Palmieri snatched the handcuffs off the table. "Then let me make it perfectly clear: I'm arresting you unless you give me Segreto or his daughter. Then I'll ask them my own questions. It's clear the answer is there somewhere."

I would die before I turned Valentina over to the GDF. And I promised her I wouldn't involve her father.

We stared at one another. Palmieri's eyes were almost manic, blazing with hatred and resentment. I slipped my hands into my trouser pockets and remained calm. "Is this because I fucked your wife?"

He let out a growl right before his fist connected with my cheek. I stumbled back a half step, my face now on fire. I straightened and looked down at him. Slowly, my hands clenched into fists, while the need for violence, for retribution made me tremble. I spoke softly, but with deadly intent. "You will regret this."

With a sneer, he lunged for the door and yanked it open. "*Vieni qui*, per favore!" he called into the corridor. "Today we place the great Don Benetti under arrest."

Chapter Thirty-Two

Valentina

I pushed through the back door and raced into the kitchen. "I'm here, I'm here. I'm sorry I'm late!"

The kitchen staff were at their stations, working, while Giovanni was in discussions with his sous chef. Everyone glanced up at my arrival, a sea of confused faces staring back at me.

I plopped my bag—my old purse, the one I'd carried for years—onto the stainless prep counter. Before I could say anything more, Roberto limped out from inside the office. "Ciao, signorina. Did you need something?"

"I'm here for the meeting." I gathered my hair and dragged it into a messy bun on the top of my head. "I'm so glad you all waited for me before starting."

"Val, bella. Come. Sit with me. Let's talk."

I glanced around the kitchen, but everyone was already back at work to prep for tonight's dinner service. Roberto tugged on my arm and led me into the dining room. He held out a chair for me, so I lowered myself down and put my purse on the floor. After he sat, I said, "What's going on? Was the meeting canceled?"

"The meeting was three hours ago."

I jolted in my chair. "No, that can't be right." Leaning down, I fished my cell out of my purse and opened my calendar app. "No, no, no. I'm sure I had the time as—"

Shit.

I missed the meeting.

My calendar showed the right time, but I hadn't double-checked, instead relying on my memory. Which was spotty at best these days. Ever since Luca left, in fact.

"Damn." I tossed my phone back in my purse and lowered my head into my hands. "What in the world is wrong with me?"

"Bella," he said gently, as if about to break bad news. "You don't need to push yourself so hard. Take some time off—"

"I do *not* need to take time off. There is nothing wrong with me." Except for heartbreak, but I'd get over that soon. I had to. "I'm fine."

"You are not fine. You have lost two people who are very important to you."

Luca and my father. Flavio left town the second Luca did, saying it wasn't safe for him here. He promised to contact me from a burner phone every now and again, but he wouldn't tell me where he was going.

But that loss was nothing compared to Luca's betrayal.

I shook my head. "Like I said, I'm fine. I need to be here, helping to run things."

"We can manage for a few days. You could stay with your friend Maggie. Or—"

"Roberto, I'm not going to disappear and sulk. I need to keep busy. I'm sorry I missed the meeting, but I can't sit around at home and feel sorry for myself."

"You are very stubborn."

"Yes, I know. You're the one who should be taking time off. Your leg isn't even healed yet."

He waved his hand in that elegant Italian fashion. "It's nothing. A scratch."

"Now who's lying?"

"Ciao, Val!" a deep voice called from across the room. Gabi came out from the back with a beer keg on his shoulder. He looked so much like a younger version of Luca that it physically hurt to look at him. I'd been avoiding him, actually. Partly because of Gabi's resemblance, but mainly because I didn't know what to say. *Your dad's a dick and he lied to me, and oh, did you know he was planning to kidnap me?*

Gabi set the keg on the ground and straightened. "Come stai? You missed the meeting."

Ugh. "Yes, I know. The day got away from me somehow."

His mouth twisted in a sympathetic smile.

Roberto's phone buzzed, so he got up from the table. "Perdonami, signorina."

I was left alone at the table, feeling like a failure. A failure at love, a failure at work. Wow, I was really crushing life this week.

It has to get better.

It had to. I couldn't eat or sleep. I could barely focus. All I wanted was to stay in bed and watch cooking shows on my phone. When would this terrible ache leave my chest?

You hold my heart and my soul, fiore mio. Per sempre.

Maybe, but he didn't love me. He wanted to sleep with me, maybe keep me around as a mistress for a few weeks. But he'd lied to me—and I would never believe another word he said.

"Come," Gabi said, waving me over to the bar. "Sit, bella. Keep me company while I work."

Roberto wasn't returning, so I got up and went to the bar. When I was settled, Gabi poured me a glass of juice. "Drink that. It'll help."

"I doubt it, but thank you." I sipped the juice and blinked in surprise. "I thought this was orange juice."

"Bergamot juice. Popular in Italia. Do you like it?"

"It's good. Tart. Not as sweet as orange juice."

"I keep it around to impress the ladies," he said with a wink.

I toyed with the glass and peeked up at him through my lashes. "You don't have to stay, you know. I don't need to be babysat." Or spied on, whichever the case may be.

"I'm not going anywhere. I like it here."

"Gabi, come on." I tapped my fingernail against the glass. "You could be back home, doing more than cutting limes and lemons."

"My father asked me to stay and look after you. This is a great responsibility because you mean everything to him."

I couldn't help it—a snort emerged. "We both know that isn't true."

He put down the knife he was using and braced his hands on the bar. "Val. Bella. How can you not see this? He has never allowed a woman into his life before. Leo and I have never met any of his women, other than our mothers, because he keeps them separate, capisce?"

This was immaterial. "Your father is a liar."

"He's not. But he is a man with great responsibilities on his shoulders, and sometimes he hurts people without realizing it."

The way Gabi said it . . . "Has he hurt you?"

He straightened and took up the knife again. "I am a second son. The focus has always been on Leo, the heir. As it should be."

"Not at the detriment of your mental health."

He lifted a shoulder. "Our world isn't so concerned about mental health. But being here has helped."

"You mean at the restaurant?"

"Yes, but New York in general. I like having something to do."

"You were bored at home?"

"Not bored, but my father kept me protected from most of the family business. I mostly drove old men around."

"It's better than being shot at."

"Are you kidding? I'd much rather be shot at than listen to old men fart and blow their noses all day."

He'd rather be shot at? I couldn't pretend to understand it. "I would never let a son of mine into that world."

He shook the knife at me. "Never say never, Val. My father will return one day."

And what? Knock me up? No, thank you. And even if he did, I wouldn't turn my child over to the mafia. "Can we please talk about something else? I'm done thinking about your dad."

"Allora, then we will talk about something else. You need to move back into the mansion."

"What?" My back went ramrod straight in horror. "No way. I'm staying at my house. Why in the world would I move back into that mansion?"

"Because it's safer. And I'm tired of sleeping in my car every night."

"You don't need to sleep in your car. Get a room at the inn."

"Staying at the inn won't allow me to keep watch over you."

Shock rooted me to the spot, frozen. "You're . . . sleeping in your car outside my house? Why?"

"I promised my father to watch over you. I will not let him down."

"Gabi, nothing is going to happen to me. You don't need to follow me around."

"I will not let him down," he repeated, his attention on his cutting board.

"Oh, my god." I put my face in my hands. "This is ridiculous—"

His phone vibrated on the bar, the word FRATELLO on the display. Was this Leo calling?

Smiling, Gabi wiped his hands and lifted his mobile to his ear. "Pronto."

I could hear deep rapid Italian on the other end, and Gabi's smile instantly died. "Che cazzo?" he wheezed. "No, no, no. Non capisco."

Olive skin paling, he listened as Leo went on, and I began to worry. Was this something about Luca?

I didn't care. Luca and I were history. His mafia problems were not my problems.

I nibbled my fingernail, wondering if I should leave while Gabi went back and forth with his brother. I couldn't understand what they were saying, but it sounded personal. Maybe Leo was in trouble.

Before I could get up, Gabi disconnected. Carefully, he set his phone on the bar.

"What's wrong?" I asked when he didn't say anything. "What happened?"

He swallowed. "My father is in prison. He's been arrested by the Guardia di Finanza. They oversee—"

"I know who they are." My ears were ringing now, an orchestra of horror filling my head. Arrested? Luca? "What the hell? He told me that he had people in place to make sure this kind of thing didn't happen."

"He does. We do. I don't know what the fuck happened. Leo is on his way to Roma. We'll learn more then."

I couldn't wait that long. My heart was pounding hard inside my chest, about to explode. I needed information *now*. "Call Sergio." I nudged his phone closer to him, my voice raising dramatically. "Ask him what's going on."

Gabi picked up his phone and unlocked it, while I tried to keep from freaking out. *Oh, my god*. Luca was in *prison*.

This was crazy. How had he allowed himself to get arrested?

Stomach clenching, I thought of him behind bars, caged in a tiny cell. Was he hurt? Were the guards treating him okay? I bet he was pissed to be away from his family and men.

Gabi was waiting for someone to pick up. "Zio, che cazzo?"

I folded my hands and rested my knuckles against my lips, almost like I was begging with the universe for this not to be true. I couldn't understand what Sergio was saying, but Gabi's dour expression only turned more dour. The news was not good.

Shit, shit, shit.

When Gabi rang off I nearly pounced across the bar. "What did he say?"

"My father walked into the GDF headquarters and was arrested."

319

"He *walked in?*" This made no sense. "Why in the world would he do that? He had to know they would arrest him."

"I don't know, but Sergio said we're keeping that part quiet. As far as everyone knows, the GDF arrested Luca."

This had to be a pride thing. To admit you'd walked directly into your own arrest was humiliating. "Now what? Does Sergio have the lawyers working on getting Luca out?"

Gabi put his elbows on the bar and leaned over, his forehead resting on his arms. "No. He hasn't spoken to the lawyers yet."

"So Luca *wants* to stay in prison?"

"I'm not sure if he's refusing or if the officers won't allow it."

"But that's not fair. Aren't there rules against that?"

"In Italia? Yes, but it's not like here. The process could take months, years. They haven't even brought him before a judge yet to formally press charges."

This couldn't be happening. I thought prison was a bad thing, a place all mobsters wished to avoid. "Does this make any sense to you?"

Gabi raised his head and his eyes were flat. "Not at all. Val—"

He bit off what he was about to say. "What?"

"I need to go back. I have to be there for him, for Leo. For my uncles. I . . . " He swallowed. "And I think you should come with me."

I licked my dry lips, my head still spinning with all I'd just learned. "Why would I go with you?"

"First, because I promised to look after you. I can't go back if you're here. And second, maybe you can talk some sense into him. Convince him to see the lawyer. He will listen to you."

"You don't know that. He's incredibly stubborn."

"I think you have the best chance of any of us. Leo brought it up, and I agree."

"Leo thinks you should bring me to Italy?"

He nodded. "Obviously, I won't force you. But I'm begging you to come talk to him." He put his palms together and shook his hands at me. "Per favore, bella. Help my family. Help my father see reason."

Roberto joined us at the bar and I filled him in on what was happening with Luca. "I can't believe this," he said.

"Me neither." Glancing down, I checked my phone. But there were no texts, no calls. If Luca had access to any form of communication, he hadn't wasted it on me. "Luca's family wants me to go and talk to him."

"You should," Roberto said instantly. "Italian jail, it is a dangerous place for a man like Luca. The longer he stays in there, the harder it will be to get out."

"What about the restaurant? I can't leave. You're injured and we've just reopened."

"Signorina, this is why you hired us. We will be fine."

My throat hurt from the giant ball of emotion lodged there. While I was still angry at Luca, I didn't want to see him suffer, rotting away in some dirty prison with men who would hurt him. Could I help? I wasn't sure. But I couldn't stay here and do nothing. I needed to see him, make sure he was okay.

I met Gabi's worried gaze. "I guess we're going to Italy."

Chapter Thirty-Three

Luca

L'Aquila, Italy
Supercarcere Le Costarelle

The guard knocked on the open door to my cell. "Don Benetti, your dinner."

I set my glass of wine on the end table and paused the jazz music playing on my tablet. Tonight's meal was fish delivered hot from a local restaurant. "Va bene. Bring it in."

The guard carried in a paper sack and began unpacking my meal on the dining table. Standing, I slipped my feet into my shoes and carried my wine over to the chair. I lowered myself down and placed a cloth napkin in my lap. After the guard unpacked everything, I asked, "Did you get something for yourself?"

"Yes, Don Benetti. Thank you for your generosity."

I nodded, acknowledging, and began eating. My money and reputation meant prison was more like an extended stay at a hotel. The guards were well compensated to look after my needs and I wanted for almost nothing. Food, wine, internet, books, and my large bed was outfitted with soft sheets and a plush mattress. A good number of my men were imprisoned here, so I was surrounded by family and friends. We played cards, ate together, and worked out together. It wasn't pleasant . . . but it wasn't awful.

Sergio visited daily and we discussed business, and my arrangement with the guards meant we weren't overheard. Word had traveled about my arrest. Our enemies would close in soon so I needed my brothers to be ready. If I wasn't released in the next few weeks, we could expect to face many bloody battles. My absence would be viewed as a weakness, and our world viewed weaknesses as opportunities.

Unfortunately, despite multiple requests, the testa di cazzo— Palmieri—refused to charge me or let me speak with a lawyer. I was stuck here.

The branzino was cooked to perfection, broiled and flaky, melting on my tongue. I casually watched a streaming show on my tablet as I ate, some reality nonsense that reminded me of Valentina and her terrible taste in entertainment.

Mafia Island. I snickered despite myself. She had a sense of humor, a playfulness long missing from my life, and I missed the random nonsense that came out of her mouth. Did she miss me? Or was she still angry at the way we parted?

Maybe I would ring Roberto tomorrow and ask.

Before I could finish the buttery branzino, the guard was back. "Don Benetti, a guest to see you."

Sergio had been here earlier. Was it one of my other brothers? "Who?"

"A woman."

Was it Chiara or one of the boys' mothers? "Did she give a name?"

"Valentina DiMarco."

The air left my lungs in a rush. The last name was fake, but a clear identifier. Valentina was in Italia. Here, at this prison.

What the fuck?

My chest squeezed as disbelief and indecision strangled me like a vise, and my eyes went unfocused. Gabriele and Roberto should have known better than to let her leave New York. If the GDF realized her identity, she was at risk. Palmieri would use Valentina to get to her father, exactly as he'd planned from the start, and all my efforts to keep her out of this mess would be in vain. "Tell her no."

"Perdonami, Don Benetti," he said, pulling on the collar of his uniform. "But she warned us you might refuse her. She said to tell you she won't leave until you talk to her."

Stubborn woman. It wasn't safe for her to hang about at a men's prison. She didn't speak the language and these were dangerous men. I was going to strangle my second born for this. He was supposed to be watching over her.

Carefully, I wiped my mouth with the napkin and set it on the table. After I pushed to my feet, I slipped my arms into the jumpsuit I was required to wear. Even though I wasn't a typical prisoner, appearances must be maintained in the public spaces.

The guard led me through the corridors, past other cells not nearly as fancy as mine. Curious stares followed me as I walked past, with some inmates dipping their chin in deference, but I didn't speak to any of them. The rage burning my skin wouldn't allow me to focus on anything else than the woman in the visitor's room. Valentina had much to answer for.

He unlocked the visitor room and opened the door for me. The space was empty, save one person, and my entire body jolted at the sight of her. I rocked back on my heels, but schooled my features carefully.

Fuck. Me.

She was gorgeous, even more beautiful than my memories. In person she sparkled with some indefinable quality that could never be drawn or photographed; it was a vibrance that burned bright and drew me to her. My anger withered, and in its place was a longing so

324

fierce that I wanted to howl at the unfairness of everything keeping me away from her.

My fingers itched with the need to touch her. I craved her mouth, her sighs. The way she curled into me and rubbed her tits against my chest. Her soft skin and coconut-scented hair.

But I couldn't have any of that.

I didn't know if we were being observed or not. As a precaution, I couldn't give them any idea of how much this woman meant to me. I couldn't let her become a target.

"You asshole," she started when I didn't move or speak.

I cocked my head and gave her a bland look. "Do I know you?"

Her lips parted as her brows flew up. "Really, Luca? Is that how you're going to play this?"

Rubbing my jaw, I pretended to think. "Allora, are you the woman from that club in New York City? The one who gave me a blow job in the men's toilet?"

The air in the room turned frosty, like a negotiation gone bad. "No," she said, the single word dripping with snark. "I'm the one who gave you the blow job in your car."

As if I could ever forget.

My smile was part grin, part leer. "Ah, va bene. That was nice, no? I've been bragging of your skills to the other prisoners."

I could see her thinking, wondering what was happening and why I was acting this way. But I couldn't let up—I needed her to leave.

Leaning against the wall, I propped one foot on the plaster. "Did my brother hire you to pay me a conjugal visit? Because I would not turn one down, bella."

The skin of her neck turned red and her nostrils flared. "I want answers from you." She put her arms on the table and lowered her voice to a whisper. "You walked into the GDF headquarters? Are you *insane?*"

Madre di dio. She had to stop asking questions. "That is not how this works." I pushed off from the wall and approached her slowly, my fingers unbuttoning my jumpsuit. "Would you like to get on your knees, or should I fuck you from behind on the table?"

"Stop it." She shot to her feet. "Why are you acting like this?"

"What else did you expect when you followed me from New York? It's obvious you are gagging for my dick just like you were there."

"You know what? Fuck off." She strode to the metal door leading out of the visiting room. "You can rot in here for all I care."

She raised her hand to pound on the door, but I was on her in a flash. I caged her in, pressing her flat to the unforgiving metal door, then I put my mouth to her ear and kept my voice soft. "You should not be here. It is dangerous and foolish."

Valentina inhaled sharply. "But—"

"No, fiore mio. Get the fuck out of here and go back home." Then I stumbled away from the door like she'd shoved me away. "This is your last chance, bambina. I'll fuck you so good. I'll make you scream so all the other prisoners can hear you."

Thankfully, she heeded my warning. She slapped her palm on the metal. "I'm finished! Hey, let me out!"

"Don't go so fast," I crooned. "We can have fun. Maybe one or two of the guards can join us. They would love your big—"

The metal door opened and the guard returned. "Signorina?"

Valentina glanced over her shoulder at me, her gaze lingering on my face. I watched her lick her lips, then she looked away. "I'm ready to go."

He held the door open for her and Valentina disappeared. My soul withered when the metal closed with a loud snap. I hated what I'd just done. But it was for the best. I couldn't risk anyone discovering who she really was or how we were connected. I couldn't have the GDF investigating or following her, so there had been no choice.

Guaranteeing her freedom was more important than anything else, even if it meant ruining my chances at earning her forgiveness.

I dragged my hands through my hair. I had more problems now, as well. Everything was taking too long. I still hadn't learned where

Niccolò was from D'Agostino, and now someone brought Valentina to Roma, helped her come to this prison. I suspected Gabriele, which meant he needed to be dealt with. Valentina could not stay in this country safely. It was only a matter of time before the GDF learned of her presence and tried to use her to get to her father.

I had to hurry. I went to the door and banged on it. When the guard appeared, I wasted no time in going through. "Take me back. I need to speak to my brother. Immediately."

We started off for the cells. "Would you like to use the prison phones?"

"No, I'll use one of the burners. I need privacy."

Chapter Thirty-Four

Valentina

Someone had punched him.

Someone punched that powerful, beautiful man in his beautiful face. Who? An officer? Another inmate?

As I walked through the prison corridors, I couldn't help but worry. Prison had to be hell on earth for Luca. He wasn't safe here, not with enemies at every turn, as well as guards who now had the chance to abuse the great Luca Benetti. What bruises were hiding under his clothing? Was he sleeping? The food must be terrible, especially for a food and wine snob like Luca.

I shook off the lingering anger at the hurtful things he'd said. It was clear he didn't mean them, belittling me for the benefit of whoever was watching, but I hated hearing him speak like that. Sneering at me like I was nothing, a woman "gagging" for his cock.

He preferred for me to go away, but after seeing that bruise on his cheek?

Not a chance.

On the plane earlier I researched famous mafia bosses who were put into prison. Some were killed by other prisoners, while the rest grew old and died behind bars. None were found innocent and none were released. It was a grim sentence.

Now I had a choice. I could walk outside, where Gabi was waiting, and go to Luca's home in Catanzaro. Sit around while his family tried to decide what to do.

But sitting around wasn't really my style. I needed to do *something*.

Luca's arrest was connected to the GDF and my father, the blackmail over the officer's murdered daughter. So maybe there was a way to use Flavio and get Luca released.

I had to try.

When we reached the main check point, I collected my belongings. Before the officer turned away, I said, "I would like to speak to Signore Palmieri of the GDF. Can you help me find him?"

He grimaced. "Signorina—"

"Please. I am not leaving until I meet with Signore Palmieri." I gestured to the phone on the desk. "Ring him, per favore."

He stared at me as if I told him Texan olive oil was superior to Italian. "I can't ring the GDF and have them come here on my command."

"You can and you will. Tell Palmieri that Valentina Montella is here and I'm not leaving until he meets with me." I lowered myself down into one of the two plastic chairs in the room. Then I folded my arms and stared straight ahead. I wasn't going to debate this or be intimidated into leaving. There was a slim chance I could fix this—today—and get Luca released. Nothing else mattered.

The guard muttered to himself in Italian, probably curses, then sighed several times. Just when I thought he might give up, he sat in his chair and picked up the phone, punched some buttons. There was a long conversation and I heard him say my name to someone before hanging up. Another call came in soon after and he talked for several minutes, mostly listening. He gave brief answers, then put down the handset.

We waited.

Nerves raced over my skin and my leg bounced. I picked at my fingernails and thought about Gabi waiting outside for me. We landed an hour ago and came straight here, so I had no idea if his family knew we were in Rome. But I stared at the door, worried that Sergio or another Benetti would rush through the door and try to stop me.

The guard's line buzzed. He lifted the handset and listened, then I saw his shoulders stiffen. Nodding, he repeated "va bene" a few times before ringing off.

He stood and, keys jangling, came toward me. "Signorina Montella. Follow me."

I had no idea where we were going, but I was ready to battle. I had to do whatever I could for Luca. We continued into the facility, passing offices and desks. Finally, the guard stopped, opened a door, and gestured for me to go inside.

Four cement walls and an old table greeted me. "I don't understand," I said, looking up at him. "Where's Palmieri?"

"Per favore." He waved his hand to indicate the room.

Tentatively, I stepped in. I wasn't so sure about this plan anymore. No one other than Gabi knew I was here and I was at the mercy of these strangers. I swallowed hard. "Is Palmieri coming?"

The guard didn't answer. He pulled the door shut . . . and I heard the lock engage.

I reached to check, just to be sure. Yep, he'd locked me in. Shit!

Before I let my imagination get away from me, I settled at the table and did some deep breathing. It wasn't helpful to panic until there was something to panic about. I was a U.S. citizen with rights. They couldn't leave me here forever and they couldn't hurt me.

No one knows I'm here. They can do whatever they want.

I pulled out my phone. No service. Great.

After a few deep breaths, I decided to distract myself by looking at the photos I took during my short time with Luca. He hated photos, but he let me snap a few. Thank god I hadn't deleted them when I learned the truth about us.

His handsome face filled the screen, his eyes warm and affectionate, while a secret smile played at the edges of his mouth. The dark scruff made him look sexy and dangerous, and my stomach twisted. Jesus, he was pretty. I hated that he'd lied to me, but there was nothing fake about this photo. The warmth in his eyes, the smile on his lips . . . it was real.

And there were no bruises on his cheek.

It hardened my resolve to get him out of this place. I wasn't naive —he wasn't an innocent man. No doubt he deserved to be in prison for some of the things he'd done. But the world was full of awful people who never faced consequences for their actions, men whose money and power sheltered them from repercussions.

Why should one man be made to suffer when millions more didn't?

It was like income tax. A large number of people got away with hardly paying, while the rest of us gave away so much. How on earth was that fair?

You're rationalizing because you love him.

I shoved those thoughts aside and scrolled through more photos. The wait dragged on so long that I put my phone down, concerned for my battery. I walked around, examined the room. I didn't see a camera, but I would bet anything there was one somewhere. I checked the time again.

Finally, the door opened. A man entered, his expression flat and unhappy. "Signorina." Then he spoke a stream of rapid Italian that sounded angry.

I put up my palms. "Do you speak English?"

"Of course. Do you?"

Ah. Now his attitude made sense.

He didn't believe me.

"Signore Palmieri?" When he nodded once, I continued. "I am

Valentina Montella from New York. My father is Flavio Segreto. I believe you are looking for him."

He yanked out the chair on the opposite side of the table and sat down. His tie had been loosened, the first button on his dress shirt undone. It added to his general air of aggravation. "Benetti has told you, I see."

"Luca didn't tell me. My father did."

Palmieri's demeanor changed, his gaze sharpening on mine. "So you are in regular contact with him."

"Not really. Flavio stays away to protect me. However, we did speak about your daughter." Palmieri went deathly still, but I had to get the rest out. He had to be told. "He did not kill her."

"Perdonami, signorina. But the evidence suggests otherwise."

"Evidence provided by whom? Because someone is lying to you. Don't you want to know why?"

"And what evidence do you have that your father is innocent?"

I drew in a deep breath. "At the time your daughter was killed, my mother was dying of cancer. Without my knowledge, my father was looking after her as she grew sicker and sicker. He loved her. There is no way he would've accepted a job that sent him away from her during that time."

"You can't be sure of that."

"I am one-hundred percent sure. I believe him. And you can look at his passport and her death certificate. He didn't leave New York. Someone else killed your daughter."

His fingertips drummed on the wooden table as he examined my face. Intently, as if searching for weaknesses. The approach was intimidating, and I suspected many criminals had confessed because of it. I tried to remain calm. I had the truth on my side.

"And did your father have a guess as to who might be responsible?"

"I'll tell you, but I want your word that you'll release Signore Benetti."

He laughed, but it was a dry and humorless sound. "Never would I agree to something so foolish."

"Then I won't tell you what my father said."

"You are in a prison in a strange country. Do you honestly believe you have any leverage at the moment?"

"Yes, I do. You want something from me and I want something from you."

"You are very sure of yourself." He leaned back, his jacket falling slightly open to reveal the pistol he wore. "Maybe I will keep you here, force your father to come and speak with me in person."

My mouth dried out at the threat, so I licked my lips. "It won't do any good. He won't come—and besides, he's not responsible for your daughter's death. You're wasting your time pursuing him for it."

The air in the room turned oppressive as the seconds dragged on, Palmieri's stare like black orbs of resentment. "You are asking for one of the country's most dangerous criminals to be released. Do you know how long we've tried to arrest Benetti?"

"You haven't charged him with a crime, though, which makes me think you know you can't. You don't have a charge that will stick."

"Maybe our legal system works differently here than in your country."

"It doesn't, not when it comes to due process. I looked it up."

"Maybe I will arrest you for interfering in an investigation, and you may learn our procedures yourself."

I threw up my hands in frustration. "Stop threatening me. If you want to find out what I know, then promise to release Luca."

Palmieri smoothed his mustache carefully. "If you tell me what I wish to hear, I will allow Signore Benetti's lawyers to be brought in today."

This seemed like a good compromise. "I have your word?"

"Sì, signorina. I'll give you my word."

"Flavio believes someone named Rossi is responsible for your daughter's death and he's trying to make my father the scapegoat for it."

"If that's true, then why target a man who hasn't lived in this country for almost a decade? Why not choose someone else, someone more convenient?"

"Rossi has been searching for my father since he left. My father knew Rossi was stealing from the mafia and made the mistake of trying to use the information to gain his freedom."

"Rossi is a common name here. You have no other information?"

"Investigating men in this country is your job, not mine. I'm sure there is a man by that name here who is already on your radar."

Palmieri stared at the wall, unmoving. I wondered what he was thinking, if he knew this man named Rossi and had been watching him. I hoped so, because I didn't want him backing out on our deal. I needed Luca released.

The man across from me stood and straightened his tie. "Unless there is more, you are free to go."

I rose and clasped my hands. "Don't forget your promise to let Luca's lawyers get him out today."

"I never promised to release Benetti today. But I did agree to let his lawyers in to visit."

"Good. Then it's only a matter of time until he's freed."

"Don't be so sure, signorina." Now at the door, Palmieri paused. "He had the chance to stop it, capisce? I asked him to turn you over or face arrest. Can you guess which option he chose?"

My mouth parted on a shocked breath. What on earth? Luca had allowed them to arrest him rather than turn me over?

We weren't dating or sleeping together any longer. Why not save himself from prison by letting Palmieri interview me? This made no sense.

I swear to protect you from the blood and crime.

Palmieri held the door open, regaining my attention. "Come. I'll walk you to the front."

"Grazie," I said and went by him into the hallway.

We began walking together, my shoes rapping loudly on the worn tile. "Your Italian needs work," he said. "But I suppose you will have plenty of time to perfect it here, no?"

Did he mean now, as I waited for Luca's release? "Not sure how much I can learn in a few days, but we'll see."

"A few days?" He made a dismissive sound in his throat. "Signorina, if you think Benetti will ever let you return to New York, you are fooling yourself. This life, *his* life, swallows women whole."

I had no response. He was wrong. I wasn't staying here, no matter what Luca wanted. We were through.

He stopped at the exit door and snapped at the men to open up. A buzzer sounded and Palmieri pushed it open. "Arrivederci, Signorina Montella."

I started to leave, then paused. "My deepest sympathies on the loss of your daughter, signore."

He didn't react, so I hurried out, hoping I'd done enough.

* * *

"My uncles are losing their minds."

I closed the car door and reached for the seat belt. "Why?"

"Luca called them and was very, very angry." Gabi checked the mirrors and pulled into traffic away from the prison. "They want us in Catanzaro right away."

"Are you in trouble for bringing me here?"

"I think we are both in trouble, Val."

I was worried for Gabi, but not for me. "I don't care. We did the right thing by coming."

"How did it go? Did you talk sense into my father?"

"No. He acted very strangely. Like he didn't know me. Like I was just some girl he hooked up with in New York. But when he could, he whispered that it was dangerous for me to be here."

"But you said we did the right thing."

"We did. I met with Palmieri. That was what took so long."

Gabi's mouth fell open. "Che cazzo? You talked to the GDF? Do you know how bad that is?"

"I don't care." I reached into my purse and dug out a granola bar. My nerves had been too frayed to eat earlier and I was starving. "If telling Palmieri what I know could get Luca released, then I'll gladly do it. I'm not bound by any weird code about talking to the police."

"Mamma mia, no wonder my uncles are upset."

We didn't talk much from then on. Gabi sped along the Italian freeways as we headed south. We stopped a few times for restrooms and snacks, but otherwise kept driving toward Luca's family. I tried not to worry. I hadn't done anything wrong.

Finally, we turned off the main road and drove up into the hills. It was pretty scenery, with rolling peaks and valleys, old farmhouses. The sun was shining and sheep grazed out in the fields. "So this is what the Italian countryside looks like. It's very quaint."

"Boring," Gabi said. "My father also has a house in town, as does my mother, but this is where Leo and I live. It's safer for us out here."

"Was it hard growing up away from your mother?"

"I see her all the time, so no. My father makes sure Leo and I stay close to our mothers."

"Did you ever want your father to marry her?" Gabi paused, and I hurried to say, "I'm sorry if that's too personal. It just reminds me of something Palmieri said."

"What did he say?"

"That this life swallows women whole."

Gabi tapped his fingers on the steering wheel. "You don't need to worry about that, Val."

"I know, because I'm not staying. But it's weird. Like, Luca never married and there aren't any women around. No sisters, no aunts. Your life is completely surrounded by men."

He gave me a lazy lopsided grin that reminded me of his father. "Not completely surrounded."

"Okay, we get it. You get laid a lot. Be serious. Why do you all hate women so much?"

"We don't hate women. Our housekeeper is a woman."

"Not really helping your case, Gabi."

His hands gripped the steering wheel. "I don't know why. I suppose we are trying to protect them."

"Diminishing the role of women isn't protecting them. It's smothering them. We want to participate, be equals, not be shoved aside."

"Women are at risk here. You're not as str—"

"If you say not as strong, I'm going to kick you in the junk."

Gabi shifted uncomfortably in his seat, like he was thinking about the damage I could do to his testicles. "It's getting better. There are more women running 'ndrine now. More wives running things when their husbands are imprisoned."

"But not with yours."

"Ma dai, Val! What do you want from me? I'm just the second son. Take it up with my father."

No, thanks. Staying in Catanzaro wasn't in the cards and I had my own battles back home. I needed to return to New York as soon as possible.

We drove in silence. The roads grew narrower as we climbed higher. He turned off onto an unmarked drive and kept going. It was like a maze. I'd never find my way here even with a map.

A black iron gate stretched across the road, connected to a similar fence that looked like it went on for miles. Gabi punched a few buttons on the keypad and the metal slowly swung open. As we drove through, he waved to some men gathered by the side of a small house. Guards, no doubt.

A sprawling stone villa soon came into view. Comprising three different levels, the house was built directly into the hill, almost an extension of the surrounding rock. Green plants and trees surrounded the perimeter and paths, lined the edge of the roof. Vining flowers adorned the front, while a fountain sat proudly in the middle of the circular drive. There were some smaller matching buildings off to the side, as well, but I couldn't look away from the cleverly designed massive structure.

This was no mobster's hideout. It was a super-luxurious estate worthy of a movie star.

"Wow," I breathed. "This is where you live?"

"Wait until you see the inside." He parked by a stone fountain and we got out. "Come on. They will want to yell at me right away."

"What about me?"

"They won't yell at you." He tossed his baseball hat into the back seat of the car, then ruffled his hair. "My father would skin them alive if they dared."

The words were said with absolute seriousness. It was a stark reminder of what had paid for this home—blood and crime. I couldn't forget it.

He led me higher along the path until we reached a door. Punching some numbers on a keypad, he said, "This is my father's office."

Before I could think about what I was going to say, we were inside. The room was spacious, softly lit. Modern and clean, with big abstract paintings on the walls. Classy, for a man who understood money but didn't need to show it off.

The Benetti brothers, along with another man I didn't recognize, were on their feet waiting for us. None of them looked happy.

Sergio launched into Gabi immediately, his Italian furious and fast. Gabi didn't try to speak, just stood silent, hands behind his back, and let his uncle rant at him. I couldn't take it any longer. "Stop," I told Sergio. "I'm the one you're upset with. Don't take it out on Gabi."

Luca's brother pressed his palms together and rested his fingertips on his lips. He seemed to be taking deep breaths. "Signorina, I'm trying to be respectful. But what you did today was very dangerous. You have put many things at risk, including my brother's life."

I couldn't see how this was true. "I had to speak to Palmieri. He has the power to release Luca and I thought using information regarding my father would help."

"You are playing in waters that are treacherous, signorina. There are things you don't understand."

"Then tell me."

His lip curled, like he was offended I'd dared to ask. "Those are family matters. I can't share them with anyone outside the family."

I gestured to the young man beside me. "Or Gabi, it seems."

Sergio's gaze flicked to his nephew before returning to me. "Luca decides what his sons know, and it's not your place to interfere."

"My *place*?" I gave a derisive laugh. "Yeah, I know all about my *place* in your world. Have babies and keep quiet. Right, Sergio? Well, that may work here, but it doesn't fly in New York. We aren't quiet, demure women afraid to speak up. Palmieri wanted my father, but for the wrong reasons. I explained the truth to him, and he agreed to let Luca's lawyers in. You're welcome, by the way. So untwist your panties and stop having a mantrum!"

No one said a word. Sergio appeared both angry and surprised, his brow wrinkled and jaw stiff, but I was done explaining myself.

I angled toward Gabi. "I would really like to see the rest of the house now, specifically a bedroom with a soft bed."

Gabi blinked a few times, but nodded. "Follow me."

Chapter Thirty-Five

Luca

There were no handcuffs this time.

I sat in the interrogation room, my hands free. I wasn't complaining. Maybe this was because of my lawyers? When I met with them yesterday, they intended to press the GDF to charge me or release me. This judicial purgatory was bullshit.

At least Valentina was safe. I instructed Sergio to keep her in Catanzaro at the compound until my situation was resolved. I didn't want her back in New York or in Roma. My brothers would watch over her, protect her.

Would I ever see her again? Our last encounter, with me pretending to barely know her, wasn't how I wanted her to remember me. No doubt she was still angry and I wish I had the ability to explain.

I wish I could tell her how every minute without her was like a chain around my soul, trapping me, dragging me down. How I would do it all differently, if I could. But life doesn't give us the ability to go back and right the wrongs done to those we love.

I loved her and I might never have the chance to prove it.

The door flew open. Palmieri walked through, his suit again rumpled, the circles under his eyes considerably worse. He shut the door and came toward the table where I sat.

"You look like shit," I said.

"Some of us work for a living." He didn't sit, but continued to stand next to me. "You should try it sometime."

I gave him a bland look. "I'm a businessman. Of course I work."

He shook his head at my comment, then gestured for me to stand. "Walk with me."

Che cazzo? "Where?"

"Let's go."

Without waiting for me, he strode to the door and went out into the hall. I pushed up from the chair and followed, my long legs catching up immediately. He led me down several corridors until we reached a locked door. Seconds later, we were buzzed through and then again through another locked door. This was as close to freedom as I'd experienced in almost a week. I tried to keep calm. It might not mean anything.

Palmieri kept going.

At a desk, he retrieved his service weapon and phone. He signed a few papers, then continued out the door. I cast a quick glance at the desk guard, but he ignored me, returning to his paperwork. I trailed Palmieri past the other checkpoints until we reached the main entrance.

He walked out.

I followed.

The sun hit my face and I let out the breath I'd been holding for days. I didn't know if I was free or this was a temporary reprieve, but I wasn't wasting it. Closing my eyes, I inhaled and let the air out slowly, like I was cleaning out the prison air from my lungs.

Fuck, that was nice.

Palmieri was standing at a food truck off to the side of the prison entrance. I went over. He gave the owner a few Euros, then we moved off to the side slightly. I didn't say anything. A few minutes later Palmieri handed me a sandwich wrapped in crisp paper. "This way."

He pointed to a small area with benches behind the food truck. It was visible to the prison, but not close enough to be overheard.

We sat. I unwrapped the sandwich, which was *porchetta di ariccia*. Boneless pork roll seasoned with garlic and rosemary. "Grazie," I said before taking a bite.

He began eating, like he was content to drag this out, so I asked, "Did you do it?"

"I have no idea what you're talking about."

"You wouldn't bring me out here alone if Rossi were still alive. So, congratulations."

He exhaled heavily. "There is no satisfaction to be found in another man's death, Benetti."

I took a bite of my sandwich, swallowed. "Killing is sometimes necessary. You can't dwell on the guilt. You avenged your daughter's death and that is what matters."

"This would be how you would see it."

"It's how anyone would see it, colonnello. Did he tell you why?"

"Retribution for his nephew's conviction. He thought I was in the car. He didn't realize my daughter was traveling with a nanny."

Cristo santo. Rossi had tried to assassinate Palmieri, which was a bad idea in itself, and instead killed the officer's daughter. I had no words. In my world, women and children were strictly off-limits. "There were reasons I could not help you. For that, I am sorry."

"I know. Your brotherhood code, or whatever the fuck. But I appreciate the little you did, which is why I kept you inside, where you couldn't meddle. No one will suspect you."

He wasn't telling me anything I hadn't already figured out. And with Rossi now out of the way, I had the chance to lead in southern Calabria. It was perfect. A few days in prison was worth taking the regional crown for my family. "I'm grateful. You could've been petty, considering our history." Me, fucking his wife.

After another bite of his sandwich, he said, "She was trying to get my attention. We'd been drifting apart after our daughter's death. It was grief that made her seek you out. I don't blame her—or you."

I couldn't resist taking a jab. "Are you saying that I saved your marriage?"

"No, stronzo. We divorced."

"Then why did you hit me?"

The edge of his mouth curled devilishly. "Because that is the least of what you deserve. Also, it made your arrest more believable."

"It hurt like fuck."

"Good." He chewed for a few moments. "I am resigning."

My head snapped over. "This is a mistake."

"It's done. I can't pretend to uphold the law after this."

Foolish, these "upstanding" men who think they are above the violence and pain of my world. "Do you think you are the first officer to break the law? If so, I have a long list of names to show you. And Rossi was a piece of shit."

"I know, but here—" he put his hand on his heart "—is telling me I can't go on as before. I want peace and I'll never find it in this job. Mostly thanks to men like you."

"Well, I won't be resigning."

"Which is why I must. I would hate to have to kill you, Benetti."

As if he could. "So what will you do?"

"Travel. Stay in a little house near the ocean. Sleep late. Drink wine." He crumpled up the sandwich paper in his fist. "I plan to enjoy the rest of the time I have on this earth. You should try it."

I stared unseeingly at the parking lot, the rows of cars blurring together, as I absorbed these words. "What makes you think I'm not?"

"Because I know more about your life than you can imagine. You stayed much longer in New York than necessary because of her. And even as badly you treated her in New York, she still bargained for your freedom. She came here to fight for you."

My stomach cramped at the idea of Valentina inside this prison, meeting with Palmieri. What had she been thinking? "Why do you assume I treated her badly?"

"Because she's angry. There were no tears, no heartfelt pleas on your behalf. She was cool and logical, never bemoaning your innocence. And when I warned her about you, she looked annoyed instead of defiant."

"And what was this warning?"

"That your world swallows women whole."

It wasn't wrong, but I wouldn't do that. As long as Val remained on the compound, she could do as she wished. The house was well-fortified and luxurious. Who wouldn't want to live there? And we would be safe there together. I was nearly salivating at having her so close all the time. Fucking on my bed, in my office. Out by the pool. In the woods. There was no limit to the places I would have her on my estate.

I stood and brushed the crumbs from my chest. "You don't know what you're talking about."

Rising, he chuckled, but it was dry. "Yeah, sure. You'll probably fuck it up anyway. Men like us aren't meant for relationships." He started toward the bin and tossed the paper in it. "Have a nice life, Benetti."

* * *

Valentina

Italians knew how to live well.

Sitting on the warm stone, I dangled my feet in the cool water of Luca's infinity pool. The view from up here was spectacular. The countryside stretched out around and below the house, with the sea sparkling in the distance. Hot pink outdoor chaises edged the pool in front of reflective glass windows, while flowers and plants lined the terrace. It was a Mediterranean paradise under bright sunshine, and the whole scene made me crave a mai tai. Any drink with an umbrella, actually.

I heard a door slide open and footsteps scuffed on the smooth stone. I assumed it was Gabi, as he was the only Benetti currently speaking to me, so I turned my face toward the sun. "Hey, Gabi," I greeted.

"Not quite," a deep voice said. "Here."

Leo, Luca's oldest son, was holding a frozen drink with an umbrella in it. As he sat the glass on the ground next to me, I shaded my eyes from the sun to study him. "Are you a mind reader?"

"No." He lowered himself to the edge of the pool and slipped his feet in. "But I know it gets hot out here."

"Is it poisoned?"

"No," he answered with all seriousness.

That was good enough for me. I lifted the glass and took a long sip of the cool drink. Orange and strawberry with a kick. "Yum. What is this?"

"A frozen Aperol spritz. We haven't officially met. I'm Leo." He put his hand out and we shook.

I could see the resemblance in his eyes, but he wasn't a mini-Luca like Gabi. Leo's face was thinner, more angular. His hair was lighter, as well. "It's nice to meet you."

"Tell me, why would I poison you?"

"Because you and your family are still pissed at me for meeting with Colonel Palmieri yesterday." I hadn't been invited to dinner last night. Instead, Gabi brought food and we ate together in my room. The uncles hadn't tried to stop me from wandering around today, though no one would answer me about when I could return to New York.

"I'm sorry for the way my uncles reacted, but we aren't all pissed. I'm grateful for your help."

"You are?"

"Yes, even though my father doesn't want you mixed up in all of this. He called yesterday and yelled at Sergio for a long time."

"I'm already mixed up in this. I have been since the moment your father arrived in the States. And I don't care if it made Luca mad. I had the ability to help him, so I did."

"You are brave, signorina. Not many go against my father's wishes."

"Your father's wishes don't mean shit to me right now." I was still angry and hurt, and being in his house, surrounded by his things, wasn't making me feel better.

"But you care about him."

Worse. I think I love him.

I sipped more of the frozen drink. "It doesn't matter. I'm returning to New York as soon as possible."

"You don't plan to stay?"

This life swallows women whole.

I shuddered at the words. I had my own life in New York, a business. Friends. My mother's things. I refused to get lured in by pink deck chairs and frozen cocktails. "No, I don't."

"This is too bad," Leo said, swirling his feet through the water. "It's obvious my father cares about you. I've never heard him so mad and worried before."

"It doesn't bother you?'

"What, that he cares about someone?"

"Someone who isn't your mother. Someone not much older than you. Someone who isn't Italian. None of that bothers you?"

Leo took a beat, his expression thoughtful. I could already tell he was the complete opposite of his brother, who said whatever was on his mind. Leo seemed more careful than Gabi. His personality was definitely closer to Luca's.

Finally, Leo said, "First, my mother is happy with her husband. He's a good man and takes care of her. I never had any dreams of my parents getting together. Second, I don't care about your age if you make Luca happy. And why would I care that you're American? I think American girls are hot."

"You sound like Gabi," I said with a laugh. "Pretty sure he got more phone numbers in New York than his phone can hold."

"I believe it. My brother said he enjoyed working at your restaurant." He paused. "He also says our father is in love with you."

You hold my heart and my soul, fiore mio. Per sempre.

A lump settled in my throat. If only that were true.

You didn't lie to the people you loved, trick them and use them. Even if that was how our relationship started, with his plans to use me to find my father, Luca had plenty of chances to come clean. Yet, he kept lying. Kept watching for my father, ready to pounce.

I took a deep breath and let it out slowly, my feet gliding through the cool water. "It doesn't matter. New York is my home. Your father lives here. The end."

"Admit it." He swept his hand out toward the Italian countryside. "This is better than New York."

It was pretty damn nice. But it wasn't home. Oh, and then there was the fact that I wasn't ready to be a mafia girlfriend. "You haven't seen the Hudson Valley," I said. "Especially in the fall when the leaves change color. It's so beautiful you want to cry. And a bonus? There's no one blackmailing or murdering there."

"Sure there isn't," he said under his breath.

The door opened again. Before I could see who it was, there were voices yelling in Italian. Leo straightened and immediately lifted his feet out of the pool. "What's happening?" I asked as he dried off his legs with one of the beach towels. "Is something wrong?"

"My father is here."

My body jerked, rocking me back slightly. "Here? He's out of prison?"

"Scusa, signorina. I need to change." Leo disappeared inside the house and I frowned. He'd been wearing a t-shirt and shorts, like me. Did Luca insist that his oldest son dress up every day?

I sipped my frozen Aperol Spritz and pushed those thoughts aside. Leo's clothing was something else I didn't understand about Luca's life and probably never would.

Besides, I had bigger worries.

Luca was *here*. I hadn't expected to see him again, at least not so soon. What was I going to say to him? Worse, what was he going to say to me?

My chest expanded with a strange sensation that I suspected was both anticipation and dread. Was I going to hug him or kick him in the balls? I wasn't ready. And I wanted to go home.

I wasn't his mistress or his girlfriend. I was just the woman he'd manipulated for his own ends. Luca was everything my mother warned me about, yet I'd gone along with him willingly, too naive to question what was happening.

I swirled my legs in the water and finished the drink. Being heartbroken sucked. I needed this feeling to go away. I needed to forget about Luca and bury myself in work at the trattoria.

Maybe we should add a frozen Aperol Spritz to the menu?

"Would you like to swim?"

The sound of his deep voice sent a deluge of longing through me, a flood of memories I wished I could forget. I blinked but didn't look over. "No."

He lowered himself to the stone beside me and began rolling the cuffs of his trousers. I peeked at his hands, the movements sure and swift. I loved those hands. I missed those hands.

He dipped his legs into the water one at a time. "Why not? I'm sure there is an extra suit somewhere."

"This isn't a vacation, Luca. I want to go home."

"Forgive me. I saw the empty cocktail glass and thought otherwise."

My mouth flattened as I ground my back teeth together. "You're a dick." I started to get up, but he grabbed my arm.

"Wait, per favore. I . . . " He heaved a heavy sigh. "Please, listen. I have much to say. I'm sorry, Valentina. For everything. I never should have used you to find your father."

"It's not that. It's that you kept using me even after we started sleeping together."

"I know, and I'm sorry, amore."

I kicked my feet and watched the ripples in the water. "Why not tell me, then? Why go on letting me think it was real."

"Because it *was* real." Leaning over, he put his forehead against my temple. "My soul aches for you. I am like the dirt surrounding us, dry and lifeless, and you are the water bringing me back to life. Fiore mio, my beautiful flower. You make everything better—you make *me* better. I am nothing without you."

Tears spilled over my lashes, tracking down my cheeks. I wiped them, but they kept coming. "God, Luca."

Luca wrapped an arm around me and brought me closer. "Don't cry, bella. I know I've hurt you. Let me make it up to you."

"I'm not sure you can. Even if I were willing to forgive you, what would be the point?"

"The point is to be together." He kissed the top of my head, then pressed his face into my hair. "*Ti amo*, Valentina."

The words were like a punch to the gut. I'd wanted to hear them for so long, but it no longer mattered. He was an Italian mob boss with a giant rock house and pink pool chairs. I lived in a tiny town where we didn't lock our houses at night. For god's sake, I scrubbed toilets and bought clothes from mobile apps. There wasn't a way in hell this added up.

"I have never said those words to a woman in my life," he continued softly. "Because I never found one who I wished to marry before."

My chest cracked, the pain ripping through me. God, when would this agony stop? "Don't."

"I can't. Marry me, stay here with me. Let me make you happy every single day with orgasms and purses and chicken parm. Babies. Whatever you desire, amore mio. I need you by my side."

"Luca . . . " I said shakily. I hadn't expected this from him and I had no defenses in place against his onslaught. "I can't stay here. I have a life, a business. I'm not cut out to be a mafia wife, sequestered up here in the hills with nothing to do all day."

His body stiffened against mine and his arm dropped from my shoulder. "This is where I live, the land on which generations of Don Benettis have lived. It isn't safe for me to stay anywhere else."

"You lived in Paesano," I couldn't help but point out.

"For a short time, yes. But I can't permanently run an empire there."

I rubbed at the tears, trying to stem their descent. We were quiet for several minutes, both of us unmoving.

"You are asking me to give it up," he said softly. "Which I cannot do."

"I'm not asking that. I know you won't."

"It's not a question of whether I will or won't. I'm telling you I can't. Only death passes on the title to another."

So that was that. There wasn't more to discuss, really. We both knew where the other stood. No doubt it seemed unreasonable to him that I refused to move here. After all, the estate was gorgeous and I'd want for nothing.

But I couldn't leave Paesano. I'd lost my mother too recently, her house and restaurant my only ties to her. I wasn't looking for a fresh start on the other side of the globe.

"Do you love me?" he asked.

I didn't know how to answer. Telling him the truth only made things worse. Yet I couldn't keep it from him. He deserved to know. "I think I fell in love with you the night you made me dinner."

He cupped my neck and angled me toward him. His gaze was soft but troubled as he studied me. "Valentina, I promise to give you the world if you let me."

The knot in my stomach twisted, my insides squeezing with misery. I liked problems with easy solutions, but there was no solution here. We were just two people who lived in different places and couldn't make it work.

I fought back the tears threatening to start again as I put my hand on his jaw. "I don't want the world. I have everything I need back home—except for one thing. And he can't stay there."

"Please, I am begging you to reconsider. Stay and see if you like it."

He wasn't listening. This wasn't a pair of boots to try on and return if they didn't fit. This was moving across the globe and leaving everything I knew behind. I couldn't do it.

"I can't. My answer won't change and we are delaying the inevitable." I leaned in and pressed a gentle kiss to his cheek. "And unless you're planning to hold me hostage here forever, then you have to let me go."

He swallowed loudly, then eased out of my reach. With a graceful push, he stood and adjusted the cuffs of his trousers, not caring that water soaked through the cloth. "Allora," he said softly. "I'll have Gabi fly you home."

Without a backward glance, Luca strode to the sliding door and disappeared inside the house.

Chapter Thirty-Six

Luca

I lost track of how long I'd been running.

The ache in my chest was unbearable and exercise was the only way I could think to ease it. Though it was two o'clock in the morning, I couldn't sleep. I also couldn't eat. If I started drinking instead to dull my senses, I might not ever stop.

She was gone. I'd given her everything and she didn't want it, didn't want *me*. I had to get over her and accept it.

Unless you're planning to hold me hostage here forever, then you have to let me go.

I wiped away the sweat streaming down my face. Part of me had considered keeping her here. Eventually she would come to love this place as much as I do and settle into her role as my wife.

But I couldn't do it.

Val had lost so much in her life, her choices taken away because of her mother's illness. Choices stripped because of the trattoria, because of her father. I'd done enough damage. It was time to let her be.

Besides, what did I know of love? The women in my world, including my own mother, were unhappy. The men were all killers, blackmailers. Criminals of all stripes. And I couldn't change it even if I wanted to. Chi nasce lupo, non muore agnello.

He who is born a wolf does not die a lamb.

What right did I have to bring Valentina into such a fate?

My legs burned as I increased the speed on the treadmill. I needed to forget. To get to a place where I could close my eyes without seeing her beautiful face, without memories of her slicing me from the inside out.

Movement caught my eye and I saw Leonardo enter the room. Clad in only a pair of long shorts, my oldest son walked over to the treadmill, a frown on his face. But he said nothing as he approached. My lungs were too busy forcing in air, so I could only watch as Leo bent and ripped the machine's cord out of the wall.

The treadmill died.

I gripped the handrails and tried not to fall over. "Che . . . cazzo?" I wheezed.

"You're scaring everyone. Go to bed, Papà."

"I'm . . . the boss. Don't give . . . a fuck."

Leo folded his arms across his chest. "Are you trying to kill yourself? Is that it? Because I won't let you. The uncles and guards are too afraid to come in here, but I'm not."

My legs wouldn't support my weight, so I collapsed against the wall and slowly sank to the ground. I sucked in huge gulps of air and closed my eyes. I didn't like admitting weakness, especially in front of one of my boys, but the words tumbled out in my exhaustion. "I just need to sleep."

I heard him move around, then the door to the tiny refrigerator opened and closed. "Here." Cool plastic pressed to my palm.

He'd already opened the bottle of water, so I chugged it gratefully. When I finished I said, "You don't need to worry, figlio. I'm fine."

"You're not fine." Lowering himself next to me, he rested his forearms on his bent knees. "You're very much not fine. Respectfully."

I hadn't seen much of my brothers this past week, and most of the household staff had started avoiding me.

Not even finally learning where Niccolò was from D'Agostino had given me the focus I needed. Maybe resolving that mess when Niccolò returned would snap me out of it.

"Allora, I will be fine," I said. "I'm too wired to sleep from being in a different time zone and then prison. In time I will adjust."

"I don't think it has anything to do with jet lag or prison, Papà. I think it has to do with Valentina."

The sound of her name scraped across my ragged nerves, irritating them further. "Do not say her name to me."

"Why? Do you hate her that much?"

"I don't hate her. But I don't wish to discuss her, either."

"Zio Sergio said you asked her to marry you."

I told my brother that information in confidence, the stronzo. He had no right to tell anyone else. I said nothing and used my sleeve to clean the sweat from my face.

"Papà," he said tiredly. "I know we don't talk about these things. But we can."

"Talking is pointless. She's gone. Now I can concentrate on the things that matter, like taking over Rossi's territory."

"Talking is not pointless. Or maybe it's pointless for you, but not for me. I'd like to understand you. Gabi and I both would, actually."

"What is there to understand? I've kept you close, helped raise you both for your entire lives. We talk all the time."

"But you don't tell us anything important. We learn more from Zio Dante than you, our own father. You don't talk to us about the business or your personal life. We're treated like soldati."

Soldiers, who are told what to do but not why.

I ran a hand through my wet hair. "I'm trying to protect you, figlio. You have years to learn what you need to know to lead the 'ndrina. I want you to enjoy your life while you can."

"Is that what Nonno did with you?"

I grimaced. My father taught me brutality and responsibility from a young age. He didn't care whether I was happy or not. All that mattered was being strong enough to become the next Don Benetti. "No. He told me too much. Showed me too much. Which is why I've tried to spare you and Gabi as long as possible."

"But what happens if you die? I don't want to take over and not know what I'm doing."

"You'll have your uncles to guide you." I put my hand on his knee and squeezed before letting go. "You will be an excellent don, figlio mio."

"Still, it would be nice to learn from you. I've tried so hard to prove that I'm ready, but it's like you're keeping me at a distance. And I know Gabi feels the same. It's why he acts out. And why he followed you to New York."

I stared at the ceiling. My boys shouldn't have to act out to get my attention or prove themselves as worthy. They were Benettis and my sons—which meant they were worthy. "Perdonami. I am a good don but a shitty father. I was only trying to give you both the life I never had."

"Ma dai, Papà. You *are* a good father. Most men in your position don't care about their bastards, even if they are sons. We're grateful for the life you've given us. But we're not little boys any more. We're men. And it's time to let us help lead."

Emotion squeezed my chest like a fist. They were good boys, smart and loyal. The empire was in excellent hands after I died, and this pleased me enormously. "Okay."

"Really?"

"Do not question your don, figlio mio. His decisions are final."

"Does that include the decision to let Val go back to New York?" When I didn't say anything, he bumped his knee against mine. "I like her. And Gabi does, too."

I liked her, too. But it didn't matter. "She lives in New York and has no interest in moving here."

"And?"

"And what else can I do? She asked me to let her go." I shrugged. What more was there to say?

Leonardo was quiet for a long time, then he spoke softly. "I once asked you something and I've never forgotten your answer. Every time Gabi and I visited our mothers for the weekend, you sent five guards with each of us. It seemed like a lot of trouble for two days. And when I asked you why we went so often when the security risk was so high, you said, 'Sometimes in life the reward outweighs the risk.'"

I didn't remember the conversation, but it sounded like something I would say. "I wanted you both to remain close to your mothers. No good comes from taking little boys away from the person who gave them life."

"Papà, this also applies to you. Go after her. Reap your reward."

His advice irritated me. Hadn't he been listening? "She doesn't want to move to Catanzaro and I can't force her."

"So live there."

My head snapped over and I scowled at him. "You know this is impossible. Even if I wanted to turn everything over to you, I can't."

He put up his palms to face me. "I'm not angling to become don. What I mean is that you don't need to run the family from here."

My mouth fell open. "To do so would be the height of irresponsibility. The risk—" I bit off the rest of what I was going to say.

"Exactly," he returned smugly. "The risk is nothing in comparison to what you gain."

"I could be killed."

"Gabi said the mansion was well-fortified. And you can fly back here whenever you like. The two of you can stay here for months at a time. Allora, you could split the year in half."

"You make it sound so easy."

"It will be a headache for security, but the rest is easy. This isn't Nonno's day without computers and mobile phones. Our business is international and so is technology."

I rubbed my jaw and straightened my legs. "Why are you pushing this so hard?"

"Because I'd like to see you happy. And maybe if you're happy in your own relationship, maybe you'll let me marry Bianca."

"*Stai zitto!*" I snapped, telling him to shut up. "No talk of marriage, especially to a girl I haven't chosen."

He grinned, not repentant in the least. "I said maybe."

Leonardo wasn't fooling me. The fact that he'd raised the possibility told me he'd been thinking about it. "I'm telling your uncles to keep a closer eye on you."

"Does this mean you're going to live in Paesano?"

I didn't answer. It wasn't as simple as that. This was a decision I couldn't make alone. My brothers needed to be involved, as splitting my time between two countries would reorganize our family structure. A small army would be required to keep the estate in New York safe, as well as to keep Valentina protected wherever she went.

And if I did move there, would she want to marry me? She was so young, her whole life ahead of her, and my world was death and destruction. It hardly seemed fair.

I have everything I need back home—except for one thing.

Leonardo took the empty water bottle from my hand and replaced it with a fresh one. "Gabi also said there is opportunity there. The locals are weak and a mess, and Vito D'Agostino is in Toronto. He could be a resource."

"Yes, he told me."

"Could be fun, Papà. We haven't had a turf war in years."

I shoved his head and ruffled his hair. "You were four. How would you even remember?"

My son laughed then pushed to his feet. Reaching out, he offered a hand. "Come on. You need a shower and your bed."

I was too tired to fight him. Too tired for everything. "When did you get so smart?"

He held open the door to the gym for me. "I've always been

smart. Which is why I hope you'll listen to me when I say that if you love her, you shouldn't let her go."

Chapter Thirty-Seven

Valentina

Two weeks later

T he bell jangled as I walked into the café. Sam was all alone behind the counter, sipping an iced coffee and scrolling on her phone. She had her nose ring in today and her black hair was braided into two pigtails. With her pale skin, she looked very Wednesday Adams.

She glanced up as I drew closer. "Val, have you finished this book for book club yet? It's so *boring*. I suggested a dark romance, but they picked this one instead. I'm forty percent in and no one has even banged yet."

I set my wallet and keys on the counter. "No, I haven't started it. To be honest I'll probably skip book club this weekend."

Wincing, Sam looked up from her tablet. "I'm sorry. I totally forgot."

"It's okay. I've only just mentioned it, so how could you forget?"

"I mean that I forgot about the man who shall not be named."

"It's okay. You can say his name. The entire town knows."

When I returned from Italy, everyone was talking about what had happened. From the fire and the shooting, to my father, then how Luca was arrested . . . and it was no secret that he'd broken my heart.

"Still, you don't need any reminders of that giant dick hole. Do you want your usual?"

"Yes, please."

As Sam went behind the espresso machine, I asked, "Where's Bev?"

"Running late." She lifted her eyebrows meaningfully.

Bev had a date with Roberto last night, which could only mean one thing. "Stop. Are you serious?"

"Girl, this is the third time this week."

"What! How did I miss this?"

"Maybe because I don't want to talk about how my grandmother is getting laid more than me these days."

That was fair. "But Roberto hasn't said anything either, that dog."

The door blew open and Bev hurried in, her hair wild. "I'm here! I'm so sorry I'm late. My alarm didn't go off."

Sam and I exchanged an amused look over the alarm excuse. "No worries, Gram," Sam said. "We've been pretty slow this morning anyway."

Bev darted into the back and when she returned I could see that the buttons on her shirt didn't line up. "Did you get dressed in the dark?" I asked, pointing to her shirt.

The older woman glanced down. "Oh, shoot." She quickly refastened the buttons correctly. "Mercury must be in retrograde right now. I just cannot keep up."

I pressed my lips together, trying not to laugh, as Sam rolled her eyes. "Yep, it's Mercury alright."

"What did I miss?" Bev's head swiveled between the two of us as she wrapped an apron around her waist.

"Not much," Sam said as she sprayed whipped cream on my iced coffee. "We're still not mentioning you-know-who and Val isn't sure if she's going to book club."

"Oh, Val. Honey." Bev grabbed my wrist and squeezed. "Just give it time. I know you probably don't want advice, but my mother used to say men are like the bus. If you miss one, another is coming along right behind it."

None of them were like Luca, though. Every man I knew paled in comparison. The pressure behind my sternum increased, making it hard to breathe. I missed him so badly. I couldn't allow myself to cry anymore, though. This had been my choice. "Thanks, Bev. I'll keep that in mind."

"I still think you should've moved to Italy," Sam said.

"Move to Italy?" Bev's eyebrows climbed. "He asked you to move there?"

Only Sam and Maggie knew of my final conversation with Luca. Well, now Bev knew too. "Yes, he asked me to marry him and move there."

Sam put my drink on the counter. "Sorry, Val. I have a big mouth."

"You turned him down?" Bev waved away my attempt to pay for my drink. "Tell me why."

"Isn't it obvious?"

"Not to me." Bev looked at her granddaughter. "Do you understand it?"

Sam shook her head. "Not even a little. A man like that—rich and handsome—who wants to marry me and take me to an estate in Italy? Y'all would definitely never see the likes of me ever again."

"Hello?" I interrupted. "I have a business here. A life, friends. My mother's house. I can't just up and go."

Bev's smile was soft as she reached for my hand. She started walking around the counter. "Come with me. I want to show you something."

"Bev, I have to get to the restaurant."

"No, you don't," she said, leading me toward the far wall. "Roberto wasn't even dressed when I left. You have time."

I didn't comment, though it took all my self-control not to bring up Mercury again.

We stopped in front of a row of familiar photographs. Each one was of the Leaning Tower of Pisa from a different angle. I knew them well.

"Your mother took these photos for me," Bev said. "When she was studying over there and met your father."

"Yes, I remember. I love them." After her death I spent a long time looking at these photos, imagining her standing in front of the famous landmark.

Bev reached to take a frame off the wall. "Have you ever read what she wrote on the back?"

My muscles locked in surprise. "She wrote on the photos?"

"Just this one. And I think it might help you to see it."

The photo was clipped into the frame. It took Bev some maneuvering but she finally got it out. "Here." She handed me the large photo and I flipped it over.

Sure enough, there was my mother's elegant script.

Bev,

What a time this was! I wish you had been able to visit.

Next time, no excuses! Life is short and there is too much joy to experience in the world. We shouldn't let anything hold us back. Enjoy the pictures.

Love,
Abby

I couldn't speak, my heartbeat rushing in my ears. *Life is too short.* If she'd only known. There weren't any more trips because I'd been born eight months later. Then she died sixteen years after that.

We shouldn't let anything hold us back.

Tears stung my eyelids. She'd been so determined, so fierce. Independent and strong. And she'd raised me to be the same. So what happened? Why was I afraid of leaving this town?

"Every day I regret not taking that trip," Bev said gently. "But I convinced myself the café wouldn't survive if I closed down or let someone else run it for two weeks. I was more worried about money than happiness. And that's part of what's wrong with our culture. We value all the wrong things."

"It's not money," I whispered. "The trattoria is her legacy, just like her house and garden. The peeling wallpaper and expired boxes of pudding I can't stand to throw away. She's still here and I'm afraid to let her go."

Bev pulled me into her warm body. She smelled like vanilla. "Honey, you aren't letting your mother go. Those are just *things.* Your mother will always be with you, no matter where you are."

I knew this in theory, but it was still hard to accept. "You think I should move to Italy."

"I think you should put yourself first for a change. Do what makes you happy."

Taking in a deep breath, I pulled away and dabbed at my eyes with my fingertips. I didn't want to ruin my mascara. "I'll think about it."

"Good. Now, go get your drink before it melts and Sam starts yelling."

We both knew Sam was pretty chill, but I returned the photo to Bev and went to the counter. Chuck, the only realtor in town, was paying for his coffee as I gathered my keys, wallet and drink. We knew each other from high school. "Hey, Val," he said.

"Hi, Chuck. How are you?"

"Never better." He slipped two dollars into the cafe's tip jar.

Sam leaned against the counter. "Chuck was saying the Portofino mansion has sold."

I nearly dropped my iced coffee. Images of espressos on the terrace and long showers assaulted me. Picking out ties and cuddling and purses and sex. Lots and lots of sex.

Luca's former house . . . sold? Now someone else bought that tacky house.

God, the universe hated me.

They were both staring at me oddly. I blurted, "Congrats on the commission, Chuck. See you around."

And I got the hell out of there before I started crying *again*.

Chapter Thirty-Eight

Valentina

Book Club was in full swing.

Nearly every single man in town was packed into the trattoria's bar, hungry gazes watching the women in the corner. Instead of drinking with my friends, though, I poured drinks for customers and helped behind the bar. It kept me busy, as well as prevented my friends from grilling me about Luca.

The new bartender, Quincy—who was Anne Marie's son—didn't know a Manhattan from a Long Island Iced Tea, but I couldn't complain. Quincy had stepped in after Gabi returned to Italy to go be a mafia prince. I missed Gabi, but he and I texted regularly. He sounded busy, but happy. He never mentioned his father and I never asked.

Had Luca started sleeping with his mistress again?

The thought caused my empty stomach to turn over, so I popped an olive in my mouth and looked around. Roberto hovered near the front, even though I told him to go home ages ago. There was no reason for both of us to be here, and I'd close down after my friends left. Giovanni's team was almost done with dinner service, and then we'd only have the bar to worry about.

A few minutes later I made change for a beer. When I turned, Maggie was at the bar, frowning at me. I gave the customer his money. "Thanks, Carl. Let me know when you need a refill." He turned toward his buddies and I rested on the bar closer to Maggie. "Need anything?"

My friend's response was instant. "Yes. You."

"I'm right here."

"Val, god dammit. This is pissing me off. Come sit with us."

"I don't want to. They're all looking at me with sad, pitying eyes. The second I sit down, they'll want to hear what happened. Honestly, I don't have the energy."

"It's only because they care about you. And I'll tell them to not raise the topic of Luca Benetti tonight, I promise." She put her hand over her heart.

"Maybe later. Let me help Quincy a little longer. Okay?"

Maggie pointed at me. "I'm coming back in thirty minutes and I won't take no for an answer."

"But—"

"If you refuse, I will tell Carl about the crush you had on him in seventh grade and how you used to walk by his house every day after school even though he wasn't on your way. At all."

Horrified, I watched Carl spin at the sound of his name. "What?"

"Nothing," I said at the same time Maggie said, "Oh hey, Carl."

"Were you guys talking about me?" He appeared adorably confused.

"I don't know." Maggie raised an eyebrow in my direction. "Were we?"

"You are the worst." To Carl, I said, "Ignore her. She's stuck in middle school."

Carl rejoined his friends and I waved Maggie away. "Get lost, Fiorentino."

A few minutes later the computer froze and needed to be

rebooted. I was standing with my back to the bar, entering in the information to restart the computer, when I noticed everything had gone quiet. I glanced into the mirror to see what was going on.

I jerked in surprise and my elbow bumped the computer. No, this couldn't be. Was I imagining him?

Luca.

Luca was here, at the bar. A now empty bar.

What the hell? Why was he here?

A loud ringing echoed in my ears as I faced him. He looked good. His hair was a little longer and the bruise on his cheek was almost non-existent. A few days' worth of scruff graced his jaw, gray whiskers dotted in among the dark brown. His intense stare was locked on my face and my tongue felt thick as I blurted, "What are you doing here?"

"Ordering a drink. I heard this place has a good wine selection."

"I don't understand."

"A Valpolicella, I think."

I needed time to think, so with a shaking hand I poured him a glass of the red wine. "Should I start a tab, or did you want to cash out?"

"A tab. I'm going to be here a lot."

I stared, unsure what to say. Then I noticed everyone staring at us, the room as silent as a tomb. I jerked my thumb toward the kitchen. "Come with me."

I didn't wait to see if he followed. I walked out from the bar and went through the swinging door. The usual hustle and bustle greeted me, the familiar sounds of a professional kitchen during service. When I reached my office I heard Giovanni greeting Luca like an old friend. They chatted in Italian, but I unlocked the door and went inside, pacing back and forth as I tried to figure out why Luca was here. We'd said everything that needed to be said in Catanzaro.

Maybe he was here on business?

Finally, the knob turned and he strode inside, all masculine grace and leashed power in his dark navy suit. I recognized the tie as one I'd chosen for him all those days ago. "Tell me what's going on."

One eyebrow quirked. "Isn't it obvious?"

"No, not to me. Are you in town for business?"

"Sort of." He set the wine glass on a file cabinet. "I'm moving here."

My stomach dropped at the same time as my jaw. "What? You're kidding."

"Not permanently. I'll set up here, then go back and forth to Catanzaro."

Moving here. My brain tripped over these words. It made no sense. "Why?"

"For you. I want to marry you and you want to live here. I hoped we could compromise. We'll split our time between Paesano and Catanzaro."

Needing to ground myself in reality, I gripped the edge of the desk. Was this really happening? "Isn't that dangerous for you?"

"Yes, and for you. But I brought a small army with me to keep us safe."

"And so, what? You'll vacation here while I work?"

"Not vacation. I'll work, too."

His smile grew, and there was something devious in the depths of his eyes. Like he had plans in the works. I didn't care about those plans, not yet. I still couldn't believe he was serious. "You bought the Portofino mansion."

He nodded once. "You heard. Good."

"Of course I heard. No one can keep a secret in this town."

"Roberto can."

"Oh, my god. No wonder he was hanging around tonight. He knew you were coming."

Luca reached inside his coat pocket and took out a small box. My heart leapt into my throat as he flipped open the box and took out a ring. I saw a flash of white, but I was concentrating on his face, not his hands.

Luca met my eyes, his expression serious. "Valentina, you are everything to me. I have tried breathing and eating and existing without you, and I can't do it. So I will move heaven and earth to give you what you need, if only you stay by my side. Marry me, have a life with me in both places. Because it doesn't matter where we are, as long as you are with me, amore mio."

"You're really willing to live here for half the year?"

"If you are willing to live in Catanzaro for the other half, then yes."

We shouldn't let anything hold us back.

My mother's words. She wouldn't want me wrapped up in Luca's world, but she would want me to be happy. And she would want me with a man willing to do anything for me. Like move across the globe for six months out of the year.

He shifted on his feet. "You may take more time to think about this. I know it is a big decision for you."

"Yes."

"So think, fiore mio. I'll give you a few days—"

"That was my answer. Yes, I'll marry you. Yes, I'll live in Catanzaro for part of the year. Yes, yes, yes!"

"Thank fuck."

He was on me in a flash, his strong arms pulling me into his chest. I wrapped myself around him and held on, his familiar scent filling my head. God, I'd missed him.

We clung together for a long beat, then he grabbed my face in both his hands and kissed me. His lips were soft, and he tasted like wine and mint and a lifetime of promises. I gave as good as I got, telling him without words that I was in this for the long haul.

When we finally parted, he pressed his forehead to mine. "Ti amo, baby."

"Ti amo, Luca."

He gave me a brief, hard kiss then picked up my hand. "I hope you like it."

The diamond ring was over the top. A cushion cut stone, with smaller diamonds surrounding it like a halo, all in a platinum setting. "It's . . . stunning. I'm almost afraid to wear it around."

"But you will. I want everyone to know you're mine."

For some inexplicable reason, that caveman declaration caused my heart to flip over. "I'm yours. And I love it." I pushed up to kiss him. "Grazie, bello."

He growled low in his throat, his fingers tightening on my skin. "I love when you speak my language."

"Then I'll hire a tutor and learn it properly. I mean, we'll be living there for half the year. I'd better understand what you and your brothers are saying."

"This makes me very happy. Come, I want to fuck you in a bed."

He started to tug on my hand, but I stayed put. "Wait. Tell me what you're planning to do while you're here. Are you starting another criminal empire in New York?"

Luca placed his hands on my shoulders. "I love you and we will share a life together. But it's for your own protection if you stay out of the business and leave it to me, capisce?"

I held onto the edges of his suit jacket. "Luca, I visited you in prison once. I don't want to live through that again."

"You won't. Amore, I went to the GDF headquarters purposely so they would put me in prison. You see, the man who killed Palmieri's daughter was the boss of the region. I couldn't name him and betray the brotherhood. So I dropped enough clues for Palmieri to figure it out, then insulted him to get arrested. Being in prison ensured that I couldn't be blamed for what needed to happen—not by the GDF *or* the 'ndrina. Thankfully, Palmieri is a smart man and did what had to be done. Then he let me go."

"That was all planned? Holy shit. You're very smart."

His mouth curved into a sly grin. "This is true. I am very smart. Any other questions before I take you to the mansion and fuck you into the mattress?"

"What about the fire? I thought the mansion was in bad shape?"

"The garage, yes, and I'll have it rebuilt. Andiamo, fiore. That's enough talking." He flicked open the door and held it for me. I grabbed my bag from under the desk, which caused Luca's smile to widen. "I see you are still using my gifts."

I was carrying one of the expensive handbags he bought me. "Only because these are too pretty not to use. It had nothing to do with you."

"You missed me," he whispered as I walked by him.

I had, but I wasn't admitting it. Yet. I walked through the kitchen on my way to the dining room. The staff all stopped what they were doing to watch us go by, their gazes curious. "We're back together," I announced.

A round of congratulations echoed down the line, but I tried to appear professional. "Thank you. See you all in the morning."

I started to push on the swinging door, but Luca held my arm. "Wait."

Bending, he picked me up, bridal-style. I yelped and held on to his neck. "What are you doing?"

"I have watched this movie, *An Officer and a Gentleman*. It's very corny, but romantic. And we have a tradition to uphold for book club, no?"

"Oh, god." I buried my face into his throat. "I'm never going to live this down."

Quickly, Luca strode through the swinging door and we were in the dining room. All the conversation slowly stopped as the diners noticed us. I could feel my cheeks burning, a mixture of happiness and embarrassment. But mostly happiness.

"Finally!" This was from Maggie, who was now on her feet. "About time, you two!"

Someone started applauding, and then more people joined in. I covered my face with my free hand. "Stop it. Oh, my god. Luca, put me down. This is mortifying."

"Not a chance, amore." He kept going toward the exit. As he walked, Luca shouted something to Roberto in Italian.

"What did you say to Roberto?" I asked.

"I told him to give everyone a bottle of champagne to toast us and bill me."

We reached the front door, but he didn't set me down. The night was warm and mild, stars twinkling overhead in the perfect romantic backdrop as he carried me. How did I get so lucky?

"I know you wanted a bed tonight," I said in his ear. "But I was wondering . . . Think the cemetery is empty tonight?"

He started walking faster. "Don't worry, little girl. I'll take good care of you."

Epilogue

Luca

Three weeks later

I sat with my back to the wall.

Gabriele was in the chair on my left, Leonardo on my right. The late hour meant the trattoria was empty, save the kitchen staff.

I didn't like having meetings at night. They kept me away from Valentina, and I'd much prefer to be fucking her at the moment.

This meant I was pissed off.

I drummed my fingers on the wooden table. Leonardo reached for his wine, while Gabriele checked his mobile once more. Where the fuck were they?

The door opened.

My cousin Niccolò walked in, followed by another man. The stranger was well dressed, probably mid-30s. He looked very similar to his brother.

I stood, as did my sons, and Niccolò started in my direction. "Don Benetti—"

"You will fucking wait, stronzo." Ignoring him, I held out my hand to greet the stranger first. "Luca Benetti."

"Vito D'Agostino." He shook my hand. "A pleasure, Don Benetti. My brother speaks highly of you."

"We are appreciative of his help. Thank you for coming down from Toronto."

I sat, as did everyone else, except Gabriele, who gave his seat up to Niccolò. My cousin had the good sense to remain quiet. I would deal with him later, when it was just family.

As Leonardo poured wine for the table, I asked, "How do you like Canada?"

"It's fucking cold." Vito shook his head. "I thought I wouldn't mind it, but *fuck*."

I wasn't looking forward to the winters in New York. I would convince Valentina to stay in Catanzaro during those months. "And you took over for Mancini. How is business?"

"Things have settled down. We've secured the territory and expanded."

"It must be nice to have your brother's resources."

Vito sipped his wine and set the glass down carefully. "I believe in being direct, Don Benetti. So if you're asking whether Enzo is running Toronto with me, then the answer is no. I am doing this alone."

It was what I'd been told, but I'd needed to be sure. "I also believe in being direct. You should know that my family is settling here."

If he was surprised, he masked it well. "In this area or Manhattan?"

"This area. I will go back and forth to Catanzaro, but my brother Dante will reside here permanently, as will my son." I indicated Gabriele.

"I'm assuming this has something to do with the woman you brought to meet my brother."

I dipped my chin in acknowledgment. "My fiancée, who runs this restaurant."

"*Congratulazioni.*" He lifted his wine glass in a toast. "I wish you many happy years together."

"Cin cin." We all drank. I pointed to the ring on his finger. "I hadn't heard you were married. Congratulations, as well."

He held up his hand and smirked. "Not married. Not interested, either. This ensures it stays that way."

Everyone laughed except for me. I was once so foolish, but then I met Valentina. Now I needed to marry her, make her forever mine, for my own peace of mind. "I wanted to inform you of my intentions so there are no misunderstandings later."

Vito's fingers stilled, his eyes going flat. "What are your intentions?"

"There is a casino an hour away, poorly run. We plan to start there, then expand as necessary. How are you finding the MCs?" Some motorcycle clubs in North America dabbled in trafficking.

"Stupid and a pain in the ass."

Good. That meant they would be easy to eliminate here. "I want to establish a trade with you. The chemicals for crystal in exchange for South American coke. We'll use drones. Boats, when necessary."

"I'll agree to that. What about the casino? Need any help?"

"I might want to borrow some of your men. Temporarily, until things settle down."

"And in return?"

"What are you asking for?"

"Ten percent of the casino."

I laughed. "Please."

"Eight."

"Ma dai, I would never agree to such a high percentage."

"And I would remind you that I have just saved your cousin from making a very big mistake."

I pressed my lips together. I didn't like it, but Vito was right. And I was going to strangle my cousin. "Three."

Vito nodded once. "We'll work out all of the details later. Who should we talk to? Dante?"

"I'll be here at least until the holidays. How quickly can you get your men here?"

"Next week."

"Va bene." I rose and buttoned my suit coat. "Where are you staying?"

"I prefer to return to Toronto immediately."

Smart of him. I shook his hand once more. "My thanks for your help with my cousin."

"Good luck," he returned. "And I hope you change the name of this town. It's fucking stupid."

He departed, three of his men behind him, and I lowered myself into the chair once more. "Sit your fucking ass down, Niccolò."

"Luca, forgive me."

Gabriele smacked the back of Niccolò's head. "That's Don Benetti, stronzo."

Our cousin winced, then put his palms together, prayer-style. "Don Benetti, I'm here to beg for your forgiveness. I never meant to cause so much trouble."

"And yet you did. Tell me what the fuck happened."

"I lost a shipment."

"The fuck?" This was Gabriele, who leaned into his cousin's face. "You should have called!"

I put a hand on Gabriele's arm. Very quietly, I said, "Start explaining."

"Don Rossi asked me to accompany his man and deliver a truck full of coke to Belgium. He said you recommended me and I didn't want to disappoint you."

That fuck. Rossi set everything up from the start. "Go on."

"Rossi's man came down with food poisoning an hour outside of town. He said to drop him off and continue on. I didn't know what to do, but it was a massive shipment and I knew what was at stake."

Niccolò shifted in his seat and his voice dropped in volume. "I stopped for drinks in Lucerne, and the truck was stolen."

I sighed heavily and rubbed my eyes. "How much?"

He hung his head. "It was so much, much more coke than I'd ever seen. Don Rossi said it was five hundred kilos."

"Porca puttana!" said Leonardo. "That's more than thirty-eight million Euros!"

"I know!" He put his face in his hands. "That is why I tried to make it right."

"That was stupid of you," I said. "You should have contacted someone immediately."

"I did, Don Benetti, I swear!" exclaimed Niccolò. "I called Don Rossi first. He said not to bother you because you were leaving for New York on urgent business and he would fill you in."

Bastardo! Too bad that stronzo Rossi was dead. I'd like to kill him myself over this. "What else did he say?"

"He said he would kill me if I didn't find that truck. And he said you would kill me if he didn't."

I hated to think it, but this was clever of Rossi. He had to do something to keep Niccolò out of the way, and kidnapping or killing my cousin would've forced me to retaliate. Better to create confusion and issue vague threats.

"I panicked," continued Niccolò. "I knew I couldn't find that truck. So I thought if I could steal coke from someone else, it could replace what I'd lost."

Again, stupid. "Where did you go?"

"I rented a van and drove to Munich. It was the closest city where I knew some soldiers. I hoped to follow them for a day or so, then see where their storage facility was."

Mamma mia, this boy. "Stealing from another family puts ours at risk, idiota."

"It was dumb, I know. I was desperate. I didn't know what else to do."

My voice grew hard. "You contact me or Sergio. Then we *tell* you what to do."

"I know, I know. Mi dispiace."

I stared at the wall, my irritation mounting. "I traded a favor with D'Agostino to find you, for fuck's sake. His hackers caught you on camera in Munich, watching a Cosa Nostra warehouse, because you did nothing to disguise your appearance."

"I didn't think anyone was looking for me. And I was in a panic. I didn't know what would happen if I returned empty handed."

I slapped my palm on the table, rattling the flatware and glasses. "You should be more worried about what will happen now, considering all that has transpired because of your disappearance."

He paled, sweat beading on his upper lip. "Per favore, Don Benetti. I'll find a way to make this right."

"Get out of my sight. I need to decide how I'm handling this. Go with Gabriele."

My younger son left with Niccolò, and I swirled the wine in my glass, thinking.

"Papà," Leonardo said. "He meant no harm."

"Meaning no harm and causing no harm are two different things, figlio mio. Niccolò didn't think and has caused a great deal of harm."

"But Rossi put all this in motion to get Segreto and clean up his mistake with Palmieri. It seems Niccolò was just a pawn, no?"

"Yes. Rossi stole back his own truck and sent Niccolò into hiding. Then Rossi needed to force me to find Segreto, so he convinced me Niccolò was in custody. No one else has the contacts we do, so I was his best hope."

Leonardo whistled. "You must admit, it's pretty clever."

Anger flooded my veins and my fingers curled into a fist on the table. "That old fuck. I don't like being used."

My son lifted his shoulders. "You wouldn't be here with Val otherwise."

Of course he would see it this way.

The swinging door leading to the kitchen cracked and my

woman's face peeked out. A smile tugged at my lips. "We're finished," I called, beckoning her forward with two fingers.

She pushed through and started toward us. "I didn't hear any yelling, so that's a good sign, right?"

I scooted my chair back and patted my lap. "I never yell, fiore mio."

My son made a noise, but I ignored him as my woman slid onto my thighs. She smelled like garlic and lemons, and her soft curves melted into me. I wrapped an arm around her back and held her close, my face pressed into her neck. All the tension from my body disappeared like someone pulled a string to unwind me.

"Leo," she said, smoothing my tie. "Are you hungry? They're wrapping the donation bags right now, but I'm sure you can grab something, if you'd like."

"Donation bags?" he asked.

"Every night we donate the extra food to the shelter."

"Grazie, but I ate earlier."

My son didn't move, just continued to scroll on his phone. I glared at him. "Leave us."

That got his attention. His eyebrows flew up as he lowered his phone. "But you're my ride."

"Then wait in the kitchen."

He smirked, but stood. "This is nice, seeing you two. I wouldn't have thought it possible, but you are a miracle worker, Val."

"Careful, figlio."

"Luca, stop," my woman said. "Thank you, Leo."

Leonardo went into the kitchen. I nuzzled Valentina's neck, enjoying the velvety feel of her skin. She arched to give me better access. "Are you done being the king of mafia island?"

I chuckled. "For tonight, yes."

"You were, like, so hot. I peeked through the window a few times. You looked very serious, very in charge."

"Amore, I am always in charge."

"Because you make the rules."

"That is right." I pulled her closer. "And do you know what I want most right now?"

"To go home and fuck all night long?"

"No."

She leaned away to see my face, her brow lowered in confusion. "No?"

I shook my head. "I want to fuck you, shower and get in our robes. Then lie in bed and eat sundaes with you."

Her smile sent a flutter straight through my heart. "And watch reality tv?"

I heaved a dramatic sigh. "If we must."

She kissed me sweetly. "You are the best fiancée, Luca Benetti."

"And after next week, I'll be the best husband." I nibbled at her lips, which she allowed, then froze.

"Wait, next week?"

"Yes. I'm tired of waiting." I placed her on the ground, stood, then slapped her ass. "I want you as my wife."

"No, this is crazy. I haven't even thought about our wedding."

I grabbed her ponytail and held her tight, tilting her face toward mine. "Then plan it, amore. Because it's happening next week."

"What about Flavio? I might . . ."

She paused to nibble her lip. I knew what she was about to say. Based on our recent discussions, I knew she was worried about having Flavio around. I took her hand and led her to the door. "Valentina, if you want him to walk you down the aisle, then do it. I am not a fan of your father's after he shot Roberto, set a fire in my home, and kidnapped you. But I won't stop you from having him present at your wedding."

"I don't even know where to find him."

"I do." Leaning my head back, I shouted, "Figlio! Andiamo!"

Leonardo and Aldo came out of the trattoria's kitchen, each of them holding a sandwich. "Papà," my son called. "Do you want a sandwich?"

"No." Then I put my mouth near my woman's ear. "I have plenty to eat at home."

* * *

Thank you for reading
EMPIRE OF TEMPTATION!

* * *

Want to know what comes next in
the New York State of Mafia Series?

EMPIRE OF SEDUCTION
with Vito D'Agostino and Maggie Fiorentino

Coming June 2025
Preorder it now!

About the Author

Mila Finelli is the dark contemporary pen name of *USA Today* bestselling historical author Joanna Shupe, who finally decided to write the filthy mafia kings she's been dreaming about for years. She's addicted to coffee, travel, and books with bad men.

Visit Mila's website at milafinelli.com.

Join Mila's Famiglia on Facebook.

Want more mafia?
Sign up for Mila's newsletter and get a FREE Mafia Mistress bonus story!

Also by Mila Finelli

THE KINGS OF ITALY SERIES

MAFIA MISTRESS

MAFIA DARLING

MAFIA MADMAN

MAFIA TARGET

MAFIA DEVIL

MAFIA VIRGIN

* * *

Start at the beginning with Mafia Mistress,

Book 1 in the Kings of Italy series!

MAFIA MISTRESS

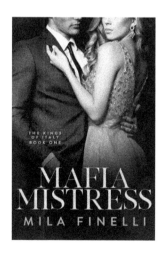

FAUSTO

I am the darkness, the man whose illicit empire stretches around the globe. Not many have the courage for what needs to be done to maintain power . . . but I do.

And I always get what I want.

Including my son's fiancée.

She's mine now, and I'll use Francesca any way I see fit. She's the perfect match to my twisted desires, and I'll keep her close, ready and waiting at my disposal.

Even if she fights me at every turn.

FRANCESCA

I was stolen away and held prisoner in Italy, a bride for a mafia king's only heir.

Except I'm no innocent, and it's the king himself—the man called il Diavolo —who appeals to me in sinful ways I never dreamed. Fausto's wickedness draws me in, his power like a drug. And when the devil decides he wants me, I'm helpless to resist him—even if it means giving myself to him, body and soul.

He may think he can control me, but this king is about to find out who's really the boss.

MAFIA MISTRESS is available in eBook, Print and Audio.

www.ingramcontent.com/pod-product-compliance
Lightning Source LLC
Chambersburg PA
CBHW052233070125
20022CB00028B/391